Also by Piper CJ

The Night and Its Moon

The Night and Its Moon
The Sun and Its Shade

the Sun and its Shade

PIPER CJ

Bloom books

Content Warning:
This book contains consensual breath play.

Published by Bloom Books, an imprint of Sourcebooks
P.O. Box 4410, Naperville, Illinois 60567-4410
(630) 961-3900
sourcebooks.com

Printed and bound in the United States of America.
VP 10 9 8 7 6 5 4 3 2

I'd like to use this opportunity
to tell Henry Cavill that I too am a nerd
and then put my phone number in the dedication.

Henry Cavill as Geralt?

You get it.

I get it.

Did you know he was late for his *Superman* audition
because he was playing *WoW*? We're both gamers.

I did know that.

So can I give him a shout-out?

You may not.

part 1

ballad of terrasen	*victoria carbol*
call of the sea	*claudie mackula*
shum	*go_a*
heroes	*the sidh*
i see fire	*peter hollens*

part 2

the path of silence	*anne sophie versnaeyen*
warrior	*anilah*
menuett	*faun*
selig	*helium vola*
í tokuni	*eivør*

part 3

song of the witch	*victoria carbol*
kingdom fall	*claire wyndham*
hard to kill	*beth crowley*
a taste of elegance	*anne sophie versnaeyen*
start a war	*klergy, valerie broussard*

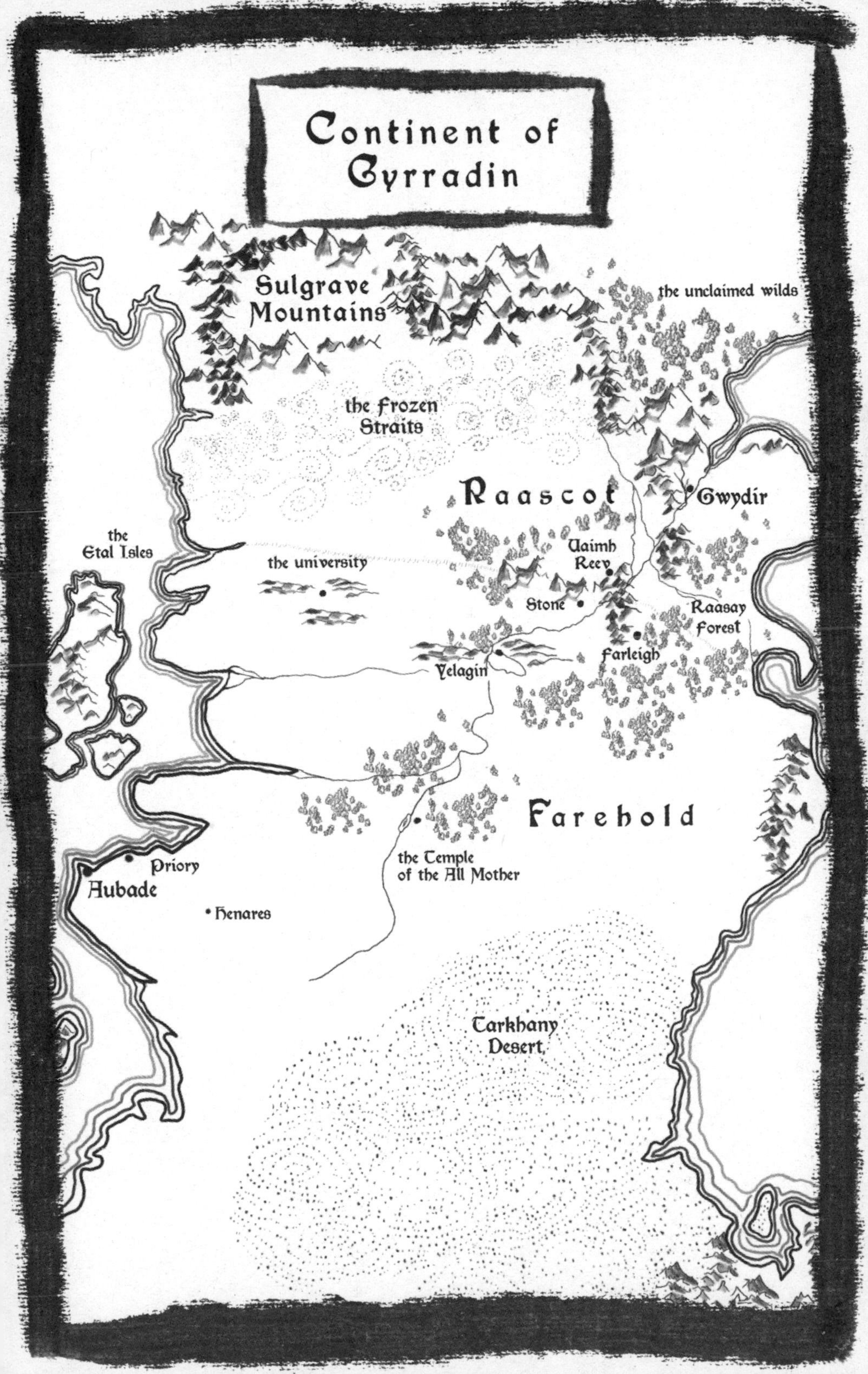
Continent of Gyrradin
Sulgrave Mountains
the unclaimed wilds
the Frozen Straits
Raascot
Gwydir
the Etal Isles
Uaimh Reev
the university
Stone
Raasay Forest
Farleigh
Yelagin
Farehold
Priory
Aubade
the Temple of the All Mother
Henares
Tarkhany Desert

Pronunciation Guide

Characters

Amaris: ah-MAR-iss
Achard: A-kard
Ceres: SERE-iss
Gadriel: GA-dree-ell
Malik: MAL-ik

Moirai: moy-RAI
Samael: sam-eye-ELL
Odrin: OH-drin
Zaccai: za-KAI

Places

Aubade: obeyed
Farleigh: far-LAY
Gyrradin: GEER-a-din
Gwydir: gwih-DEER

Henares: hen-AIR-ess
Raascot: RA-scott
Yelagin: YELL-a-ghin
Uaimh Reev: OOM reev

Monsters

Ag'drurath: AG-drath
Ag'imni: ag-IM-nee
Beseul: beh-ZOOL

Sustron: SUS-trun
Vageth: VA-geth

Prologue

C INNAMON, CARDAMOM, PEPPER." AMARIS MUMBLED THE words to her quietly. "And plums. Always plums."

The way she inhaled was like sipping wine, as if she were savoring each delicate scent. Amaris had always said that Nox smelled like dark spices and the sweet, ripe fruit they'd had the chance to try on rare occasions. She'd also stated more than once that it was the best smell in the world, better than baked bread or perfume or chocolate.

She cuddled into Nox, sleepily muttering something about comfort, safety, and home.

Dreams were cruelties. They were painful reminders of what wasn't and what would never be. They weren't memories, truths, or even hopes. They were reminders of all the things that hadn't—or couldn't—come to pass.

"I wish you were here," Nox said quietly, running her fingers through silken, pearly strands of hair. Her heart wanted to swell with its fullness at the girl's presence, but instead, it squeezed, strangled with the knowledge that Amaris was little more than a phantom. Nox had been so desperate to hold her again. Seeing the rippling corners of consciousness that presented themselves only in dreams, she couldn't bring herself to soak in the joy she'd wanted so badly to feel.

Amaris unraveled herself from the hug to look up into Nox's face, the light violet of her eyes catching against the filtered light. Shadows obscured her lovely features ever so slightly. Her white brows stitched together in the middle with a tinge of confusion as she looked up at her.

"I am here."

Nox murmured, "Right now, that's all that matters."

"I don't want to do this without you," Amaris said quietly against the skin of her neck.

"You have me," Nox promised. Nox's heart cracked at the speech, knowing that in this, as with all dreams, her subconscious supplied her with what she wanted to hear. "And I know you're alive. Wherever you are, you're alive."

"How do you know?"

"I would feel it," she whispered.

"I am," Amaris said with low, sleepy certainty.

"You are what?"

"I'm okay."

Nox hated herself for conjuring a healthy, loving Amaris when, for all she knew, the one who held her heart had tumbled to the jagged cliffs and lay comatose after falling from the back of a dragon. All Nox had wanted was to keep her safe. She'd done all she could to help the snowflake, too small, too delicate for the cruelties of the world as she'd been dragged into the coliseum.

But Amaris hadn't been fragile. She hadn't been powerless or defenseless. She was nothing like the snowflake Nox had known and loved in Farleigh. She had been capable and quick and strong. She'd been agile and brave. She was someone Nox didn't know. Not anymore.

Nox didn't want danger or adventure or trials. She didn't want dragons or dungeons or assassins. She hated the castles, the guards, and the welts that she knew throbbed on her skin even as she slept on the forest floor from the biting twigs and stinging insects. She rejected all of it. All Nox desired was a pantry filled with root vegetables and a quiet life that left them to rest in each other's arms. Even in her dreams, she didn't dare let herself hope for more than this simple exchange. Nox had locked her feelings up so tightly that even her unconscious mind wouldn't allow her to want or to wish.

Her heart shattered, each crack like the tension of a frozen lake. It broke under some terrible impact as her ice began to fracture, feeling the first of her tears as they fell.

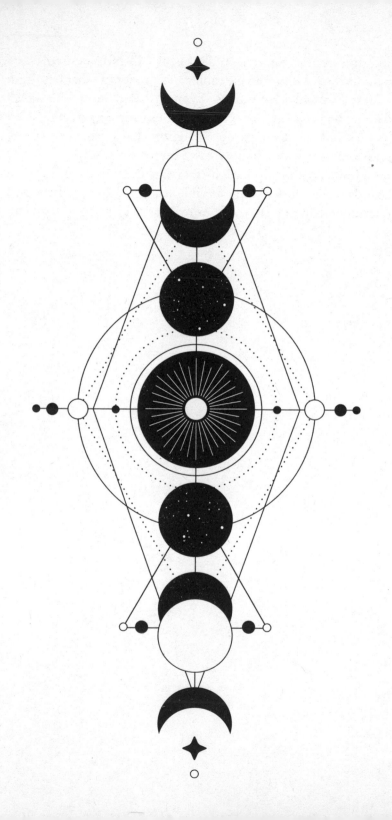

PART ONE

Something Worthy

·One

THERE IS A METALLIC SCENT TO BLOOD, ONE AMARIS RECOG-
nized instantly. The iron, rust, and salt left its tang in the
air as it exited in slow, methodical drops. She'd known the
odor of blood when it clung to lifeless bodies baked by the
sun. She recognized the smell of hot, angry liquid that spilled
either from you or over you in violent buckets. And then she
knew the distinct discomfort that came with knowing that
the bloodied scent filling her nostrils was not her own.

Gadriel.

Her hand had been slick with his blood. It had soaked her
lap through the night as she'd held him. Even now, she could
feel the itch of dried blood against her skin.

Amaris wanted to open her eyes, but they were too heavy,
too tired as she tried to shake herself from her dreams. Her
limbs were no longer strong and flexible. Her head was no
longer sharp and clear. She was alive, but that was all she
knew. She was okay but no longer a human girl of flesh and
life and joy. She was made of ice and stone. She was a statue,
chiseled from the slab she now rested on just as Uaimh Reev
had been hewn from its granite mountain. Voices burbled
around her in nonsensical rhythms, too excitable for her ears

to discern as they crowded over one another. She was vaguely aware that if she were to open her eyes, a violent, bright light would assault them, and she certainly didn't want that.

A word scratched at her ear from one of the voices. *Ag'imni.*

They had him—whoever they were. Her friend was here, and they could not see him for what he was. The dragon had not carried them beyond Farehold's borders.

She had to get up.

Amaris pulled at the life within her, willing it to stir. An external force acted on her instead. Hands jostled her, rolling her body onto her side, then her back somewhere beyond the blackness of her closed eyelids. A sharp prick on her arm. A liquid splashed across her lips. There was tugging and scrubbing and the wet sounds of washing and bandages.

She was there for all of it and none of it.

She forced herself to overcome her fear of the light, fighting with her body to open her eyes. At first, her vision was scarcely two slits, squinting against the bright light that punished her vision.

There were so many people in the room. Why were there so many people?

Several were above her chatting about this and that. She heard the words, the questions, the noises. Her pulse? Yes, she had one. The numbers they ascribed to it meant nothing to her. Her pupil dilation? Yes, that was also given some measurement. Her body's temperature? Too cold, they had said. One saw her stir and began to speak to her, snapping his fingers to gain her attention. Her head lolled to the side, rolling away from the stranger. Over their shoulders and with a crowd of his own, she was able to make out the battered shape of a winged man, leather straps binding him to a table. His arms, legs, torso, and head were all bound, secured to the sheet on which he rested. This was the jolt she needed.

Her eyes opened fully, taking in the studious, unfamiliar faces overhead.

"My friend—" Her throat scratched with the effort. The exertion of speaking nearly sent her back into oblivion.

"Our veterinarian is looking at it now. What can you tell me about what happened? Is the ag'imni the ag'drurath's rider?"

Another voice, louder and deeper with age, shushed the first voice. The second man scolded, "Our responsibilities lie with our patient. Save your curiosities for the creature or you will be dismissed from the room."

"Don't take him," she whispered, eyes shutting once more.

"What's that?"

The deeper voice belonged to a man who may have been in his fifties, though she'd never been particularly adept at guessing ages. He sounded comfortingly human. She squinted through a curtain of lashes, attempting to block out the light as she assessed whether he was friend or foe. The man had salt-and-pepper hair and wore white. His posture, like his voice, carried the authority of years of experience. He lifted a small, white fae light to Amaris's eyes and she winced.

"Good, good. Your pupils are showing great cognitive function. Are you able to speak?"

Her voice felt like it fought through cotton to find its way to her lips. Her throat was so dry, her mouth was stuck with the feeling. She tried to push herself up, echoing the same two words as before. "My friend—"

He cut her off again.

"Miss, can you tell me your name?"

She swallowed, throat on fire as she found her dry, sandpaper mouth unable to summon saliva. She croaked out her name to the crowd in three raspy syllables. Several of the younger faces around her scratched the name into their parchment studiously. She made another motion to bring herself upright.

"Please, don't attempt to move. Your beast is safe and appears stable, though we don't understand enough about its species to assess its condition. You were in a hypothermic shock when we found you. The creature appears to have suffered a head wound and is rather battered, but as my interning associate has previously stated, the veterinarian is tending to it now." Then, to himself, he mused with a smile, "Though I do have to say it's rather exciting to have the opportunity to study an ag'imni. We've never captured a live specimen."

"Please, let him go," Amaris rasped, eyes closed once more.

The hands pressed her down again as she felt the sting in her arm once more. Her world drifted away, and she let the warmth of the darkness consume her.

When Amaris woke, she had the sense of the passage of time. There were no windows in her room, but she knew that if she were to have looked, the night would have fallen. She took in the room around her to see it dimly lit with the warm glow of a single lantern on a desk. Cabinets lined the wall, accompanied by a long stretch of utensils on a counter and a number of books. In the corner, a sharp-faced young girl with bobbed, mousy hair and foxlike features who couldn't have been a day over sixteen, sat scribbling notes onto a parchment stuck to a wooden slab. A fae light was latched to her slab, gently illuminating her features.

Amaris recognized her. It was the girl from the forest.

"Hello?" Amaris called softly.

The girl jolted, short hair whipping around her face as she snapped her head up. Caught by surprise, the wooden slab nearly tumbled to the ground. "I'll go get the healer."

"Wait," Amaris commanded. She hadn't intended to flex her persuasion, but the human reacted instantly. The girl obeyed.

"Come here," Amaris said quietly, and the girl approached. She wasn't trying to use her ability, but it did come in handy. Her throat felt unusable. She desperately needed water. "You're the one who found us in the woods?"

The girl quickly admitted that yes, she and her friends had been the ones who'd discovered them. She'd also been the one who had sought out the healer and guided the professor to where Amaris and the ag'imni had been lying on the forest floor.

"I'm Cora. I'm only a second-year student, so I'm not really qualified to interact with the patients. I'm here taking notes on your condition for the healer. I really should go fetch him."

Amaris attempted to nod an acknowledgment, but her neck was rigid. Her muscles were stiff. She knew that if she could see herself in a mirror, she'd be covered with bruises from her tumble as she'd crashed from the dragon's back, through the canopies, and onto the forest floor.

"Tell me what's happened with my friend."

"The ag'imni?"

"Where is he?" Amaris pushed.

"It's alive. We took it to a secure room where it can be watched through glass so as not to harm any of us." Cora made a face that Amaris assumed was an attempt at bravery. The girl was afraid of the demon they held. "While we understand from the way it accompanied you that it might be tame, we don't know if its amicability extends to those other than yourself. Our Master of Beasts and head veterinarian have instructed us not to take chances. It has not yet awoken, but we've kept it restrained just to be safe."

Amaris's stomach roiled. She swallowed rising bile at the information. They were keeping Gadriel like an animal.

Amaris pushed herself up to her elbows, her head an ocean of uncomfortable sensations from the movement. "Can I have a healing tonic?"

"Please, you were very close to death when we brought you in. You're not supposed to exert yourself while you regain your strength. What you need is sleep and warmth for stabilization, not tonics."

Amaris coughed, touching a hand to her throat. Cora understood the gesture and rushed to the counter. She procured a tin cup, filling it with water from a nearby pitcher.

Amaris drank deeply, a small dribble escaping the edge of the cup and dripping off her chin. Her throat burned as the water washed over her inflamed passages.

She didn't want to waste time.

Throwing her legs over the edge of the bed, Amaris allowed her head to find its equilibrium. The girl made a useless cautioning gesture, but Amaris ignored her. She planted her hands on the lip of the bed while the world dotted with stars. It took a moment for the blackness to ebb and the humming in her ears to quiet. She looked at the student once more. "Remind me of your name again?"

The girl responded in a bright, polite voice, "I'm called Cora."

Amaris made a resigned exhalation as she once again flexed her persuasion, morality be damned. "That's right. Cora, take me to see my friend."

Cora escorted Amaris from her room and down the corridor. Time passed with unbearable slowness as they went down two spiraling flights of stairs into the belly of the basement. They were still in the healers' hall, though now they seemed to be deep underground and on the far side of the building.

Cora opened a door marked as a laboratory and led them into a strange room with three stone walls and one wall of exceptionally thick glass—a window to another room rather than the outside world. The glass took up three-quarters of the wall itself, with the remaining quarter dedicated to a metallic door. Amaris had never seen anything like it.

Cora stopped in front of the glass barrier that separated an onlooker from the dark fae inside. There was no one in the observational room at this hour. The building was hushed with the night.

Gadriel was all alone.

Amaris tried the metal handle but found it locked. She watched Gadriel's form through the glass that separated them, but the sounds of the handle hadn't caused him to stir. She set her face into a steely expression as she turned to the student with another attempt at persuasion.

"Cora, open this door."

Cora frowned and tried to obey, but even as she twisted the handle, she answered, "I don't have a key." She continued twisting at the handle.

Amaris's eyes widened as she watched the girl raise a hand as if to claw at the door. Fear gripped Amaris in a flash as she watched Cora bring her fingernails down against the obstruction, and she cried out a horrified order to cease.

"Stop! Stop what you're doing. I'm sorry. I don't need you to open the door," Amaris said, disgust so thick it was nearly palpable. "I do need to know how I can get to my friend. How can I find a key?"

Persuasion was useful, but she'd been sloppy. She would need to be exceedingly careful before utilizing her gift. If she hadn't told Cora to stop, would the girl have clawed until her fingers were bloodied? What were the limits to the powers of persuasion and obedience? The horror of the moment stretched between them. Amaris's face melted in apology at the sight of the welts already swelling on the girl's hand. Cora's lips parted to ask what had happened, but then she closed her mouth again. She looked both confused and terrified—the same expression Malik had worn when Amaris had wielded her power on him.

Her heart squeezed painfully as she thought of Malik.

She closed her eyes as she blinked away the memories of her brothers in the cell across from her, seeing their faces as they'd stared helplessly through the bars. They were two of the bravest and strongest men she knew, and they'd been unable to protect her as she'd been dragged onto the sands to face the ag'drurath.

Her last words had been to beg Nox to save them.

She couldn't think of them now.

The only person she could help was Gadriel.

She stared at his motionless body through the

floor-to-ceiling window and saw how he had been strapped to the table in his cell. They had not only bound his wrists and ankles but his torso, his lower section, and his forehead, all with thickly padded, buckled leather straps. The university seemed to be taking no chances with an ag'imni in their possession.

From behind the thick barrier of glass, Amaris saw the tears to his once-powerful wings. Black feathers dangled helplessly from the tattered wings that remained pinned beneath him, like a crow secured to a table. Dried blood matted both his hair and feathers. She knew it had been his blood that had filled her nose as they had been hoisted into the building together on entry.

How was she supposed to help him from this side of the glass?

"Cora." Amaris didn't tear her eyes from where they roamed over Gadriel as she spoke. "Who is in charge?"

The girl fidgeted. She answered out of either politeness or fear. "In our sick ward, we have the Master Healer. You are under his care, as are the medical assistants who serve him. In this wing, we have a few other creatures who fall under the supervision of the Master of Beasts when they've taken ill. And then of course, the university's headmaster oversees all seven departments, from healing and math and literature to zoology, cultures, magics, and manufacturing. Headmaster Arnout's specialization is theology. Isn't that interesting for the master of academia? My concentration is in healing."

Cora's words came out as nervous babble. She was undoubtedly still feeling residual fear from her bizarre attempt to scratch through the door. It only made Amaris's guilt swell.

Amaris's hand slipped from the glass. "Do you have any healer's magic?"

Cora looked a bit glum. "No, I simply study the medicines, tonics, and poisons. I can stitch and set and wrap, and by the time I leave the university, I'll be able to aid any village in Farehold. Wellness shouldn't be a privilege to only those born with power, don't you think?"

8

Truth be told, Amaris had no idea what to think.

She didn't know much about the university aside from the childhood whispers at Farleigh. If an orphan had displayed a rare aptitude for magic, it wouldn't be long before a university ambassador came to claim them if the church didn't snatch them first, though that had only happened once or twice in Amaris's fifteen years at the mill. Her peers had fancifully insisted that those with magic were whisked off to help develop and hone their skills. More sinister rumors persisted about the university's intent and its need to capture those with such inclinations to dissect, study, and understand. A horrible image came to mind of the informational text Amaris had found in her room at the reev and its anatomical sketches that had been diagrammed from autopsies. What future might they have in mind for someone like Gadriel?

Amaris's voice hitched with urgency. "Cora, I need to be able to speak to someone in charge. It's important and it can't wait. Can you find someone for me?"

Again, it wasn't a command. The girl hedged but nodded and scuttled off down the hall. Amaris listened to Cora's footsteps grow quieter and quieter. She pressed her hand to the glass once more, refusing to look away from Gadriel's too-still form.

They were finally alone.

"Wake up," she pleaded with him through the glass. "Wake up!" But this was not how her persuasion worked. He was fae, and he could neither see her nor hear her. She pounded her fist against the glass, face falling in anger over how helpless she felt. "Damn it, Gad, wake up! You don't get to die like this! I was supposed to take off your head in the coliseum, remember? Don't you think I should get a say in when you die? It's not now." More quietly, she said, "It's not like this."

She was hit with a powerful wave of emotion that she wasn't prepared to understand. What was pushing her to the edge of tears? Was it fear? Helplessness? Anger? Amaris grabbed for the airtight box within herself to shove each and every emotion inside. She could neither focus nor do what needed to be done if her heart was squeezed so tightly. The last thing she slipped into the cage was the sight of how very, very still he lay.

This time, the box fought back.

A new wave of feeling assaulted her as she was struck with how he had held her against the dragon's back for hours, clutching her tightly, no matter how it had burned his muscles or tired him. She could still feel the shock and thump of their downward descent as his tattered wings had slowed their fall just long enough for him to cocoon her in safety while he absorbed the blows from the trees and their outstretched branches. Amaris fought a second flood of tears as she pictured his crumpled body and how it had been so motionless against the rock.

He'd entered the castle, had his wings slashed to ribbons, battled a dragon, and cushioned the plummet to the ground all for her.

All she wanted was for him to be alive.

She scrunched her face against the wave of pain as she banged her fist once against the glass. "You shouldn't have come to Aubade. I told you not to come."

Every bad thing that had happened to him was her fault. Gadriel was strapped lifelessly to a table because of her. If he hadn't stumbled across a girl in the forest with the ability to see them many moons ago, he would be safe with his men right now. His life would be better if he'd never met her. Yet she felt a strange, pained twist when she considered the alternative.

She was too tired to be responsible for controlling her feelings. If she didn't get some rest, everything she fought so hard to suppress would bubble over. Her mind would go to Nox. She'd think of how Nox had come for her in the dungeon, had held her, had done everything she could to save her. She'd think of the kiss…

Goddess, she needed to sleep.

Her fingers began to tingle with numbness. Her hand had gone pale and bloodless from how long she'd kept it pressed to the glass. Footsteps echoed through the hall, tearing her attention from the fae within. Amaris released her hand from where it had touched the barrier between them, leaving a small, clammy print in its wake.

The door opened.

"Hello," Amaris said quickly. "Thank you for seeing me. I'm sorry it's so late."

A rather plain woman in her forties with hair slicked back accompanied Cora. The stranger appeared to have been rudely awoken. Her face was both shrewd and annoyed as she eyed Amaris and the ag'imni beyond the glass. Though the woman was in a structured autumn jacket and normal walking shoes, she wore a white linen nightdress. She extended her hand to Amaris.

"It's fine," came her brusque words. "I'm Master Neele, Master of Beasts and overseer of our zoological department. I'm in charge of your creature's case here in the veterinary wing. Thank you for bringing your ag'imni to our doors. We're very excited for this opportunity, regardless of the hour."

Amaris understood precisely what was happening. These men and women of science and education saw Gadriel for what he could offer them: knowledge of the demons. What did the time of night matter when a man was being strapped down and contained like an animal?

"Yes, about that...Master Neele, thank you and everyone here for your efforts in taking care of us. I appreciate your intentions. However, there has been a mistake, and I need you to listen carefully."

Master Neele's face remained impassive while she listened to Amaris describe the dark fae and the perception enchantment at the border between Farehold and Raascot with all the passion and gravity she could muster in her exhausted state. Amaris informed the woman hastily that Gadriel, her friend, was no ag'imni nor any beast of the night. When she finished explaining their situation, she waited expectantly for Master Neele to show a sign of remorse or understanding.

The severe woman merely responded with tight, pursed lips, "I will have to speak with the Master of Magics in the morning to discuss this further. Cora, please see our patient back to her room."

Amaris flexed her fingers with stress, unsure about the morality of her next move. Just beyond the glass, Gadriel was dying. She couldn't believe the woman was going to leave after everything she'd been told. It was unconscionable to leave him strapped to this table like a monster.

Amaris drew in staccato inhalations as she struggled to stay calm. She overcame her aversion to her gift and summoned it once again, speaking in a quick, commanding voice. "Master Neele, open this door."

The woman straightened her shoulders. She turned back to look at Amaris with painful slowness. She narrowed her eyes with dark, unmistakable loathing before responding with one word. "No."

She left without a second glance over her shoulder, shoes clacking on the stones of the basement.

Amaris stood in shock at the utter fucking uselessness of her gift. Master Neele's ears had been round. Her features had not been the beauty of the fae. The woman was unmistakably human. Amaris flexed her fingers so tightly that her nails bit into the palm of her hand while she continued to blink numbly through the baffling exchange. Without another word, Cora escorted her back to the medical room.

Amaris shook her head at her own confusion, trapped in silent debate with herself. First the priestess, then Queen Moirai, now Master Neele. She grappled with the limitations of her power and how she could possibly know when her gift would or wouldn't work. She couldn't fathom the purpose of such an ability if it was utterly meaningless every time she genuinely needed it.

Cora helped her onto her bed and informed her that another intern would be along to keep watch for the rest of the night. She rubbed at her palms absently as if not fully understanding why the anomalous welts on her hands pained her. Amaris hid the shame from her face, looking away from the hurt she'd caused.

The student bid Amaris good night and disappeared into the hallway.

Once she disappeared, Amaris was up from her bed, opening every drawer, pillaging every cupboard, studying every label and tonic and container in the room. There were strange names and unfamiliar smells, barbaric objects and tools meant for incisions, informational scrolls and medical terminology strewn about her chamber. Once she'd snooped through every conceivable object and was satisfied that there was nothing useful for her here, she began the long, sleepless process of waiting until the sun came up.

TWO

AFTER BEING EXAMINED, STUCK, POKED, AND PRODDED ONE final time, Amaris was deemed fit for movement. She blanched at the inedible plate of unsalted, boiled chicken, boiled carrots, some sort of greasy corn cake, and a fresh pitcher of water.

"Do you have any salt?"

"Salt isn't very good for your blood pressure." The assistant shook their head before walking off.

Amaris missed the cooking at Uaimh Reev and thought of stewed apples and meat pies while she choked down as much as she could of the flavorless meal. She frowned at the unseasoned chicken. Even campfires flavored things with char and smoke. She ate the corn cake and pushed the carrots around on her plate until someone returned. She was more than happy to abandon what was left of the slop as an unfamiliar student led her to what she was told would be a meeting with the university's masters.

Amaris remained tense and exhausted, unable to appreciate her surroundings as she marched toward the assemblage. They exited the healers' hall and passed numerous stone and ivy-covered buildings to reach what appeared to be an administrative building at the campus's heart. She hadn't thought to ask for a cloak and chafed her arms for warmth as they moved through the chilly, overcast day. She knew she should have been paying attention to the doors, halls, and turns they'd taken before they reached the room used for ceremonial meetings. Odrin and Samael would have been disappointed at how little she did to keep her wits about her.

"Please, go ahead," the student said. "They're ready for you."

He held the door open with a hand, ushering her in. The door closed behind her with the heavy click of ominous finality.

Amaris was struck by a sense of déjà vu as she entered the room.

The rooms looked nothing alike, yet she'd done this once before.

Once again, several humans and someone fully fae sat at a large table. The familiar sense of dread and unbelonging that had stabbed through her when she'd pleaded her case to the men of Uaimh Reev pressed down on her now. This time, she beheld the impassive, unreadable faces of the masters.

"Thank you for meeting with me," she said, voice too quiet for the big room.

The overhead lights in the room had been suspended through a clever design meant to conceal the twining, giving the lights the illusions of floating. There were nine in the room, if she counted herself. She assumed she was before the heads of the seven departments that Cora had mentioned, and in the center sat their headmaster.

"Welcome to the university, Miss Amaris," replied a stoic man in black robes. His clothes were not simply the dull black of night but had elaborate swirls and designs of the moon and the stars spiraling in contrast, glossy obsidian thread set against the matte black of the fabric. The man's eyes were sharp, though his skin was papery with age. She scanned the faces, confirming the presence of only one fae. Amaris recognized the shrewd Master of Beasts as the woman to his right, and the only other familiar face, that of the Master Healer, was seated three down from the left of the one currently speaking. "I'm Headmaster Arnout, and though you seem to have come to us through rather unfortunate circumstances, I'm pleased to introduce you to my staff. Master Neele has informed me that you summoned her for a conversation last night regarding your creature companion, and we are willing to hold an audience with you regarding how we proceed." He gestured magnanimously for Amaris to go ahead. "Please, for the council, state your case."

Amaris didn't understand what case there was to be made. The man didn't seem to hold sinister intent. Nevertheless, his implication troubled her. If she failed to persuade them, would they vote amongst themselves to keep Gadriel under lock and key? There was no case. There was only the truth.

"First, I think I need to introduce myself appropriately. I'm Amaris of Uaimh Reev, and I serve the reevers."

This was mildly interesting at best to the onlookers, save for one or two perked brows at the mention of the organization. Amaris took a breath, steadying her nerves. The room grew uncomfortably cold as she shrank beneath the stares of the masters. Remembering how the Master of Beasts had glared at her in the middle of the night when she'd attempted her command, Amaris opted to start with diplomacy.

"The man strapped to your table is fae. He's no monster," she began, controlling emotion from leaching into her voice. "I understand why you look into the room and see an ag'imni. I sympathize with why you've taken the protective measures to tie him down and place him in a glass observatory." While the words made her temper flare as she thought of her wounded, captured friend, she pressed on. "You're seeing the result of an illusion. A perception curse has been on the border between Raascot and Farehold for twenty years. When a northman crosses into the southern kingdom, he is perceived as a demon."

She waited for them to ask further questions or chatter amongst themselves, but they did not. They listened, no flicker of emotion or feeling on their faces.

Her hands flexed into fists. "My companion is a fae named Gadriel. He is no demon, though as I've said, I understand it's how you perceive him because of the curse. He doesn't need a veterinarian. He requires the medical attention of a healer." Her voice hitched. "Please, I'm very worried about him. When we fell, he took the blows from several branches and landed on a rock. You have him strapped to a table, and I have no way of knowing if he's all right. Right now, I'm not asking for you to believe me. I know members of the university value what can be seen by eyes and ears far more than the words of a stranger. But if you help me to get him the medical attention he needs, I'll gladly prove to you that he is not the monster you think he is."

"Fell?" asked someone. The single word, a question, came from a stout man with a mustache whose stature was nearly a head and shoulders shorter than his colleagues.

Amaris winced. She didn't expect that they'd appreciate her explanation. "Yes...did you happen to see an ag'drurath in these lands yesterday?"

At long last, the masters stirred.

"We traveled on the creature from the city of Aubade."

The Master of Beasts frowned at this. "The ag'drurath are known for being familiars with the ag'imni. You wish for us to believe that you and your *friend* rode on the back of the dragon, and yet he is not ag'imni?"

Amaris clenched her jaw. "We didn't ride it so much as... we grabbed onto its spine and held on for hours, praying to the goddess we wouldn't be shaken loose. The situation was...complicated."

"And why," the headmaster asked, "would you do that?"

Ah yes, this was a great question indeed. Why would they cling to the spine of an ag'drurath in any way that wouldn't paint them as in direct defiance of the queen and as traitors to

Farehold? Amaris wasn't sure how long it took information to disseminate on the continent. It would have been impossible for word of the capital's disaster to have reached the university this quickly. At least she hoped as much.

Instead, Amaris offered weakly, "It was the only escape from a dangerous situation. We were lucky to make it out alive. If we'd had any other option..." She let her words drift away.

She didn't understand why the masters weren't moving. She couldn't comprehend what was so broken within them that they demonstrated neither emotion nor compassion.

"Now, please," she said, her voice verging on begging, "I need to ensure that he is, in fact, still alive. I don't think he's been properly treated, as none of you see him as fae. Don't let an illusion stand between a man and the medical care he needs."

The lone fae at the table held up one slender finger. She was a serene-looking woman of unknowable age, who may have been thirty or three thousand years old for all the difference it made in the life of the immortal. While the others were in elaborate robes, hers were black and gray and made of thick, linen layers. An unpleasant nostalgia reminded Amaris of the matrons, for better or for worse. Even if the attire was matronly, the woman's face was anything but. Her vibrant, jewel-green eyes were far too large to belong to a human. Her ears pointed in their telltale elfin way. Her skin was the bronze of the northern fae with dark hair braided in numerous twists behind her ears.

She spoke with a cool, low tone. "If we are to believe that this companion is in fact a fae of Raascot, yet we cannot see him due to an enchantment, how is it that you see the man for what he is?"

The headmaster nodded. "The Master of Magics asks an excellent question. I am quite curious to hear the answer myself."

Amaris eyed the masters, wondering how many of them

18

possessed magic. She calculated her odds at persuasion, should she need to argue her way out of the predicament. She decided to answer honestly—if only partly. "My gift is the power to see rightly. I possess the magic to discern enchantments. It's proven rather useful."

There was a murmur of discussion amongst the masters at her revelation. Amaris was asked to step out of the room while the eight deliberated. She reentered the hall and slumped to the floor, her back to the wall. Though she had slumbered like the dead in her hypothermic state, the sleepless night and stress that had followed wore heavily on her. She closed her eyes and rested her head against the cool stones of the corridor.

While she and Gadriel were sequestered within the walls of the university, she wondered if her brothers were safe. She thought of Nox and the wide, coal-dark eyes that had stared into hers as she'd begged her to save them as she was dragged to her fate. She'd tried so hard to keep her memories and feelings for Nox in an airtight box, locked in chains. The unnamed relationship was a suffocating, overpowering monster within her that she needed to slay time and time again, shoving the kraken-like creature down into the cage within herself, unable to look it in the eye. While it was in the box, Amaris was able to go days, weeks, months, or years without feeling pain or sorrow or longing. She didn't think of Nox. She couldn't allow herself to experience the bites or scratches that came from letting oneself feel.

The raw emotion and its fangs belonged inside the box. At times like these, the tentacles would pound at its lid, breaking through from their enclosure. The pain swept her feet out from beneath her, stopping her in her tracks, stealing her breath as tears bubbled to the surface.

In the dungeon, Nox had come for her. In her moments of despair, Nox had found her, clung to her, held her, stroked her hair, and freed her. The way Nox had kissed her had undone the years of careful chains and locks around the airtight space within her, unleashing its monster. Nox's mouth had shattered the box, allowing the creature to freely roam, swimming around the blood and gore that remained of her heart.

Amaris's breath caught as she heard Nox's words.

I love you.

She hugged her knees tightly, burying her face in her lap.

Nox had said it in Farleigh many years ago. Amaris had heard it then without hearing anything at all. But then in the dungeon, she had understood the weight of those words as the many-armed sea monster wrapped its tentacles around her soul, squeezing until she couldn't breathe.

I love you.

"Amaris?" The call came from behind the closed door.

Her face shot up. She hoped her eyes weren't red, as she wasn't sure that these masters were ones for compassion. She stifled her tears, rose to her feet, and let herself back into the room.

Without the grandeur of pause, Headmaster Arnout gave his proclamation.

"For today, the Master Healer and Master of Magics will accompany you to your companion. We will give your friend three days and three nights to show recovery through healings meant for men and fae. If these methods fail, the Master of Beasts will resume her veterinary care."

Relief splashed over Amaris, but the headmaster was not finished speaking.

"If your companion makes a recovery under our healers, we will require demonstrations of his cognizance and person-hood before he will be untethered. Even then, it is for the safety of our students and staff that the ag'imni will remain in the security of his observation chambers unless Master Fehu says otherwise. If you're amenable to this agreement, Amaris of Uaimh Reev, the masters will escort you now."

She was able to ascertain from the fae woman's presence that she, the Master of Magics, was Master Fehu.

Amaris thought of Gadriel's bloodied, unmoving head. She pictured the matted hair she'd stroked while she sang her haunting melodies into the freezing hours of the night. She thought once more of how he'd held her to him so tightly on the back of the ag'drurath.

This was not how he died.

Three

D ON'T GET ME WRONG. WE LOVE SEEING YOU LIKE THAT, BUT you're going to need something more practical if we have any hope of traveling," Ash said as he eyed Nox's tattered dress.

Malik frowned sympathetically as he evaluated her. Red welts lined her arms, her cheeks, and the exposed places of her chest and legs from the scratching fingers of twigs and brambles.

Malik grimaced at Ash's choice of words. It didn't feel right to objectify their newly acquired travel partner. Not only had she saved them, but clearly she and Amaris knew each other exceedingly well.

Nox made a half-hearted motion to as if she were going to cover herself, then waved it away as if to indicate her sense of shame had been cast to the wind. She'd been in the same plunging, thin silk dress ever since they'd met her. When he'd asked if all the women of Aubade wore such lovely things around the castle, she'd made it clear that this particular dress had been for Eramus—"hell's forsaken Captain of the Guard, may he rest in pieces." A faint smile had crossed her lips as she'd referenced him, presumably recalling the delectable crunch of justice that resounded through the coliseum when the ag'drurath seized the captain in its rows of draconian teeth, only to be spat up and discarded on the sand. The reevers hadn't known the captain, but they inferred from Nox that the man had met a fitting end.

The trees and thorns had torn her dress to glossy ribbons, slashing not only the bottom but snagging and pulling at where it had draped down her back and snapping one of its hair-thin straps. The reevers had shed the gaudiest aspects of their courtly apparel on the cliffs of Aubade—their clothes still a holdover from their visit to Queen Moirai—but remained in stuffy finery. Still, their shirts and pants were a welcome comfort compared to the nearly naked traveling companion they'd acquired. Malik wished he'd kept his jacket so he might have had something to offer her, but he refused to make her continue on their travels in her current state.

"Just stay here," Malik said from behind a dilapidated structure.

"I can do it," Nox countered.

"No, no. I've got it."

The country sounds of animals and the buzz of summer insects hummed in the air. Ash scratched at his arms, slapping away invisible bugs. Sweat beaded on their lips in the midday heat. They'd left the safety of the trees behind in favor of seeing if they could scavenge necessary items from a nearby farm. Ash agreed to wait with Nox behind a chicken coop while Malik picked his way through the farmyard. Robbing countryfolk was not something he wanted to be known for, but desperate times called for desperate measures.

Malik heard a noise from within the house and froze in the grass, shooting a look between the small home ahead and where the others waited. With nowhere to hide in the open air of the yard, he opted for speed over stealth as he bounded across the yard and reached the clothesline. If he could just hurry up and get back to them...

Malik mumbled a prayer for forgiveness as he plucked the drying clothes from the twine across the farmyard. He selected pants and shirts and stockings not only for Nox but so that he and Ash might slip into something that would draw less attention. He'd just yanked the final homespun tunic from the line when a woman burst from the house.

Her voice was a crack of angry thunder against the blue sky. "What do you think you're doing! Thief!"

He took off like a fox caught in the henhouse as he sprinted for the others, absconding with his plunder. Nox and Ash scrambled after him while the woman hurled threats and obscenities. A chicken clucked and flapped its wings in their path, nearly tripping Malik with its sudden movement. All three were laughing by the time they made it safely through the tree line.

"I'm sorry!" Malik threw over his shoulder, and truly he was. He tucked the clothes under his arm as he matched pace with the others. The reevers were not thieves, nor would they ever take from countryfolk under normal circumstances. These, however, were not normal circumstances.

Their running slowed once they were sure no one was chasing them.

Nox giggled, doubled over from the exertion of escape. She lifted a single hand from her knees, extending it for her share of the spoils.

"Here you are." Malik placed a shirt and pants in her still-wriggling fingers. Clearly she wasn't used to running. She smiled at him in thanks, and he felt his cheeks heat. He averted his eyes, but she'd seen him. He didn't miss the soft chuckle she'd stifled, which only worsened his flush. Her laughter wasn't unkind. As far as he could tell, nothing about her seemed unkind.

She held the stolen clothes for a long moment.

"Are you going to be gentlemen, or will you be paying me to put on a show?" she asked in a humorless deadpan.

They mumbled hurried apologies while they busied themselves looking at the trees. If he hadn't been red before, he knew he had to match the ruby-red barn they'd left behind. He heard the gentle sounds of what was undoubtedly silk tumbling to the grass, cotton over skin, and the gentle rustle of hair.

He couldn't speak for Ash's resolution in self-control, but resisting the urge to turn was no small feat. Their new companion wasn't just pretty. Nox had been glowing with an ethereal light from deep beneath her skin from the moment they'd met her. Her glossy black hair was like fresh, wet ink as it tumbled down her shoulders. Her eyes were hypnotic, drawing all who looked upon her into their depths. Her body—

Malik scolded himself at the wayward direction of his thoughts, squinting up at the trees for any distraction. They'd never survive traveling with her if they allowed themselves to think of her in such a way. They'd spent years with Amaris, and she had been their brother in arms. Nox did have one strike against her for once attempting to lure Ash into her spiderweb in Yelagin, but they'd promised to let bygones be bygones.

"You're safe," Nox called, wry smile in her voice. "Consider your decency protected for another day."

"Ash has no sense of decency."

"Hey," Ash objected. "That is entirely true, but not something we need to tell the lady."

The cut of the tunic and trousers she now wore indicated they were meant for a young boy, but Malik was instantly convinced Nox would have looked stunning in a vegetable sack. He had no doubt that if they entered the city dressed like this, all the women would be seen in too-short trousers ending at their shins and in loose, flowy tunics after their envious eyes saw Nox in her apparel. Loose tunics of white fabric that didn't offer the top coverage or support of a—

Malik chastised himself again, muscle ticking in his jaw as he gritted his teeth to stop himself from a verbal curse.

"So you and Amaris seemed to know each other?" he asked, both to change the topic and ease the tension. He knew the barest edges of the answer, if only from the intimacy of the women's reunion in the cell. He wasn't sure how much

Nox was willing to share but felt he should give her the opportunity for openness. He wanted her to feel safe enough to be honest with them.

Nox bit her lip. "We do. We grew up together in the orphanage. I hadn't seen her for years before..."

They nodded. Perhaps now was not the time for discussions of deeper meanings and long-lost loves. Nor was it the time for thoughts of the jail or their escape from the castle.

"For the last three years, she has been with us," Ash said. "Your friend is a reever now, and quite a good one. She's knocked Malik on his ass a time or two."

Malik made an appreciative face. Ash wasn't wrong.

"And you?" Nox cocked her head to the side, looking at Ash.

Ash scowled, but it was with amusement. "Yes, she's also better than I. I blame it on her size. She's quicker on her feet than the rest of us. Maybe that's why women didn't train at the reev for the last hundred years—it was too embarrassing for the men to be outpaced time after time."

Nox's smile stirred between pride and regret. "I'm sorry that I never got to see that side of her."

Ash seemed to consider this. "I assumed she'd always been something of a fighter. She looked pretty beaten up when she arrived at the reev."

Nox's face fell. "Her scars?"

Ash nodded. "They were still healing when we met her. Odrin had mentioned they had come from a fight when she'd escaped her mill."

Nox shook her head. "I guess I don't know what happened in the moments between when I left her at the stairs and when she made her way to you."

Ash's eyebrows bunched apologetically as he said, "I'm really sorry for what you two went through. It's not right. It's—"

Malik took the discomfort in the way Nox shifted her weight from one foot to the other as his cue to intervene. He clapped his hands together. "Ash, how about we show we're truly sorry with actions instead of words. I'll catch a bird, you pluck it, and we'll make dinner. How's that sound, m'lady?"

✦

Nox was full. She felt safe. She wasn't freezing or scared or any of the emotions she'd expected she might feel while on the run. She looked to the reevers, evaluating them carefully from the far side of the fire.

She'd done her best to clear the air with Ash given their encounter in the lakeside tavern in Yelagin, though she wouldn't blame him if he maintained a wall of cautious distance. Malik, on the other hand, presented to all the world as if he possessed the genial warmth of the sun embodied. She absently mused that a man of his character would be better suited serving as king of the land than amongst the obscure ranks of the reevers, then promptly reflected on the curiousness of the thought. She wasn't sure if she'd ever met men she hadn't instantly mistrusted before these two. It might be too early to know for sure, but she almost felt as if she didn't hate them. How odd.

They maintained polite chatter around the fire, though most of Nox's responses sent the men into awkward, contemplative silences, which a sadistic part of her enjoyed. If her dress hadn't been enough of an indicator, Nox made it clear that she was not ashamed of her life as a courtesan. The men didn't know half of how it served her more than she served it, nor did she feel compelled to tell them.

"So how long do we stay out in the forest?" Nox asked.

"Oh, this is our life now. New identities, new home in the woods. Welcome to the family. I hope you like trees." Ash was too busy cleaning the sword he'd stolen from the centurion to look at her while he responded.

Smart-ass.

Sarcasm aside, they began making plans for the following day. They would return to Aubade to gather as much

27

intelligence as they could regarding Queen Moirai's next moves. As the queen's powers of illusion were no longer entirely undetected—particularly given the bloody spectacle of Amaris's escape and the near destruction of her coliseum—they had no doubt the queen would be mobilizing whatever task force was necessary to keep her secret. They also had no doubt that Amaris was currently the queen's most public enemy.

"Do you think she's in danger?" Nox asked.

"From the queen?" Malik responded. "Definitely. From anything else? I think she can handle herself."

It was hard to imagine the truth of those words. Soft, gentle Amaris, guarded like a secret, too precious for splinters or labor or to be seen on market day, could now knock men on their asses and, in Malik's unbothered words, handle herself. Nox picked the final bits of meat from a bone, musing at how her moonlit counterpart wasn't the only one who had changed.

After dinner, Ash stood off to the side practicing a few movements and lunges with his sword. The reevers still carried the weapons from the guards they'd disarmed in their escape from the dungeon, and Ash had made comments about wanting to ensure that he was as comfortable with its weight as he would have been with his own sword. Nox watched his graceful strikes, arcs, and steps with the weapon.

Malik cautiously took a seat beside her on a log and brandished a small knife. "How are you with a weapon?"

Nox looked up at him and considered the question. He was tall even while seated, requiring the lift of her chin as she regarded him. She tilted her head to the side while she contemplated it, studying his features, wondering what he must be hiding. His face was friendly enough. His blond hair and green eyes didn't seem to hold any underlying malice, but she'd been wrong before. She was confident that no man could be as good-hearted as he presented himself to be. Nox had too much evidence to the contrary.

28

She had never needed anything sharper than her mind as a force for destruction. She was the weapon. She wasn't in the mood to explain, so she simply said, "I suppose I've never used one."

"Here." He didn't wait for her to react before pushing its hilt gently into her hand. "First things first, it's not a dead fish. You need to firmly grasp it."

She wrapped her fingers around it more tightly.

"Good. The way you're holding it right now is the forward grip, also called the hammer grip. When you point up like this, it's effective for parrying. You have more reach, should you need it. But since you don't have a lot of experience with defensive maneuvers, I'm going to make a suggestion. Now, if you switch your grip," Malik said as he reached around to reposition her hold, his calloused hands rough against her cream-soft fingers. He twisted the knife downward. "Holding it backward like this is your ice-pick grip. It will be more impactful whether you need to pierce armor or just a rib cage. Use the strength of your body's weight and gravity should you need to slash or plunge it into something or someone."

She cocked her head once more. "You're trying to teach me to wield a knife?"

"In a perfect world, no one would need these things. But you've managed to wind up with our lot, and we have a penchant for getting ourselves into trouble. If a vageth comes at us in the middle of the night, I'm not going to let it rip your throat out. Still, you should know the basics of how to defend yourself."

He stood and extended a hand. She slipped her fingers over his palm, though her gaze remained heavy with suspicion.

Malik helped her to her feet, and she eyed him almost as if he were a dog that had learned to speak. It was almost difficult to listen to him over the sound of her own cautious inner monologue. She was aware of him speaking but was preoccupied with the peculiarity of the event itself. Malik demonstrated a few basic moves and had Nox attempt them, correcting her stance and her posture. She appreciated his awareness of his surroundings, as he seemed to take notice of the way she bristled when he touched her. He adapted, keeping his contact to a minimum.

In truth, Nox wasn't sure how to categorize such an exchange. At Farleigh, the boys had been children, and none of them had been her friends. At the Selkie, men had been a mixture of patrons and prey. It was a curious sensation to meet men who complicated her worldview on the sex, and she wasn't quite sure how to handle the cognitive dissonance that clattered through her mind. She used the bricks of her skepticism to build a barrier between whatever game he was playing at and whatever she had to offer. Nox wasn't sure what his angle was, but she had been on the goddess's lighted earth long enough to understand that nothing came for free.

They could only practice swinging the knives for so long before it was time to sleep. After the men snuffed out the fire, Nox curled under her blanket, clutching the knife.

Whether it was the safety of the weapon in her hands or the comfort she felt surrounded by the reevers, she was able to drift off into her dreams. She didn't have to be in the forest. She didn't have to be escaping Aubade. She could close her eyes in one world and open them in another. When she was little, it had been a lovely way to escape the toils of life by using her sleeping hours to run through poppy fields on a warm summer day with no fear of snakes or insects or the tear of cockleburs.

And then there were the different kinds of dreams, the ones that didn't feel like dreams at all. She'd close her eyes in one world and open them when her sleeping mind brought her to Amaris. Sometimes it hurt more than it helped.

Occasionally her dreams would play in her mind as if they were reliving old memories. Sometimes they created entirely new memories altogether. In one fit of sleep, Nox had seen them and how their life may have looked together. She had envisioned herself burning dinner in the kitchen they shared and Amaris politely eating it anyway so she wouldn't hurt her feelings. She imagined the small goat they'd own and tend in their country cottage, far from prying eyes, gossiping neighbors, and social obligations. She allowed herself to see what it would be like to wake up in the morning and have her eyes flutter open only for the snowy young woman to be the first thing she saw, wrapping her fingers around the hand beside hers, bronze and pearl contrasting lovingly as Amaris nestled more deeply into early-morning sleep. She could see them drinking tea, growing old, and spending their lives in a world where there had never been a Madame or assassins or a curse.

Even in her dreams, the yearning was unrequited. She wanted, but that was all it was: a want. She longed to lean in close and wait on bated breath to see if Amaris would return the kiss, one that would swirl of juniper and cinnamon where their mouths met. Nox wanted to know if she would pull her in tight and hold her and accept her for all she was and the weight of what she wasn't.

There was a weaving of energy, of air, of tantric thirst and wishes and desperation as she hovered so close, clutching so tightly. The pulse between heartbeats would pass on the air between them. Nox would make herself and her intentions clear, but for her to know that Amaris felt the same way, that this wasn't a fabrication of her selfish, wishful heart, the final inch of the space between them needed to be Amaris's choice. She pressed herself into Amaris and let desperation and hope linger between them as thick as honey.

All she could do was act with love, with patience, with intention. The rest was up to fate.

Nox shook herself awake with a chatter of her teeth.

Though it was summer, the early hours still made her muscles ache with chill. The cold roused her from whatever brief, calm escape she'd been allowed in her dreams. It was time for them to collect their things and wander into the city to see how two reevers and a succubus might best kill the queen.

Four

T HE HEALER, WHOM THE STUDENTS REFERRED TO AS
Master Dagaz, patiently listened to Amaris while she
described the features on the winged man strapped to the
table. Master Dagaz had responded as he would with a fae
or human patient, collecting tonics and bandages appropriate for a male fae. Meanwhile, the fae Master of Magics sat
in the corner of the room with a statuesque grace while
they worked, her too-large eyes missing nothing. Outside
the room, a rather disgruntled Master of Beasts continued
to visit as the hours passed. The woman made no effort to
hide her displeasure that the rare opportunity to study a live
ag'imni was being denied. At least Master Neele, though
obnoxious, did not interfere.

"He can't stay strapped to the table like this. It's inhumane."

"Well, for our safety…"

"Please. Would you do it to a human with a head injury?
You can't treat his head if it's strapped to the table like a
rabid dog."

After exchanging a long, silent look with the Master of
Magics, the healer conceded to removing all the restraints save
for the primary buckle around Gadriel's lap. Dagaz reasoned

that this way, the demon would have a semblance of freedom and the ability to sit without the true capability of lurching across the room to maul them where they stood without warning. Amaris held Gadriel's hand while the attendants bustled around her, following every indication for where a cut or bruise may have been challenging to distinguish on the blackened gray of a demon's amphibious skin. She only saw the shallow breaths of a beautifully handsome face and what remained of his angelic wings.

"I know you'd like to be present to help, but have we checked your vitality lately? I don't believe you're getting enough sleep. The bruises under your eyes are as positively purple as the irises themselves. My assistant did inform me you'd requested a tonic, but it's a mistake to make my students rely on magical means of healing should they find themselves without external resources. The body doesn't need unnatural interventions when the only culprit is—"

"Sleep. Yes, yes. I'll be fine. Is there anything that can be done for his wings?"

The healer frowned at her clear disregard for his expertise. "Many northern fae may possess a magic for their wings, but we have no such winged fae at the university. I can call the Master of Literature and put a cohort of archival students in search of a remedy, but I don't believe anything can be promised to you or your companion."

Amaris sucked in a frustrated breath, then perked with an idea. She left Gadriel's side when she heard the angry pacing of Master Neele once more at their door. She nearly collided with the impatient woman just beyond the door that had been left ajar, presumably for rapid escape from monsters.

"Master Neele." She leveled a look at the Master of Beasts. If the woman refused to make herself scarce, she may as well find a way to be useful. "Are there any other creatures in your stables with the gift of flight?"

The woman glared at her. She had apparently taken to seeing Amaris as something of an adversary. Before Amaris had interfered, the zoology department had been so close to possessing a demon. "There are two species of creature under my oversight with wings, yes."

Amaris nodded. "If one of them were to have their wings damaged, what would you do?"

Master Neele had ice in her breath as she responded, "I would put the creature out of its misery."

✦

Gadriel stirred.

Amaris shuffled from where her head had been bowed in a drowsy attempt at rest. Her hand was clammy from holding his throughout the night.

His first words came out in a groan. "Where am I?"

Amaris's inner fire ignited, nearly choking her on its joy. She threw her arms around him, pressing her face into the feathers and skin and clothes he'd been wearing for days. "Goddess be damned, demon, if you scare me like that again, I will kill you myself."

His voice was muffled as he nearly gagged on her hair. "Have you been holding my hand?"

Amaris unraveled her arms from where she'd gripped him, cooling her outburst. She shook her palm, wiping the sweaty evidence onto her trousers. "Call it my maternal instincts. I thought you were going to die." Despite her best attempts at stoicism, relief colored her voice. She continued before he could ask another question. "Goddess, you scared me."

His hands went to his temples as he rubbed at a headache. "Careful, witchling. You're starting to sound like you care about me."

She decided they would both be better off if she ignored his goading. "Gad, we're at the university. We're still in Farehold. You should be aware just so we're on the same page. Everyone here sees you as a demon, so I'm going to need you to try to hold back from being a violent monster for at least a few days. Try to muster some civility."

He chuckled but winced at the effort. "My head is killing me."

"I'll get you something for the pain."

He grabbed her arm before she could leave his side. "No, it's just a headache. A blow to the head will do that." She looked to where his hands wrapped around her forearm and thought of how he'd reached for her in Moirai's castle. It had been so intimate, so filled with hope for his people. She dragged her gaze from looking at the compression of his fingers against her arm, meeting his gaze as he asked, "How long was I out?"

Amaris pulled away on instinct. Regret prickled through her the moment he relinquished his hold. "A few days. When we jumped from that ag'drurath..." A resurgence of emotion coursed through her despite her best attempts to master her feelings. She shook away the sensation and leveled her voice. She told herself it was the sleep deprivation. Nothing more. "You absorbed most of the impact. A few students found us in the forest and brought us here. Try not to get angry at what I'm about to say, but I'm pretty sure they want to keep you in their zoo to study you as their first live demon specimen."

Outrage flashed. "Don't get angry?"

"I'm handling it."

"Like you handled the queen and her attacks on our forces?"

He probably hadn't meant to hurt, but Amaris felt the weight of her failure in the single question. She'd been dispatched for a single task and had failed in a most spectacular fashion. Not only had she failed to persuade the queen, but she hadn't even possessed the wherewithal to plead for help from the court, the guards, or anything that might have saved them. Utter worthlessness crushed her.

His expression softened as he watched her. His voice was gentler when he spoke again. "I didn't mean it like that, Amaris. We're no worse off now than we were before. So what if this didn't work? There's more than one way to skin a cat."

"What psychopath invented that saying?" she mumbled. "Cats should get to keep their fur."

"I'm just saying, if our first plan didn't pan out, then it's on to the next."

She grimaced and stood to fetch water as the student had done for her the other night. He'd rarely used her true name, save for moments of gravity. She extended the glass to him as she said, "I appreciate your optimism, but I think there's a chance we're far worse off now than before. The queen has declared reevers to be enemies of the throne. You were there. You saw how she incited the crowd to see Uaimh Reev as traitors after centuries as the protectors of the north and south. I wouldn't be surprised if Moirai was making an attempt to rally for whatever move comes after the discovery of the illusion."

He used his hands as leverage to prop himself up. She watched as his eyes fixed on the belt that bound him to the bed. It was a simple enough buckle to undo as a fae, though perhaps if he'd truly been ag'imni, the smallest of puzzles would have proven impossible. Gadriel leaned into her while he tested his muscles. He flexed his hands, then his legs. The wince of pain as he attempted to flare his wings was clear across his face.

Amaris twisted her mouth. "What do fae do in the north if their wings are damaged?"

Gadriel closed his eyes, taking his time before he answered. "What do birds do in the south when their wings have been clipped?"

Amaris deflated. She dug deep to conjure an expression of ease, even if it wasn't entirely convincing. "Fortunately for you and your pessimism, we're at the continent's seat of knowledge. If anyone can think of a bright idea for my favorite demon, it's them."

"I'm your favorite demon now?"

"Absolutely. My favorite demon right behind Zaccai and Uriah. I don't have enough information on Silvanus yet to know if I like him better than you."

36

There was a knock at the door and the healer entered, accompanied by two of his students.

Amaris nodded in acknowledgment. "Gad, this is the man in charge of the healers' hall, Master Dagaz. Master Dagaz, this is Gadriel. He's Raascot's general."

"It's a pleasure to meet you, General Gadriel." The man made a small bow to let them know he would be approaching.

Amaris spoke again. "Thanks to your help, he's awake. Before the two of you speak, I need to make it clear that the perception spell works on all facets of perception. You won't be able to trust any of your senses. This is the most comforting way I can prepare you for the shrieks you're about to hear. Ask whatever you need to, and I'll translate."

The Master Healer dipped his chin again. Politely, he addressed Gadriel by his formal title as he said, "General, please describe your state to Amaris. I need to know your areas of discomfort along with their severity. After that, I will have a few questions by way of cognitive tests before we proceed."

To his credit, Dagaz did not cringe, nor did he show any signs of fear while Gadriel spoke. Amaris once again considered the courage it must take to stand in the presence of a perceived monster as the Master Healer maintained an unfazed, stately composure. She quickly explained that Gadriel had a throbbing headache and that he suspected several of his bones to be broken, from his battered ribs and dislocated shoulder to a fractured collarbone. His legs, while purple with bruises, were otherwise undamaged. The healer nodded along and expressed satisfaction that the tonics seemed to be working.

"We'll get you one more bottle just to be safe. I can't rightly assess what would be appropriate for your height and weight, given... Well, between Amaris's estimation of your height and weight, I think it's safe to assume you'll require a second dose." Dagaz motioned for his assistant to grab another brown glass jar. He offered the tonic directly to Gadriel, who drained it in a single swallow. Master Dagaz continued, "Now,

I'll ask a number of questions to test for concussion. Please answer them as quickly as possible while your companion translates. In which kingdom are you presently?"

"Farehold."

"How did you come to the university?"

"We arrived by ag'drurath."

"Who sits on the throne in Gwydir?"

"King Ceres."

"What sort of creature are you?"

"Fae."

"Your rank is?"

"General."

"Who is this woman to you?"

"We fought together in Aubade."

Amaris translated everything rapidly, tripping over the final answer. She stifled her hurt at the truth in his words, the inexplicable urge to bring her hand to her chest as the response pricked her. He was right. They were not friends, nor should she have led herself to believe any different. She was a useful reever with the ability to see through enchantments.

That was that.

Master Dagaz thanked him and then, with Gadriel's permission, began to press on the abdomen of the ag'imni. Gadriel made small faces of discomfort, but it was determined that he had no internal wounds that would prevent him from getting up and moving about over the next few days. As the healer stepped out, the Master of Magics stepped in to take his place. Unlike Dagaz, she offered no bow.

The emerald-eyed woman entered with the smell of red wine and falling rain. The room filled with the clashing scents, battling the black cherries and spice Amaris affiliated so strongly with Gadriel.

Amaris kept the tightness from her voice as she offered a similar speech about her role as translator. The Master of Magics lifted a thin finger to silence her. "I am Fehu, Master of Magics at this university," she said, talking over Amaris and speaking directly to Gadriel. Her voice was the clean, sharp noise of polished steel. "Please introduce yourself."

He faced her. "I'm Gadriel. I serve as King Ceres's general."

Amaris pursed her lips slightly but remained silent as she regarded Fehu's face.

"Allow me to introduce myself. My father shared the wings of the northern fae, but my mother, though fae and a naturalized citizen of Raascot, was born in the south. Alas, I have not been blessed with your gift for flight. I have lived and educated others here on the grounds of Farehold's university for the past two centuries. General, can you tell me, have you made contact with others of northern descent while here in the south? Do others of northern blood possess the predilection for comprehension?"

Amaris looked at her quizzically. "You can understand him?"

Fehu shot Amaris a silencing look before returning her attentions to the general.

Gadriel shook his head. "The first year was chaos. For the first several months of the curse, my men didn't understand what had happened. Once we realized that the southern kingdom took us for monsters, we made painstaking efforts to avoid detection. My second-in-command has the power of dampening, which has aided us greatly. We always travel by night, and we make no efforts to interact with those in the south. I'm afraid I can offer little information on those of Raascot blood within southern borders."

Fehu arched a slim brow. "And yet you've come upon this girl?"

"She attempted to shoot one of my men with an arrow. I intervened."

Amaris sucked on her teeth as she recalled their origin story. That was precisely what had happened. She had drawn her bow on Zaccai, and Gadriel had pressed a dagger to her throat. No wonder they had no hope of considering themselves friends. Gadriel had seen her for her usefulness, nothing more. He'd protected her and helped her as one might any valuable asset, not for her humanity. And here she'd been begging for the masters to see *him* as a person. She thought of how she'd cradled his head in her lap and winced with humiliation at the memory. He'd needed neither her concern nor her coddling.

"How is it that you understand me now?"

Fehu dipped her head to acknowledge the question. "I see the ag'imni before me that I am meant to perceive. As I was approaching the hall, I could hear both the sounds of a monster and those of a man, interwoven. I suspect that my northern blood has offered me a link to its people, though at this point, that's all it is—a hypothesis. Perhaps it is not your presence in Farehold but merely the act of crossing that results in your susceptibility to the enchantment. If this is the case, I suspect that if I were to leave Farehold's lands and reenter, the curse would not spare me. My assumption is that I too would be ag'imni to my colleagues. This will be the focal area of study for my students moving forward, as this is the first border curse that I've encountered. Quite fascinating."

Amaris decided with thinly veiled annoyance that this conversation did not require her presence. She went to the corner of the room and made herself comfortable in a chair. She busied herself picking dirt from under her nails while the two northern fae bonded over their many commonalities and whatever deep and important bloodlines intrinsically connected them.

Gadriel spoke to Fehu about as much as he was able—save for the classified details of the mission privy to only Ceres and his troops. Fehu made the executive decision that Gadriel no longer needed to be contained to the observational room, and the other masters supported her motion—however reluctantly—to have him relocated to proper rooms.

Amaris excused herself unceremoniously somewhere in the middle of the fae's conversations. Less than an hour later, she heard him settling into the room across the hall and was glad her door was shut. She was too drained for interaction.

Amaris sat on her bed and stared at a blank wall—no art, no tapestries, no clocks or plants or nice things, just sterile nothingness. At first, her thoughts went to the reevers. She used the blank wall as a canvas, remembering their faces as she was dragged away. Ash had held the iron bars with his hands. Malik had looked so heartbroken at his inability to intervene. She wondered if they had made it out, if they were safe, if they were with Nox.

Nox...

Amaris heard the door across the hall open and hugged her knees to her chest, maintaining her glazed stare at the wall. She didn't look at Gadriel as he entered.

"Hey," he offered weakly.

She dismissed his greeting, words unfocused and disinterested. "I don't remember doing a summoning spell."

"The demon bit is getting old."

The wall continued to hold her attention.

From her peripheral, she could see how Gadriel leaned against the doorframe and narrowed his eyes. Even if she hadn't been able to see him, his tight tone would have betrayed his feelings. "Are you not going to speak to me? After I saved you in Aubade?"

Her eyes flashed then, glowering up at him. "You saved me? I'm sorry, didn't you get yourself caught in the castle? Wasn't it I who had the plan of distraction? Wasn't it Nox who sent out the man to show us how to chop off the dragon's leg?"

"Who's Nox?"

That was one question too far. It reminded Amaris of a very important detail that she'd allowed herself to forget: they didn't know each other.

She had no energy for fury or vitriol, but with the deadened weight of her exhaustion, she answered him. She returned her glazed eyes to the wall as she spoke in a far-off voice. "Go away, Gadriel."

He flexed his hands at his sides. Amaris may not have been heated, but he certainly was. He gripped her doorway as his irritation burned. Even from the corner of her eye, she could see the way the muscles in his jaw feathered. "My wings look like this because of you, Amaris."

Fine. If he wanted a fight, she'd give it to him.

Her face hardened as she faced him fully. "Your wings are broken because you imposed your agenda on the reevers, demon. Your wings are like that because of your king and because of your decision as a general to force me out of my dispatch and into yours. You will never fly again because you came to the castle in Aubade when I specifically told you to leave. You did that to yourself, Gadriel." She dropped her voice to a whisper as she looked away. "Get out."

The venom of her words dripped between them like a third presence in the room.

Amaris thought for a long minute that he might yell. Good. Let him yell. He was probably a great military leader, but she wasn't his to command. She'd been following Samael's dispatch, Odrin's training, and fighting alongside her brothers. She'd come to know that Gadriel was not a man used to disobedience, and he'd never taken fondly to her disregard for his rank. That was his problem, not hers. She didn't give a shit if he was a general, a king, or a fucking god.

After all, she was just someone he'd fought with in Aubade.

Gadriel remained frozen in the moment, presumably locked in debate over how to respond.

Amaris did not look at him, wondering what kept him from speaking. He stayed perfectly still for several excruciating heartbeats. She wished if he were going to curse at her, he would just do it and be done with it. Maybe they could scream. Maybe they'd stand and throw things and let the anger break free like a dam, disillusionment and betrayal pouring out as their lakes emptied.

Instead, he left.

Several moments passed before she looked up to the space where he had stood and saw the fractured indentations his white-knuckled grip had left on the doorway.

Five

T HE REEVERS INFORMED NOX THAT THE LAST TIME THEY'D
entered Priory had been on horseback in broad daylight.
Now, if they wanted to get into Aubade, they'd first have
to navigate the outlying coastal community that acted as its
safeguard.

Nox led the way. Her three years in Priory hadn't included
extensive experience beyond the Selkie, but her knowledge
of its geography far exceeded theirs.

"I just need to make one stop first," Nox whispered.

Malik's brow furrowed as he asked, "Where?"

"My—" She stopped herself before calling it home. Unless
Millicent had thrown her belongings onto the street, everything Nox owned remained in her room at the Selkie. Her
stolen farm clothes may have sufficed in the forest, but she
couldn't risk the out-of-place appearance drawing speculative eyes within Aubade. Shoes, cloaks, clothes, papers, notes,
information, and—if she was lucky—answers waited within
the brothel. She shook her head before answering, "Just trust
me. I'll be quick."

The late hour had emptied the streets. Their only companions were mewling cats and the spoiled smells of meats common

to the congestion of cities. The moon peeked between clouds, revealing itself intermittently as they navigated the city until they stopped in the alley across from a town house. Even from where they waited in the gloom, Nox could see the telltale iron mermaid tail emblazoned on its front door.

"Wait here."

"Wait," Malik whispered. "What do you need in there?"

Annoyance over being questioned fluttered through her. "My things."

"We'll get you new things!"

She glared. "Just give me a moment."

Malik moved to stand between her and the building. "It looks like whoever lives there has gone to sleep for the night."

"No one in that house sleeps."

Malik's mouth turned down. "I'll come with you."

"Not this time."

Nox didn't wait for the retort. She was certain these men defined themselves by their usefulness and probably didn't know what to make of her dismissal. Perhaps the reevers weren't accustomed to taking orders, but she was so self-assured that they found little space to argue.

It took three seconds for Nox to cross the street and disappear into the wall of shadows along the building's side. The town house's curtains were always drawn for the privacy of its patrons, though even through the thick, silk shades, the glow of life behind their fabrics should have been blazing. Malik was right. The house looked darkened as if its residents were asleep, but that couldn't be the case. This was a home for creatures of the night.

She sidled along the edge of the brothel and pressed her face to the window. Nox closed her eyes to help herself focus. She listened against the glass but heard nothing from the brothel. Somewhere in the distance, a baby cried. A horse clip-clopped down the cobblestones a few streets over. Alley cats mewled. But inside the Selkie, nothing stirred.

When she'd left, she'd sworn never to return. As it turned

out, her promise was worth about as much as the shredded gown she'd abandoned on the forest floor.

Rather than risk the front door, Nox went directly for the windows. She tested shutters, windowsills, and panes until an unlatched lip wiggled under her fingers. She stilled once again, straining her ears for any sign of life. She poked her head into the shadows, brows knit in confusion as she listened. When nothing moved, she pulled herself up over the ledge and jumped down into the house, landing on the balls of her feet with feline grace.

She had never seen the Selkie empty before.

Something about its silence demanded quiet in response. She chose her steps carefully, refusing to break the quiet around her. The salon was vacant, save for the ghosts of traumatic memories that haunted the very air. Overturned chairs and silk plumes were awry. Bottles of liqueurs, garnishes, spices, and preserved foods were still behind the bar, though several were shattered. A few pint glasses and a single wineglass sat on the bar top, one of them still nearly full. The mingled smells of alcohols and perfumes lingered.

There was nothing in the lounge for her.

Nox crept across the salon and up the stairs toward the girls' rooms, peeking her head into the bedchambers as she passed, but no one appeared around any corner or behind any door. The beds were left unmade. Several of the rooms displayed clothes torn and strewn about the floor. Wherever they'd gone, this had not been a peaceable exit.

She headed for her old room.

Nox checked her desk for her notes and found them untouched. They seemed useless now. Her drawings of Amaris's abductor had been etched into her memory. She had pored over every minute detail of the assassin she'd seen in Farleigh, meditating on it like a prayer for years only to learn that Amaris lived and fought happily beside these men—men Amaris loved so much that her final words had not been for Nox but a command to save them.

She couldn't explain the tiny sliver that embedded itself at the memory. Jealousy, pain, sorrow, and regret burrowed themselves just below her skin. She closed her eyes against the memory of Amaris's plea—her parting thoughts of the one she loved.

Her drawings, her journal entries—they were of no use now.

Nox fetched a black hooded cloak from her closet and a few small trinkets, like a black ribbon to tie her hair away from her face and a necklace, should she need to barter. She changed out her footwear into the most sensible pair that remained in her wardrobe—flat, comfortable, padded leather shoes.

Though the queen's city had fallen into riots as the dragon had torn from the coliseum and citizens had run for the streets, she couldn't believe Priory had been as affected as Aubade. The ghostly quiet of the Selkie's halls led her to believe the pleasure house and the girls within had not been spared.

Nox took a few steps from her room into the dark of the hall.

Perhaps if there were any answers, they'd be in Millicent's office. If the All Mother was particularly benevolent, perhaps the Madame's dragon-like hoard of crowns had remained untouched.

Nox had just started toward the Madame's office when she heard the distinct sounds of rustling.

She froze, knowing those weren't the sounds of an animal.

Her heart skidded as she fumbled with the memory of what she was supposed to do. Nox pressed herself against the wall and reached for the knife Malik had given her from where it had been tucked in her pants. Her fingers wrapped around the hilt. She looked at the blade in her hand and remembered that she should flip her grip into what he'd called the ice-pick hold. A smile flickered on her lips despite her fear, knowing Malik would have been proud.

She crept sideways along the wall, drawing closer to the sound.

Someone was definitely in the office.

While the rest of the house was as black as death, the tiny flicker of candlelight licked its way out from the space beneath the closed door onto the plush carpet of the hall. Nox was nearly at the door as she listened for signs of who might be inside.

In her heart of hearts, she'd promised the Madame that she would kill her. If the moment had come, she wasn't sure whether she was ready.

She tightened her hold on the dagger, ready to plunge it downward. The disturbance of objects being moved around and papers shuffling continued to filter from behind the door. Her fingers slid to the knob, and she took several rallying breaths.

You want her dead, she told herself. *You can make that happen.*

With one final breath for courage, Nox threw open the door and leapt into the space beyond the doorway, dagger aloft.

Cici loosed the shrill squeak of a dying mouse.

"Cici?" Nox's adrenaline rang in her ears. "What the hell are you doing here?"

The short-haired girl threw a hand to her chest as if to catch her heart from flying from its cage. "You scared the shit out of me, Nox! Fuck!" She stared with wide eyes for a few long moments, and then as quickly as her fear came upon her, it was over. She resumed her rifling of drawers and the objects within as if Nox had never entered.

"What are you looking for?" It was the first question that came to mind, until Nox remembered there was a much more pressing issue. "What happened to everyone?"

Cici didn't stop shuffling through papers. "I'm looking for my contract. I want to light that life deed on fire so that if that bitch ever comes back, she has no proof of ownership."

If Cici was fine, that left one final orphan unaccounted for. Nox asked, "Have you seen Emily?"

Cici shook her head, focused wholly on her search. She got down on her knees, looking under the desk, tearing through the drawers while she spoke. "First you left, then Emily. You came back after you fell ill, but Em never did. Everything seemed fine for a little while. You got better, Millicent was in a good mood, business was great, but then the night after you went to the Bird and the Pony, the whole place went to hell. Guards stormed in here the next morning. They practically dragged Millicent out by her hair."

Nox felt as if she'd been slapped. "Why?"

Cici stopped then, finally regarding her with her full attention. "Where have you been, under a rock? The city was sacked. Some dragon escaped from the castle, and the riots that followed...well, if I had to guess, your head is probably up on the chopping block too."

"*My* head?" Nox clarified, certain Cici had made a mistake.

"Every man saw you there that night and saw the captain leave with you. They traced the connection to the Selkie almost immediately. That's what you get for being too good at your job—notoriety and a reputation. Apparently, the captain acted against the crown immediately after your encounter with him. He was a loyal man of service for umpteen years and then he flips for a traitor the moment he meets a whore? There's a story to be followed."

"What?" Nox asked breathlessly.

Cici tapped the side of her nose as if indicating someone were sniffing out the clues. "You did this. I'm not mad about it. I have no dog in this fight."

Nox's heart quickened. She hadn't killed him, not really. She had merely influenced him. She couldn't be blamed for that, could she?

"I don't understand."

The girl looked exasperated. "Are you just trying to make sure we have our stories straight? Because I'm a little busy. I know, Nox. The crown knows. Everyone knows. You and Millicent conspired with the Captain of the Guard against Queen Moirai. It's done with. I don't give a shit. I don't care who you overthrow or what powers you usurp. Conspiring is treason. If I were you, I'd get out of here." Cici grabbed a small bag and had it arcing through the air toward her. "Here. I've already taken two pouches."

The weight of the coins clanged in Nox's hand as she caught the bag out of the air.

"Where is everyone else? All the girls?"

Cici stopped again. Her posture softened, and for the first time, she did not seem annoyed. Her shoulders slumped slightly with the weight of whatever truth rested on them. She eyed Nox sadly, taking her time to feel the questions and the heaviness of its answer. "Some of them ran. Others were taken during the riots. We were a house without a madame—a group of unprotected women in a city that sees no value in whether we live or die. What do you think happened?"

It wasn't a question.

Nox simply stood there at the revelation, a deer in the snow. Her memories flitted to the night she'd entered the Bird and the Pony. She didn't know how the men could have recognized her or what they would have speculated. Yes, she had sent Eramus into the ring that day to face the ag'drurath, but there was no evidence known to man or fae that could link her to it. Right?

"Give me a moment."

Nox left for a moment down the hall and returned to Millicent's office with a black velvet satchel meant to carry things to and from the market. If the Madame was gone, Nox felt she was owed some reparations. Most of Millicent's treasures were bulky, gaudy, and ostentatious, but there were a few things that had always piqued her interest. When Millicent had explained the enchanted carriage, she had also referenced several other spelled objects that she had acquired over the years. While Nox wasn't entirely sure what use she'd have for them, she reached for the only magic objects she could find.

She turned for the door. "Cici?"

With thinly controlled impatience, Cici replied, "What?"

Nox crossed the space between them and hugged Cici goodbye. The girl stiffened uncomfortably in Nox's arms. Nox didn't know why she did it. She wasn't a hugger. It just felt like the right thing to do.

With that, Nox walked down the plush rug of the corridor, only the rustling noises of a girl and her papers to break the pressing quiet. Aside from her cloak, her walking shoes, and a coin purse, she'd grabbed the only three things she knew to have power. The first was a candle that never grew smaller, no matter how long it burned. The second was a pocket watch that didn't tell the time but had an arrow to point wherever you wanted to go. The third was an elaborate black quill that could write on any parchment and have its message received anywhere in the world by whoever possessed its matching counterpart.

She reached the window in the salon and looked over one last time at the gloomy phantoms in the vanilla-scented lounge.

Nox pulled up the hood of the cloak as she slipped through the window, landing silently in her soft, leather shoes. She was exposed by the pool of light between homes for the briefest of moments as she crossed the street to where the men were waiting.

"Nice cloak. Did you bring us anything?" It was Ash's way of greeting.

"Why yes, I have an emerald dress that would complement your skin tone beautifully." Then to Malik, she asked, "Don't you think Ash would make a marvelous woman?"

"I've always told him so."

"No time like the present, Ash. The closets in the Selkie are ripe for the picking."

He mock scowled between the two of them. "You laugh, but I'll have you eat your words when you see just how stunning I am in a gown."

They continued their way through the city, Nox with a small smile on her lips. She found herself starting to wonder if these men might be her friends.

Six

TWO GUARDS STOOD AT THE ENTRY TO THE WALLED CITY OF Aubade, torchlight glinting off their metallic breastplates. Nox and the reevers watched from the shadows as citizens filtered in and out of the choke point. Each civilian was inspected, their scrolls thoroughly examined before they were admitted into the royal city. Papers for safe passage had always been necessary when entering any of the continent's walled cities, but it was safe to assume there would be no lenience in security given the recent riots. The men whispered their ploys to slither in, undetected.

"You're not going to slip past," Nox said impatiently.

"I think you need to have a little more faith. We're very sneaky."

"With your fae ears? You stick out like a sore thumb, redhead. You may be the worst spies of all time."

Ash tugged his hair out of its knot and gave it a tussle to ensure the points of his ears were concealed. He made an unappreciative face.

Nox rolled her eyes. "Follow me and do your best to look subservient."

"What?"

But Nox was already making her way toward the guard. Ash and Malik jogged to keep up. The hood of her black cloak was up as she approached the guards. She lifted it, flashing them her most charming smile. First, she eyed one and then let her eyes slide to the other, as if she couldn't quite decide which man was more delectable.

Nox struck a gentle tone—not seduction but a voice meant to disarm and stir thoughts of benevolence. "Well, hello, gentlemen."

"M'lady," one managed to stutter.

"I hope you haven't found much trouble this evening? The roads have been so dangerous, I can't tell you how glad I am to be off them."

The guards grunted some form of agreement. Surely the last few days had been hell in the wake of the ag'drurath and whatever anarchy had rippled from the disturbance.

She gave an apologetic smile as if she truly felt for their plight. Then, as if mildly inconvenienced, she wiggled her fingers at Malik. "Boy, my papers."

The honest bewilderment on Malik's face shone in the flickering torchlight. The guards turned their eyes to him expectantly. He blinked in confusion, then lifted his hands in a hopeless gesture but understood the ploy the moment his palms had begun to rise. He patted his shirt, then his pockets. He widened his eyes further and then struck a tone between panic and contrition.

"My lady, I'm so sorry. I have no idea…"

Nox spun on him, flashing anger mingled with potent fear. "How could you—" Then she made a show of catching herself and controlling her temper. She smoothed her cloak and made an effort to look the part of a proper lady, catching her breath despite her extreme dismay. "I want to extend my forgiveness, but you may have just cost me my entrance into the city, which could very well have greater consequences for our safety than you realize. Do you know how dangerous it is on nights like these?" She turned to the guards with a defeated look. "Do you gentlemen know who might house me tonight? My aunt is within Aubade's walls, and she's fallen ill. She won't be able to send papers for my admittance until the morning. I know no one in the city on this side of the wall." Nox feigned hurt and surprise at a thought that crossed her mind. "That is, my aunt will deliver the papers if she's well enough to write them. Oh, no…" She began to wring her hands.

"Oh, don't fret, m'lady." One of the guards looked as if his heart were genuinely breaking for her. His face practically proclaimed that these were no times for such a radiant personage to be unprotected on the wrong side of the wall. While the other sentry seemed to be taking pity, it was nothing like the ache painted on the first guard's features.

Excellent, she thought. She only needed one. Nox focused her attention on him, looking up at him with the helpless eyes of a doe. She did not cry, as it would not serve her to oversell her part. She sniffed as if battling tears in an attempt to show strength. The best tactic in negotiations was the willingness to walk away, and she knew it to be true even now.

"I love my aunt very much. I know she'll understand why I cannot be by her bedside tonight."

Shadows from the night and the flickering torches exasperated the guard's deeply etched concern. His face betrayed every emotion. He would not stand for it. The guard spoke for his compatriot without giving the other man a chance to argue. "That's ridiculous, that is. We check papers to keep illegals and infiltrators out, not maidens helping their sick aunt. Please, go to your aunt."

Nox looked as if she might hug him. "Oh, thank you. And what may I call you, sir?"

He blushed deeply at that. The sentry was truly kicking the dirt under the weight of her gaze like a shy child. "I'm no sir, m'lady. I'm just a sentry. My name's Vescus."

She put a hand to his arm, face beaming with her bottomless well of appreciation. "I will never forget your kindness, Sir Vescus."

53

As the three passed through the gates, Vescus slapped Malik upside the head for his negligence. The reever's hand flew to the back of his head instinctively at the hurt. Nox could feel the guard's longing stare as he watched the object of what would surely be a tale he told for ages to come—his one true love, the one who got away.

Nox flashed a warning look at Malik, urging him not to react to the slap. He lowered the hand from the back of his head. The men continued following Nox until she had led them around the corner.

Once they were out of both sight and earshot, the men began to give her slow, impressed claps as they shook their heads in amazement. She bowed deeply, her teeth glinting. Her eyes sparkled as she broke their admiration with a taunt to Ash. "If you had worn that emerald dress, we could have given your charms a whirl instead."

"There's always next time."

"I may be no good with a sword, but I earn my keep."

"You're no good with a sword *yet*," Ash corrected. He clapped a comforting, companionable hand on her shoulder as they made for the castle.

✦

While the three rightly suspected that the queen had put out word for the reevers, it was doubtful that their sketches and descriptions had been spread amongst every innkeeper in Farehold. Ash and Malik waited in the shadows behind a tavern and sent Nox in alone to secure them a room for the night, along with two warm loaves of bread dotted with sprouted grains. To avoid the suspicions of traveling with her companions, she only purchased one room on the second floor of the inn. Once she'd settled into her rented room, she locked the bedroom door, opened the window, and extended an outstretched arm to help the reevers scramble up the side of the wall.

Nox helped Ash up first, as he was lighter and quicker

54

on his feet. She left the faeling to hoist up Malik, since she'd probably dislocate her shoulder if she needed to swing him into the room.

It was easy to find shelter in the forest. In the cities of men, amongst their filth and between their architectures and structures, one could not simply lie down for a night's rest and expect to wake up unbothered in the morning. Now that they were all safely under a roof and away from prying eyes, it was time to strategize.

"It's only fair that you know, I'm also wanted by the crown."

They both looked surprised. "For what?"

"You remember my knight friend who ran into the coliseum?"

They didn't have to respond. Their faces said enough. Yes, of course they remembered the utterly bizarre situation. Anyone present would recall the vacant shell of a man who'd sprinted after a serpentine demon to his own death at Nox's bidding.

"He was the Captain of the Guard. Understandably, I'm wanted for treason. I still think it's safer for me to talk to innkeepers than you, but you're traveling with a dangerous fugitive."

"So are you."

"Excellent. We're all in good company."

Ash and Malik sprawled on the floor of the inn while Nox took the bed. She ripped off half of one loaf of the bread for herself, passing the rest to the reevers. She sat on the foot of the bed, her legs dangling off the ledge with her elbows on her knees, chin propped up in her hands.

"Even if there weren't a bounty on my head, I don't think I could flirt my way into the castle. And if I did, do we know what we're looking for?"

"I, for one, would like my sword back," Malik responded through a mouthful of bread. The crackling fire, safe in its hearth, blazed behind him. The fire's glow against his hair ringed him in an angelic halo. "I think Amaris would be a sight happier to see us if we were able to find Cobb as well."

"Cobb?"

"Her horse."

Nox's face twitched, brows lowering and lip puckering almost imperceptibly. Each and every reminder that Amaris had an entirely separate life—one utterly foreign to her—stung.

Ash didn't seem to notice the way Nox's energy shifted as he continued to consider her question. "We were sent on dispatch from the reev to find out why the queen is ordering the slaughter of northmen. If we're to believe Amaris, then the queen possesses the power of illusion. What we don't know is why she would curse the border or why she would use her power to maintain the illusion of a crown prince."

"How could Moirai do that? What is she?" Nox asked.

The reevers shook their heads, but it was Malik who said, "Your guess is as good as ours. Nothing we saw made sense to anyone but Amaris. Moirai has to be a witch."

Nox chewed on her lip. "A client of mine had seen the queen once and called her a paranoid woman who was always sequestered in her rooms. I can't imagine how it drains her to have to focus her magic like that."

There was a shuffling and adjusting of postures that may have implied the men were undergoing a triumphant effort not to picture what it meant to be one of Nox's clients.

"From what's been taught of curses, they're a one-time use of powerful magic, not something maintained," Ash said. "The illusion of a crown prince, though, has to require an incredible focus—particularly as she is not simply charming someone else to look like the prince but conjuring him from the air around her. Unless she were fae, of course, though she certainly doesn't look it. The queen must be on the verge of burnout after every one of the boy's appearances."

"And we have no idea why she would conjure a prince?"

Malik considered the question. He planted his weight

on his hands on the floor behind him. "Maybe there was a prince? We know the queen's daughter passed away a long time ago, and the crown prince was her son, right? Queen Moirai reigns as his grandmother and regent."

They nodded along.

Nox thought of the royal family, chewing her lip. "By the time I was old enough for the matrons to teach us about politics, the princess had already been long dead. The orphanage didn't bother to update itself with portraits of the prince, so our impressions of the royal family were rather outdated. I never knew what he looked like."

Malik had a few years on the other two. "We didn't follow the crown particularly closely in my village. I was already in my early schooling by the time the princess left the earth to be with the All Mother, so I do have a few memories of it. Before that, though, I remember how the teachers celebrated the day the kingdom announced the birth of her son. Isn't that funny? We had cakes and pies as if we'd won some grand tournament."

Nox was quiet. She had not found it amusing. "I doubt the fanfare would have been nearly so grand if Princess Daphne had borne the kingdom a daughter."

No, she thought, life was not kind to women. They were not celebrated for the grand achievement of being born with something between their legs. She knew more than most that a girl had to find a way to navigate the dangers of this world, whether it was through Amaris's brandishing of swords or Nox's charm and intellect, lest she be chewed up and spit out by the continent.

Ash prompted Malik to continue, asking, "And what of Princess Daphne's husband?"

Malik frowned while he searched his memories for the information. "He hadn't been of royal blood and had no claim to the throne, from what I recall, so he was of little relevance after she died. The man had some vaguely noble title and lands. I want to say that it was an advantageous alliance, but

I was too young and too bored by politics to have retained much of the information. I guarantee that whatever was happening outside during playtime was far more interesting than talk of princesses and politics."

"How do you think the queen has made it this far without anyone knowing that she was a witch?" Nox asked.

Ash ventured, "I suppose there was truly no way to know any better. Think about it. Consider if you possessed the gift of illusion. If you were a child who created an imaginary friend, those around her would perceive a true being of flesh and blood. They wouldn't know of your power. There's a chance that, for a time, neither would you. It would be a very easy power to keep hidden in plain sight. She may not have even realized she had it in the beginning."

Nox wondered at this. How many of those around her were witches or in possession of small magics? She had thought Millicent just a wicked human until the woman had taken off her long, black glove in the carriage and touched her with death. She had lived with and spent every moment with Amaris for fifteen years and never knew that the girl she loved so well, the one she knew inside and out, could see through enchantments. The reevers before her regarded her as a beautiful creature, yes, but they had no idea what dark magic sourced her beauty. Ash was part fae, and as such, he possessed elegant features and graceful speed and would not experience the ravages of age the same as his fully human peers. Nox supposed she was also part fae and pondered the aging process for faelings living in secret, their human halves interfering with any true immortality. She briefly wondered how long would she maintain her youthful face.

"Malik?"

He blinked a bit at the use of his name. "Hmm?"

"What do they teach in the villages about fae and magic? Princesses and politics may not have been important, but do they teach children in school about these things?"

He frowned. "Farehold just doesn't have the population

58

to support more than distrust of magic. It's a very human kingdom, save for a few stray fae and halflings like this mutt."

"Proud mutt," Ash said, stuffing what remained of the bread in his mouth.

Malik continued, "We aren't discouraged from talking about it, but it isn't formally taught. There are no classes beyond what we're told of history. It's largely speculative."

Nox nodded. "That seems like a good way for misinformation to spread."

He agreed.

"Do you have any access to magic?"

"Who, me? No. I'm just a human." He said it almost with a tinge of disappointment.

Ash swallowed, chiding, "You're no human. You're a reever."

This made the golden young man smile. He had a kind, honest smile that made him winsome in nearly every way. Nox felt that if he had ever been sent to her room, perhaps it wouldn't have been such a terrible night. She certainly would have let him live, and if she couldn't have guaranteed his life, she would have refused the patron altogether as she had the omnilinguist many moons ago. But no, she was confident that Malik would not be the sort to frequent establishments like the Selkie. There was a goodness about him that made her certain his feet had never darkened any such doorstep. She appreciated him all the more for it.

"What about you?" Malik asked her. "Are you just incredibly charming to gatekeeping sentries, or is there a power under all that dark hair?"

"There is."

The men's postures stilled, exchanging glances before looking at her expectantly, but she offered nothing more. Seeing the secret and not wanting to disregard her wish for silence, Ash finally pressed, "Is it anything that will help us get into the castle?"

Nox thought of Eramus and his treasury of weapons. She

thought of the men at the Bird and the Pony and how they'd clapped their captain on the back as he'd left the establishment with his arm around a true beauty. She thought of the smell of the blood of maidens before her as she entered the armory and the sound of the click as he'd locked the door behind them.

"No."

Seven

THERE WAS A HUSHED, SACROSANCT BEAUTY TO THE UNIVER-
sity campus with its stones, its ivy, its lichen-covered
boulders, and the emerald of its hills. The forest's tall pines
lined one far side of the grounds, creating a natural barrier
between the rest of the world and the haven of knowledge.
The buildings were hewn from whatever natural stone broke
the earth this far north, creating a dark uniformity to the
buildings, though each had its own distinct shape. There was
an intermingling of age and vitality to the university that
Uaimh Reev hadn't possessed. Though these buildings were
as old as the continent, they'd been preserved with care for
both modern needs and to honor the history the architecture
represented.

Amaris had been in the middle of eating another bland
meal in the healers' hall when Cora had arrived with a pleasant
smile and an offer to take her out of her cramped quarters. All
too excited to escape her windowless tomb, Amaris jumped
at the opportunity for a tour.

The chilled air was a welcome relief. The mist carried
the fresh scents of grass, rain, and conifers at all hours of the
day and night. It was a peculiar climate compared to the crisp

air at the reev, the warmth of the southern coast, or the days spent in northeastern Farleigh.

Cora had always been pleasant, but Amaris had underestimated just how precocious the clever girl could be. Cora was more than happy to explain everything about the university's history, the various subjects, the livelihood of the students, and everything in between. Knowing the girl to be fully human from how she'd responded to Amaris's persuasion on the night she'd tried to free Gadriel, Amaris asked her how she came to study here.

"My mother did have an aptitude for the small magics, yes. She was sought out by the university at the age of fifteen when word spread about her ability to speak to metal. The metalsmiths and forgers had told of her talent, coming to her with tricky armors and requesting reinforced blades and complex weapons. Though she was younger at the time than I am, she could bend any metal to her wish. She was quite clever. Still is." Cora smiled while she led Amaris around the buildings.

Amaris listened with one ear while wondering if the sky was ever blue in this part of Farehold. Perhaps she'd be cursed to see dense, gray clouds for as long as her feet remained planted on its grounds. Her gaze returned to her tour guide. Perhaps Cora was sunshine enough for them both.

"She studied here and met my father," the girl was explaining. "He was also a student of manufacturing, though he is fully human—no magic to his name. You see, any metalsmith can apprentice under another in his town, but those who come to the university come to be the best. He didn't just want to learn about metals. He wanted to learn about leathers and ships and architecture. He studied mechanisms and fabrications and all the things the university had to offer. Whatever he couldn't do with his hands, my mother could do with her gift. Together they were the most successful creators in Farehold. They served the queen for twenty years together as her manufacturers. Once I was old enough, even though I hadn't demonstrated any aptitudes for magic, they sent me off to try my hand at a few departments and see where I might best educate myself."

"So manufacturers can be humans?"

Cora laughed. "Any subject can be human or fae. Humans just have to work, and the fae get to cheat."

It pleased Amaris to know that this was not a university merely for those born with gifts. While the magically inclined were often recruited and studied on the graces of the school, human attendees were required to pay a tuition fee. Cora said she didn't mind, but her mother had thrown a fit amongst the alumni about the discrimination the university displayed by taxing only nonmagical students.

Humans shouldn't be excluded from the university any more than women should be excluded from Uaimh Reev, Amaris thought. Of course, just as she'd undergone her share of struggles at the reev, the human population would surely face prejudice and unnecessary hardships and feel as though the cards were stacked against them. Maybe they'd sculpt a new future, a more inclusive future, one chip in the marble at a time.

While her mind danced between humans and fae, Amaris had a thought. "Cora, can you draw?"

Cora nodded pleasantly. "I'm something of an artist, if I do say so myself. Ever since I was a child. I prefer to paint, but sketching is far more practical. Though creativity rarely pays the bills." She sighed. It was apparent from the defeat in her tone that this was a conversation she'd had before.

Amaris frowned. "Is that what you would do with your life? Art?"

Cora smiled, but the expression was no longer happy. "It's not pragmatic."

Only the squish of their feet on damp grass filled the space between them as they walked. Amaris understood that being a classically trained healer was realistic. It was safe. It would surely make her parents very, very proud.

"Can I tell you something?"

The girl nodded.

Amaris chose her words creatively, knowing that the details were unimportant. "I was also given a specific path to make money. My fate had been decided for me, and it would have been very profitable. My...*career*...had been ascribed without my input."

Cora didn't look at her as they continued walking, and Amaris knew her words struck a chord. Cora prompted Amaris to continue. "And?"

"And they were right. It would have been a profession that I'm sure would have made a lot of people very happy," Amaris said. Agnes, Millicent, and a horde of patrons would have been very pleased at the very least. "I may have been great at it. I may have bathed in riches. But I would have been miserable. I didn't know what I wanted to do, but I knew it wasn't that."

The girl looked at her then. "And now? Do you make money?"

The question was downright comical. "None at all!" Amaris beamed. "I've never had less to my name. But I'm free."

Cora blew out a breath of air. She kept her eyes fixed on the grassy knolls, the stone, the ivy as she said, "Why do you ask about drawing?"

Amaris had nearly forgotten the reason she'd inquired in the first place. "I was wondering if you might draw a picture of what you see when you look at Gadriel? I've only ever seen him as fae. I know he looks terrifying to everyone else, and I feel like I need to be able to see what they see, even just once." She didn't add that seeing him as a demon might give her a sense of sick satisfaction after what he'd put her through.

Their conversation reached a lull as they approached an enormous building. Amaris had been particularly interested in the library ever since the healer had mentioned the Master of Literature and the information at his disposal. It was their true destination in the day's tour. The energy shifted the moment Cora led her through enormous doors to a closed atrium. She spoke to a nervous-looking girl behind the front desk about escorting Amaris through the archives. Walls separated the stacks beyond them from where they stood in the foyer. The new student's voice was wrought with distress as she said she would need to speak to whoever supervised her. Her supervisor had then sent a runner to fetch word from the Master of Literature, creating quite the ordeal. Amaris wasn't sure why her presence was such a source of contention, but she had nothing better to do than wait.

After a small, fidgeting eternity, they received word that she was allowed to see their collections, so long as she remained in the escort of a university student.

It took Amaris precisely two seconds to understand why this collection was such a well-guarded secret.

Her eyes widened, lips parting slightly as she inhaled at the sight of the library before her. She was hit with the smells of leather and paper and wisdom. She looked upward as she rotated with slow, deliberate awe.

The center of the room was circular, with a brightly colored mosaic of tiles sprawled on the floor displaying a map of the continent and its kingdoms. Overhead was a stained-glass window of yellows and reds and blues and purples, encompassing nearly the entire roof. The archives themselves appeared to be seven floors high, each lined with colorful leather books. Some books were a deep burgundy with gilded letters, matching sets nearly thirty editions long. Others were forest green with markings embossed in silver. There were black books and brown books, tall books and tiny books, long, thin scrolls and even some text that appeared to be chiseled into stone. The collection of books was as colorful and beautiful as the artistic glass above. Leather-bound books, tattered paper journals, scrolls, texts, and all assortments of information had been neatly organized in the most expansive collection anywhere on the continent, if not the globe.

"Wow," Amaris said in a single, low breath.

"It's really something, isn't it?"

"Something…" Amaris repeated as she again spun in a slow, evaluating circle, straining as she took in each of the seven layers of the balconies overhead and the knowledge and mysteries every text held.

Cora clasped her hands in front of her. "Is there anything in particular you'd like to know?"

Amaris blinked. She returned her attention to Cora and leafed through her brain as if it were little more than a book in the library, searching for what it was she wanted to know. Should she research curses? Perhaps her time would best be spent reading records of the relations between Farehold and Raascot? Would there be texts about the reevers and the history of their keep? Could she simply ignore all these and find a romance novel where a dangerous and mysterious prince kidnapped a young maiden and took her to his castle, tempting her night after night until they fell in love?

"Where might I find something about the dark fae and their wings?"

She was surprised at her own question. Though she did not find herself particularly fond of Gadriel, his words had stung. She did blame herself for his state. She had struck back with equal force in their verbal spar, but if there were any solution to his tattered wings, she'd like to find out.

Cora led her to an array of neatly organized mahogany desks. Each desk had six small drawers across the top and six small drawers below, along with a place to sit and write. She explained that each desk represented a subject, and each drawer contained the names of authors and location references to the texts. For example, one desk was dedicated entirely to cultures, so if one wanted to read about the history and people of the Etal Isles, they would simply sit at that mahogany desk and flip through the alphabetically arranged authors until they found the title that interested them.

Amaris never would have been able to navigate the

complex organizational system of letters and numbers to find the knowledge she required without Cora's help. It was a tedious task, but Cora helped Amaris locate three separate books dedicated to the dark fae—Raascot fae, as they were academically named. There had been more titles and more authors on the subject, but several of them seemed geared toward religious speculation or zealous contemplation, so Amaris chose to keep her research as scientific as possible. Cora led her over three different floors, plucking books from the shelves and plopping them in Amaris's arms before setting off to find the next. She led Amaris to a small, wooden desk by a slitted window. Once she was satisfied with her little collection, Cora excused herself to find books for her own studies and said she'd check back in later.

"Try to stay here. It's a big library, and I may never find you again if you wander off to another alcove. Happy studies!"

Left to her own devices, Amaris leafed through page after page of information.

The first book spent its time categorizing magics into dichotomies of light and dark. The master—whose name was a collection of unpronounceable syllables—had taken particular interest in trying to trace familial ties regarding magical abilities. Amaris had been told that power, unlike hair color, did not transfer from parent to child. This author argued to the contrary, though their evidence seemed thin and unsubstantiated.

The second text seemed to be of a more historical nature, written with an anthropological angle and covering the migration of fae and relocation of those who manifested certain abilities. It was a collaborative piece by a team of archaeologists as well as a documentarian who recorded several tales from the few surviving fae who had been alive for the last thousand years or so. Even in that text, the author couldn't avoid the reason *why* the dark fae had been forced out of Farehold: some powers were terrifying. Roughly three sentences suggested rather conspiratorially that the migration had begun centuries prior to the earliest records of magical prejudice when, upon finding the climate near what was now Aubade favorable, efforts had been made to uproot the royal family from their ancestral home in the mountains to the mild southwestern coasts, creating a toppling effect of relocation. The rumor was unsubstantiated, and the text quickly redirected to dark gifts and the protection of the light gifts. Farehold had been a push, and Raascot had been its pull, offering asylum to all who migrated from the ever-growing hostility of the southern kingdom.

The books seemed to agree on two things: dark fae existed, and somehow the predilection for wings was passed through the lineage of pure-blooded fae as a genetic trait.

"Great. You exist and you do indeed have wings," Amaris muttered dryly to her book. She had hoped to discover a reference to healing and maintenance of the wings, but instead, she was only able to read about a handful of powers affiliated with the northern fae categorized as dark magics, then contrasted against the light.

Regardless of the text, the author, or the intent, the underlying theme was the same: the continent's dark fae had been pushed north centuries ago. Some fae could call the darkness itself, extinguishing candles and lanterns and filling a room with night even if it were the middle of the day. Some fae possessed voyeurism, an ability to remain unseen to anyone around them, save for the glow of their eyes. Other dark fae were said to possess powers of fear and the ability to project those fears onto those around them. There were records of shape-shifters, succubi and incubi, the power to influence bonds and relationships that might dissolve marriages or falsely connect allegiances, consorting with and reanimating the dead, and even those who could invade the mind, planting memories and thoughts and beliefs that were never there to begin with. Amaris shuddered as she read the list but considered her own power. Surely persuasion would have been listed amongst the powers affiliated with dark fae, even if she herself was not wicked and had no intentions of using such gifts for evil purposes.

Perhaps all these unsavory powers could have altruistic uses. Or maybe the southern kingdom had been right to herd the menaces northward. The text in her hands did its best to remain objective, recording only facts and withholding its commentary.

She'd always preferred studying monsters over history, but this book was difficult to put down. She was absorbing its primary theme like a sponge soaked up water. She'd dragged her finger across page after page, the sound of skin on paper a fruitless, raspy thing. Despite the knowledge she'd gleaned, she'd scanned for one word only: wings.

Instead, she saw scholar after scholar end in the same conclusion. Despite Raascot's size and population, without the contamination of Farehold blood, northern fae would have long family lines of dark fae, as none of the light gifts intermingled. This seemingly ensured their children would also be presented with darker gifts. The same could be said to have happened in the south, as fae and faelings born in Farehold rarely seemed to manifest powers that the peoples around them deemed corrupt or cursed.

Amaris shut the book and rubbed her fingers against the pressure building behind her eyes. She hadn't asked Gadriel what other powers he might possess and wasn't sure if she wanted to know. Though she didn't particularly crave his company, she didn't think he was evil nor fear him. Then again, after all she'd read, perhaps she should.

Amaris placed her books on a cart to be reshelved and returned to where she'd been abandoned, closing her eyes against the swirl of knowledge and information. She lowered her head to the desk and rested it on her hands until Cora came to find her.

"Amaris?"

She opened her eyes. Cora's mouth wiggled off to the side as if fighting the urge to say something.

"Yes?"

Cora kept her tongue for another moment, then said, "So instead of studying, I drew you a picture."

"You did!" Amaris's eyes widened, extending her hand excitedly for the page.

Rather than hand it to her, Cora slid into the chair across the desk from her. "Before I show it to you, will you tell me what he looks like? What he really looks like?"

"Gadriel?"

Cora dipped her chin with the barest of cautious nods.

Amaris blinked, withdrawing her hand. She rested her forearms on the desk and reeled in her emotions. She didn't want to describe Gadriel. It only took a heartbeat of reflection to know that she didn't want to talk about him because she was angry with him, and it would pain her to call him beautiful. He didn't deserve it.

Yet she sat in a building of academic scholarship. Lying would not serve her.

Amaris nodded. "Sure. Yes, I can do that." She exhaled and propped her chin on her hands, leaning her weight forward as she pictured him. It didn't take long for Gadriel's face to populate, followed by his shoulders, his body, his cocky half smile. She sighed and began.

"He's northern—something like Master Fehu. He doesn't have her jewel-toned eyes though, which must be from her southern side. His are like night." As were Nox's, she thought. "His wings…well, he's injured at present. But picture a crow or an angel. The big, black feathers of a bird. They were so strong before…" She stopped herself, moving on to his next feature. She inhaled and exhaled slowly, struggling with admitting to his features without sounding resigned. "He's lovely, of course. He's fae, so how couldn't he be? But he's also a general, meaning he isn't just lithe or thin like many fae but well trained, tall, muscular. His hair is black—as black as his wings. He's… he's very handsome. How's that? Do you need more?"

Cora's eyebrows pinched. She frowned and pulled out the

page, holding it so only she could see what she'd drawn. Conflict and concern etched themselves on her youthful features as she asked, "And you've never seen it any other way? This is always what you see when you look at it—him, I mean?"

Amaris confirmed, "Yes, I've always seen him like this."

Cora exhaled slowly. "Well, that makes sense then. I don't see how you could have befriended him if you saw what the rest of us see." She passed the page to Amaris, who grabbed it a bit too eagerly.

Her mouth opened ever so slightly, face tensing nearly imperceptibly as she looked at the nightmare on paper. Ripped, cobweb wings, almost like those of a bat, joined his back in projectile spines. Though bipedal, the ag'imni's arms and legs bent at terrifying angles, as if its joints were too sharp, too rigid for a truly humanoid creature. The enormous black eyes had been etched again and again and again with Cora's charcoal as if to emphasize the abysmal trenches within them. The teeth, the talons, the sheer terror seeped through the page.

"You're very talented," Amaris said quietly, voice low as an oath. "I feel your fear when I look at this. You've captured an emotion. And...I'm sorry. I'm sorry that you see him that way. I hope your nightmares—"

"No monster can give me nightmares any more than the stress of final examinations already do. But...you really think it's good? The art, I mean?"

Amaris nodded, handing it back to her.

"Don't you want to keep it?"

Amaris frowned. "No. It's perfect. It's wonderful. And no, I don't think I can hold on to that version of him. But thank you for letting me see it. Truly."

Buoyed by the compliment at her artistic skill, Cora was cheerful once more. She smiled as she led them through the stacks and toward the exit, proudly boasting how the university contained all the world's knowledge as if it had been a personal achievement of hers.

"I am sorry you didn't have any luck," Cora said sympathetically. "Someone has to know something, and if they do, it'll be on those shelves. I'm sure of it."

"If we come back, I'll look up avian healing rather than fae. We'll approach it from a different angle."

Cora nodded confidently. "If the answer is anywhere, it's there!" As they headed toward the healer's building once more, she made a gesturing sweep to the tallest building on campus. "The library holds all the continent's knowledge, and the tower holds all the continent's magic."

It had been said so cheerily, so flippantly.

Amaris said nothing as the girl dropped her off at her room with a friendly wave and flitted off to her studies.

She didn't check on Gadriel, letting herself directly into her room and shutting the door, nor did she attempt to sleep that night.

As she took off her shoes and crawled on top of the bed, she knew in no uncertain terms that she would not be closing the door to her mind. Her shoulders, her back, her legs all lay wooden and lifeless as she stared up at the ceiling. Her eyes burned with exhaustion, but she couldn't keep Cora's comment from her mind. A distant memory of a mystical glen and the Tree of Life colored her vision. She could remember the words of the priestess ringing through her as clearly as a bell.

"Magic is energy. It is neither created nor destroyed. It exists before it takes shape and maintains its presence after it is uttered. If you find the orb of its physical shape, there too you will find your answers."

That was what the priestess had said at the Temple of the All Mother. When Amaris had asked if the holy woman had the orb and inquired as to where she could find it, the response had been simple:

"It is held where all magic's secrets are held. You will find it there."

Amaris was motionless for what felt like hours as she

thought of Cora's innocent remark. *"The tower holds all the continent's magic."*

Her eyelids began to droop as she played the conversations in her head over and over. Her body relaxed as her limbs melted into the mattress beneath her, the voices in her mind playing on a loop like a lullaby. As she found herself drifting into the clutches of sleep, she did so with the conviction that she was lying only a few buildings away from the orb.

Eight

G ADRIEL LET HIMSELF INTO AMARIS'S ROOM THE NEXT
morning without knocking.

"Hey!" Her temper flared, muscles going rigid in reaction.
"I could have been changing!"

"I'm sorry." He stared directly at where she sat fully
clothed on her bed. "Are you naked?"

Her eyes narrowed. "What do you want?"

"I want you to talk to me." Gadriel didn't sit next to her
on the bed but grabbed a chair from the corner of her room
and carried it over. He spun it so its tall back faced Amaris.
He mounted the chair like a horse, resting his folded arms on
the chair's back. He wore the distinct long-suffering expression of patience. Though she couldn't quite put a name to the
way he eyed her, it conjured the memory of a matron preparing to talk to a peer at Farleigh. "I'm not sure what happened
yesterday, but I've done my best to give you space. What's
bothering you, demon whisperer? You're surlier than usual."

He rested his chin on his folded arms as his eyes looked
expectantly into hers. His face was stern but not unkind. He
had the sharp, squared jaw and darkened features that told her
any enemy who met him in an alleyway would have trembled

upon seeing him, even in his beautiful fae form. Amaris was unmoved by the goddess-granted looks of the fae. She wanted him to leave and allow her to glower in peace.

"You have a problem with my sunny disposition? Sorry, General, it's just my moon time." She scowled.

"That's a bullshit excuse, and I hope you don't take me for the kind of man who would buy it. Tell me why you're angry."

Amaris fought the urge to roll her eyes, knowing it would make her look childish. She wanted to tell him she was angry that he had ever entered her life. She wanted to let him know that he had alienated her from the reevers and then promptly gotten himself captured so that she was nearly forced to behead him in the coliseum. She fought the urge to tell him that she hated him. But all she could think about was the sting of how he'd answered the masters' inquiries when he'd said, "We fought together in Aubade."

She couldn't fathom how it could serve her to tell him. The only outcome would be his realization that she was sensitive to his perception of her. Her response was reactionary, emotional, and something she needed to get over, not discuss. Her misunderstanding was not his burden to bear but hers to grow through. It was a dry, bitter pill she was still attempting to swallow. The only cure for this sort of disillusion was time and a bucket of cold water.

The Raascot fae were not friends. Gadriel did not consider them so much as companions. To think, she had started to feel... No, she shut down whatever vein she'd opened when her foolish, gullible heart had led her to think they were anything else. It had been reflective of her immaturity. It had been a weakness, a misunderstanding, a weak, stupid hope that she'd conflated with truth. They were merely two people—or fae or half fae or witch or whatever they were—who happened to share a common enemy.

She didn't say any of those things. Instead, she exhaled slowly. "I think I know where they're keeping the orb."

This wasn't the answer he'd expected. "They, as in the university? You think they have information about the curse?"

She averted her gaze, lip twitching to fight off a sneer. She nodded once at the space on the wall that held her attention.

He followed her gaze briefly to the blank wall before returning his eyes fully to her. Gadriel appeared moderately amused by her insistence on displeasure. "So you've discovered where the information is, and this infuriates you. That makes perfect sense."

She wasn't sure why he had to antagonize her like this. She looked at him again, keeping her tone low. "I'm going to find the orb because Samael dispatched me specifically to learn Moirai's role and intent in the slaughtering of northerners."

"And to be clear, you think you're better equipped than a general with hundreds of years of experience?" He didn't voice the underlying implication that she was young and knew little of the world. She'd undergone some of the best training on the continent, short-lived as it may have been compared to his centuries.

He was baiting her for a reaction. He was good at that, but she didn't want to fight. It wouldn't help her heal or move on if she rose to the occasion. She closed her eyes, resisting. "I don't doubt your skill, your know-how, or your value in these matters. But this is my mission, and it has nothing to do with you."

From the look on his face, one might have thought she'd struck him. Gadriel leaned away from where he'd been supporting himself on the back of his chair and gestured to his body, his wings. The ever-patient expression was now one of irritation. "Nothing to do with me? This has everything to do with me."

Amaris looked away again. "I'll let you know what I find out."

"Amaris, talk to me."

She did not.

"Reever, I need you to look at me."

Still, she refused. From the corner of her eye, she could see the same controlled flash of anger she had seen in the doorway last night. He did not handle disrespect well.

"Amaris—"

"Fuck off!"

His movement was so fast, she hadn't seen it happen at all. It was just like in the forest, how she'd had her arrow ready, perched for the kill, when suddenly his knife was at her throat, holding her close. His ability to disarm her and the unfair advantage the fae had with speed and dexterity enraged her. Gadriel had grabbed her chin between his thumb and index finger in a motion too swift for her to fight off.

"Gad!" She jerked her neck to shake him, but he held his grip firm, his eyes boring into hers as he held her still.

Gadriel's dark eyes had the larger-than-normal irises known to the fae, both lovely and terrifying as he stared intently. "I said, look at me. How are we supposed to fight together or trust each other if you're building a wall between us? I can feel you constructing it brick by brick. You can tell me what happened, or you can continue whatever petty hostility toward me you've built, but if we're in a war, I should at least understand the battlefield. Talk to me."

This was precisely why she was angry. Moments like these when he forced a connection—when he lulled her into the stupid assumption that they had been friendly, at the very least. Perhaps after her years with the reevers, she'd trained herself to look for companionship in fellow warriors, and her mistaken faith in that had made her think them to be something they were not. If he were honest and simply voiced what he wanted from her—a mouthpiece in his escapades— they wouldn't have needed such deception.

"You aren't my general. I don't have to tell you anything. Go find your men to command."

He held his grip on her chin. She hoped he could feel the fire in her eyes, intending every second that pulsed between them to burn. She stared back with defiance. One second passed, then another. Her anger swelled with nowhere to go. She couldn't fight. She couldn't flee.

When he didn't release her, she spat.

A thrill of fear gripped her stomach the moment the water left her mouth as a flash flood of adrenaline coursed through her. She didn't know why she'd done it. Maybe she'd wanted to piss him off. Maybe she'd just wanted him to leave. But it was too late. She'd angered the monster.

Tiny droplets of her disrespect glistened on his face.

A terrifying calm settled over him as he went perfectly still. He released his hold of her face. He stared for a moment longer, his face neither threatening nor friendly. He stood to leave the room, allowing fear to leach into her through his unruffled feathers. Her heart thundered within her chest as she stared at the back of his head, but even if she hadn't already begun to regret the action of her own volition, he was about to make her regret it.

"You're lucky I need you alive."

"Fuck you."

Those words had been the golden scissors that cut the proverbial thread.

He wheeled on her with the speed and ferocity of a creature of the night. She could see the rage that scalded him. He made no move to intimidate or smash or wound; a man with this intensity did not need to resort to such things when his gaze was enough to burn ice and snow, but this time, he had a hand in her hair, pulling her head back to look up at him. His grip was not tight, nor did it hurt, but it was an act that demanded a modicum of respect from the brat she knew he perceived. His words came out in a growl as he said, "If you spit on me again, I will cut that tongue right out of your pretty mouth."

He released his hand from her hair and stalked from the room.

An infuriated, confused blush spread from her cheeks to her chest. Her hand flew to her hair, touching the place where he'd grabbed at her roots. An indefinable sensation spread to the tips of her innermost being. She felt it—whatever it was—in her toes, in her capillaries, in her throat, and as a throb in more than one entirely too-sensitive place within herself. She despised him. She wanted to kick him. She wanted to scream. She wanted… No. She stopped herself from thinking of anything beyond her fury. The idea that her body would respond so defiantly against the convictions of her mind felt like a betrayal.

She couldn't fathom why she cared so much about his anger. She had no idea why he was so bothered that she'd shut him out, save for a general's pomp and circumstance of needing respect. All she was to him now was someone he had fought with in Aubade. All she'd been before that was a set of purple eyes able to see the fae. She had every right to be angry, and she clutched her resentment tightly to her chest while a bonfire of emotions burned pink, red, and violet within her.

Nine

A MARIS HAD PLAYED THE ROLE OF ASSASSIN, AMBASSADOR, gladiator, captive, and commodity. One title she had yet to earn was that of cat burglar. If tonight went well, she could add it to her ever-growing list of life experiences.

She picked her way through the shadows across the back of the healer's building as she headed for the Tower of Magics. It was long past midnight. Her blank, sterile room had neither clock nor window, but after the building had gone silent with the lateness of the night, she'd crept outside and watched the moon as it crossed the sky, dipping between the concealing blots of clouds and marking the hour. Though the weather had been summery along the southwestern coast, the temperature felt unseasonably chilly in this part of the kingdom. It didn't take long for her to regret not bringing a cloak, but she didn't want to risk returning to her room. Sticking to the shadows, she made it to the back of the math building when a rustle behind her made her freeze.

Her back straightened and she spun to the shadows.

She wasn't sure if she was relieved or angry at who she saw. "What the hell are you doing here?"

She knew him well enough to assume he would have

smiled if he weren't so tired with having to deflect her need for antagonism. "If I had to guess, I'd say it's the same thing you are. You see, I don't know if you've heard, but the orb containing the border's curse might be somewhere on this campus."

"Go back to your room!"

He chuckled. It was not loud enough to draw attention but just for genuine amusement to escape his lips. Perhaps no one had spoken to him like this in the better part of a century. She knew he found her both belligerent and unswayed by his title of power. She also refused to be charmed by his smart-ass remarks.

Ignoring him quickly proved impossible. As she darted from the shelter of one building's shadows to the next, she could feel Gadriel close behind. They were only a few hundred feet from their target, and there'd been no signs of life to give them away. She gave up on trying to shake him from her trail as she reached the tower. There was only one entrance at its circular base.

Quieting her breath, she turned the handle and pushed her way inside.

Amaris stiffened. Gadriel went rigid at her side.

She wouldn't have been surprised if she had found a guard or a student surveilling the tower. She also wouldn't have been shocked to see Master Fehu and her enormous, gem-bright eyes glaring disapprovingly at them. She wouldn't even have been shocked if a vageth had been chained to the door to gnash trespassers between its needle-sharp teeth. Instead, they found no security. No hellhounds, demons, or sentinels. Just…magic.

Her lips parted in silent surprise, eyes widening to match as she drank in her surroundings. Her mouth dried as she struggled to understand what she was seeing.

Inside, the Tower of Magics had to be ten times the size it appeared from its exterior. While the outside had been looming and enormous of its own accord, whatever magic expanded it had created an estate that appeared the size of the entire university yet within the walls of only one of its buildings.

"Holy shit," she gasped. "I didn't know this was possible."

She didn't tear her eyes from the enormity of the room. Gadriel made no effort to keep the awe from his voice as he agreed, "It's incredible."

The space, though vast, was not entirely open. They had roughly ten arms' lengths to freely navigate before the enormous room was gated beyond further entry. They were permitted to see everything that they could not touch.

The pair took a few cautious steps forward to examine the iron bars prohibiting their access. The entryway was grand, but it allowed only for stairs to lead up and to the right, curving slightly as the staircase wrapped around the enormity of the enchanted tower. While the stairs awaited them, they couldn't tear their eyes from what stretched before them, locked behind an iron gate. Runes were etched into every bar, inscribing the iron with reinforcing enchantments. Behind the bars was a library, though it was nothing like the whimsical, colorful library Amaris had already seen. This darkened archive vibrated with power.

While the library had been neatly shelved in numerous rows, many of the books behind the thick iron bars stood alone, kept like exotic animals separated into cages. A large book in the center of the room seemed to cast its own light, enclosed in a showcase of rune-etched tempered glass. The runes lined every side, every seam of the tome. The book's sparkling light illuminated much of the ominous library before them, banishing shadows and revealing the oddities around it. The book nearest to it emanated a chilling frost, its cold mist cascading down its side and pooling on the floor below. Another glass case contained thick tomes that were a red shade like that of embers, glowing as if the fire within them were kept to a controlled smolder. Another book was pinned to the floor to prevent it from moving. Amaris stared at the book as it struggled against its bindings like a living animal.

She knew instinctively that these were not books intended for knowledge. The pages locked behind the giant prison cell of the Tower of Magics were meant for power.

While curiosity urged her to look around, her eyes returned to the book in the center of the room with a magnetic need. Its glittering light beckon her forward. She knew she couldn't reach it, couldn't touch it. But maybe if she could just get a bit closer...

She extended her fingers.

"Amaris, don't!"

Gadriel's voice sounded a moment too late.

She wrapped her fingers around the iron bars to lean in closer, then leapt backward with a pained yelp as lightning coursed through her. A silver crackle accompanied the loud pop as white-hot fire jolted her to her core. Nothing remained of her reverie. Gadriel's hands gripped her on either side from behind to keep her from tumbling backward, but the moment was over as soon as it had started. Amaris gaped in horror between her open palm and the bars that separated her from the call of the bright book. She shook her hands, blowing the heat away from them, but small welts were already beginning to form.

"How did it do that?" she gasped at the bars.

"Are you okay?" he asked.

She tried to shake his hands from her shoulders, but he didn't release her.

"It's lightning," he said cautiously. "Shock can stop your heart."

"My heart is fine! But my hand—" She twisted to look up at him. Her answer must have been satisfactory, as he slipped his hands away.

He examined the runes briefly before saying, "Manufacturing is a tricky, difficult business. Something like this?" He gestured to the iron bars. "It probably took at least four fae, though I suppose someplace like the university would be the best location for such a task."

She blinked at him, blowing on the welts swelling across her palm. "It takes four fae to do what?"

He continued studying it. "You need a manufacturer, and you need someone who possesses the power you desire. So in addition to whoever was trained in manufacturing and runes, it probably required a fae who could summon lightning, or whatever static shocked you just now. You'd also need someone who could speak to metal to contain the spells. And a fae shield, or someone who works in containment. I guess at the university, it would be easy enough to rally students and their abilities to consider it little more than a class project."

"Containment?" She rubbed her palms again.

"Shields and containment are often considered benign powers. They're not uncommon in Farehold. They're useful in most jail cells. We even have them on our bars in Gwydir." He looked at her hand again. "Are you sure you're okay?"

Her injured hand went to her chest as if she'd be able to feel whether the lightning had damaged her most vital organ. It continued thundering anxiously within her chest. "It was just a shock. I'm fine."

"Let's go." Gadriel urged them toward the stairs, but Amaris continued to hear the gentle temptations of the book. She shook it from her head, tearing her thoughts from its mysteries as they came to the second floor, exiting the stair-well to see what secrets rested on the landing.

After the magic of the first floor, the mundanity of the second floor was something of a disappointment. They paced the halls and looked behind door after door but discovered only classrooms, laboratories, and offices. Some were lined with desks, others with what appeared to be bar tables topped with glasses and beakers and bowls. Some rooms had large chalkboards at the front, and others had their chairs placed in such a way to create a circle, regarding whatever would have presented itself in the room's center. A set of double doors opened to reveal what appeared to be a gymnasium of some variety. A raised platform in the middle could have been for anything from showcasing one's abilities to dueling with magics for all they knew. If they had been at Uaimh Reev, it would have been an excellent platform for sparring in front of the other reevers.

As the second level appeared to hold no useful secrets, they advanced to the third.

They'd scarcely taken five steps from the stairs when a chill snaked down Amaris's spine, stopping her in her tracks. She took a half step back and bumped into Gadriel. A quick look at the tension in his face told her that the slithering anxiety had not spared him either.

The third landing was simply one large, dark pool that appeared to encompass the enormity of the entire level. Neither of them moved toward the lip of the ocean of black water. She flinched as she caught a noiseless splash, followed by a ripple from somewhere in the middle of the pool. What remained of Gadriel's tattered wings flared protectively around them. He put a hand on her lower back and ushered her hastily to the stairs once more. She was too grateful to escape the ominous ocean to bother snapping at Gadriel for touching her.

They mounted the stairs once more.

The fourth level had an iron grate similar to the one that had separated them from the library below. Once more, iron bars etched with runes prevented the pair from advancing. It didn't, however, stop them from peering at the museum of antiquities inside. This time, she knew better than to touch the bars.

While the library had held books, this room was filled with treasure. Enchanted items littered every corner, practically singing of their power. An amethyst necklace seemed to reverberate from where it sat on the supportive black-velvet neck of a partial mannequin mount. A harp made her fingers itch with the need to pluck its strings. A mirror on the far side of the room seemed to be showing not their reflections but two separate onlookers entirely. Gadriel and Amaris shot looks over their shoulders at nearly the same time, startled by whatever the mirror was reflecting, to see if any unwanted entity had joined them in the room. From instruments and tools to utensils and household items, the room was a museum of spelled objects. Despite the wonders of this forbidden treasure trove, some of which appeared spherical in nature, none appeared to be an orb that would offer the answers they needed.

"Spelled objects?" she asked, looking at him.

"Manufacturing."

"And you don't know anything else about manufacturing?"

"I'm a general. I command troops and make war plans. What about you? Do you know anything about roof thatching? Or how to bake pastries? Or—"

"Fine, I get it." Her irritation flared, though she supposed he had a point. She shouldn't have wasted her time looking up books on the northern fae and their wings when she could have been educating herself on more useful aspects of magic.

"There's no door," she said as she looked into the room. "The same with the library in the basement. There's no door. How do they get in and out?"

"Your guess is as good as mine, though I'm assuming the lack of locks is its own layer of security."

"What if it's in there? What if the orb is among those items?"

"Do you see anything that looks like an orb?"

She peered through the barrier at the objects in the vaguely threatening museum before them. "No, but that doesn't mean it isn't there."

"Let's keep going. If we don't find what we're looking for, we can always come back and let you break in to steal that purple necklace."

Amaris was pretty sure he'd only said it because taunting was one of the few things that forced her hand at interaction.

She denied the bid for connection. Instead, she turned her back and returned to the endless, spiraling stairwell.

Once again, they found an arrangement of classrooms, these with somewhat different configurations from the ones below. Amaris wondered if the students who were forced to trudge up five flights of stairs were in a more advanced or trusted level of their studies. The daily dedication from the burning in their thighs as they ascended these steps would spur their motivation onward.

Each floor held something more bizarre and ominous than the floor before it. Every so often, these curiosities and horrors were interspersed by levels of classrooms and offices. One particularly chilling level was dedicated to a neat row of narrow, empty beds. They didn't speak as they took a few steps into the room, scanning the vacant hall. Her stomach roiled at the familiarity of rows of cots as she thought of the dormitories in Farleigh. These beds had been plucked from nightmares, each accompanied by silently dangling chains, from iron manacles and leather straps to golden clamps and silver restraints. Amaris didn't want to imagine what terrors would have to befall a person to be strapped into one of the beds in the Tower of Magics and hoped she never would.

She was the first to turn from the silent room as she led them away from reminders of her orphanage, of imprisonment, of being stashed away until someone decided her fate. She'd taken her destiny into her own hands then, and she'd do it again now.

Gadriel followed as they mounted level after level, stair after stair.

Eight levels. Ten levels. Fifteen levels. Thirty? One hundred? She'd lost count, and her imagination had a tendency toward hyperbole.

She had no idea how many centuries of combat training Gadriel had under his belt. The physical tax of climbing flight after flight in a never-ending ascent would have been challenging but expected from him and his veteran status.

Amaris had spent years running up and down the sheer face of a mountain. It comforted her to hear him stifle his panting intakes of breath just as she struggled with her own. Her thighs burned in a way they hadn't in more seasons than she could count. She gasped for air, face reddening as she wondered how long it had been since she'd gone on a run. She thought absently of Ash practicing his movements each night over the fire before they smothered its flames and wondered if she should have been taking the opportunity to maintain her stamina.

Whether it had been twenty thousand steps or a three-mile vertical climb, time and height had lost all meaning.

They were climbing and climbing and climbing, and then suddenly, they weren't.

"Wha—"

Gadriel nearly toppled into her from the cease in forward motion. He used his hand to brace himself against her back as he jolted to a stop with a grunt. She came up short where the stairwell ended, not in a typical landing but in a walled-off door in the midst of the stairs. She pressed a hand into it to give it a shove, but nothing budged.

Amaris panted up at it, craning her neck, straining for breath as she read its inscription. She was acutely aware of Gadriel. Fortunately, she was overheated enough to wish he'd step away. The athletic need for space spoke over the voice that whispered for him to stay close.

She squinted through the sweat dripping over her brows at the obstruction. The door was made of wood seemingly thicker than the hull of a ship, so old it looked practically petrified into the stone of the tower around it. A large band of iron arched across its top and ran its way along the sides of the door, all etched with runes. Carved in deep, crude slashes into the door was an inscription:

Entry Forbidden. Perish Within.

Gadriel caught his breath as he read the words.

"That looks promising."

Amaris lifted her shirt to wipe the sweat from her forehead. She panted, "I think you mispronounced ominous."

"Well, it seems like if I were to hide the magic of the continent, that's precisely the kind of warning I'd want to put on my door."

Amaris leaned against the cool stone of the tower's outer wall.

"Can we," she huffed, "take a break"—another set of ragged breaths—"before we enter? Since we perish within and everything? If we have to fight a monster, I need a minute to prepare myself."

From where she leaned, Amaris reached up to feel along the barricade's ledges for a latch, but the door had no handle and no foreseeable means of passage. It blocked their ascension with the stoic ferocity of an impenetrable sentinel. Amaris rolled her cheek onto the stone, allowing its rocks to chill her, lowering her body temperature.

Gadriel found his breath far more quickly. He approached the door, resting one hand on the center, and closed his eyes. Resisting the unwise urge to slump into a nap, Amaris eyed him with exhausted curiosity. His dark hair had curled slightly with his sweat. The wet salt glistened on his forehead and made his black clothes cling to him. She saw his eyes tighten behind their closed lids. He pushed a second hand into the door, and she saw his lips moving, talking to it as if it were a friend. His wings twitched behind him as he pushed his weight into the door.

The sound of mechanisms moving came quietly from within, followed by the distinct click of a lock. The door began to slowly creak open.

"What the hell was that?"

Gadriel looked impressed with himself. He leaned back and raised his eyebrows, holding back a smirk.

"What sort of nefarious dark fae power is able to unlock enchanted doors?"

He rolled his eyes. "Power? This is just a knack, hardly

one of my powers. What sense of superiority does your diamond hair give you that your powers are any less threatening than those of the 'dark fae'? Just wait until you see what I can really do."

He had put the term for his people in quotes in the air, clearly exasperated by her insistence on referring to him and the winged fae of Raascot as such. It was no secret that the southern kingdom looked down its nose at the north and their so-called unsavory gifts.

"Wait, what you said about manufacturers—"

"Right now, witchling? Is right now the best time to talk about manufacturers?" His hand stilled on the door.

"I was just curious if you could make a key with your... knack. Something that could open any door, even enchanted doors."

He grinned. "Way ahead of you."

"You have one?"

"I do, in Raascot. Like I said, it was made together with a manufacturer. Now, this is terribly fascinating, but don't we have a border curse to break?"

Gadriel pushed the door the rest of the way open and led them into the upward-curving stairwell beyond. Amaris rallied her energy to follow.

One final landing brought their seemingly mountainous ascent of the stairs to a halt. Gadriel stopped the moment his feet hit the final step, and it was Amaris's turn to nearly collide with him. She raised her hands to make contact with his broad, muscled back, hand planting between the wings on his sweat-soaked shirt just before running headlong into him.

"Well? Share the secrets," she said, pushing to the front. She lightly grazed the ligament of his wing to bend it so that she could maneuver around him as he extended what he could of his wings to block out whatever stood before them.

As she made her way to his side, her lips parted in a silent gasp.

Blue. So much blue. Everything was radiantly, vibratingly, blindly blue.

In the middle of the room was an expanse of shelves so tall and vast that she found it to be truly unfathomable that this should exist anywhere in the goddess's lighted kingdom. The shelves did not run in a length like a mortal may have arranged but rather twisted upward in an incomprehensible, hollow spiral, shaped as if someone had taken a ladder and rotated it until it coiled in on itself. She had never seen such a shape occur in nature. She stared up and up and up into the piercing blue lights on the endless corkscrew of shelves.

It was not the shelves themselves that had made Amaris gasp or Gadriel flare his wings in a protective gesture but the incredible things that rested on them.

This was it.

They'd found what they were looking for.

No longer were they in the darkened rooms of a hushed tower. This final chamber was aglow with the ethereal blue of tens of thousands of fae lights shimmering from the radiance of the orbs that rested on each and every shelf, seemingly ten thousand feet high. She saw no limit to the spheres or end to their ominous blue glow, banishing all shadows with their permeating sheen, infinitely twisting on the shelves.

The shelves rested on a stone island in the middle of the room, surrounded by a black sea of nothing. She and Gadriel remained on the landing, separated from their goal. She couldn't fathom how deep the pit must be if even the intense blue of the orbs didn't pierce its enchanted depths.

"There must be thousands...millions..."

Gadriel took a step as if to advance toward the orbs, and Amaris let out a sharp, strangled scream. With panicked urgency, she grabbed the nearest thing she could grasp: the exposed tendon of his wing. He was about to turn in anger, pain, and horror when he felt the gravitational pull. The pit began to claim his weight, tugging him downward. Gadriel reached back for her, his hands outstretched in return to grip a fistful of her tunic by the front, nearly ripping her shirt as Amaris planted her feet on the step below them, forcing her weight into the backward pull of the staircase.

"Come *on!*" She strained with everything she had. Her cry was a sharp, loud sound as she attempted to yank him toward her. He continued clutching her shirt, confusion melting away as he realized what Amaris had seen from the start.

There was no floor.

Gadriel grunted against the exertion as he tried to find balance. Thanks to Amaris's grasp, he had been able to spin as he toppled backward through the floor, body half-submerged in what seemed to be liquid stone. He was so much heavier than her, and his wings weighed him down tremendously. The ground of the blue glowing room had dissipated as if made of mist, enveloping him within it.

His growl reverberated off the stones as he grappled for a foothold. Through gritted teeth, he said, "I've almost got it, just—"

"Don't you dare let go!" She continued her rallying cries as she pulled on his wing, knowing from his grimace that she may as well have been grabbing exposed bone.

He rammed his knee into the stone at her feet. He used his newfound leverage to hoist his body through the deceptive stone flooring. Finally succeeding in pulling himself up, he rolled toward Amaris's legs as he returned to the safety of the staircase. He hauled himself to a sitting position, shock and pain clear on his face.

"What the fuck was that!"

Amaris continued panting. She wanted to laugh from the absurd combination of relief, terror, and vulgarity that had come from his mouth. Her legs burned, her lungs had given out, and now every remaining drop of her reserves had been hurled into saving the demon fae from plummeting to his death.

"You nearly walked off the edge!" She just barely bit off the end of the sentence to prevent herself from calling him a reckless jackass. It had taken her a while to muster her strength, but now that she'd caught her breath, she could have hit him. She thought she still might.

"What edge!"

The fury with which she gestured held no kindness or sympathy. "The goddess-damned edge, Gadriel! The fucking edge! How can I be expected to go after the orb I need and look out for your carelessness!" She was practically frothing. "You're so distracted looking up at the orbs that you can't bother to check your surroundings? What kind of general are you?"

Gadriel was still gulping in mouthfuls of air. "What edge, Amaris?"

Still angry, she paused in her expression of rage. Somewhere mixed with the dry cotton in her mouth and the tangy rush of adrenaline was the terrifying flavor of a familiar memory. Her heart skidded, skipping one beat and then tripling its pace to make up for the lost rhythm.

What prince?

Amaris looked from Gadriel to the black void of the abyss. She lowered to her knees, peering over the lip of the stone on all fours. The pit should have landed on the floor beneath it, but the mouth of the crater before them showed no trace of a bottom. The blackness was endless, swallowing all traces of light. She nudged her knees back from the edge, unconsciously shuffling closer to him.

How often would she play the role of a madwoman as she pointed out things unseen? Whatever magic had enchanted the tower for its height and size had also managed to create an illusion-clad moat around the shelves of blue orbs.

"There's a chasm between us and the orbs." She stopped herself from asking him if he could see it. She knew the answer. His face looked precisely the way Ash's and Malik's had looked as they'd knelt before Moirai in the throne room.

Still reeling from the shocking force of his near tumble with death, he said, "I only see the floor."

Amaris nodded, arms still burning. "So I gathered. How's your wing?"

He made a pained expression. "They can't get any more broken than they already are."

She was still firmly planted on her hands and knees, clutching the ground with everything available to her. Whatever cavity she saw, Gadriel took her at her word. She also understood the foreboding message etched into the doorway a bit more clearly. The first barricade had been the enchanted door. The second would have been the invisible moat that swallowed all trespassers who'd refused to heed its warning.

"Anyone who makes it past the door is meant to plunge to their death."

"That's..." He searched for the word. She thought of a number of words to end the sentence for him: cruel, inhumane, evil. Instead, he decided on "...effective."

She laughed a single, terse laugh. It was effective indeed.

"How wide is the gap?" he asked.

She shook her head. "I can't jump it."

He breathed again. "Can I?"

She frowned. "If you could fly, yes."

He shook his head. "No, if I spread my wings, I can still catch the updraft, even with them torn. Would I be able to land on the other side?"

She couldn't conceal how startled she felt, nor did she attempt to. She gaped at him, lips parted and mouth wide. There were layers upon layers as to why she was unnerved by his question. It shook her to her core.

Gadriel was not simply asking if he could jump far, nor was he asking what she saw. The man was implying that he would trust her with his life no matter how she answered. If she told him that he could make the jump, even knowing he would fall to his death, she felt confident he would take the leap. Amaris wanted to bring a hand to her mouth to cover her shock. Instead, she found Gadriel's arm. Her anger, her hurt, the sense of rejection she'd held close to her chest melted as she shook her head. She looked to him with more gentleness than she had in days when she spoke.

"It's too wide to jump, Gad."

He assessed her. "Are you saying the gap is genuinely too wide to jump, even with wings, or are you saying it's a frightening distance to jump?"

"I'm saying I don't want you to jump."

The moment hung between them. She had held her anger like a lump of hot coal for days, no matter how it blistered or burned her hands. Scalding objects were meant to be dropped, not clutched. Ever since he had spoken to the masters and established their relationship, she'd let it consume her. Her bitterness had been like drinking poison while expecting him to be the one who suffered. It hurt only her.

Amaris's resentment, however potent, was not great enough to want him dead. She could see him eyeing the space between the landing and the shelving, estimating the stretch between where they sat and the answers they sought.

"Gadriel…"

"Can I make the jump with my wings?"

She closed her eyes. She searched for whatever detached shreds of assessment rested somewhere within her. She asked herself how would she answer if this were a training course for the reevers. She examined it as if it were a challenge for someone trained for survival. She reached for objectivity, stripped of emotion, but her grip on it was loose.

Amaris opened her eyes and examined the void before them once more. Her eyes remained trained on the pit as she slowly exhaled. Her gaze dragged from where it began on their threshold to where it ended on the bluish glowing shelves.

"It's not just a deep pit, Gad. It's a bottomless pit."

"That's not what I'm asking."

She closed her eyes once more, knowing she couldn't answer while staring into the darkness. She reopened them slowly and trained them on Gadriel. "I don't think I could make the jump, but maybe you could. *Maybe.* I see, perhaps, three arms' lengths of stone between the lip of the chasm and the first shelf on the opposite side. You've found for yourself how little room there is between the top step and the cavity. I don't think you could get the running start you'd need to make the jump."

Gadriel considered this. He planted himself from where he rested on the top step and began to lean forward, cautiously feeling along the stone for where the floor fell away to the illusion. He saw only solid stone flooring from where they stood to where the orbs rested, but his fingers felt their way through the enchantment.

"You saw it for yourself when we leapt from the ag'drurath. I was still able to catch a lot of wind and slow our fall. That was with me holding on to your dead weight. I think I can make the jump and then plant myself for you to leap for me."

She blinked. "You mean for me to jump over this pit?"

His lips pulled upward in a crooked smile. "I'll catch you."

She tried to shake her head but saw no leeway in his gaze. Her heart stuttered again. She had been sent on a mission by Samael at Uaimh Reev, but was she willing to die for it? Gadriel seemed prepared to perish for his cause. His king and his people were suffering and falling to the metallic arrows of Queen Moirai's men every day because of this curse. He would sooner allow himself to fall to his death than give up when they were so close to an explanation for the curse that plagued the border.

Amaris couldn't place her emotions: sadness, anxiety, fear. She didn't understand if they were for him or for herself, but she continued forcing calming breaths into her lungs. "If you sprint and leap exactly when I tell you to and flare your wings, you're going to have to dive for the opposite side. You can't reach feetfirst, or I don't think you'll make it."

He nodded and began to stand.

"Gadriel." She was still on the floor looking up at him. She couldn't find the words.

He met her worried gaze with steadiness. She absorbed the way his eyes refracted bluish in the glow from the orbs. He offered the same, crooked smile. "Tell me later."

Amaris stood and shook her nervous energy from her hands.

He backed a few steps downward and began to gear up, loosening his body. He looked to Amaris for the go-ahead. She couldn't breathe. She looked again from the edge of the pit to where he'd need to land to make it safely to the other side. Finally, she turned to him and gave a single nod. Gadriel began to sprint on powerful legs, pounding up the steps.

She had one chance to give him the force he needed. She filled her lungs with air, ready to scream. One chance, and only one.

Three seconds. Two. One.

"Now!" she cried.

He propelled himself upward, spreading the remnants of his once-angelic wings. Flickers of blue-white light could be seen through the tears in the outstretched parts of his expanse. Time moved in slow motion as she watched him cross the vast, dark void beneath them. His wings filling the space of the cavern, Gadriel extended his body forward, angling himself like an arrow. He dove for the opposite side, reaching for the stones near the shelf. He hit the floor with a loud whack like meat on a butcher's block and shuddered from the impact, sliding forward until he nearly collided with the shelves.

He'd made it.

Amaris jumped up from where she stood, crying in relief. He was alive. Her heart leapt at his survival, wiggling against the dance that ached to burst out of her. She grinned against the shock, clutching her knees with her hands. "I don't know how the hell you didn't die."

He rolled out to the side extending one vulgar finger. Amaris laughed with a relief akin to euphoria.

He'd made it, he'd made it, *he'd made it.*

Gadriel knelt and began reaching for the edge. His fingers found the place where the floor gave way to the illusion. He rose to a half crouch, half kneel as one foot planted its grip on the floor. "You ready?"

The entire space was filled with the intense glow of the orbs, but the pit was so black, no light pierced its inky depths. She couldn't tear her eyes from the void. Her heart felt like a wild bird trying to escape the cage of her chest.

"Right now?" Fear punctured her joy, the brief celebration cut short as elation sunk to the stones at her feet. "Definitely not."

"Do you trust me?"

The question took the air from her lungs.

Did she? She searched herself for the answer.

She shook her head as if to say no, but as she looked into the glow of his face, she was filled with…something. It wasn't cool, like relief. It wasn't dark, like numbness. It was a warmth. It had a heat of its own. Reassurance spread through her, however distantly. The same coal she'd used to burn her hands in resentment warmed her now, an ember in her chest. She wasn't sure how or why, but she believed he would not let her die.

Gadriel remained unwavering. He waited, hand extended toward her.

Her dread was dizzying.

"Stop looking down," he commanded.

"You really are a demon."

"If you listen to me, you might realize I'm invested in keeping you alive."

She swallowed and fixed her eyes on Gadriel. The obsidian darkness did not disappear just because she refused to look into its depths. Her life had never been so literally in anyone's hands.

She could turn around. She could go back down the stairs. She could leave the university, abandon the reevers, forget about the fae. She could start a new life, take on a new name, become a seamstress.

She didn't have to jump.

Amaris took several calming breaths, though the effort was hardly effective. Her heart was doing her no favors. Her hands trembled. Her legs quivered. Perhaps it had been easier for Gadriel to leap without truly seeing the vastness of the chasm beneath them. She took one backward step, then another.

"Now or never, witchling. You'll make it worse for yourself if you delay."

"Just jump?"

"Jump, and trust that I will catch you."

This would be like carrying herself on her runs up the mountain, she thought. She would place one foot in front of the other, leaping in upward strides as if to throw herself over a landslide where the trail had broken. Amaris pictured the daily mountainside trail runs at Uaimh Reev. She envisioned the first time she'd passed Malik and Ash and the delight she'd felt at the shock on their faces.

She wound herself up. There was no looking back now.

She gave herself over entirely to the momentum of her stride. Her legs summoned every tendon, every fiber, every run, every day in the ring. She leaped with the power of a stallion as her foot pushed away from the edge of the pit and she flung herself into the open air. Gadriel had one arm outstretched, the other bracing himself against the lip to hold on.

When Gadriel jumped, everything had moved in slow motion.

As she leapt, the world went in double time. One moment, she was pushing off from the ledge, and the next, she was falling into the void. Too fast. No time. Falling. Down, down, *down* in the second it took to blink. Gravity claimed her, belly in her throat as she realized she had not cleared the gap. The pit began to swallow her whole. She saw the change in his eyes as they shifted from determination to panic.

Amaris didn't even have time to scream as the chasm readied itself to claim its victim.

Gadriel threw himself forward to grab her, his torn wings

beating backward against her pull. He gripped Amaris around the forearm with bruising strength, clinging to her with everything he possessed. He summoned all the tenacity and power that remained in his wings, beating them back like the ag'drurath attempting to take flight. Amaris's mouth was ajar, hung on its hinges in a silent shriek. Her eyes widened to take in the fear in his face as he battled everything inside himself to hoist her up. His wings beat harder as he attempted to shift his weight backward. He'd lost so much ground when he'd extended himself for her.

He growled, releasing a thundering sound as he yanked, tightening his viselike grip around her wrist, nearly breaking her arm with his powerful hold.

She could see the agony in his eyes as his shredded wings pounded against the air to haul her up, but their view went in only one direction. Amaris knew he couldn't see her from where she dangled below the stony ledge. He wouldn't be able to look into her face as she fell to her death. Perhaps Gadriel could only see his arm as it was swallowed by the liquid stones of the illusion and the disappearing tips of his broken wings as they flapped against the gaping mouth of the pit.

"Gad." She barely choked out his name. Her opposite hand swung upward, fingernails clawing into his arm from where it flexed. His torn wings continued their endless beat as if pumping to the beat of a frenzied song, the drumbeat of her death. There was no sound except that made by the rhythmic percussion of his wings and the deep, relentless noise tearing through his throat as he pulled.

"Hold on," he said through gritted teeth. The tendons in his neck flexed, a muscle in his jaw throbbing along with the blood vessels that swelled against the glow of the orbs. She felt it the moment the tide turned in the battle for her life. The movements were slow, but between the rhythm of his wings and the gasps of his strength, she knew he was winning as he hoisted her onto the edge. The cool stones scraped her arms as he pulled her upward.

Her loose arm grabbed the edge, wedging an elbow on the cool stone. Gadriel continued to pull her until the lip of the edge made contact with her chest. She resisted the urge to grab onto his clothes, knowing she'd be little more than a drowning victim bringing a rescuer underwater. The stone made contact with her belly, which was the final space she needed to throw her knee up over the ledge.

Amaris used the leverage against the stone and scrambled with all her might. With the gasps of a final heave, she toppled onto the ground and panted against the cold floor. Gadriel collapsed half atop her as he slumped over where he'd been. Emotions washed over her in a conflicting, chaotic flood. She was swept up between her fear of death and the gravity of the fall and the joy, trust, and gratitude. Her heart swelled with one wave after the other, and she was the cliff against which they crashed. Gadriel released the iron grip he had on her and rolled to his side, pain painted across his face. Her forearm was already purple from the force of the grip he'd used in his unwillingness to let her go.

She had trusted him, and he had not failed her.

"Are you okay?" Amaris found her voice long enough to take the focus off herself and onto his wings.

"No," he grunted. Despite his response, he pushed himself into a sitting position. Pulsing pain was clear on his face. "Remind me not to bet on you in long jump."

She could have cried from the laugh of relief that clawed its way up from her belly as she echoed incredible, joyous truths. They were alive. Gadriel was okay. She had made it. They may have to pitch a tent and live among the orbs, though, because she wasn't sure she'd ever be willing to attempt that leap again. The two brought themselves into sitting positions and exchanged wild looks of delirious joy mingled with terror at their brush with death.

For now, all that mattered was that he had trusted her, and she had trusted him.

Ten

A MARIS WASN'T SURE HOW SHE WAS SUPPOSED TO CARRY ON with their mission as if she hadn't narrowly avoided a fall to her death. It seemed like the kind of traumatic event that had earned them a bit of a reverent pause. Maybe there would come a time to comprehend how they'd narrowly avoided dual funerals, but such thoughts would have to wait. Somewhere on the twisting shelves behind her, she would find the curse.

"Come on." Gadriel's voice was gruff as he helped her to her feet. Though still in what appeared to be unfathomable amounts of pain, he was a warrior in both profession and spirit.

Mindful of the edge, they began examining the room. The first thing to draw her attention, of course, was the million, brilliant blue orbs. The second thing was the bottomless pit of despair. The third thing she noticed was perhaps the most problematic of them all. There seemed to be no markings nor system of organization. Each orb was a self-contained world of blue-white luminosity with no way of knowing what was what. Gadriel stood beside her, though a bit unsteadily as if still woozy from all she'd inflicted on him. She opened her mouth to ask him for ideas, but he shook his head as if preempting her question. Neither of them had any clue how to search for the information they needed. She had expected some ornate labels, some etched dates or information.

"Any thoughts?" He squared his shoulders behind her.

Nothing gave her any indication as to what to do or what she was looking at. Figuring she needed to start somewhere, Amaris extended her fingers to the orb nearest her.

It happened so quickly, she scarcely had time to react.

The world melted away before she had a chance to catch her breath. The last thing she felt as the world spun was Gadriel wrapping a steadying arm around her waist, and then he was gone.

The sensation was like being plunged underwater.

Everything changed.

She was no longer in a stone tower. Gone was the magical glow. Instead, she found herself in the glittering shards of what may have been a throne room made of brilliant white stone, so pure it could have been porcelain. Amaris spun around to take in the faces and figures that crowded around her, gasping to understand the sights before her. Everyone was richly dressed in loose-fitting finery that conjured images of laurels and sea spray. The royal room was filled with the ethereal, olive-toned faces, with various hair and eye colors, all radiating with the angelic loveliness known only to fae. A man—a human man—knelt before the throne. His face was red with his tears. A fae stood amidst the crowd with a crown of gilded leaves.

"Our people have been sullied for the last time."

Amaris stumbled around the throne room as she looked from face to face, but no eyes met her own. Gadriel had not come with her. Her head spun as she struggled to make sense of her surroundings. Her heart skipped as if shocked by another bolt of lightning as she panicked, desperate to understand where she'd been transported. She reached for a fae in a loose gown, but the tips of Amaris's fingers dashed through the woman's shoulder as if it were made of mist. She tried to gasp, but no sound came from her throat. She was a phantom.

The commotion at the center of the room forced her attention.

"Please," begged the human. His face was filthy. A long, unkempt beard and tattered clothing suggested this man had been in a dungeon. She blinked in confusion between the ornate fae and the tear-stained face of the man who knelt before him.

The crowned fae's voice boomed with fury. "For as long as I stand on this earth, my life's work will be the purity of our people."

"Your Majesty—"

"I swear it! Never again will humans be allowed to do what's happened here!"

"Don't—"

"There will be no salvation. There will be no rescue. No one will come for you, your children, or your children's children. Seek us all you will, insect! You will not perceive us. This is my vow!"

A scream tore from the man, a pain ripping from his throat as an ungodly light exploded from his eyes and mouth. Light shot from his fingertips, his joints, his toes. The human evaporated into vapor.

The throne room lost its shape like wet paint dripping in globs down a canvas. The echo of the man's screams melted with it. In its place, the vibrant blues of the orbs and the stone walls of the tower transitioned into view.

Amaris drew a ragged breath as if breaking the surface tension of a pond as she reemerged from beneath the water. She whipped to Gadriel, surprised to see he was still holding her. He stabilized her back and sternum as she wobbled, doubtlessly wary of avoiding whatever possibility they had of tumbling over the edge once more. The orb slipped from her hands, but gravity did not claim it. The circle of magic floated of its own volition to rejoin its spherical equals amidst the shelves.

She wanted to curse, to vomit, to scream until her voice

mingled with the memory of the man as he disintegrated. Amaris continued to pant, still feeling as if she'd swum up from the sea floor.

She brought her thin fingers to grip the calloused hands that steadied her front, flushing at how he had inadvertently grazed her breast. She moved his hand aside but did not release it. His eyes were wide. She had no idea how it had looked to him on the outside when she'd been taken to see what the orb contained.

"What just happened?" From his wide eyes, he looked like he'd just witnessed hell.

"It was a curse," she sputtered, head shaking. "At first I thought maybe I'd traveled. I thought I…" She looked at Gadriel, struggling to explain the panic that had surged through her when she'd thought she'd been spirited to a new land without him. She swallowed against her realization as she said, "I don't know how I know. I just do. I…I don't know how to explain any of it. There were fae, and there was a human. Oh my goddess, I have no idea. I…I don't know what I saw…but I saw a curse."

"Our curse?" he asked, voice mingled with hope and trepidation alike.

"No. They didn't look like they were from Raascot or Farehold. I've never seen anyone or anyplace like it. It was about…sullying? Purity?" She struggled to make sense of the world, still struggling to differentiate past from present as if she'd witnessed a particularly vivid dream. "It wasn't us. There were no wings. It was so bizarre. Gadriel, I don't know what we're supposed to do. I have no idea how to find what we're looking for."

"You were here," he said carefully, "but you weren't. The moment you touched the orb, you stopped responding. I'm not sure it's safe."

"You're right," she said, voice dry. "Let's go back home."

"I'm just saying—"

"You're saying," Amaris cut him off, "that you'd prefer a

foolproof option. That's very general-like of you. But I didn't go anywhere. Nothing happened. The moment the curse was over, I was back."

He remained unconvinced.

Her gaze touched Gadriel's cautious eyes as she said, "See this with me."

Gadriel frowned uncertainly. He looked down to where he was still holding Amaris's elbow, stabilizing her from her first encounter with seeing the visions within an orb.

Amaris grumbled but understood the wisdom in his caution. "Would you prefer that we sit?"

"I would prefer to keep us alive, yes."

She complied. She settled on the ground, then grabbed his hand and guided it along with her own so that their fingers met the blue glow of a new orb simultaneously.

Once again, there was the sensation of being plunged into chilly, breathless depths.

In one moment, he was looking to her inquisitively in the tower, and in the next, they were flooded with the colors and vibrancy of an autumn day. The air smelled of dying leaves and apples. A woman was holding an infant tight to her breast as she drew pained, broken breaths. The sounds of hooves filled the air as horses thundered into view, hoisting banners adorned with the colors and sigils of a kingdom Amaris didn't recognize. Anxiety nudged her once more, but this time, she wasn't alone. She looked at Gadriel and watched his face harden as he took in his surroundings with the calculating expression of a general. Amaris wasn't sure how travel worked between orbs, but she was unwilling to let magic take one without the other. She wrapped her fingers around what she could of his broad forearm. Her heart ached with confusion, sorrow, and empathy for the mother on the ground.

The woman before them sobbed so loudly that her breaths cut between cries and gasps. The woman laid the babe to the leaf-covered ground, and the infant was nearly swallowed by the oranges and reds of the earth. She threw out her arms to the goddess and yelled, voice thick with broken emotion, "Please, goddess, hear me. With my last breath, I beseech you that this child will never be touched by man. Never will she or her kin have harm brought to them by this king. Bless her with life in everything that I give to you now." A shimmer exploded from the woman as gold descended on the glen. The baby in the leaves began to cry as its mother disintegrated into a plume of metallic, glimmering dust.

The autumnal day fell away like rain on glass as the gloom of the tower colored their vision once again. The jarring sensation of leaving the orb behind and rejoining the world made her head spin. She was still clutching Gadriel's arm as their wide eyes locked onto each other.

"Was that a blessing?"

Amaris blinked wordlessly in response. She and Gadriel wore matching faces of bewilderment. "The first one I touched was a fae curse. The human also evaporated into gold dust. Do you think that really happens when there's a blessing or a curse?"

Gadriel frowned. "I...I don't know. But I don't think so. It may just be the magical representation of the blessing or curse brought to life. But I'm a general, not a—"

"Manufacturer?"

"I was going to say student of magic, but clearly you're still stuck on that."

Their orb had already abandoned their hands and returned itself to its place on the shelf.

Gadriel took a partial step away from the coiling shelves in their vast expanse. "We can't stand here and watch all of them. That would take..." His words drifted off as the sheer number of orbs overwhelmed him. If they watched every single blessing or curse in this tower, it may have taken them two centuries before they found the one they needed.

"I have no idea what to do. I kept us from falling into the pit. I think I've contributed enough."

"*You* kept us out of the pit?"

She sighed. She didn't want to fight, and she was quite sure he didn't either, even if he couldn't help himself from being a smart-ass. They were tired. They were overwhelmed. It was hard not to feel like they'd faced death only to come up against a puzzle with no solution.

They began to circle the shelves, eyeing orb after orb. No matter how they scrutinized, there were no distinguishable markings, no patterns. No helpful names or dates adorned the shelves. She hadn't expected a sign that said *Look up here, Amaris,* but surely there would have been some indication as to what the orbs possessed. Instead, there was nothing but the azure burn of lighted sphere after sphere. Amaris felt in her stomach that for her luck, the orb she needed would be one hundred feet above them on a shelf unreachable to anyone without functional wings.

They had nearly completed their fruitless circling of the shelves when a break in the ledges revealed itself. She understood the girth of the shelves as they'd appeared to coil the width of a house. It wound like a cave, aquamarine in the ethereal, underwater light that it cast over their features. The breach was that of a triangular space, the sharp opening between two shelves where they failed to connect. Inside, fully illuminated by the glow of the orbs, sat a man.

Her breath caught in her throat in surprise. She looked immediately to Gadriel, but he had gone still beside her. There had been no indication that they would find life in this tower. The man's presence was more jarring than the blessings and curses themselves. She blinked rapidly to ensure she wasn't hallucinating.

The man was as statuesque as something belonging in the courtyards of the villages or in city squares. The stranger sat on a single chair and was dressed in what may have been a hermit's rags. His beard fell well below the height of the chair, coiling to a wispy white point several arms' lengths beyond where his bare feet rested on the stone. His cheeks were sunken into paper-thin gauntness as if his years exceeded the life meant for any mortal, human or fae. His fingers were scarcely more than bones with the knobby gristle of joints and aged skin stretched over them. His hands grasped a staff that was topped with an orb identical to those that coiled above him in the towering cage of his shelved blessings and curses. She took a step forward to examine the man, then another. Amaris's eyes found the sunken pits of the man's eyes. It was as if his horrible eyes were made of the same milky, misty blue spheres as the magical orbs themselves. He showed signs of neither death nor life.

This guardian of the magics of the world, bound to the curses and blessings of the land, was something entirely *other*.

He did not shift nor blink nor breathe.

Gadriel rested a hand on her shoulder protectively, cautioning her advance. Amaris motioned with her upper arm to free herself from the weight of his palm as she took several careful steps forward.

Amaris looked over her shoulder, briefly catching the vigilance in Gadriel's militant expression as he followed, taking the deliberate, wary steps of someone prepared for sudden battle.

They were nearly to the center of the room when the man spoke.

Amaris yelped in surprise, her entire body flinching against the break in silence.

He said, "You've stolen knowledge with the fumbling grasps of children. Your fingers reach for things unknown, and your hands hold blessings and curses your mind cannot understand."

Amaris opened her mouth as if to respond but said nothing. She stood her ground.

The hermit's wispy, wind-swept voice continued as if speaking in riddles. "If knowledge is meant for you, it will find you. Step forward." The man held his right hand aloft, palm outstretched before him. His staff remained unmoving in the clutch of his left hand.

She knew what he wanted. Not bothering to weigh the consequences, Amaris's feet moved forward.

"Don't." Gadriel grabbed her hand.

Rather than stopping, Amaris pulled him with her as she closed the gap between herself and the ancient man. She understood intrinsically that he needed to touch her. Once she was squarely in front of him, the old man raised his outstretched fingers and pressed his weathered hand to her forehead.

She was hit with an excruciating crack of lightning.

Amaris fell to her knees. A cry of pain clawed its way from her throat. From a distant somewhere, she felt Gadriel's attempts to yank her from under the man's grasp, but the elderly man's palm remained fused to her head in an unnatural welding of bodies. The blue glow from the spheres around them matched that of the light that shot from under his palm as it drilled itself into Amaris's forehead. The ancient guardian of the orbs was unmoving, his milky eyes impassive. The luster of his eyes and his staff intensified as the orbs around them seemed to pulse in response.

Gadriel grabbed her with both hands as he tried to tear her from where she had melted into the hand, but her single, unbroken cry stopped only when the guardian released his palm.

When he freed Amaris, it was not with any physical movement but with an untethering of magic. She fell backward onto the ground, head stopped from smacking against the stones by Gadriel's nimble reaction. Paying no mind to the pair on the floor, the guardian raised his staff skyward.

Gadriel spun on the man as if ready to fight, but the hermit was deathly still.

It took a moment to discern what was happening. The pulsations of his staff appeared to call to an orb. A single sphere released itself from where it perched on the shelves hundreds of feet above them. It floated downward with the unearthly grace and speed of a feather, not constricted by the laws of gravity or time. The small blue globe containing the mysteries of the universe descended until it levitated in the space between the decrepit man and where Amaris had crumpled to the floor.

The guardian spoke. "Take the knowledge that was meant for you and seek nothing further. Leave this place, steal no more from the blessings and curses, and receive only what is yours to behold."

His message was little more than wind against dust.

This was it.

Amaris looked at Gadriel, imploring him with one pleading glance to go with her as she took the curse into her palms. She reached for it, and he joined her.

The sapphire lights gave way to cream-colored stone, once again giving her the melting sensation of paint and plunging of water as the world blurred from present to past. They were no longer in the tower. They stood, feet planted on the ground, in the caramels and beiges of the southwestern coast. Gadriel remained beside her as they observed the curse, little more than phantoms drifting through time and space.

While Amaris did not recognize the room in the vision, she knew they were in the browns and custards of Castle Aubade. Her eyes went immediately to a figure on the floor. A dark-winged fae held up a defensive arm, angelic wings outspread as if hiding something beneath himself with them. His face was hardened in defiance. His words came out in an angry snarl. "What made you so hateful!"

"Don't speak of my hate! You know nothing! You know—"

"I'll tell you what I know! I know that you can force me to leave today, Moirai, but I cannot be kept away. I will come back day after day, night after night, year after year. No matter what shields you throw up or how many men you lose to this foolish battle, I cannot be kept away!"

Amaris whipped to see the woman who towered above him.

The terrible laugh that rippled through the room belonged

to the younger, healthier face of Queen Moirai, gold-brown hair tumbling loosely around her shoulders. She was never beautiful, but the years of stress and grief and hate had not yet carved themselves into her features. Her laugh contained no joy. Her words dripped with venom as she spoke. Her eyes sparkled with malice.

"Return all you like! Return every day. Fly to her every night. No matter how you plead or seek, the people of Farehold will see you for the demon you really are!"

The man's face was one of stone-set defiance. "Your hate is your undoing, witch! Nothing you could say would—"

The queen threw her hands in front of herself and unleashed a scream that came not only from within her body but from the tremors of the earth. The disembodied chorus of countless hellish shrieks tore from within her in an unholy binding. The castle shook. The man flared his wings, protecting whatever hid beneath them.

With the legion of ten thousand hateful voices, she cried, "Never again will you or your people find welcome in these lands! Everywhere you turn, wherever you look for comfort or sanctuary, you will find only terror! The death you've brought upon this castle will reverberate throughout the lands, demon!"

"You dare to damn—"

His words were cut short like a sword through his sentence. His face slipped from defiance to a look of petrification as she screamed, her voice carrying through the air around them. It tore through her as the stones around her trembled. The fae tucked his head inward, but it did not appear as though he were cowering. He seemed to be holding someone in his arms, still sheltered beneath his wings.

Moirai's hate permeated the room. "Your people are a cancer on this earth, and no matter what price I must pay, I will purge you and your people from my lands. You are never to enter Farehold again without being seen as I see you: as the scourge of hell and all its plagues!"

Gold light filled the room as both the queen and the fae disintegrated into a tumbling powder of glistening, metallic beauty.

Amaris felt the jerking motion of being forced above the water one final time.

The cream-colored stones slid away, but bluish orbs did not replace them. The dripping, wet melding of Aubade was giving way to darkness. Amaris succumbed to the sensation of falling. She plummeted downward through the tower, into the pit, hurtling toward the earth. Amaris barely had the sense of mind to reach for Gadriel as the final dot of bluish curses and blessings was expunged from her vision as some force from the glowing staff of the elderly man flew them downward and blackness engulfed her.

The guardian had thrust them from the tower with one incredible push of magic.

Down, down, down.

Before she could blink, Amaris was flung onto her back. The door to the tower slammed shut before her. The wind had been knocked from her lungs. She gasped for oxygen but couldn't catch her breath. Fighting off the urge to panic, she remembered all the times she'd been beaten to her back in the sparring ring. Amaris forced herself to focus on her senses. She could feel damp grass underneath her. The moon dipped its way between intermittent clouds overhead. She could smell the dew, the ivy, the chill of the night. She had landed not with the force of a plummet from ten thousand steps but merely as if chucked from the threshold of the tower door.

Finally calming, she reached within herself to find her air and forced the breath into her lungs. Her tunic was smeared with grass stains. Her head throbbed. After several steadying breaths, she rolled to see Gadriel.

He was still blinking up at the scattered clouds that hid the moon. The moon did not illuminate as the spheres of curses had, and she struggled to adjust her eyesight to see what he was thinking.

Irrespective of the unspeakable horrors they had experienced, the surprises, the pitfalls, the magic, the curses, something was different. There was an eerie silence to the way his mood shifted.

Gadriel brought himself solemnly to his feet and extended an arm to Amaris. She took his hand and raised herself up, waiting for her vision to level as the rush of blood to her head threatened to make her legs too weak to walk after their tremendous fall. There had been more exercise tonight than she'd had in weeks, and that was before she considered the mental taxation of what they had seen. The pair began walking in silence to where their rooms in the healers' building awaited them. She wanted to talk to him, wanted to ask about Queen Moirai's words, but his posture kept her silent. She trailed slightly behind him, not bothering to hide in the shadows, taking the shortest route from the tower to the rooms, allowing the moon to light their path whenever it spied them between the clouds.

✦

Twenty minutes of silence.

How much longer did she have to wait before breaking whatever had muted him?

They had been in Amaris's room for nearly half an hour without a single word exchanged. Amaris didn't know why they were keeping silent, but her inner voice urged her into patience, no matter how she burned with questions. Gadriel sat on her bed, and Amaris had taken to pacing the room while she waited for him to speak. She had no idea as to the hour, but they'd been out all night. Surely, dawn was nearly upon them.

Finally, Gadriel spoke. "I thought this would give us the answers we needed. For twenty years, I've believed that finding the curse would tell us what we needed to know to end the blight on the land."

"But?" Impatience and anxiety raked through Amaris after their long stretch of quiet.

"How could he have kept this from me?"

"Who?"

"How does he expect me to help him, to serve him, to be on these missions when he can't even..." Gadriel was not talking to her. He was running through an incredulous stream of emotions as he demanded answers of the same blank, sterile wall that had consumed Amaris days prior.

"Gadriel, what is it? What do you know?"

"It feels like the more I know, the less I understand." He looked up at her briefly, then back to the wall. "Like perhaps I'm holding a small piece to the puzzle without knowing how many pieces remain and with no pictures to reference what I hope to uncover. How many keys will we need to find before we can unlock this door?"

Amaris readied herself for the question that had been eating at her. "I could see Moirai, but we knew it was her curse from the beginning... What about the man on the floor? Did you know the winged fae from the vision?"

Gadriel let out a gruff, humorless noise mixed between a laugh and a scoff. "Indeed, I do. That was my cousin, King Ceres."

Eleven

N OX SUCKED HER TEETH IN IRRITATION. SHE DID HER BEST
to keep herself from looking at the reevers like she was
a mother regarding children. The stakeout in Aubade was
not the heroic mission of three savvy spymasters that one
may have hoped. Malik and Ash, while trained in combat
and nearly invincible on the battlefield, were not particularly helpful in matters of infiltrating a castle. Despite
Malik's confidence that they could "make it pretty far" if
they just "hacked and slashed," Nox continued to temper
the excitable assassins as they brainstormed from their
room at the inn. She was able to draw several diagrams of
the castle both from her own experiences and the reevers'
descriptions.

"If you don't have any better plans, I don't know why
you have to keep throwing water on ours," Ash grumbled. He
made a not too subtle comment about ditching Nox at a silk
shop to occupy herself with whatever women fancied while
they took care of the mission themselves.

Nox rubbed at her temple, her head in her hands. "I
don't have to provide a better alternative to know when I'm
hearing something stupid."

"All I hear is you being part of the problem rather than part of the solution."

She chased the men away to fetch breakfast while she continued her blueprints. Her thoughts had always come out more clearly when she could put pen to paper. The innkeeper had been happy to sell them several loose sheets of parchment for a few pennies along with a small container of ink. Recalling she'd fetched a quill from Millicent's office, she didn't bother with buying a pen from the old man who seemed to believe that his quills were worth triple that of the paper.

Bent over her desk, she noticed something curious.

Her brows knit as she struggled to understand what she was seeing.

A blotch of dark ink began to bleed in the corner as if blooming from within the page itself. She used her thumb to rub at the ink, but the contact had no effect. Words blotted across the top of the page as if emerging upward from the underside of the paper. Nox stifled a sound of surprise and snatched the page, checking the front and pack, but the words continued to form. It was a single question.

Why are you drawing the castle?

She blinked rapidly, alone in the room with a phantom penman. Her heart sounded its warning. Nox had heard Millicent but hadn't considered the consequences of wielding a magical object. Aside from the Madame's carriage, she'd never, to her knowledge, wielded an item that held genuine power. Nox's mouth dried as she realized the sensitive nature of all she'd been writing. The quill tumbled from her hand as panic descended. She began to scan her papers, reading every line, every sketch, every diagram for signs of their true intent. While it was an extremely suspicious collection, nowhere did it say something as damning as *We plan to sack the castle.*

Nox forced herself to calm as she tried to remember

exactly what Millicent had said about the quill. The Madame had mentioned only that it had a twin: there was a counterpart to this black plume somewhere in the world. With a still-racing heart, Nox wondered if the owner was within the castle, or worse, if it were the queen herself.

She shoved the spelled quill back into her black velvet bag, kicking herself for using a cursed object. Nox crumpled the pages and threw the diagrams along with the phantom's question into the fire still cheerily burning on her hearth. She remained bent over the fire, disposing of the evidence, when the doorknob wiggled.

The reevers returned with plates of food, including a tray for her. She carefully dusted her hands of any proof of her mistake as they opened the door.

Malik put the food down on the desk and was quick to speak. "Eat up. As it turns out, we're in luck. We don't have to enter the castle after all. The queen is on the move."

She glanced at the tray he'd set down for her but didn't touch her food. "What do you mean?"

"There were whispers of it all over the taproom this morning. Raascot colors and banners were spotted camping outside Priory. Everyone's on edge thinking the north is attempting an invasion. The whole town is buzzing."

Ash spoke before she had the chance. "If Raascot's men look like ag'imni on this side of the border, we know one thing for certain: whoever is wearing Raascot's colors and holding their emblems cannot be northmen."

The slab of salted pork slowly lost its heat as Nox ignored it. "You think the queen has dressed her own men in northern colors? Why would she do that?" But even as she spoke, she began to verbally process the answer.

They looked at one another. "I doubt it's to foster peace relations."

Nox nodded. "And in the wake of her dragon escaping and the riots, maybe she'd think the city looks particularly vulnerable."

"Exactly," Ash agreed. "It would be the perfect opportunity for the north to strike."

"Eggs are disgusting if you let them get cold," Malik said, gesturing to the untouched tray.

Nox waved him away. "That's fine. I'm not hungry."

"Bullshit. We haven't properly eaten in days. At least eat the muffin."

"I don't—"

"It's blackberry."

Nox returned to the desk, approaching the food. She thought better of it and began to gather her things. She stepped into her leather shoes and slipped into the black cloak. Malik fussed over her, nearly forcing her to take a few bites of pork and eggs before they left. When she didn't touch the muffin, he carried it out, announcing that she'd have food for later when she realized she was, in fact, hungry. She decided that she would not tell the men about her error with the quill and resolved never to use it again.

The innkeeper eyed them as the three left the home together, doubtless wondering why a pretty young woman who had checked in alone was now departing with two men. She wasn't sure why she did it, but the part of her that enjoyed stirring the pot made quick eye contact with the innkeeper as they left. Nox winked at him, heavy with implication, just as they crossed the threshold. She didn't miss the way his eyes flared with surprise. She hoped he would take it as confirmation of his dastardly suspicions and procure gossip for years to come.

The tiny deceit warmed her.

Men were so simple.

Twelve

A T HER BEHEST, ASH KEPT HIS HOOD UP. BETWEEN HIS EARS and his reddish hair, he was a beacon for suspicion. Nox convinced them that three ominously hooded figures skulking out of Aubade would draw more curious eyes than they wanted to risk, so she and Malik walked confidently forward as if they owned the city, features exposed for all the world. She was relieved that there had been a change of sentries at the gate so that she wouldn't need to explain to her noble savior Vescus that her aunt had made a miraculous recovery in the night and they would now be abandoning the aforementioned relative. Unlike those entering, the guards waved all exiting through the gate without so much as a second glance. The sentries cared only about who dared to penetrate their city's walls, not parties who left.

Priory was not a small city, and it was a long, tiring walk through its cobbled streets, over its square, between its alleys, as they made their way to the other side. Nox's feet were swollen and aching from walking on stone, but it would do her no good to begin complaining.

They were at Priory's edge before the three felt that they could speak openly.

"How are we supposed to find men dressed in northern colors? Do we just start asking around?" Malik frowned as he looked to the road, slowly circling to the huts that dotted the hills, the glistening horizon of the western sea, and the trees that populated all around them.

"I thought you said they were outside Priory?"

"We are outside Priory. I don't know if you realize this, but there are four cardinal directions outside Priory, though I suppose we could scratch west off our checklist unless we want to start swimming." Ash smirked to himself.

Nox's face flashed in irritation. "You mean to tell me that the gossips at the inn were so loose-lipped that they loudly spoke of seeing men in northern colors, and you couldn't ask any follow-up questions? Do you just want us to each pick a direction and hope we find them? What was your plan?"

"Hey! I seem to recall offering several excellent plans."

"Hacking your way into the castle was not an excellent plan!"

Everyone knew Nox was right, but the men were cross with her nonetheless. There was a helplessness to the way their shoulders slumped as they looked around them. Unless they wanted to divide into three parties and hope that the goddess reunited them with useful information, there was nothing to guide them.

"Oh!" Nox lit with the exclamation.

They looked to her expectantly for the continuation of a sentence, but she was preoccupied. She plunged a hand into her velvet bag and fished through the coin pouch, ignoring the soft texture of the quill and waxy candlestick until her fingers closed around something metallic. She brought the accessory to the surface and held it out before her triumphantly.

Malik's mouth twisted into a frown. "That's a beautiful watch, Nox."

She bit back her laugh, "No! This object... Well, honestly, I've never attempted to use it. Let's give it a whirl."

She opened the pocket watch and regarded the three

hands of its face: hour, minute and second. Nox looked at it for a moment, feeling extraordinarily silly as she did so. This seemed like an exercise in lunacy. Nox closed her eyes and held the object close to her mouth. She wasn't sure how the enchantment worked, but she whispered, "Show me Castle Aubade."

The effect was instant.

The large hand swung in a circle, completing three quick rotations before it began to rock in a pendulum motion on only the watch's leftmost side, tightening its triangulation, slowing its bob until it settled on one location. Their eyes followed the hour hand as their gazes left the watch's arrow and trailed slowly upward to where the castle stood on a hill several miles away. The arrow of the hour hand was pointing directly at the queen's castle.

"Aha!"

"What…"

Nox grinned and grabbed Malik's hand, dragging him several feet in another direction. She whispered for him to come closer, only loosely aware of how his cheeks reddened with their proximity.

"Tell it to find Ash," she whispered.

She leaned in conspiratorially, closing the gap between them as she pressed the pocket watch into his palm. She was too entranced by the spelled object to appreciate the nervous tremble of his hand. If Nox could have heard his thoughts, she may have empathized enough to take several steps backward. She wouldn't have wanted to make him feel uncomfortable, after all.

✦

Malik's throat bobbed and he hoped she missed how loudly he'd swallowed. Try as he might, he couldn't keep the blush of shyness from coloring his neck. Goddess, she smelled good. The brush of her skin was the softest touch of velvet. Somehow, after days of travel, she still smelled like fresh plum pie sprinkled with cinnamon as it cooled on the window ledge.

Her eyes twinkled with excitement as she urged him to focus on the watch, and while he didn't want to let her down, it took a moment to tear his eyes from her dark lashes, her berry-dark lips, or the golden skin that looked impossibly soft.

He blinked several times, forcing himself to lean away from her as he sharpened his focus on the pocket watch.

This was about the watch, nothing more. The object had resumed its normal ticking. In the moments it had taken for them to relocate, the watch once more told them the time, no longer betraying its point toward Moirai and her kingdom. Nox's graceful fingers pointed urgently toward their redheaded friend, and Malik complied.

"Show me Ash?" he asked, voice thick with uncertainty.

Nox pressed herself into him to stare intently at the watch, leaving no room for Malik to breathe. She appeared lost in her fascination as its hands once more spun in three quick rotations before locating the faeling, arms dangling at his sides, unsure as to why he had been abandoned. The two stared, their eyes drawing a line from the watch to Ash. Malik's mouth was open with his unspoken questions, but Nox beamed at Malik in success. He heated more than he thought possible at the unadulterated excitement in her expression. Goddess, he hated how transparent he was.

Nox dragged him back to where Ash stood and explained everything. "The Madame had once told me about the enchanted objects in her office. This pocket watch is meant to show you the way to wherever you want to go."

Ash took the golden watch and turned it over in his hands. It once again revealed only the hour, ticking with the absolute mundanity of any common watch. It seemed from Ash's face that he wanted to be skeptical, but evidence didn't lie. The object had proven itself twice already.

"That's amazing," he murmured appreciatively. "Manufactured objects are so rare. I've never had one."

Malik peered in genuine interest as he asked, "Do you have anything else in that bag of yours?"

She nodded proudly. "I paid for our room last night, didn't I?"

He offered a half-apologetic grimace. "I'm sure you'll find ways for us to repay you."

"I also stole a candle with a wick that will never run out. It's spelled to maintain its size no matter how long it burns."

"You didn't think to tell us about these things?"

"Honestly, I had no way of knowing whether they worked. My Madame could have been filling our head with fish tales for all I was willing to believe. She wasn't known for her honesty."

"You're incredible." Malik gaped at her.

She smiled. "What would you do without me?"

With a tone too serious for the occasion, he responded, "I have no intentions of finding out."

✦

Nox whispered the intent to find the men dressed in Raascot colors, and the watch pointed them east-northeast, straying from the regency's road and forcing them into the forest.

Once more, they were amongst the brown trunks, bushes, brambles, and thorns. The escape from the thicket had been short-lived. It had been refreshing to spend a night in the warmth and safety of an inn, but Nox was confident that if she'd braved the woods before, she could do it again—this time in superior footwear.

"Am I crazy, or have the bugs multiplied?" Ash swatted at a gnat.

"The undergrowth also seems a thousand times thicker," Nox agreed.

"You two are going to make traveling really unpleasant unless you learn to stop and smell the roses."

"*You* smell the roses," Nox grumbled without bothering

to look at Malik. "I'm just trying to keep twigs from poking out my eyes."

Uncaring how many times they nearly tripped over fallen logs or how many mosquito bites they acquired, the watch urged them onward. They took a small detour when the object pointed them directly over a swamp, and Nox insisted on no uncertain terms that they would be walking around it, not through it. She announced with some matter of conviction that all bogs were filled with leeches and monsters.

Finally, they reached a break in the trees.

The small village was roughly half a day's walk from Priory, set apart from the road and nestled in the forest with no logical entrance or exit that they could see. It was just past dinnertime, with the sun slowly turning its yellow rays into the orange glow of evening as it began to lower. Priory may have been where folk too poor to afford the luxuries of the walled city of Aubade lived, but this village removed the classes of wealth one, two, or three steps further. Hovels dotted a small clearing, thatched roofs evidence of townsfolk strewn about. The people of this village could only afford what they could build with their own hands.

It had been a surprise—though a welcome one—to come upon the village. At least Nox thought so at first. The closer they drew, the less certain she felt of their fortune. Smoke did not rise from the chimneys of these homes. Chickens did not cluck. There was no evidence of horses or livestock. No signs of life came from the rows of homes that lined the forest clearing, as if the town had been abandoned, left only to the ghosts. The town was not old enough for these to be ruins, nor was it decrepit enough to make them believe it had been left alone for any stretch of time.

It was very, very eerie.

Nox looked to one reever, then the other. She could see it on their faces. Without knowing why, they shared a tangible dread as they began to walk through the silent village, following their pocket watch wherever it led.

"What do you think happened here?" Nox asked.

Malik opened his mouth to answer, but a small sound drew their attention. Someone had opened and then quickly shuttered a window. The travelers paused, tensed with a preparation to run as they scanned for which house had stirred.

A wide-eyed woman's face emerged from the crack in a door, frantic as she beckoned them forward. Their feet were glued to the grass underfoot for a moment at the bizarre sight They exchanged looks, but the haste of her demanding hand and intensity of her face drew them to her.

"Get in, get in!"

The village woman ushered them into her home, closing the door with what seemed to be unnecessary carefulness before bolting it behind her. Two young children playing noiselessly with faceless dolls paused and looked curiously up at the strangers. One small room made up the home, with a partial wall creating a shoddy separation for the hay-stuffed bed that lay on the ground. Its fireplace was filled with black cinders and remnants of long-cold logs.

The woman's eyes darted wildly with horror as she took them in. Her questions came out in a hushed, angry breath. "Are you mad? What are you doing out there?"

Nox wasn't sure what insanity they'd stumbled into, but whatever terror gripped this village had driven the woman into some deranged state. She didn't have to speak to Ash or Malik to verify their regret that they'd entered her home. This had been a mistake. When the three offered no words, the woman pushed the information on them with a low urgency.

"There are demons in these woods!"

The reevers visibly relaxed. They had been traveling through the woods for several hours and seen only the trees, leaves, and underbrush of a perfectly typical forest. There had been no claw marks of sustrons or evidence of vageth dens.

In a normal voice, Ash asked, "You've seen the ag'imni?"

She shushed them, her sound cracking with paranoia. The woman craned her neck to listen as if their presence may have already summoned whatever superstitious demons she was referring to. After several ragged breaths, the woman returned her gaze to the three. "No! It's the spider!"

The room filled with a pitying smugness. It was a placating thing, almost a tangible energy. There was a naivete to the woman that further softened Nox and the men around her as they pitied the plight of the indigent. Nox knit her brows together sympathetically. She touched the woman's arm in what was meant as a comforting gesture. "Thank you for looking out for us, but I think we can handle a few spiders. If you'll excuse us—"

The woman threw her body between the strangers and the door. "The motion will attract it! And goddess, please be quiet! If you speak again, you'll bring it upon us all!"

They had expected to find the queen's men dressed in Raascot clothing, and instead, they had wandered into the thatched-roof home of a madwoman.

"Ma'am," Ash said, doing his best to be diplomatic as he raised his hands to pacify her, "we don't want any trouble."

She looked like she might cry. Her hair, though pulled back, had several erratic strands poking out in all directions around her face as if to emphasize how often she clutched her head in terror, tugging it loose from its bun. Her voice was thick with her intensity despite the whisper she struggled to maintain. "I'm begging you, please don't make any more sound. You'll draw it to us."

They didn't have time to say more.

A searing pain stabbed through their ears as a sound erupted from the bowels of hell itself.

A scream tore through the village, no mortal cry but something of scraping iron, strangulation, ice, and blood. It was the goddess's divine humor that had chosen the spans of the woman's rants to unleash a terror on the people. Nox felt as if the noise used the opening in her ear to burrow into the very center of her. The children clutched their heads, eyes wide in fear, while the others winced against the horrible noise. The hovel reverberated with the sound. This was not the scream of a man nor that of a beast. This was the banshee shriek of the undead. The woman choked a sob and threw her body over her children. The little ones began to cry, and she fought desperately to shush them, her trembling hand covering their mouths as tears spilled over her eyes. The three were motionless, frozen with the bloodcurdling sound as it tore through the village once more.

"The spider!" the woman wept.

Thirteen

G ONE WERE ALL THOUGHTS OF THE VILLAGER'S INSANITY. Nox felt adrenaline connect them as if they shared a lightning rod.

Ash was the first to action. He put his back to the wall and cracked the window's shutter with the barest of movements. Beyond the closed doors of the sorry villagers' homes, a monster ripped up the ground with every deafening step.

The creature that thundered its path through the village was no ag'imni.

Ash paled against the nightmare.

"I don't understand," he breathed.

From what Nox understood of reevers, she'd expected them to know everything. Yet she watched the face of a man unable to fully comprehend what he saw. She leaned until she found a gap in the window, eyes locking onto the monster as it tore through the skin of the earth. Eight horrible legs, prickled with barbs and glistening with a heinous liquid, tore from hovel to hovel, ripping chunks of mortar from the homes as it careened between the spaces. The abdomen was that of a spider, but the twisted torso and breasts of a woman rose from this godless creature, larger than a horse. Her ribs jutted terribly against her night-dark skin. The spider had the long, wet hair of something that had just crawled from the swamps of the earth. As if her eight legs were an insufficient number of appendages, two long humanoid arms covered in jagged spikes descended from her shoulders. When she threw back her face to scream, her jaw unhinged like a snake. While a woman should have had two eyes, the spider had dozens of black, glinting beads clustering the expanse of her unearthly face.

Nox looked into the gaping maw of a true demon.

The cries of the village woman mingled with the innocent wails of her children bubbled up from behind them, filling the house. The mournful wails of the villagers were the sounds of people who knew they were about to die.

"I really wish she had just been crazy," Nox said, voice disembodied in her shock.

Ash looked at Malik. "You ready?"

Malik had already unsheathed his sword, muscles flexed. "Born ready."

"Wait!" Nox's eyes flitted desperately from one to the other. Chill claimed her as the blood drained from her face, pooling in her fingers and toes. Her dry lips moved uselessly, unable to find an argument to get them to stay. Were they just going to charge at a demon? No plan? No strategy?

"We've got this," Ash promised.

"You two? Alone?"

He barely spared a moment for his shrug. "All of us."

They unbolted the door and were out before she had time to beg.

Nox rushed to the window and clutched at its ledge uselessly as the men sprinted from the small house. She held her breath and watched as they split up on instinct, flanking the spider. While she still felt herself unable to breathe, unable to process, the reevers were already springing to action against the All Mother's most wretched creation. The orange evening light made the creature glow with the reddish fires of hell as it glinted across her demonic, too-wet hair. The she-devil whipped her tendrils of hair as she looked from one to the other and then slashed a spiked hand at Malik. Her scream rattled the windows of the homes that were doubtlessly filled with other terrified villagers, praying she wouldn't turn their attentions to them once she'd eaten the men before her. Her claws were ones that had killed, her mouth one that consumed.

Nox's knuckles turned white as she tightened her hold on the ledge, eyeing the men. The reevers had no room for fear.

Malik made a defensive maneuver and sprang backward, away from the creature. They used the grassy stretch that ran between the village's homes as their sparring ring with the monster at its center. Ash took the opportunity of distraction to slash at one of her legs with his weapon. His sword clanged against the thorny appendage as if it were made of metal. His face flinched from the unexpected sound, groaning with whatever disappointment tore from his belly. With speed seemingly too fast for a creature her size, the spider had swung the attentions of her numerous beady coal-black eyes to the half fae. Ash was in a crouch, tempting the beast to dive for him. As she did, he struck her arm. This time, his sword connected with flesh, slicing into the blackened meat of the creature. She let out an angered noise, spurred into a maddened frenzy.

It had seemed that he may be fast enough to outsmart her, but Ash wasn't able to roll from her swipe as her humanoid hand made contact with his chest, throwing him into a home. He crunched against the wall and slumped to the ground. The sound of his impact sickened Nox. She felt a cold sweat collect across her face and chest as she watched the men. Her utter uselessness consumed her, helpless as the demon advanced.

Hearing the worthless metal clang against the spider's legs, Malik avoided her arachnoid limbs altogether. The man sprang with the power of his entire weight, jumping with the force of years of training and gripping the hilt of his blade as he brought his sword toward the spider's abdomen in a downward plunge. His weapon met its mark, but it did not puncture the spider's skin. Instead, the sword glanced off the abdomen with the grating noise of nails on a chalkboard as if the beast was composed of some hard, black exoskeleton.

Malik was caught on unsteady feet as the sword jolted sideways. His face barely registered his dismay as his blade scraped uselessly against her. Nox gasped as the spider twisted her torso and grabbed for him, wickedly elongated barbed fingers wrapping around his chest. His reflection showed in the spider's eyes dozens of times, too many horrid eyes for any one creature of the earth. Her withered, black-gray breasts heaved in something like delight. The spider unhinged her jaw to reveal the needle-sharp glints of blackened teeth as she prepared her gullet to bite into Malik. Nox's lips were parted in a silent, worthless scream, knowing the creature would bite him in half before the reever could escape. Time was moving in slow motion. The spider was lifting Malik to her lips. Ash was getting to his feet from where he'd been struck against the wall, but he wouldn't be able to free his friend in time.

"No," Nox begged the goddess. "Not like this."

The seconds slowed and time stretched into an infinite stagnancy while Nox watched the nightmare unfold. She knew she was about to watch the head of a man as it was gnawed from where it connected to his shoulders. She was about to see the reevers die. The inevitability lengthened like taffy, stretching out her breaths into long, horrible moments. This was how it felt to watch someone else's life flash before one's eyes.

Cool metal against her skin called to her for attention. Nox felt for the small knife Malik had given her. What could it do against a beast that could not be pierced by swords? If she just stood there, the two reevers would perish in the next few seconds. She didn't have time. She didn't have minutes. She didn't have moments. She had heartbeats at best. The spider was going to eat him. Not comprehending what she was doing, Nox sprang from the house, leaving the trembling village woman and her crying children behind.

"Hey!" Nox hurled her intention at the spider.

A wave of sulfur hit her as she smelled the demon's foul odor roll from her body, rotten eggs and spoiled meat gagging her with its cloud.

Nox joined the oranges and reds of the evening as if plunging into the very fires of hell. She planted her feet on the ground before the spider, mustering every drop of power she could imitate. Her eyes went between the spider and Malik. He looked as if he wanted to scream for her to stop, to run, but his lungs were so crushed by the beast that he was unable to find the sound. He clawed at the talons that gripped him.

"Look at me!" she cried for the spider once more with angry, antagonistic intent.

The demon whipped her head from her meal and bellowed a shrill, angered response. The many black, sunken eyes and their horrible gleams homed in on Nox. With an unhinged, animalistic speed, the spider began to barrel toward her, Malik still in her grasp.

Oh shit. Oh fuck. Oh, goddess damn it.

Nox hadn't had a plan.

Every fraction of a moment contained the image of a demonic she-devil closing the grassy space between where she had towered, lit in the cinders of sunset, and where Nox currently stood. Houses disappeared behind the spider's barrage of legs and the expanse of her abdomen.

Fight or flight was said to be the typical reaction in times of danger, but Nox was frozen to the ground, choked by the smell of decaying bodies and rancid meat. The spider was nearly upon her before the weight of invisible hands shoved her to the side, some unknowable force from within her rallying her survival instincts. She may not have possessed any conscious will to live, but something deeper, something more primal forced her to action.

Nox turned and ran. She ran faster than she'd ever run

133

before. She tore through time and space, feet pounding into the grass, arms pumping, heart thundering, eyes watering as she sprinted. She ran away from the sun, away from the demon, away from the vibrant reds of the fiery sky. She wasn't even sure if she remembered to breathe.

She needed to create time for Ash to free their friend.

If she could get the spider to follow her long enough for Ash to find his weapon and take on the spider, Malik might be spared.

There! A turn! Her thoughts sharpened, thinking only of each next step that might bring her one second closer to survival.

She took it at the last possible moment, feet skidding to the side as she wound between the tiny village homes in tight serpentine patterns. Her hand stretched out to steady herself against the grass as her turns were so sharp, they brought her nearly horizontal with the ground.

A sound let her know that Ash had made another slash at the creature. Nox pushed her back against the side of a house, panting from both terror and exertion. Her body trembled so badly she could hardly see the tree line before her. A cry from one of the men told her that they needed her.

What the fuck kind of skills do I possess? Her thoughts cursed as she looked around. *I can't fucking seduce the spider into submission!*

The gleam of the setting sun reflecting off metal caught her eye. She didn't allow herself to relax against the wall for more than a second. A tree stump behind the home had a solitary axe stuck into its trunk. The remnants of chopped, abandoned pieces of wood and neatly stacked piles of cleaved logs behind the house forced her attention forward. Nox ran to it. She clutched the handle with both hands but could barely free it from how it had been lodged into the trunk. She grunted her pathetic pleas for the trunk to release its captive, but she had no upper body strength. No feats of physical exertion had ever been required of her.

Another shout from Malik rose through the homes, and she tapped into a new wave of intensity, desperate to free the humble weapon. The stump relinquished its hold on the axe, and she tumbled backward, landing on her backside with the weapon in both hands.

There was time. Not much, but there was time.

She would not let him die.

The red sky around them cast a dramatic view of the hellfire from which this demon had surely crawled. The creature did not look at her as Ash swung again. It was all the faeling could do to keep moving as she reached for him. The demon had caught him once before. All she needed was one more strike before she'd dispose of the annoyance long enough for the golden reever to be in her mouth. The spider needed no weapons as every barbed leg, every strike of her clawed talons, every horrendous cry from her throat was a weapon in and of itself. Malik's hands were bloodied from where he had beaten and struggled against the barbed arms of the spider.

While the spider crushed her intended meal in her fingers, her furious eyes stayed on the fae as he dove and slashed. Ash wasn't trying to defeat the spider any longer; he was merely drawing her gaze away from her food.

Carried forward by an incomprehensible bout of insanity, Nox sprinted as close as she dared to go and lifted the axe above her head.

"Hey! Bitch!"

The spider thrust her many-eyed stare toward Nox, wet hair whipping like ink around her.

Nox pulled the axe back and hurled it with the force of twenty-one years of fury at the spider's womanly torso. She watched it twirl through the air with the inertia of some unknowable force.

The goddess made her aim true.

By the miraculous grace of the All Mother, the axe stuck. The blade meant for chopping firewood embedded into the sternum of the demon as if it were merely another trunk in the forest. Black blood began to ooze from where the weapon pieced the spider's skin.

Malik crumpled to the ground as she released her hold on him. He didn't move. The creature's awareness of the men seemed to slip from her mind as she clawed at her breasts, trying to free herself from the axe that Nox had buried in her body. While the spider's fingerlike talons thrashed and gripped for the axe, Ash seized what may have been his only opportunity.

He lifted his sword with two hands to behead the monster. His arms buckled from the tremendous collision, but his blade didn't miss. He severed the womanlike head from the demonic torso. The sharp, high crunch of meat, bone, and blood joined her final cry as the monster found one cognizant moment to unleash awareness of her decapitation. Black blood spurted in a horrid fountain from the head and throat. The long, wet hair clung to her face as her head flew from her shoulders with the force of the descent, skidding to a stop against a village home, snakelike jaw unhinged in an unholy scream. The creature stood on all eight legs for a moment, hands still thrashing with the remnants of life as she clutched at the stump at her neck. Her hands stayed at her throat as she collapsed to the ground with a mighty thud, barbed legs twitching as black, viscous poison leached from the fatal blow.

Her head rolled toward Nox, who kicked it farther away from the body with a horrible, disgusting thump as her foot connected with the black, syrupy fluid.

The danger had not passed.

Ash stood over the slain beast. He remained doubled over, heaving for air. Nox ran past the faeling to where Malik remained on the ground and fell to her knees. She rolled him onto his back and saw the barest upward turn of his lips as he smiled at her. The death rattle of ragged breaths was the only sound between them. Bits of blood began to dribble down from his mouth.

"No." She shook her head. "No, no, no, no, no." Nox clutched at his clothes uselessly, willing him to be better. She was no healer, but she knew the creature had to have crushed something vital within him that caused his very blood to bubble up.

Ash was on his knees at their side, but she barely noticed him. She watched him grab uselessly at pockets, patting himself for healing tonics that did not exist. Ash's color drained from his face, and with deathly stillness and widened eyes, he stared at Malik.

He had the look of a man who had done all he could. He had distracted, he had fought, and he had beheaded. But it wasn't enough to save his friend.

Malik coughed weakly, a small sputter of blood coming up with the movement. "Hey," he groaned. "At least we took her down with us."

"You're not going to die. You're going to be fine. You're not going to die." Nox shook her head uselessly. Her hair tumbled over her shoulders, creating a night-black curtain around them as she stared down into his face, defiantly denying the All Mother the soul of the golden-haired man.

Ash remained frozen where he knelt.

Too weak to move his head to regard his friend, Malik's face stayed fixed on Nox, lily-pad-green eyes staring deeply into hers. His bloodied lips were still caught in a half smile. "Amaris would be so proud of you."

The words strangled her.

"Don't talk. Shh, shh." Nox began to cry. Her shoulders shook with the effort to contain her sob as it choked her. The hot salt of her tears rained down on him as she clutched at his shirt. She was vaguely aware of the villagers opening their doors and watching the commotion in the center of their small village. The red of the setting sun was bleeding into the dark of night, its last ember glows casting the remnants of warmth on Malik's face.

He began to close his eyes, his green pools of life twinkling out.

"No!" Whatever force had urged her from the house to confront the spider commanded her now. She hadn't known what strength she possessed then, nor did she know now. Without understanding her motives, she clutched her fingers into handfuls of Malik's blood-soaked tunic. The tremor of Malik's last breath of air hissed from his lungs as Nox lowered her mouth to Malik's, capturing his final exhale before it could fully escape.

This was no kiss.

Her lips locked around his. With a single push of air, she offered him the glow of whatever magic she possessed: a life that had not belonged to her. The spark she had devoured from the Captain of the Guard many moons ago traveled from its humming cage behind her ribs, ripping its way from where it had lit her skin and embedded in her soul. It rose from her heart, beyond her lungs, passed through her throat, over her tongue, beyond her teeth, and through her lips into his.

She gave him everything she had to give.

Relinquishing the life force that had never been hers, her world went black as she collapsed to her side.

Fourteen

I T WAS DARK. IT WASN'T THE BLACK ABYSS SHE'D EXPECTED
from the far side of death. It wasn't the void of nothingness, nor the star-soaked dark of night. She frowned into the
gloom as she struggled to understand what was happening.

"Where am I?"

Nox's voice was hoarse as she addressed an empty room.
No fire crackled; no life stirred. She tried to move but
couldn't. She blinked against the gloom but saw nothing,
heard no one. She tried to bring a hand to her face but felt
as though her arms were made of lead. The only noise in the
quiet room was that of her slow, intentional breaths. There
was a hitch to the way her lungs pulled and released the air.

A familiar fear crept into her. It was not the panic of
spiders or the terror of men, nor the fright of Millicent and her
outstretched arm. This was a fear of horrid recognition as she
attempted to wiggle her limbs, fighting a surge of panic. Nox
struggled to control the shallow pants of her rising breaths as
she battled for control over her body, just as she'd had to after
the immobilizing grip of the Madame's deathly touch.

She'd only recovered when she'd been fed a life, taking a
soul from someone who no longer deserved it.

Souls.

She realized with clarity that she had offered the life she'd stolen to Malik.

Her fingers twitched from somewhere beneath their scratchy blankets. She searched her body for awareness. Her shoes had been taken off. Other than the leather shoes, she was still fully clothed under the blanket's warmth. Her feet jerked slightly against the irritation of rough wool. She continued to explore her body, searching for injuries. Her muscles spasmed as she willed her life into them, though they did not rise. With the tiniest relief, she realized she was not the husk she had once been. Though unable to rise or move, she knew that she would find the strength if she continued to try.

This was different.

She forced herself to remain calm. She'd hyperventilate if she continued to panic.

"Hello?" Nox called out again, grateful for the use of her voice, as she'd been unable to speak as she'd lain in her silken cage at the Selkie.

The door cracked open then, and a small candle glowed in its space. The village woman they had met when they'd first entered this goddess-forsaken cluster of cursed country homes hustled over to her. The matronly woman's eyes widened as she observed Nox and her stress-creased state.

"You're awake!" The village woman held the candle closer to her. In the other hand, she held a bowl. The woman began to dab at Nox's forehead with a damp rag. "We put you in here so no one would disturb you, love. The owner of this home…" Her voice trailed off. "Well, after he was killed, we haven't had much use for it. It seemed as good a place as any for you to rest."

"How long have I been sleeping?"

The woman's face was kind. Whatever terror had gripped her as the village had been in the clutches of the spider had seeped from her features. She was nearly unrecognizable now that her shoulders had relaxed and fear no longer painted itself onto her face. "Nearly three days, love. Your friends have gone to fetch a healer. I did expect them to be back by now, but I imagine after slaying that demon, they're bound to be awful tired."

"The spider—"

"Chopped up and buried in more pieces than kindling."

Nox blinked. Her mind stepped back a few paces at the information. The woman had used the plural when referring to the reevers: friends. That had to mean Malik was not only alive but he was on his feet and able to travel.

Nox's arms and legs twitched again from beneath her blanket as she searched for a way to rally her appendages. The motion was noticeable enough that the woman offered a gentle chastisement.

"Shush now, little love. Just you rest. We owe you our lives, we do. You'll be well cared for until your friends return. Do you think you can eat?"

Eat? Nox wasn't sure how she would be expected to chew or swallow when she didn't have the strength to raise her head. She merely looked to the woman, brows moving in her unspoken question.

"I'll fetch you some broth." The woman lit a candle as she left the one-room house so that Nox was no longer alone with the shadows. The candle was small, but in the absolute darkness of night, even the smallest of lights set the entire world aglow. The shadows of the dead man's house disappeared against its tiny, orange strength as it kept her company in the dark. Whoever had inhabited this hovel was currently rotting in the stomach acids of the dead spider, deep below the earth.

In the Selkie, she'd been left alone with her thoughts for days.

She'd barely stared at the candle for a few minutes before her maternal companion returned to her bedside. One of her children accompanied her, clutching the fabric of her dress

141

in their fingers. The woman ignored the toddler and ladled careful spoonfuls of broth onto Nox's lips, ensuring that nothing was too hot to scald or burn. Nox hadn't realized how hungry she was until her stomach cramped at the small liquid.

Three days of sleep, the woman had said.

Three days without eating or drinking. Three days in which she had been dead to the world. The woman chatted, if only to hear the sound of her own voice as it replaced the gloom with friendly babbles. She paused in the middle of the meal to light a fire on the hearth, and she spoke the names of the dead. The woman carried on talking cheerfully, dribbling spoon after spoon of broth into Nox's mouth, mopping up anything that cascaded down her chin.

Then she shared everything she could of the spider. They didn't know what had conjured the demon, she said, nor what made it cling to their small forest town, but if it hadn't been for the courage of its three saviors, they'd still be in the demon's spindly grip.

The woman fretted after Nox as if the girl were her own daughter.

Nox was too weak to do much except absorb the woman's care. Her chest tightened as she realized no one had ever stroked her hair the way this woman did now. No one had fed her spoonfuls of soup when she was sick. No one had dabbed at her face or sat beside her in times of need. Amaris had been the only person to keep her company, holding her hand in those days after the long, bloodied lines had broken her back. Amaris had clung to her silently and Nox had healed slowly, quietly, while meditating on that love. Now that she knew what cursed gifts she possessed, some broken part of her wondered if that was the reason her scars had faded to their thin, nearly imperceptible lines. Had she sipped from the cup of Amaris's love the same way she sucked the life force from her prey?

Her mind wandered elsewhere as she stared up into the woman's warm face.

Nox had never had a mother.

It hadn't bothered her much, as it was hard to miss what she'd never known.

Agnes had treated Nox with favoritism, but Farleigh's Gray Matron had never fussed like this. Agnes hadn't tended to her wounds or asked about her feelings or told stories of her family. This was the first time in Nox's life she experienced maternal care, and she nearly choked on it.

The villager seemed to sense her shift in energy and clucked her tongue gently. "There, there. Don't be sad, little love. Your friends will return swiftly, I'm sure of it. If the All Mother emboldened you to survive that demon, surely she will see you healthy and on your feet in no time."

The woman's prediction was accurate.

Before dawn broke, the reevers were at her door. The village woman had kept a wakeful watch through the night, cooing comforting stories of deserts and dragons, forbidden loves between kingdoms, and the goddess and her saving mercies, never allowing Nox to feel a moment of fear or abandonment. When Malik and Ash burst through the door, Nox nearly possessed the strength to sit up on her own.

She recognized true joy shining in their eyes at their relief that she'd survived.

A frail, somewhat pretty woman in her forties took cautious steps behind them. She was plainly dressed in simple country clothes, her curled hair in one loose braid down her back. The woman, with her timid energy, made no attempt to push past the reevers.

Malik was at Nox's side in a heartbeat, grasping her hand in both of his. He kissed her limp knuckles, and she tried to tighten her grasp around his hand but couldn't find the strength.

"Goddess above, Nox. You saved me," he said, moving one hand to her hair. There was so much gratitude, so much affection in the touch. Malik only sat by her for a moment before he was on his feet again, ushering the small woman to take over at Nox's side.

They explained through the commotion that filled the following minutes that they'd been able to find someone trained in healing rather quickly, but the first healer was of the strictly medical variety. Given that Nox's injury seemed to be of a magical nature, it had taken everything they possessed to track down a person blessed with the ability to heal rather than simply the education of proper herbs and wrappings. If it hadn't been for the pocket watch and its enchanted hands, they may never have come upon the middle-aged woman who accompanied them now. She'd been alarmed, they said, when two armed assassins identifying themselves as men from Uaimh Reev had interrupted dinner with her family, but she'd obliged and answered their call.

The healer placed a hand on Nox's forehead and frowned. Nox's illness was most definitely of a magical nature, the healer agreed. She didn't speak much, merely made faint expressions of dismay as she moved her hands over Nox, pressing and prodding. Through her touch, Nox was able to find more movement in her arms and legs. The frown lines around the woman's lips and brows deepened while she concentrated, pulling on some deep magic. The healer was not calling on the knitting of wounds or the regenerative properties of cells. Instead, she muttered her claim to search for whatever absence, whatever lack presented itself in Nox now.

There was no curse, she said. There was no wound. There was only a void.

The healer lifted her hands from where they had pressed into Nox's head. Nox did her best to push herself into a sitting position but was still unable.

"And," the healer said quietly, turning to the reevers, "is this her normal appearance?"

"No," Ash said, tone matter-of-fact. "She looks different, but it's hard to describe how. Her hair has lost its luster. It was like ink before. Her skin used to glow…sort of. Now it's sallow. Her eyes weren't this flat."

"She was beautiful then, and she's beautiful now," Malik amended quietly.

"Hmm." The healer made a slow, speculative noise as her eyes went from Nox, then to Malik. The healer spoke to the reevers, asking, "Will you try something for me?"

The men made no attempt to shield their surprise. Nox was quite certain of their answer. Of course, they would do anything she asked. They had traveled for days to fetch the healer, after all. A reassuring voice in her head told her they would pluck flowers from forbidden gardens, collect antidotes from wicked creatures, or sacrifice swans to the All Mother if the healer had asked.

Instead, the woman simply said, "Will you sit with her? Hold her hand? I'll be back soon."

Without waiting for an explanation as to the anticlimactic request, Ash was near her feet, resting his chin somewhere on her leg. He gave her foot a comforting squeeze. Malik settled much closer to her face, holding her hand as the woman had suggested. The green of his forest-knit eyes sparkled with so many indiscernible emotions.

"You saved me," he repeated with low reverence.

The light behind Malik's gaze now glowed with whatever stolen effervescence she had possessed.

Nox's chest tightened as she regarded him. She'd never truly studied his features. Then again, she hadn't had occasion to lie quietly and behold her friends before now. Malik was still in his twenties, but perhaps either in the middle of the decade or cresting its edge. Stubble grazed across his chin and jaw, catching in the glow of the fire that had been lit in the small room. He looked at her so kindly.

He was truly, deeply good.

At her feet, Ash peered up at her with the golds and reds of autumn. His eyes had always been a gilded glow, his hair the dark embers of a forgotten, dying fire. Whenever she'd gotten close to him, she'd been faintly aware of the smell of apples, and she was curious if that might be a gift of the fae. He was Amaris's friend, her trusted companion. He fought with Malik, and he protected those he loved. Nox knew that Ash would have fought for her if the occasion had called for it. She knew he had fought for her as much as he'd fought for the reever and the villagers and the forces of peace as he'd slain the spider. She had no doubt that he would put his life on the line, time and time again, if it had been what honor demanded.

Who the hell are these men?

She had no idea what these two stood to gain from her friendship. They had fought and trained with Amaris and counted her as their brother in arms, so of course they would have fought for her as their fellow reever. As Amaris's friend, surely, Nox would receive the benefit of the doubt in their eyes, but nothing more than that. She had picked the locks to their cells in the dungeon of Castle Aubade—perhaps their dedication was the result of some life debt that they felt they owed her.

Nox found her strength as she wiggled herself from her prone position onto her elbows and then finally propped her back against the pillows. Malik helped, stacking a second pillow behind her as she sat. She offered a weak, grim smile at the men.

In her peripheral vision, she caught the healer from where the woman leaned in the doorway. The woman had a somewhat sad though satisfied smile on her mouth. "I thought as much," she whispered.

Fifteen

G ADRIEL SLEPT SOUNDLY BESIDE AMARIS, STILL PROPPED ON
her bed with his head against the cool wall. His steady,
rhythmic breathing was as soothing as rain against a window.

After the events in the tower, they'd barely clung to
consciousness long enough to get back to the healers' hall.
Their conversation hadn't lasted long before drifting into the
comfortable lull of sleep. They were weak, their thoughts
were scattered, and they carried the confusing swirl of brushes
with magic and death. It had been all they could do to hold
themselves together.

She looked around blearily, eyes opening slowly. It took
a moment for her sight to adjust as she tried to blink the fog
of sleep from her eyes.

Amaris had curled into a tight ball like a cat against her
pillow. It took a moment to adjust to the dull, sterile room with
its desk, cabinets, and the absence of the decorative touches
anyone could call home. She jerked her legs up, realizing her feet
had found warmth on Gadriel's lap in the night. Embarrassed
at the vulnerability of her prone state, she moved a little too
quickly to get her limbs under control. In her haste to right
herself, she nearly kicked him in a particularly sensitive place.

The jolt set the man stirring. "What?" He blinked his eyes open. He stretched, face revealing a new layer of pain and stiffness.

"Oh fuck," he groaned, voice low with controlled misery.

Amaris was stiff with the discomfort that one felt after fitfully sleeping in their clothes. She cleared her throat, voice sounding as though she was in something of a daze. "Did last night really happen?"

Gadriel had put his head in his hands. "Part of me wishes it hadn't."

She unraveled from the bed. She'd spent plenty of time examining her room in the healers' hall and knew the cabinets were well-stocked with clean gauze, disinfecting astringent, numbing agents for the pain, and healing tonics. She grabbed vials of the latter two and returned to the bed, handing him a few bottles of liquid. He took the healing tonic but waved away the painkiller.

She threw back one of each and tossed the empty bottles.

Before she returned to the bed, she poured two glasses of water. "And here I'd thought you were a general because you were the strongest and the bravest. I didn't realize you held a nepotism title."

Gadriel took the cup from her and drained it completely with a satisfied sound, a small stream of water running down his chin. He wiped it with the back of his hand. The black clothes that had stuck to his body with sweat were still creased in the shape of his muscles, the salt crafting them into whatever craters and curves his upper body possessed. Amaris lifted her eyes from him as she turned to refill his cup. It wasn't expected of her, but movement gave her something to do with her nervous energy.

"You don't think it was relevant to mention King Ceres was your cousin?"

It took a long moment for him to respond.

"He's not a bad man, you know," Gadriel said quietly. "I'm sure you've heard rumors of his reputation. Of his...

mental state. Everyone has. But Ceres ruled kindly and with a fair hand for hundreds of years until one day, he didn't."

"Until Moirai's curse?" She lifted another full glass of water to the winged fae.

Gadriel pursed his lips. He took a sip from the second glass of water and considered the issue at hand. He reiterated, "Ceres is kind."

Amaris rejoined him on the bed, leaning her head against the wall. Her eyes felt so dry, so strained from their night in the tower. She didn't know how long they'd slept, but it couldn't have been more than an hour or two. Every fiber within her ached from their snag against death's talons. "What happened?"

Gadriel dipped his chin. His hair still curled slightly from where the night's fight to survive had made it unruly. She had always known him to be large, but as she sat beside him on the small bed in the healer's room, she truly absorbed what a towering figure Gadriel was. Even stripped of his wings, he would have been enormous. His shoulders and chest were broad. His legs were powerful. But with the wings, he engulfed the space around him, making her feel elfin in his presence. Her pride would have urged her to stand, to pace to make herself feel bigger, but her exhaustion pressed her into the bed. It was too small of a space for them to comfortably share, but neither had the energy to move.

"He fell in love" was all Gadriel said.

There was a romanticism to the sentence that quieted her. The thought was beautiful and terrible all at once. It was a satisfying answer but also raised an entirely new set of questions. Amaris though that perhaps if she were another person, someone who still lived at Farleigh and found herself helpless, pretty, and clinging to tales and adventures from the lips of others, the sentence would have been enough. Now she couldn't spare herself the report on behalf of romantic ideologies. She had a mission. If she couldn't comprehend the queen's motives, how was she to understand the curse? How

149

could she do anything about the slaughter of Raascot citizens in the south?

He was lucky she was tired, because it kept her from genuine irritation. Instead, her lips turned down as she felt a headache begin to pulse between her ears. "Gad, you haven't shared everything with me about your mission to the south. I shouldn't have had to find out you and Ceres were cousins from the curse. Is there anything else that might be relevant? Anything I might need to know?"

He looked at her with an unnamed emotion. Some part of her told her that she was seeing sadness, though she didn't understand why. "Nothing I can share." He looked away again.

"Gadriel." She said his name slowly, waiting for his dark eyes to meet hers. If his hair was any indication of how the sweat and night's operation had left them, hers must have been a sorry sight to behold. She needed twelve hours of rest and a hot, soapy bath to scrub away the scents of sweat, climbing ten thousand steps, and nearly plummeting to her death. Perhaps it was a good thing there was no mirror in the room. Amaris had no way of confirming how self-conscious she should feel.

Still alert at his name on her lips, he waited expectantly.

She picked her words carefully. "I know I haven't been entirely pleasant."

He chuckled at that. It was one single, fatigued exhalation of amusement.

She did her best to ignore the laugh, inhaling through her nose. "My point is, I don't have to like you to prove that I'm here for this mission, whatever it is. Samael gave me purpose when he and the reevers took me in. Before him—before the reevers—I had nothing to live for. My dispatch seemed so simple when I was sent south to meet with Queen Moirai, but now…"

She paused for effect, studying his expression. His lower lip was lifted, puckering subtly in a small frown. His eyebrows met in the middle with her words. Amaris was able to ask her final question.

"What aren't you telling me?"

His sigh wasn't loud, but it was still disquieting against the stillness of the room.

"I know that you reevers take an oath to serve no king. Your egalitarian league is no military. I don't expect you to understand why there are some things I've been sworn to keep concealed. It's treason. I'm Ceres's general. If the king's military head is sharing his secrets, well…when you reveal classified information, you are tried and imprisoned."

He gestured as if he expected his retinue to be there in the room. It had been a long time since Zaccai had sat at his side. She idly wondered where were his fellow winged fae were now.

"I'm clearly not here for espionage, Gadriel. I'm not going to sell your secrets or brand you a traitor. If we're to work together…" Amaris pressed. He was right—she didn't understand why anything would be so confidential that he wouldn't even share it with her.

Gadriel wasn't looking at her, but neither was he avoiding her gaze. His eyes were in the soft focus of the middle distance, lost to memory.

"I can tell you about him," Gadriel said quietly.

"That's all I'm asking."

His eyes remained glazed as he stayed in his thoughts. "He's my cousin and my king. Ceres and I grew up together. He was born only thirty years before me, which, for fae, is nearly like being twins." He chuckled lightly. "We were brothers for much of our upbringing. We played together, trained together, drank together. We would even prowl the same taverns for women together for a time."

He smiled, lost to whatever unwholesome thought caught his lips in a twitch. She allowed him his unsavory memory until he continued.

"Ceres was born to rule, and I mean that in the truest

151

sense. I preferred fighting and sparring. I liked strategy and combat, while he was the most diplomatic person I'd ever met. He always knew how to see things at their core. No bullshit could slide by Ceres. He had the patience and discernment of a god. He took the time to truly listen to the people." Gadriel rubbed at his eyes. "I don't know how much you've learned about the continent's history, but Raascot suffered greatly when the south first sealed off its borders. Its people felt the weight of its discrimination long before our reign. When Ceres took the crown, he led by example. Darkness was something you expressed, not something you inherently were. Imagine the power of this message for two hundred years as he reassured his people. After all, his powers were everything the southerners feared them to be. Whatever corrupt or evil powers those in the south whispered about, Ceres possessed. He was a beacon for how everything one might use for wrong could instead be used for good."

She parted her lips to ask about his abilities but stopped herself. She was grateful Gadriel was talking to her at all after his great speech on militant secrecy. Any interruption might break his reverie.

"He was a very involved leader, so it wasn't uncommon for him to travel. I'd be with our troops, visiting various camps and overseeing the forces, doing my job, living my life. Meanwhile, Ceres would visit cities across Raascot, meeting with the mayors of villages, even going on diplomatic missions without bothering to bring bodyguards. He truly saw the good in everyone. He was powerful enough that no one thought to worry. He's a hard man to kill."

Gadriel spoke with the slow, crushed energy of someone telling a tragedy. Amaris recognized his cadence from the books she'd read and the tones of the matrons who'd gathered them to hear the classics at story time years and years ago. Novels and poems and songs were written with the sort of intentional, gradual inflections that he used now as he spoke so lovingly and brokenly of his cousin.

His story began to dissolve, taking on a less consistent flow, his message little more than a ramble as he reached the haunting conclusion.

"We didn't even know it had happened until it was too late. None of us did. He was fine. He was great, whole, wise, and quick. Ceres was himself. He hadn't brought anyone with him when he visited Farehold. It wasn't out of the ordinary for him to go. None of it was. Ceres regularly went away for weeks at a time. I have no idea how often he was away from his throne, and we assumed he was in neighboring villages or meeting with nobility when he was really with her. I don't know how many months or years it went on. I should know. A general should know these things about their monarch."

"With who?" Her question was barely a whisper. Amaris didn't want to break the dreamlike energy in the room. She wasn't even sure she'd asked it out loud.

The quiet lasted too long. His pause went on for an incomprehensible length of time before he spoke again. When his lips parted, he sounded like he might cry.

"I don't know. When he came back, he had cracked. Something had broken in him. I haven't recognized Ceres in years."

"He didn't tell you anything?"

"He wasn't *him* anymore."

"How can that be?"

If she hadn't been so tired, she might have felt impatient. Amaris wanted to grill him, wanted to tear into whatever he was holding back from her, but she could do nothing aside from wait. Her lids grew heavy again as the rise and fall of his breath became a sort of lullaby. She listened to the air as he pushed it in and out of his lungs, allowing her eyes to flutter to a close. So rhythmic. So steady. The smell of leather and pepper and black cherries mixed with sweat, matching his inhalations and exhalations as she felt herself begin to doze.

She'd nearly nodded off before he spoke again.

"I don't know what happened. None of us do. What we

know is that whoever he loved destroyed him. The only thing he has ever told us is that his son was in the south. He was convinced that Moirai was keeping his child from him. It didn't matter how we questioned him or what the council had to say. Even when we were alone, I begged him to talk to me, but he wasn't the same. Whatever had shattered in him had healed in some hardened, damaged way. That feeling you get when someone you care about is closing off from you and there's nothing you can do to stop it…it's unbearable."

She winced at that, wondering if even a small part of him was referring to her.

"For the last twenty years, he hasn't been a king to any of us. Raascot has gone without a ruler. All his men are on this mission to find a son that may or may not exist, if your priestess at the Temple of the All Mother is to be believed. He hasn't helped his people; he hasn't regarded his lands. The north has fallen to the anarchy of his abandonment. All we can do is carry out his broken folly, sent to our death while he searches for his son. It's as if he thinks his child will bring her back."

"You know she's dead? The one he loved?"

He made a helpless gesture.

"How can that happen? How could love shatter him?"

He looked up at her, his gaze coming back into focus. "I've had love in my life, but I haven't been *in* love. Not like that. Seeing him…I wonder if it's truly love if it doesn't have the power to destroy you."

She swallowed, disquieted by the shift in the conversation. "Why would you say that?"

He tilted his head ever so slightly. "Are you asking what I could know about love?"

"If you've never been *in* love…"

"Have you had your heart broken?"

Her back straightened. She'd clamped down on thoughts of Nox, catching them and stuffing them into her airtight box. Nox had never broken her heart. In fact, Nox's steadfastness was her truest north star. No, she hadn't had her heart broken.

Unless… A moment itched at her. "Yes. Not romantically, but there was a moment when I thought I'd lost the reevers. I thought I'd lost my only family."

"And? Did you handle it well?"

No.

The answer rang through her as clear and sharp as a bell that she couldn't unring. She'd handled it with spectacular humiliation in her desperation to remain connected, in her fear of abandonment, in her need to keep her family together. She'd cracked, if only for a moment. Fortunately, she hadn't possessed a kingdom doomed to suffer under the weight of her perceived loss.

Her silence was answer enough.

"Family can break your heart when you love them. Fuck, a damn horse can break your heart if you care for it and it passes. So I don't know. Maybe I don't know anything about it. Maybe none of us do. But with Ceres on the throne, it's been on my mind for decades…" His thought trailed off as his eyes unfocused once more, rejoining the exhaustion of the middle distance. "They seem opposed, don't they? Guarantees and love? You can choose security, cautious distance, sex, fun, companionship, but love is vulnerability."

She was too tired, and the world was too heavy. She couldn't begin to process his words or why he would share them, except that he'd seen his cousin—his king—fracture. The most terrible evidence of the king's shattered heart was Raascot's destruction left in its wake.

This was the bitter burden Gadriel bore. This was the hardship that slumped his mighty shoulders. Now she finally understood the task that had been laid at his feet by the half-mad king he had loved and revered for so many years. Countless northern fae had fallen to the shredding arrows of the south while Ceres searched its lands for his son, not caring what Farehold saw, not caring about the ag'imni curse at its borders, consumed solely with his need to be reunited with whatever piece remained of his beloved.

"What if there is no child?"

It felt so insulting for her to say something like that after he had shown her his soul, but she had to ask.

His intake of air may have been a laugh under different circumstances, but Gadriel was not smiling. "I don't think it matters."

She considered this. If the king in the north truly had gone mad, those sacrificed would be unimportant. It was with the slow seep of water soaking a fabric that Amaris began to understand Gadriel's plight. Comprehension didn't crash in at once like a lock clicking into place, nor was empathy taken for granted. This creeping realization brought everything into clarity. He'd been so willing to accept the smallest sliver of hope when it had been shown to him. He had stumbled across Amaris in the glen and felt for the first time that, even if there were no heir, even if their mission was pointless, even if the heartbroken king continued to condemn his men to die, perhaps one person could help to end the bloodshed.

Gadriel would carry on looking for the king's son, whether or not one existed. He would follow his duties to their bitter end. Amaris, however, might be able to use her gifts to keep even a few of his men alive. She thought of the emotion that had flashed in his eyes—a dream akin to desperation—as he'd gripped her face in the castle before she'd met the queen.

We have never had a hope like this.

Gadriel had seen the barest glimpse of a possible future where his troops, his family, his countrymen, his friends, were not sent south of the border to die.

She considered all she'd learned, not only from him but from Queen Moirai, from her powers of illusion, and from the orb and its curse. She'd spent days burning with her own anger toward Gadriel. She had felt nothing but bitterness that he hadn't considered her a friend, merely a means to an end. As she regarded him now, she understood the value of any tool that would hinder the tide of bloodshed. Her hand found the place where his own was resting. She dared to touch him gently.

"How can I help?"

Gadriel looked down at where her fingers grazed the skin of his forearm, then up at her. A ghost of a smile crossed him as he asked, "Are we calling a truce?"

"Maybe I'm tired of fighting."

Perhaps it was the exhaustion or the raw emotion of the story, but he lifted the arm she'd been touching, reaching it around her as if to hold her. The movement was so unconscious. She responded with a long-forgotten familiar instinct, tucking herself into the space between his arm and his body. She didn't realize what she'd done until the wave of salt, leather, and pepper hit her, but Gadriel had already relaxed, ready to fall back to sleep. Amaris would have shaken him off, would have wiggled away, but it felt...nice.

It felt more than nice.

Her eyes drifted shut once more. Her stomach felt something like a flutter. Her body felt something more. An influx of blood, a pulse, a throb, a want rushed through her, mingling with the swirling scents that belonged only to him. She was too sleepy to fight the feeling, even if she knew she didn't want to feel any of it. She was too tired to fight the flashes of how he'd held on to her as she'd almost fallen to her death. Fatigue kept her from blocking out how he'd yanked her hair to make her look at him. She didn't want to take ownership of how it made her flush. She was too exhausted to scold herself to guard whatever treacherous reaction she felt blooming and clutching her in depths far below her stomach.

Now was not the time to analyze any of it. Now was the time to sleep.

His eyes remained closed as well as he tilted his face skyward, resting his head against the wall. Gadriel just shook his head. "I don't know exactly how you'll be able to help make things right, witchling, just that I know you can. I know you have a role in this. If we go back to Raascot, I think you can help Ceres more than you'd ever realize. You might be the only person he'd listen to."

Amaris considered their puzzle pieces, her brain too foggy to attempt to assemble them into a logical image. Could they fix the jigsaw after they'd slept? For now, there was no picture aside from the angry face of the southern queen. Moirai had the power of illusion. She had cursed the king for his presence in the south. She had been conjuring the image of a crown prince. Moirai was at the center of everything.

But why?

A horrible thought poked at Amaris. It prodded her until she was forced to give it a modicum of attention, despite her drowsy state. It was nearly strong enough to stir her from the fatigue that was pulling them both under its waters once more.

"Gadriel," she began slowly, waiting for him to make an acknowledging sound so she knew he hadn't fallen asleep. "I need you to think hard on what I'm about to ask you."

He tilted his chin down to look at her, sleep looming over him with immediacy.

Amaris yawned slowly as she asked her question. "Is there any possibility King Ceres's lover was the princess?"

Sixteen

T HE TIME HAD COME.

In their conversation, Amaris and Gadriel decided a reever and a general no longer had a place at the university. After plummeting from the back of the ag'drurath, this institution had been their salvation. They had healed and learned more than they had thought possible. Its magic had revealed keys to locked doors that they hadn't known existed. But the more they learned, the more questions they had. If they wanted any hope of solving the questions that plagued them, they needed to be in Raascot.

"When do we leave?" she asked. It was all she could think to say while still clinging to the edges of consciousness.

"As soon as possible. But if we're in Farehold, we're going to have to travel by night."

"Oh yeah, the ag'imni thing." She smacked her lips sleep-ily, eyes closed.

He made a face. "Go to sleep."

"I think we need to say goodbye." Her eyes had fluttered open again. The weight of his arm was so comforting. "They've given us so much…"

"We sleep for the rest of the day, we say goodbye, and then we pack up."

They slept.

Amaris was awake before Gadriel. After her brain and body had the opportunity to stitch together once more, she returned to feeling embarrassed at the intimacy of their contact. Maybe she'd missed how it had felt when she'd curled up against Nox as they wasted the day tucked into pantries or huddled on the cots. Perhaps it was the sort of closeness she'd taken for granted—an arm around her, a shoulder to rest on, a pure, consistent comfort—something her unconscious mind had sought out while she slept. But he was not Nox. She unraveled herself from the vulnerable position and slipped away while the man continued to sleep. She had to express her gratitude to the masters before they left. It was the polite thing to do.

First, she paced the floors of the healers' hall. A student caught her in her stroll and suggested that she might find the Master Healer in the library near the medical texts, so off she went. The chilly afternoon air felt refreshing against her skin. For the first time since visiting the university, the sun was shining. She wandered each of the library's seven floors in her search for the Master Healer. Coming up empty-handed, she returned to the hall.

A slender shape stood outside the door, blocking her path with a quiet, patient fortitude. Amaris was surprised to find Master Fehu waiting for her at the entrance to the healers' hall, still dressed in simple gray linens in a way that reminded her too much of Farleigh and its matrons.

The woman was as statuesque as ever. Somehow, the Master of Magics never seemed to move. Her shoulders did not rise and fall with breath, and her hair did not so much as flutter in the wind. The woman was a living painting. It was clear from the way the master angled herself that she'd been waiting for Amaris, who was once again struck with the combination of scents, something like petrichor and deep red wine.

"Master Fehu, hello—"

"Please, follow me, won't you?" The fae woman was not making a request, regardless of how it was worded. The master moved from where she's been planted in front of the building. Amaris looked beyond the closed door to where Gadriel hopefully continued his healing sleep. Unsure of how to proceed, she did the only thing she could think to do and followed the master. Though the Master of Magics had never done anything to validate the emotion, she had an incredible knack for making Amaris feel uncomfortable, as if always on the verge of being scolded for a crime she hadn't realized she'd committed.

The master did not speak as she led the way across the campus. The long walk across the grassy lawns and between the stones and moss of the buildings grew more ominous as the time stretched on. The weather was the nicest it had been since her arrival, so she knew it wasn't the sunny day cursing her with the chill that slithered down her spine. It wasn't until they were near the manufacturing hall that Master Fehu came to a stop. Her sharpened steel voice was impassive when she spoke.

"I watched you depart from my tower last night."

Again, it was not a question. A small part of Amaris knew there was wisdom in certain fear. She stiffened but remained otherwise motionless.

She said nothing in response.

The master wasn't bothered by her silence. Unruffled, she continued, "I don't know what the magic revealed to you, but I suspect if it were mine to know, it would have been offered to me as well of its own accord."

She stretched a hand before her, sweeping over the mossy green grounds to where the final building at the edge of the campus rested. It had been easy to take the rugged greenery for granted throughout their stay at the university. Farleigh had been forested in a way that had never given way to mountains. Aubade had been dry and coastal. This was where the pale foxes of the highlands were born and bred.

The earth was a stunning display of the continent's jagged, emerald beauty.

"You and I are due for a conversation," said Fehu, "but first, there's something you need to see."

"In here?" Amaris asked, looking at the building. She hedged uncomfortably at Fehu's words. Perhaps she was in more trouble for entering the Tower of Magics than the master had indicated. She chewed on her lip and looked at the manufacturing building. Cora hadn't taken them inside on their tour, so she had no idea what to expect within its walls. Though she couldn't justify the emotion, entering a strange building with Fehu felt like she was living out a children's cautionary tale about entering a witch's den and being boiled in a cauldron.

"The Master Manufacturer and I would like to show you something."

Master Fehu led Amaris into the building past the smell of molten metals, blown glasses, and several kilns. She again thought of Cora, whose mother could speak to metal. Her thoughts went to Cora's father, who had come to the university as a human to learn to create things with advancements and technologies unbeknownst to the humans of the continent. They'd been a match made by the All Mother.

"Did you know," began the master as she led Amaris through heated corridors and past cold blasts of energy emitting from unfathomable creations within the rooms, "that I have led as Master of Magics for two hundred years, and I have never crossed into the Hall of Orbs?"

Ice clotted Amaris's blood at the words. Between the enormous door, its ominous warning, and the bottomless moat of shadow meant to trap all who entered, the blessings and curses of the land were well-guarded secrets. The master knew everything, then. Amaris didn't know how the fae woman had guessed their activities, but she knew. Fehu's voice held no hint of emotion as she continued.

"There has never been a reason for their magics to

divulge themselves to me. Imagine my surprise when two strangers were here for scarcely more than a few days and found themselves under the grips of blessings or curses that I've never been able to fathom." She continued walking, her feet silent on the stones. Whatever blessings granted the fair folk grace and weightlessness prevented her footsteps from reverberating against the rocks.

Fehu paused before a closed, iron door. "Perhaps it was not for a fae like me to uncover."

Amaris twisted her lips unhelpfully before offering, "I'm half fae, and Gadriel is fully fae."

She felt stupid for opening her mouth under the weight of the woman's gaze.

The Master of Magics arched a curious eyebrow, which was far more telling an expression than the impassive features had ever revealed. If Amaris were better at reading faces, perhaps she could have discerned what it was the woman expressed as her lip twitched at the corner. "Are you?"

Amaris's brows creased at the cryptic response.

"I'll call upon you later for this discussion." Master Fehu opened the door and gestured for Amaris to step inside.

Behind a desk, the short, stout man who had spoken at their meeting beamed up from his place behind the desk. It seemed too large for his stature; the room was too big for his frame. His office exemplified the stereotype of the erratic professor, with stacks of books and oddities in disorganized piles throughout the room. He hopped down from his chair and came to the hall to clasp Amaris by the hand, his voice positively overflowing with delight.

"My dear, you're here!"

"Master Manufacturer," Amaris said politely, realizing she didn't know the man's name. She'd hoped it might be an opportunity for him to alleviate the social faux pas and introduce himself, but alas, he did not.

"I'm so glad you've arrived! There's something rather marvelous that needs your attention. Come with me!"

Amaris tried to smile but felt deeply confused. "I'm sorry. I don't know that I'd be very useful. I don't understand much about manufacturing."

"Ah." He waved his hand as he went to the door. "People rarely do. You're in good company. Never fear. I know plenty enough about it for the both of us. Now, on we go!"

The jolly man led Amaris and Master Fehu a few rooms beyond. He kept up his happy chatter while Fehu remained characteristically stoic. It was with an iron clatter that he pulled out a heavy key ring and unlocked a door. Whatever secrets remained behind it were ones that needed safekeeping. The door opened slowly, and they crossed over the threshold into a room with low, reddish lighting. Toward the center was a device showcasing a textile she couldn't quite comprehend. A wooden contraption held some sort of fabric, stretching it from one end of the room to the other in a taut display. What was she seeing?

His eyes darted between the fabric and the reever rapidly, positively twinkling. The Master Manufacturer grinned widely. "Quite clever, isn't it? Go ahead, touch it! Feel it for yourself."

Amaris stretched her hand out and pressed the tips of her fingers against the material. She allowed her touch to graze against the unfamiliar sensation. Something firm yet soft to the touch was spread to its maximum expanse before her. It reminded her of silk, though the texture had no true match in her mind. It was unlike anything she'd felt. She marveled at the curious bolt of fabric before her.

The master positively glimmered with his own ingenuity as he handed her a knife he'd procured from one of his numerous pockets. "Be my guest."

While it seemed improper, she felt confident she was meant to stab the membranous material. She looked to the manufacturer, then to Master Fehu, but both inclined their heads expectantly from Amaris to the fabric.

With exceeding hesitance, she obliged. She raised the

small knife and attempted to plunge it into the silken fabric. The blade made a weak indentation before sliding to the side like a rain droplet over glass. Frowning, Amaris attempted once more to stab the bolt outstretched before her. For the second time, her knife was unable to puncture whatever it was she beheld.

"Positively brilliant." The Master Manufacturer was admiring his own handiwork. "This particular project has been under my oversight for years, but we've never had occasion to test it out quite like this! A few of my students have offered to leap from the tower." He laughed at that. "But I can think of no better recipient than our guests."

Amaris frowned at him. It seemed as though he was offering the fabric to her, though she couldn't understand why.

"Of course, the fabrication process is in our records, dear. We have replicated it many times to ensure that we weren't letting go of anything too precious. I doubt you'd be able to re-create it even if you sold it to the cleverest of engineers. Though if they do manage to replicate it, then they deserve the knowledge! It's no small feat! Go ahead, then! What do you think?"

She shook her head. "What do I think about what?"

The Master Manufacturer looked a bit put out as he threw up his hands. "For his wings! What do you think about this for your fae companion's wings?"

✦

Amaris had seen happiness before. She'd seen the excitement on a four-year-old's face as a family had plucked her from the orphanage to live with them in a new home, far away from the dreary life at Farleigh. She'd witnessed Odrin's glowing face the first time Amaris bested Ash in the sparring ring and the night she'd taken her oath. She'd cried over Nox's weeping face through the iron bars of her prison as the woman had clutched her with every cell of strength she possessed, reunited at long last. Yet she had never seen the truly unbridled, childlike joy that she watched on Gadriel's face as he flapped his reinforced wings. He took to the sky, the fabric not only fortifying his wings but somehow making them strong, faster, enhanced in nearly every way.

They'd worked with incredible speed and the marvelous art and science of manufacturing under the supervision of both Master Dagaz as the healer who oversaw the surgical adherence and the manufacturer who bound the material. It had taken very little time before Gadriel was a new man entirely.

It was not an exact match to the texture and coloration of what remained of his great, angelic wings, but the fabric had the iridescence of the inky rainbows held within the black depths of oil. It was easy to see the spaces where his feathers had broken and torn, but now instead of slashes and emptiness, there was the reinforced fabric of glossy, impenetrable hope.

He shot upward, energized by the new life breathed into him. The energy he radiated was as though he'd had the best night's sleep of his life, was drunk on the finest wine, and had a bride-to-be accept his proposal all in one moment. His stress was gone. The problems had disappeared. The world was whole. Gadriel twirled and spun like a bird released from its cage, tearing into the blue sky. He was an angel against the sun, an eclipse barely dotted against the bright, hot disk of bliss that beamed down on them. Amaris nearly clapped from the secondhand joy she felt watching the winged fae climb skyward and then plunge for the earth, tearing himself from gravity at its final moments. The Master Manufacturer and Master of Magics stood with her while they surveilled Gadriel in his unhinged expression of pure ecstasy. The Master Manufacturer truly was clapping, zealous with delight at his handiwork.

It was a sight unlike any other.

Amaris knew the masters were watching the demonic form of an ag'imni and grinned inwardly at how ridiculous it must be to see the terrifying shape of the most horrible demon in the tomes of the bestiary as he soared and danced through the air with unabashed giddiness. If he had been on two feet rather than outstretched wings, she may have described his movements as frolicking.

Gadriel dove for Amaris and swept her up in his arms. He'd snatched her before she knew what was happening. She let out an unintentional yelp from the unexpected motion as they shot skyward, ground disappearing beneath her. Her stomach abandoned its place and leapt into her throat before free-falling once again as the fae defied the forces of sky and earth. He spun her once, her equilibrium dancing into starlight. Her breath was stolen in a rush of wind and the scent of pepper. After one quick, tight hug, he returned her to the ground and continued his elated flight around the campus. She struggled to find her footing as he resumed his excessive display of glee.

The sight was downright silly.

The Master Manufacturer's face was aglow with his pride and satisfaction as he saw the object of his careful work put to such miraculous use. Even Master Fehu seemed to be containing the ghostly gem of a smile behind otherwise unreadable features.

Gadriel's wings had been restored.

For one wonderful moment, nothing else mattered.

Seventeen

IT TOOK ROUGHLY A DAY OF FLEX AND FLUTTER FOR GADRIEL to fully adapt to his new wings. While he kept to the skies, Amaris had the time she needed to say her goodbyes. The masters, however, had mixed feelings about their departure.

Master Neele was decidedly sour that efforts were not being made to detain the ag'imni, and she had not offered any parting farewells. Master Dagaz expressed his pleasure over the opportunity to display "blind healing" for his students, wherein he was able to administer proper care and medication without the ability to correctly assess his patient. The Master Manufacturer was still aglow with his delight that his magnificent invention had gone from inception to actuality as it flapped and soared through the sky on Gadriel's outstretched wings, so glad to see such a beautiful creation put to use. The faculty members were not a particularly sentimental bunch, and after their unceremonious goodbyes, they scattered across the campus, most wishing the two well on their way.

Gadriel and Amaris took dinner in their rooms and prepared themselves for a comfortable night's sleep before they'd undoubtedly return to the dirt, campfires, and pine needles of the forest floor. They'd been saved in more ways than one. Their days had been restful, healing, and eye-opening. Gadriel had his wings. They had both witnessed the birth of the border's curse. They were lost to their own thoughts as they waited for sleep to take them in their rooms that night.

A soft knock on her door pulled Amaris's attention.

Despite the late hour, Master Fehu eased her way in, followed by the rush of an oncoming storm and the rich smell of freshly poured wine. Something about the fae and their inborn perfumes was meant to be lovely—compelling, even—but this particular cloud of rain and wine put Amaris on edge the way a deer might turn toward a snapping twig in the underbrush.

"Good evening, Amaris." The master took Amaris's door—which had been left ajar, should Gadriel need her—as an invitation to let herself inside. "I was wondering if we might chat?"

Unlike the lanterns and blinding fae lights that filled the room during daylight hours, three nighttime candles flickered on the bedside table, offering a softened light meant to quiet one's thoughts at the end of the day. Their glow had been soothing when Amaris was alone, but now with the master present, the romanticism of three simple candles felt borderline inappropriate.

If she'd had a moment to collect herself, she would have lit a lantern.

Instead, Amaris nodded and gestured for the chair.

"Of course." Amaris carefully tested her boundaries. "Perhaps we might both learn from each other before we lose the chance."

Master Fehu's jewel-green eyes glittered. "Are there questions you have for me?"

Amaris wasn't sure where to start. She could ask about the climate or if the food was always so terrible, but the shallowness of such small talk seemed transparent. Instead, she started with something innocent, something irrelevant, just to make conversation. "Why is a Master of Theology the headmaster? Is this a religious institution?"

Fehu smiled with genuine amusement, jeweled eyes twinkling. "Have you heard the saying that theology is queen and philosophy its handmaiden?"

Amaris had not.

"The implication is that all things—magic, literature, math, all of it—can be understood if we grasp the nature of the divine. It's at the center of mystery and thus begs the most of knowledge and inquiry. Master Arnout is secular and yet a diligent student of the continent's power. I suspect he'd be very interested in you remaining here at the university."

"Me?"

Fehu tilted her head to the side, an action that seemed both examining and predatory. Perhaps Amaris's opening question had not been a wise choice in generating conversation. She scrambled for a second question, anxious to change the topic.

"There's something I've only noticed a few times, always around fae. Gadriel, my friend Ash, even you...there's a perfume. A scent. Is that—"

"Yes."

Fehu did not elaborate.

Maybe Amaris should have just asked about the weather. If Fehu was going to give cryptic, truncated responses, then they might as well have been about the overcast skies and boiled chicken. Amaris tapped her fingers rhythmically against the mattress in her discomfort.

The simple room in the healers' hall was cramped and seemed unsuitable for someone as timeless and elegant as Fehu, but the master had taken a seat and looked Amaris in the eye with her too-large irises. The fae woman held up a small pendant with a rough-cut amethyst stone set in a handkerchief. She handed the handkerchief to Amaris.

"I was wondering if you might look at this for me and tell me what you see?"

Amaris frowned, stretching out her hand for the object. She accepted the pendant and plucked it from its cloth, turning it over in her palm. She moved it between her fingers, examining the gem. There were no inscriptions, no decorative properties, nothing of the sort. The amethyst was not heavy, nor was its chain. She shook her head unhelpfully. "I'm not sure what I'm supposed to be looking for?"

Master Fehu extended her arm and grabbed first for the handkerchief, then the pendant between its fabric. Amaris hadn't realized that the master had intentionally been avoiding direct contact with the jewelry.

"What was it?"

Master Fehu seemed disinterested as she answered, "A cursed object. I was curious if your gift to see through enchantments would offer you any indication as to whether something inanimate possessed any magical properties. Perhaps your eyes, intended for sight, could spot such things from afar. It seems your gift does not extend so far."

Amaris's face flashed between worry and offense. "You let me touch it? Am I cursed, then?"

"Hardly." The master waved the question away. "The curse is meant to nullify the powers of only the fae in contact with it."

"It would have rendered my powers useless?"

Master Fehu eyed her. The woman was unreadable, her face chiseled from some fine stone. There was something behind the lack of expression that Amaris nearly recognized as an emotion, but she couldn't articulate what it was that she saw.

"You are perfectly fine, I assure you." It was all the master said on the matter before letting her thoughts redirect themselves. "What other abilities have you revealed?"

"Can I ask you a question first?"

Fehu arched a brow. "You may."

"Why have you taken an interest in me? In us?"

This question clearly bored her. "If you can't see the uniqueness of your position, then I hardly know how to begin to explain it to you."

"There are lots of fae at the university. Fae, humans with the small magics, perhaps witches…"

Fehu laughed quietly. "People say the strangest things, don't they?"

Amaris's brows furrowed. "What do you mean?"

"I mean, you would benefit immensely from studying. You would flourish from proper education. Ignorance is no one's fault, but once you're made aware of your lack, the choice to remain oblivious is when you become culpable. Is that a choice you're willing to make for yourself in good conscience?"

This was what she'd heard whispers of in Farleigh. The university whisked away anyone who displayed abilities, whether to study or be studied. Amaris was still unnerved that the master had risked the purple crystal on her bare skin, whether or not the effects from the contact would have been temporary. It was a crude way to test whatever theory Fehu was brewing about the limits of her power. Amaris didn't let herself ruminate on the seed of distrust she felt, as there had been another question posed. She shifted her focus and considered whether she should tell the woman the goddess-honest answer to her question.

The candlelight danced, and the ever-growing wary feeling Amaris held swelled within her stomach. She couldn't name her unease.

Fehu broke the quiet with a flat question. "Now will you tell me? What you know of your abilities, that is?"

Flame and shadow from the candles continued to dance across Fehu's features while she waited stoically for an answer. She prodded Amaris's face as if her eyes were the sharpest knife, intent on carving through skull and picking her brain for answers.

Amaris didn't know how to be evasive enough for someone as piercing as the Master of Magics, so as honestly as she could, she said, "I didn't know about my powers as a child. I was fifteen when I learned of my first one, and it was by accident. I was in a meeting with the reevers and unknowingly commanded them to accept me and allow me to train with them. Samael is the fae who sits at the head of Uaimh Reev and identified my ability for what it was, as it's ineffective on fae. It seems to only work on pure humans."

"What do you mean by that?"

"By what?"

"He identified your ability to see through enchantments?"

Oh.

"I'm silver tongued, as Samael called it—our leader—"

"I know Samael."

Amaris wasn't sure if she had the time or energy to ask how or why Master Fehu knew the fac who oversaw Uaimh Reev, but she didn't have the desire to prolong their encounter enough to ask. She pushed forward. "I can give commands that are followed by those who are purely human. I didn't know what I was doing until there was a fae in the room to tell me why it was happening. Samael, that is. He's the one who taught me what it was and that it could be used for good...or that I could try to use it for good."

"You ascribe purity to the humans affected. Why is that?"

Amaris frowned. "It seems that humans born with any of the small magics show a resistance to persuasion."

"Humans with the small magics," Fehu repeated quietly to herself, something that might have been amusement on the edges of her rumination. "How have you come to this conclusion?"

Fehu was everything Amaris had expected from a scientist. The master's questions were not heavy with curiosity or intrigue but the cross-examinations of a professor challenging their student's assertions.

Amaris decided to utilize the only common denominator that she and the Master of Magics shared: Master Neele. She explained with some hesitation and allowing the appropriate amount of guilt to color her voice how she'd attempted to persuade the Master of Beasts to open the door so that she might free Gadriel on their first night on campus and how the woman had merely glared at her—a glare as if she knew that a manipulation had been attempted. Amaris was carefully avoiding examples that would betray her as the traitor to the Farehold throne that she was.

Her deerlike sense continued to anxiously prick as the master stared at her. She couldn't name the underlying threat and did her best to reassure herself that she only felt this way because she'd been so shielded from the world. Her mind was doubtlessly playing tricks on her, or her lack of exposure to the fae had resulted in an underlying predilection for mistrust.

No, she decided, it was not because Fehu was fae, nor was it because she had blood from Raascot. Amaris didn't feel this way around Gadriel, even when she'd been angry with him. She'd been intimidated by Samael, but she wasn't afraid of him. Amaris had never felt this way about Zaccai. She'd always loved and trusted Ash.

This was a new feeling.

Master Fehu's lip twitched upward almost imperceptibly.

"Master Neele has no fae blood in her lineage. She does not possess what you've called 'the small magics.'"

Amaris blinked. "She must."

Again, some flicker of an emotion. "Your conviction tells me your experiences have been replicable. Would you share them with me?"

Fehu worded her questions with the innocence of curiosity. It was such a clever way to extract information. She demanded proof in the politest way possible. It was unnerving, as was everything about her. The deer within Amaris tensed to run for the opposing tree line.

She called to mind an example that would not divulge her subversion of the crown, involving a wooded glen, a waterfall, and a beautiful woman. Amaris thought of the Tree of Life and how it had hummed with energy.

Once again, she chose her words carefully. "Many weeks ago, my traveling companions and I visited the Temple of the

All Mother. We had reason to believe that there might be an item of power that could help us understand the curse that both affected them and impacted my dispatch. The temple's priestess implied that since magic was an energy that could be neither created nor destroyed, it continued to exist in a physical form after being spoken into the world. She said there was an orb of such power—the very one we found here in the tower. However, at the time, I didn't know how to acquire the orb. I did what I thought was right for my dispatch. I commanded the priestess to give it to me, and she laughed. It had no effect on her."

The barest of smiles crossed Fehu's mouth but did not reach her eyes. She raised one arm vertically enough that her loose, gray sleeve was pulled backward by the earth's downward tug. Her upper arm was parallel to the ground, her elbow forming its perpendicular. A silver brace cuffed the fae woman's wrist, nearly covering the length between an outstretched forefinger and thumb, flat against the small of her forearm. The jewelry seemed very plain from where Amaris sat as it reflected the soft glow from the warm, independent flames of her candles. If there were runes etched into the piece, she could not see them in the dim lighting.

"I suspect you have been attempting to use your abilities on those clever enough to have warded themselves against the influences of the magics of the mind." Fehu said it so coolly that it almost made Amaris feel embarrassed. It was as though this should have been obvious to her. "Of course, wards do very little against physical and elemental magic— unless, of course, one is wearing a shield. A spelled object like this likely won't protect its wearer from being drowned in a flood or caught in a fire, but it would certainly shield someone from your persuasion."

"That doesn't make sense." Amaris shook her head as she reflected on her experience. "They had no way of knowing I had this ability."

The master donned her disappointment like a crown. It

was the first unconcealed emotion that Fehu wore openly. "I implore you to forgo your journey to spend some time educating yourself, child. The world brims with things beyond the limits of your exposure. The egoism of assuming your magic is the only one worth protecting against should not be a source of pride."

Amaris had been chided and felt appropriately embarrassed.

Master Fehu continued, "Do you know what a fear caster is?"

Amaris did not, though she certainly knew something of fear.

"Fear casting," the master went on, "is an ability often manifested in the lineages of the so-called dark fae or those who tend toward the northern bloodline. One with this ability doesn't need to know you to learn of your deepest terrors. It's innate. Their ability grants them not only access to that which one fears but allows them to project it into the victim's eyes. It happens in a moment. The victim will believe their fear is present, you see. Their hallucinations can drive them to terrible ends. Decades ago, when Master Neele was a student here at the university, a peer used his gift on her in such a way. Master Neele has not taken off her protective wards in thirty-five years. Wards are expensive, rare, difficult to craft. They come with a number of drawbacks. But for someone like Neele, nothing could convince her to take off her ward."

The story was short and simple. Perhaps it was Neele's story alone to explain what that fear was or how it had been used. The event itself did not matter, only the result. Amaris was to understand that the Master of Beasts had acquired a ward after her horrid encounter and never took it off.

She tested another question. "If the priestess and Master Neele had not been wearing their charms, would my persuasion have been effective?"

"As an ambassador of an institute for thought and education, I am inclined to inform you that yes, it would be entirely probable—if not expected—that your power would have acted as intended. Wards are taxed with the power required to absorb the blow from any of the magics thrown at them, so it's likely you'd see a reaction from its wearer. Whether your priestess laughed with amusement or the master glared with her disapproval, they were responding to the sensation of the ward as it absorbed your blow. However, the morality of such an inquiry is rather gray, Amaris. Do you find yourself in need of such a gift, that you would wish for them to remove their protective wards?"

Amaris blushed. Part of her wished she could trust Master Fehu. She thought of how helpful it would be to consort with the most formidable wealth of magical knowledge in Farehold when discussing Queen Moirai and her wicked power. Perhaps their plight wouldn't feel nearly as daunting if they could rally the university's masters to their cause. However, she wouldn't ask treason of anyone. She wouldn't risk the sensitive knowledge of their mission in any hands beyond their own.

"I suppose I'm just trying to understand myself better."

"As should we all."

"Powers of the mind—they don't work on other fae, correct?"

Fehu arched a brow at this. "Why would you ask this?"

Everything felt like the wrong thing to say, the wrong thing to ask. Fehu's question alone implied that Amaris had made an error, though she wasn't sure how.

She twisted her mouth to the side in thought before shrugging. "In Uaimh Reev, Samael told me that my persuasion didn't work on him because he was fae. My sparring partner was chosen because, as a faeling with a human parent, he'd be more resistant to my persuasions."

Fehu considered the information. "Perhaps your ability has such a limitation, then, though I cannot tell you why. That's not true of all magics of the mind. Depending on the strength of the one wielding the ability, a fae would be just as susceptible as a human to many powers of the mind. This is why I, though fully fae, wear my ward."

Fehu's too-large emerald eyes continued to roam Amaris's face, studying her as if she was searching for something.

"Why doesn't everyone wear a ward?" Amaris asked.

Fehu nodded at this. "You did mention you know little of manufacturing. The same is true of most. Each spelled object, each magical item, each manufactured gift or ward or invention in this world requires at least two parties to compose, if not many more. One who is goddess-gifted and trained in the ability to manufacture and the other who has the power with which they intend to imbue the item."

"So if I wanted to make a dampener..."

"You would need both a manufacturer and someone who can naturally dampen. This sort of collaboration, training, education, and time makes the creation of objects slow and challenging. Many do not wish to share their gifts. If you had the ability to speak mind to mind and created infinite objects so that everyone was able to communicate in secrecy without opening their mouths, wouldn't it feel as though it lessened your own ability? Some even consider manufacturers to be thieves, taking pieces of power that should belong to no one."

"That sounds rather selfish."

"Is it?"

Fehu allowed another uncomfortable pause to stretch between them, broken only by the candlelight on bare walls as she carefully watched the way Amaris fidgeted beneath the weight of her gaze. Amaris wanted her to leave. It was night-time, and her last with access to a proper bed. Her anxiety grew with every flicker of the candle. She realized she hadn't unclenched her jaw in the fifteen minutes Fehu had been in her room, though she didn't know how to politely ask the woman to leave.

"What other trials have you attempted to manifest your abilities?"

The question confused her. Master Fehu had an excellent way of making her feel exceedingly stupid. "What do you mean?"

The master was the picture of patience. "I mean precisely what I have asked. What trials and exercises have you undertaken in order to better understand your abilities?"

"Trials?"

"Trials," Fehu repeated, voice betrayed by a cutting impatience.

Amaris blinked several times. "Well…none."

If she had suspected Fehu to have been disappointed before, the suspicion was solidified into evidence as the strength of the expression formed its lines across her perfect, ageless face. Amaris's answer had fallen short of anything resembling satisfactory. Fehu's monotonous voice confirmed any lingering suspicions of disappointment.

"You've merely stumbled on an ability to persuade because a male fae told you that you were able to do so and years later stumbled on your gift of sight because yet another fae informed you of your gift. Is that correct?"

The discomfort of incomprehensible heat and sweat prickled Amaris with embarrassment. She felt so naked before the Master of Magics, as if she didn't know herself at all. She wouldn't have known how to fight or defend if others hadn't trained her. She didn't know what a ward was, and she didn't know what the fae were capable of. She didn't know of the limits or reaches of the witches and their strengths.

Amaris shook her head.

"This conversation has confirmed what I needed to know, girl. Your education has been lacking. You are untested, unproven. You will stay here, and you will train."

Amaris blanched at the absurdity of the master's statement. "I'm sorry, Master Fehu. I can't do that."

Her gut hadn't been wrong. She wished she'd done more to listen to it as it confirmed the ulterior motives of the Master of Magics.

Fehu pressed, "You present with not one but two anomalous magics. It is essential that you think not of yourself but of the greater good regarding why you must stay and test your abilities. Fate has brought you to the seat of knowledge for such a reason, child. Your age is a speck against the centuries of the fae, so perhaps you struggle for perspective. While you study under me, the Master Manufacturer would be appreciative of the opportunity to keep his invention under his oversight so it can be further perfected. The Master of Beasts would benefit greatly from the opportunity to observe and examine even the perception of the ag'imni up close. The help your fae general would lend the entire continent through his selflessness would be immeasurable. While I respect Gadriel and his task, it is you who truly require the discipline and apprenticeships that only the university can offer you. I will be your overseer."

Amaris knew with sinking certainty that fate had not brought them here.

A fleeing ag'drurath and a helpful sixteen-year-old who'd found them in the forest had carried them to the university's doorstep. Destiny didn't demand that she train, though her time with the reevers had perhaps united her with where she might find the orb. Regardless of the wisdom and power of the master before her, Amaris felt quite certain that it was greed, not providence, that urged the woman toward the desire to keep her at the university. How rare of a happening was it to be presented with an opportunity to test and study unique magical predilections? Samael had once called persuasion a gift so exceedingly rare that he'd never met anyone who possessed it.

Amaris at long last identified the layers upon layers of impassivity that had been carefully constructed to mask the woman's hunger for this acquisition. Amaris saw her reflection glistening in those dark, emerald eyes. She understood the lust to keep not one but both of them under their roof. Not only would they gain one who could rightly see but also the one who couldn't be seen at all.

Amaris had been correct to withhold her trust.

In addition to learning letters and prayers, the matrons at

Farleigh had taught her the value of agreeableness. Arguing would not buy her the distance she needed from the master. She controlled her face from revealing the anger that pulsed within her. Wisdom informed her that this was no time to be brash. Amaris couldn't risk any reason for Fehu to watch her carefully as she made her next moves. She knew she needed to be smart. To pacify. To placate.

"Honestly, I didn't even know there were such tests. How do they happen? What shape would training take?"

Fehu relaxed ever so slightly. She allowed a cautious silence to move between them before subtle eagerness entered her voice. "The classes would be under my supervision, of course. Humans, as you say, generally present with a singular gift if they have been blessed with one of what you've called the small magics, but there are nonhumans such as fae on the continent who seem to channel the forces as conductors for power. In nonhumans, gifts reveal themselves though time, concentration, and no small effort. So far, yours have been stumbled on. Any that remain will be unearthed through sheer force of effort."

"Why say nonhumans? Why not say fae?"

Fehu's lips twisted—not quite a smile, not quite a frown.

Amaris tried again, returning to her ruse. "Would we begin immediately?"

Further still, Fehu's shoulders released their tension. "I would like to see you in my office tomorrow by the ninth bell after you've had a chance to eat your breakfast. Please visit me on the first level of the Tower of Magics. If you'd like, I can have one of my apprentices fetch you."

Amaris shook her head slowly, summoning stoicism. "No, I've been to the tower. I'll be able to find you after the morning meal."

"I'm relieved to hear you say that."

Satisfied, Fehu stood with the grace of a swan. She dipped her chin slowly, an expression of acknowledgment that she had only offered to Gadriel prior to this moment.

Amaris offered a restrained smile as the woman left the room, then waited. She couldn't move too quickly and give herself away. She counted to forty-five before she stood and began to collect what she could of healing tonics and wrappings from the cabinets. She used her pillowcase as a makeshift satchel to gather the objects and left them on her bed while she crept across the hall to Gadriel's room. He was awake and raised his eyebrows at her entrance.

"We need to leave tonight."

✦

As with history's fantastical events, there would most probably be songs, poems, rumors, gossip, and outright lies that emerged from the mouths of university students who had watched or heard or discussed the events in hushed whispers in the time that would follow. It would tickle one's ear to hear how the clever masters had assumed that the two strangers at the university would not forsake the generous offers of shelter and training and containment and instead flee.

Some students recalled how Fehu and Neele had been waiting outside the healers' hall, while other students swore it was all seven masters on horseback. Others spoke of how the Master of Magics had called on defensive powers, casting shields as green as her eyes meant to cage and sending shock blasts intended to tear a bat from the air that had shaken students from their beds as if the university had been under siege. It would be deliberated for ages how the Master of Beasts had brought her trio of trained vageth, vicious hounds of the underworld that had been tethered to her through magical binds, to hunt and contain what she commanded. Other shushed party members in these retellings seemed to recall little more than a loud, disagreeable conversation.

The students would talk of how the demon ag'imni had flown, darted, and spread his terrible wings across the sky. Their voices would drop into reverie as they recalled how the silvery Amaris had reflected in the moonlight as she ducked and rolled and sprinted. Nothing else would hold much entertainment or engagement to the university's students aside from retellings of how the pair had cleverly maneuvered across the campus on their daring midnight escape. Perhaps a ballad would be written so that one might sing of the stupefying events of that night, its legend passed from tavern to tavern on the lips of bards and lutists. The climax of the ballad would end when Headmaster Arnout in his black, billowing robes had burst onto the scene like a gallant of old, silencing his masters with a strike of magic so absolute that time itself had frozen, seconds merely shards of physical glass he could pick through and reshape to his will. The song would be one about free will, corruptibility, heroes, maidens, assassins, and thirst for knowledge, the truth of it of little concern. The tale would be meant to conjure awe at thoughts of the headmaster and cast fear into any student who dared to break the will of their teachers.

Maybe one day Amaris and Gadriel would hear of their tale on the drunken lips of a sailor who told an enraptured alehouse audience a story of heroes and their fight against magic. Perhaps history would side with the captors, painting the masters as champions of knowledge and the two as untrustworthy bastards for pillaging the campus and absconding with their stolen knowledge. Yes, tales would surely be written, and maybe one day Gadriel and Amaris would hear those stories, but that day was not today.

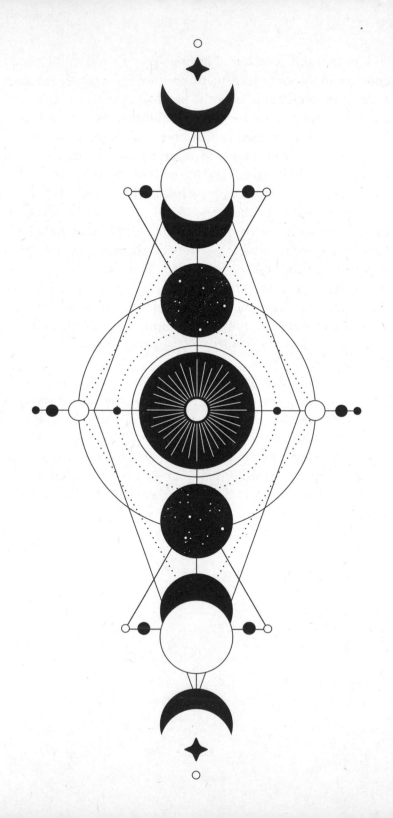

PART TWO

The Terrible Gift of Knowing

Eighteen

"HOW MANY DO YOU SEE?"
Nox looked at the men beside her as they squinted at the party below.

"It's hard to say," Ash whispered, focusing his faeling eyes on the men in the valley. "We can assume there are, what, four to a tent if this is a normal war camp? Maybe it would be easier to estimate rather than try to pick their silhouettes against their campfires."

They were supposed to feel tense, serious, surly, stoic, and all the things warriors felt, but there was an excitement that buzzed amongst them. Nox had never had the pleasure of sneaking out and exploring abandoned things as a child, but it felt a bit like breaking into Agnes's office or wandering out to the stables after dark. There was a gravity to the situation that she wasn't quite willing to grip with both hands.

"So two dozen on the conservative side, thirty-six if they're sleeping six to a tent." Nox crouched with the reevers in the thicket. Her eyes adjusted easily to the night as she scanned the gully below. They were pressed into the shelter of the underbrush on a hilltop, peering into where men in Raascot colors and banners were hidden from prying eyes in a small valley. The shelter of its hills allowed their campfires to go undetected. If it hadn't been for her pocket watch, they would never have found the war party.

"Fast math there, raven."

"Why do you call me that?"

Malik smiled. "He has a thing against using right and proper names. I don't think he's ever called Amaris by her name."

"And what does he call you?"

Malik turned to Ash. "That's a good question. Why do you call me by my name?"

Ash shrugged. "You've always felt like a Malik."

The air stilled as they retrained their eyes on the troops.

Nox had never seen Raascot's sigil before this moment. Students had been smacked on the hands with a ruler for asking about the northern kingdom while at Farleigh, and she'd encountered no northmen at the Selkie. The kingdom's absence had been curious to her when she worked the floor, as many other foreigners had come and gone. Now that she knew Raascot fae appeared as ag'imni, she fully understood why they hadn't entered her brothel.

The flags flown at this campsite were rust in color with a black symbol emblazoned on their center. The emblem contained a shield with an elaborate compass of some sort on the metallic face, with the outstretched wings of a crow on either side of the shield. Bronze, like the skin of its people, she supposed; wings for the trait that both unified them with one another and segregated them from the judgments of the south. These, of course, were no true northmen beneath the flags. These were Moirai's men.

Nox and the reevers had followed the spelled pocket watch as it had taken them first to the road that connected the corners of the continent and then as its hands swiveled them once more into the forest. It had created such a troubling, inconsistent path that they were convinced it was broken. Now that they'd found the camp, they admitted they'd been wrong to doubt the watch.

"Why were they using the main road if they were just going to go back into the forest?" Malik asked.

"To be seen." Nox understood this game. She was no stranger to manipulation. Her chess pieces had typically been shuffled around a much smaller board, playing opponents one on one in her matches of seduction. There was no reason for the games of kingdoms to be any different. Every strategic shift came with purpose.

It wouldn't make sense for the men to march out of the royal city, so she supposed they had either stayed hidden for some time amidst the dense forest, or they had merely changed into the black and copper colors of the north after creating enough distance between themselves and the castle that connections would not be drawn between them and the queen. There was both art and science to the theatrics of deceit.

Hours later, Nox and the reevers were still left with unanswered questions.

"Where are we now?" Malik blinked around them from their place on the hilltop. They weren't near any towns or villages. They were nearly a day's ride inward from the continent's road. If these men wanted to show force in the south, why had they come to such a remote location?

The other two had only shrugged. Their pocket watch told them where they wanted to go but gave no indication as to where they might currently be.

"I just don't understand," Nox said. "If their goal is to be seen, why aren't they raiding villages and sacking towns to spread word of Raascot's villainy? What is the advantage of hiding in the forest? If the queen wants to incite the people, shouldn't there be more raping and pillaging?"

"Just to be clear, we are glad that they aren't raping and pillaging, right?"

Her face fell, regretting the use of the word. Nox let her eyes flutter to a close. It was not a light matter. None of this was.

Ash made a half-amused gesture. "Maybe we should go back to the castle and just ask Queen Moirai what she's up to? 'Hey, Queen, how are you? Thanks for having us. I'm Ash. You may remember me from the day your champion dragon ransacked the city? Anyway, these are my pals. Our white-haired friend—charming girl, I'm sure you'll recall—led us to understand that you've cursed the border, have no crown prince, and are sending men in northern colors about the land. Would you care to elaborate?'"

"That's excellent. You go ask her. Malik and I will hold down the mighty fort here. Please report back with your findings."

All three smiled, though no chuckles were audible.

Their banter comforted Nox greatly. The girls under the Selkie's roof were friends of shared circumstances, not ones of choice. While they suffered the same clients and shared a common enemy in the Madame, they had very little to bond them to one another in the simple, amiable ways of easy conversation or jokes between friendlies. They didn't laugh together. They weren't quick on their feet together. It wasn't that they couldn't be or weren't smart, funny, or whole, just that work was work. Their lives required their own barriers for survival.

"I don't think I can leave Malik alone with you, I'm afraid. The man can't rub two thoughts together when you're in the room."

"Hey!" Malik protested, face reddening. It was plain he had hoped this would be the sort of thing they all politely agreed *not* to talk about.

Nox grinned at that, though it was colored with a hint of guilt. She knew the effect she had on men. "I will admit, that is my fault. Ash probably finds me less charming because of his fae blood. It can't be for any other reason, since I'm wonderful."

Ash agreed. "Yes, as the fae, I'll stay with the witch." He narrowed his eyes at Nox. "Don't think I've forgotten that

190

you tried to kill me in Yelagin, even if you do possess the magical kiss of life. Malik, you go chat with the queen. Don't be yourself, though. If you're too charming, you'll be married off and we'll find ourselves with a new king of Farehold."

They hadn't inquired as to the specifics of her powers, and she hadn't offered any explanation. The only thing they'd seen was in the wake of the spider's clutches as Malik had sputtered on the floor: they saw her as a heroine rather than someone who bartered in the giving and taking of souls. She wasn't sure she wanted them to know more. They thought of her as good. She didn't think she could take it if she watched the shift in their face when they truly understood what she was.

Ribbing aside, they'd need to understand the queen's motives to make their next move.

"I'm going in for a closer look."

The men both squinted at her as if they didn't understand the joke. Their humor had been so complementary up until now. After a moment, it became clear her comment wasn't in jest.

Ash was quick to dismiss her. "If anyone's going in, it's going to be someone trained for combat."

Nox shook her head with firm certainty. "No, if anyone's going in, it will be a forest maiden who was innocently stumbling through the woods while she gathered firewood for her family." She wiggled her axe from where it lay beside her. The villagers had plucked it from the sternum of the spider while Nox had slept. Before they'd left the village, she'd retrieved it from its stump behind the house. It was still covered in spots of black, poisonous blood. The villagers' undying gratitude toward the strangers would have granted them anything they could offer. An axe was a small token to pay.

Ash didn't like it. Malik hated it. But despite both men making their stances on her plan abundantly clear, she could see the reluctant acceptance on their faces. She had the benefit of plausible deniability on her side, and the reevers saw the wisdom in it.

"And if they have…unwholesome intentions?" Malik sounded genuinely worried for her.

She smiled, but it did not reach her eyes. He was a good man for caring about her safety in all its facets. He would remain a good man if he didn't realize how shadowed her powers truly were. "If that's the case, my intentions will be equally unwholesome."

They didn't ask her to explain her response.

She was up and moving away in the moments it took the reevers to realize the conversation had come to an end. She had no plans to strut boldly into the war camp. She was no fool. She just wanted to see if she could learn anything from the imposters as they sat around the campfires. There was something to learn, some pieces she could assemble. The picture in her mind was as though some handwritten letter had been shredded and she was left to piece it back together to discern its information. The message was there somewhere; she just couldn't see it.

Perhaps it was her dark fae blood that gave her a predisposition for sneaking, or maybe it was her years as a courtesan that forced her into a constant alluring state of career-demanded grace, but Nox was particularly adept at stealth. The men's encampment, unfortunately, did not provide many opportunities to approach them without being seen. Their location in the small valley had been advantageous not only for how it blocked out their firelight but also so that anyone approaching them would need to come from one of its two choke points. If an enemy came down from the hill, they would be far too easy to spot and pick off with an arrow long before they met the men.

She took her time working her way around the hill's backside before following the small brook that long ago created the valley. It was shallow and slow-moving, though its waters were muddy and did not look particularly inviting.

She frowned at it.

Nox wasn't afraid of men, murder chambers, madames, child mills, tempers, or kings. She didn't fear snakes, insects, or small spaces. The only things in this world that brought her true fear were the thought of harm befalling Amaris and the sort of water where you couldn't see the bottom.

She knew the stream was harmless. It was probably too small for fish. It was shallow. It wasn't fast. There were scarcely rocks at its bottom. The reeds grew thickly enough along the creek that if Nox kept low and moved slowly, no one would look her way. She could hug its bank and remain undetected.

Sounds of conversation reached her long before any discernible facial features could. Something about the men's voices felt terribly wrong. Their voices were not deep, nor were they forceful. Their cadences and squabbles sounded more like playtime bullies than soldiers arguing. Through the cattails and over the babble of the creek, she kept her eyes fixed on the silhouettes that moved against the encampment. The closer she got, the clearer her realization became. These were not men: these were boys.

Some of the boys were perhaps young adults in their late teens and early twenties, but others had such small frames, such slight builds, they could not have been older than twelve or thirteen. The armor they wore hung loosely on their bodies, clanking around with its ill-fitting size. Moirai had composed a war band of child soldiers. They seemed so small, so fragile as they squeezed between the expanse of the hills on either side. They should have been home with their mothers or in their fields plucking corn from the stalk. None of these children belonged in this valley.

Their age was not enough information. She needed to get closer.

The river tightened into a passage that she would either have to scramble over, exposing herself, or walk through. Nox removed her flat leather shoes and clutched them in her free hand. She rolled her pants above her knees and let the moment stretch on for far too long as she eyed the murky, slow stream. She made a scrunched, miserable face as she lowered her feet into the water. As she didn't immediately perish and was not consumed by a shark, she calmed herself enough to move forward. It was unspeakably horrid to find that the balls of her feet did not connect with stones or sand but that they squished into the murk of the brook's bottom. A shiver snaked up and down her body as she gagged in disgust.

The water did not reach her knees. She winced as she lowered her weight more fully into the small river until she was firmly upright. She told herself that, no, it was highly unlikely that every body of water was filled with the terrible teeth of flesh-eating eels or monstrous fish. She needed to be calm and follow the reeds on the innermost side of the creek. Nox rested her axe over her shoulder, aware that the sight of her knee-deep in the water with a weapon would probably strip the argument of her fetching firewood.

"It's a bathtub," she murmured to herself, focusing her eyes ahead. "It's a cold, gross, soapless bathtub...that may or may not contain leeches and seaweed and demons." She continued to battle the voice in her head that told her that terrors and crocodiles and monsters were hungry for her toes. She leaned into her need for knowledge, letting it drive her forward. The ripples of the stream covered the small noises she made as she advanced. She kept her body as close to the edge as possible, hoping her frame was scarcely more than a larger weed amidst the cattails. Nox willed the boys to see nothing but a stump among weeds. She was mist. She was invisible. She was one with the rock and algae and crayfish.

Her ears may not have been the peaked, arched ears of the fae, but her hearing had always been a bit more astute than those of her fully human peers. She paused against the reeds as she caught the end of a sentence said in a young male voice.

"We could go tonight," one voice was saying.

Nox was finally close enough to identify voices over the

noise of the creek. This was an older boy. He could perhaps be a young man, maybe seventeen or eighteen years of age. It was hard to make out his features between the gaps in the reeds.

"Let them sleep tonight. We'll travel tomorrow and be at the waterfall by nightfall." The second voice was slightly older, perhaps in his early twenties.

Nox had no doubt that their ranks had been arbitrarily prescribed by age. What leaders could these slightly older children be over the younger children? The reevers also had young members of their organization, but to Nox's knowledge, there was no army in the world that would allow teenagers to undergo years of strenuous training and readiness before they crested adulthood the way her companions had been trained. Uaimh Reev was the exception that proved the rule. Here at the camp, surely the youngest amongst them would follow, and the eldest of the young men would play the part of leadership.

"The boys are anxious. They'd like to get this over with."

"Their families are well compensated. The goddess will understand."

"It isn't right."

"It isn't right to put bread on the table? What isn't right is the poorest in the kingdom starving to death. The queen, long may she fucking reign, has given them a fighting chance at a life. The goddess will understand."

"It's not right," the first boy repeated quietly.

What horror was expected of them that he needed to be continually reassured by his compatriot that the All Mother would forgive them? The older boy said nothing. Perhaps it was himself that he was trying to convince.

Nox felt it then. The river monster, the horrible snake, the demons of the water, everything she feared as her toes had sunk into the muddy creek. She was going to be dragged under the water. Her feet were going to be eaten off at the shins. She was sure to drown in a watery grave.

All her long-suppressed hydrophobia bubbled to the surface in a single moment beyond her control. She felt her small, involuntary yelp escape her throat before she knew what she was doing, her terror of the unknowns that lurked below the dark, wet surfaces getting the better of her just in time to see the turtle that had brushed her calf swim lazily past her leg.

It was too late. They had seen her.

She pressed her mouth and eyes together, cursing her stupid coward's heart for its moment of weakness. A goddess-damned fucking turtle had given her away. She was going to be beheaded by a war camp of children all because she had been afraid of a turtle.

Rather than sound the alarm, the elder boy had raised a hand to still his companion. No one else in the campsite seemed to have noticed the small sound that had come from the river, nor did the boys pay any mind as one young man crept toward the reeds. The others continued their games, their jostling, their stories in the war camp beyond. The man advanced, his simple sword aloft.

Nox didn't want to be caught with a weapon. She slowly lowered her axe into the reeds, knowing its weight would prevent it from floating away. She would best be caught unarmed if she had any hope of playing the part of an innocent. Benevolent sexism was an effective tool for defense. What harm could an unarmed maiden befall them?

Her heart thudded in her chest, and she willed her breath to still, opening her eyes to ready herself for her opponent. She raised her hands meekly, palms flat and open. She hadn't been far from them, and it didn't take long before the young soldier was standing at the banks looking down at her. Her face was painted into the picture of contrition and worry, her empty hands conveying her innocence. Her mind whirled. She began to prepare a speech about how she had merely been in the woods near her home when she'd heard a commotion and had wandered into the gully to investigate. She hoped that she would be left unbothered so that they could send yet another civilian on the way to tell the villagers of Raascot's invasion. She was ready for all of it, the entire conversation on the tip of her tongue, before who she was looking at registered.

The once-rounded face of a freckled ginger peered down into where she stood in the stream. He relaxed his weapon slowly as recognition dawned on him.

"Nox?" Her name was a single word, merely a disbelieving question.

"Hi, Achard."

Nineteen

IT HAD BEEN NEARLY A DECADE SINCE THE BULLY AND HIS friends had broken into the pantry and attempted to drag Nox and Amaris to see the bishop. It had been a memory as bizarre as it was terrible. Achard and his cronies had left the orphanage before the whippings began and had never been seen or heard from again, until now.

His face had thinned, gaunt in a way that implied time had not been his friend. He was as much a young man as she was a young woman. Clad in ill-fitting armor, Achard extended an arm to help her rise from where she stood in the river. She accepted his outstretched hand, and there was a sick, suction-ing noise as the mud relinquished her feet. She carefully avoided giving away the axe's location with her movement.

Achard spoke first. "What are you doing here?"

Any hopes of playing the part of a strong captain of men seemed to have left his face. He looked back to the seventeen-year-old who had been waiting expectantly and waved the boy away, but the younger man did not obey. The boy approached and frowned when he saw Nox and her muddy, bare feet. She was still as lovely as a creature could be, though her presence in the river outside their camp had no rational explanation.

Achard spoke to the other. "She's my childhood friend."

She wasn't sure if he truly believed they had been friends but supposed now was not the time to argue the point.

"And what is your childhood friend doing in our war camp?"

"Let me handle this."

False declarations of friendship aside, their relationship held no bearing on why she could possibly be here now. The younger of the two appeared reluctant to leave the presence of a beautiful woman but tore himself away from Achard and Nox. His hormone-addled gaze trailed up and down her body in a way that made her stomach turn. Once he left, Nox took the opportunity to speak.

"I guess I feel like I could ask you the same question. Where did you go when you left Farleigh?" She decided that the best offense was a good defense and chose a tactic that had served her well at the Selkie. Men liked to talk.

A soldier would have maintained an air of strength. A warrior would have stayed standing at attention. Instead, with the weight of the continent on his shoulders, Achard sat down on the bank of the river. His action was both surprising and disarming. There was a world-weariness about him that made the freckled boy seem so much older than he was. He no longer wore the sneer of a bully but the exhaustion of someone who had done and seen far too much. She assumed he was probably tough and trusted amongst his camp, but the nostalgia of seeing Nox in the river crashed over him as if he had been flung into the body of a child once more. They were roughly the same age, and Nox marveled at that. Her patrons at the Selkie had usually stretched well into their upper years of life. Perhaps she was predisposed to seeing young men for the life they had yet to live, unlike the fated clock that seemed to be ticking over Achard's head.

Nox joined him, sitting on the ground. She dipped her feet into the river and washed the muck and mud from where it clung to her toes and ankles, easily avoiding the creek's silty bottom. There were no turtles to betray her this time.

She had almost forgotten she'd asked him a question when he answered.

Achard sounded like he had neither thought of nor spoken of these events in a long, long time. "We just left, Nox. I don't know what happened. We left, and we started walking and we never stopped walking. We slept in barns and stole from markets. We were urchins for a few years. Geoff didn't make it past our first year on the road. A cut on his leg had turned hot and sour and green. We didn't know where to look for a healer, nor could we have paid one if we had found one."

She had always thought the three boys had been killed and eaten. She had never imagined a future where they had made it out alive, even if their numbers had dwindled.

"We were half-feral before we found a farmer who told us we could live with him and the missus if we worked the land. I've been in a village called Valkov, about two days' ride from Yelagin for several years now. It's small, it's poor, and it made me miss the orphanage, believe it or not."

Nox listened to the stream, the cattails rubbing together, the crickets in the distance. She was certain he had finished speaking before she began, "If you had stayed at Farleigh, you wouldn't have ended up much better. It was a child mill, Achard. They probably would have sold you to a farmer all the same."

He considered this. "Were you bought?"

She deflated. Her voice was quiet as she said, "I was."

"And what brings you to be knee-deep in mud outside my camp?"

Without realizing it, he had given her the answer she needed. "I was escaping my master when I thought I heard a village. I had no idea I was coming upon soldiers. I was hoping to find a town among the hills. And you? You said you worked for a farmer, not an army. What brings you to be a part of such a camp?"

His laugh was dark. She wasn't sure why Achard lacked any

sense of urgency, but there was a part of her that recognized he sat on the shore with her now as someone on borrowed time. There was something in the camp, in the night, in the task at hand that did not tempt him to hurry to any return.

"Money," was all he said. It came out with a short, mirthless laugh. "It makes the world go round, doesn't it? You can never have too much, but you can always have too little."

Her brows creased as she wondered at her paths forward. Nox wanted information from the young man, but she had also been blessed by the hand of the goddess that she had been discovered by a familiar. The odds were one in…whatever the population of Farehold was. She could have been marched into the war camp by her hair like a pet to entertain the men. She could have been killed where she stood by a cruel sergeant hoping to gain power and notoriety amongst the men of his camp. Yet here she was, sliding her wet leather shoes onto her feet once again and looking at the lines on a face too young for the burdens it held.

"Can I ask you a question?" Nox's voice was too gentle to shake him fully from whatever spell of sorrow had been cast. She knew how to control her voice, understanding the enchantment of memories and their importance. The skills of her trade had prepared her for far more than a life within the walls of the Selkie.

He wasn't nodding at her but at the reeds on the opposite bank. His eyes did not find hers again as they glazed over. She recognized he was lost to his hardships, to his rabid years as a wretch fighting for survival in a cold, hungry world. Nox didn't know what he'd been through, nor did she feel that opening his wound would help either of them. While some things could be healed, other traumas were best left underneath whatever festering scab had finally covered them.

She stayed as quiet as the brook before them. "I'm sorry for coming up on your camp. I didn't realize what I was walking into one. But, Achard, have you defected to Raascot?"

She wanted to word her question as a concerned citizen

of Farehold. She edged her voice slightly as if she cared for her queen and the crown. Her tone was painted with worry for a wayward schoolboy.

He shook his head. "I can't tell you why we're in northern colors, but we have our reasons."

She chewed her lip and looked at him long enough for him to meet her stare. It took a while for his features to soften as he regarded her. Perhaps Nox no longer glowed vibrantly as she had before their battle with the spider, but she knew she still possessed charm and beauty that made her peerless. He looked into her eyes long enough for Nox to see his heart crack, and she realized this was not a game she felt good about playing. She knew the words to say and the pawns to shuffle, but there was a cruelty to the match that she couldn't name. Perhaps he was thinking of the years he'd been unkind to her, regretting them now that he understood just how unkind the world could be. He was no longer the boy she'd known in Farleigh.

"Achard, if you and your men are fighting for the north, I will keep your secret."

"Men." He blew out a terse breath at the word. She had intended for him to fixate on the cardinal direction in her gently worded accusation, but the disdain in his voice carried him elsewhere. "They're children, Nox. They're desperate children who need food, who need hope. The soldiers who conscripted us were only sent to the poorest villages. They recruited the most desperate indigents they could find."

She pressed her luck, trying to strike a balance between confused maiden and sympathetic friend, no matter how it hurt her to do so. "Raascot's soldiers preyed on Farehold's poverty, then?"

He shook his head. "I need you to leave, Nox, and not just this camp. Don't stay here. Go neither south nor north. Go to Tarkhany and find a new home in the desert. Or if you must go west, find a ship bound for the isles. I know I was never good to you or your friend, but please accept this as my chance at penance." He stood and brushed the grass from his clothes. "Goodbye, Nox."

There was no tearful farewell. There was no explanation. There was only the damp sounds of her footsteps on the sodden riverbank as she nodded, turned, and walked away from his camp.

She didn't wait for him to change his mind.

Twenty

Nox spotted them the moment she crested the hill. Despite the joy and relief on the reevers' faces, her expression did not mirror theirs.

Malik was the first to speak. "What happened? We saw them catch you!"

Ash threw him an irritated punch, hitting him squarely in the upper arm. "I could barely keep this buffoon from blowing our cover. He was ready to take on dozens of soldiers when we thought they had you. How did you get caught?"

Nox shook her head sadly. "I lost my axe."

They frowned at her. "What?"

"My axe is in the river. He stood there and watched me leave, so I couldn't get it. It's still in the water."

"Nox." Ash blinked in disbelief, presumably at her inability to distinguish the severity between misplacing a farmer's weapon and being captured by the enemy. She allowed him his incredulity, even if she disagreed with his feelings regarding the wonderful, lifesaving weapon. He said, "We'll get you a new axe. Who stood there? What happened? How did they find you? How did you get away?"

Malik ignored the redhead and pulled her into a hug, crushing her in his embrace. "I couldn't see you until the very end when we spotted two soldiers walking to the river. Neither of us had any idea how you'd infiltrated the camp until it was too late."

"Malik," she gasped.

"Yes?"

"I can't breathe."

He released her quickly and took a step back, allowing them to find their places on the ground once more. She joined them in the thicket that hid them. The reevers rested their backs against trees. Malik continued to position himself protectively over her, and she did little to fight off his attention. It was nice. She leaned against Malik for warmth and wrapped her dark cloak around her.

Despite their questions, the only things they could get out of her was that she was cold and sad, and she missed her axe. "I met someone I knew from my past. He more or less told me that Moirai is preying on the impoverished—without using her name, of course. The men in the valley are no soldiers. Those are children."

His face contorted in a pained expression as he reiterated, "Moirai has a child army?"

"I don't know what they're going to do, but it sounds like whatever it is, it's to take place tomorrow night. They mentioned 'getting it over with,' which makes me think their mission is nearing its end."

"They just told you this?"

She shook her head. The gentle feathering of her hair brushed his cheek when she moved. Her black hair concealed her deeply in the shadows of the thicket. Perhaps her intake of breath was more telling than any movement she could make in the dark. "I had attempted to approach the camp through the river. I was spotted."

"And they just let you go? You're charming, but you're not *that* charming," Ash argued.

"The young man who discovered me was someone I haven't seen in maybe eight years? He was from the orphanage."

"Well, that's…lucky."

"It was, and it wasn't. The pity I feel certainly doesn't seem lucky. All I know is that these boys and their families are being paid for whatever they're going to do. He kept saying 'the goddess will understand,' so whatever has to be done, whatever they've been paid to accomplish, I feel in my gut it's truly terrible."

"What can we do?"

She hedged for a while, breathing through the heaviness she felt in her heart. "We can find a new axe."

✦

Nox's face twisted in irritation.

Dreaming at a time like this was an irritating, disappointing, deceitful act.

A large part of her hated her dreams. The wishful swirls of the subconscious were little more than cruel reminders of what had never been and might never be. Nox was confident that somewhere in the real world, she was on a hillside overlooking a war band, not in a granite-hewn room with a fire at the hearth. The soft orange filtering in through the window appeared to be the early light of dawn. This was a dream of the mountains and far-off fantastical places. She didn't quite recognize the space around her, except for the common theme in all her most pleasant dreams.

"Hey, you," she said sadly to the false, pearly girl.

Amaris's eyes were already open and looking into her own. Amaris took Nox's hands and brushed a kiss against her knuckles. The motion surprised Nox immensely. Despite her sour mood, her lips twitched in a hint of a smile.

"Someone's in a good mood."

Amaris nodded. "Occasionally things go my way. Sometimes I have beautiful friends in my bed."

Nox sagged a bit at the word. They were friends—best

friends, in fact. She wasn't sure why her sleeping mind wanted to drill it into her over and over again. It was fucking cruel that her subconscious wouldn't allow her the fun, free escape of indulging in the relationship she'd wanted for so many years. She wanted her dreams to be an adventure where clothes were torn to ribbons and fingers were dragged down each other's bare skin and breaths gave way to gasps and moans. Why weren't her toes curling as her back arched? Instead, even her sleeping mind kept things in purgatory. It seemed as though even her innermost self didn't know if Amaris would ever love her in the same way, and maybe that was okay. Maybe her dreams were doing her a favor by echoing what she already knew to be true.

"You aren't real, you know."

"That's...an odd thing for you to say."

Nox shrugged. "Can I ask you something? Though I suppose your answer doesn't matter."

"If the answer doesn't matter, then there's no harm in asking. You can't be disappointed if you have no expectations."

Her mouth quirked further at that. Even in her dreams, Amaris was clever. She wondered if it was wishful thinking or if her brain had compiled any true memories of the girl's quick wit and way with words. Finally, she asked, "Are you happy?"

Amaris shrugged. "I think so? Then again, I don't know if I have the luxury of happiness quite yet. Life has been challenging, but I'm making progress. Goddess, I have so much to tell you. Onward and upward, right? What about you? Are you?"

"Happy?"

Amaris tilted her head expectantly.

Nox frowned at the phantom. Perhaps being able to speak to one's own subconscious was a therapeutic breakthrough for which she should be grateful. "To be honest, I have no idea. There are many things I'd like to change. In some ways, things have gotten better. In other ways, they've gotten so much worse."

Amaris made a sympathetic pout. "The fever gets hottest before it breaks."

"But why must anyone fall ill in the first place?"

They stared at each other, listening to the calm, quiet sounds of breath intermingled with the comfortable popping of the fireplace. Nox *was* grateful for the tiny graces of small comforts when she slept, feeling sad for those who only had dreamless sleep and sadder still for those who were plagued with night terrors. Her uneventful, relaxing dreams were the few times she was offered peace and reunion in a world that had been determined to tear Amaris from her arms.

Maybe they didn't need to talk.

Maybe it didn't need to be real.

Maybe she could just let herself pretend.

Nox raised a hand, appreciating just how tan her smooth, slender fingers looked against the pretty friend in her bed. She cupped her cheek and Amaris smiled, nuzzling into her hand. She turned her mouth toward Nox's palm, brushing her lips against it, sending a thrill through Nox. Not a moment went by when Nox hadn't wanted to pull her in and kiss her. She longed to claim the pale, pink mouth of the moonlit girl. This was the climax of her dream, time after time. She opened her mouth to speak to her favorite ghost when something wet hit Nox's forehead, then again on her ear, then her neck.

Twenty-One

I T WAS NOT THE WARMTH OF THE MORNING SUNLIGHT THAT woke them but gentle droplets that filtered their way through overhanging leaves in the gray morning. Nox blinked against the splash of rain to find she'd fallen asleep against Malik. Confused and disoriented, she pushed herself into a sitting position and wiped the water from her face. He stirred at her movement, blinking awake. Sporadic rain became consistent and pebble-sized. The three woke with mutual grumbles at the weather, exchanging bites of stale bread before it became too soggy with rainwater, and readied themselves for the day while the sky spit at them.

At first, the rain was merely an annoyance. The three resigned themselves to being damp and miserable, as there was nothing that could be done.

The sounds of its pitter-patter against the tents had awoken the war camp below as well, rousing the motley crew of pseudo soldiers at morning's first graying light. Nox and the reevers did their best to maintain the stoicism of warriors, but Nox huddled her wet cloak around her as if she were trying to disappear into it. She was no longer interested in being a spy. She wanted to be in a warm bed with a crackling fire with thick, dry socks and a big bowl of soup.

She was cold. She was uncomfortable. She was deeply unhappy.

It was with tangible anxiety that they watched the war party pack up their tents. The time had come, and the boys' obligations had no regard for the weather.

There was something disorganized even about the way they dismantled their tents and set to motion. There were no trained soldiers or fearsome warriors in the valley below. The boys dressed in northern clothes were merely conscripted for a single job: go forth, commit acts for Moirai, and be seen doing it as northmen.

Ash and Malik were no strangers to exercise in suboptimal conditions. They'd informed Nox that they had been forced to run up and down the mountain through treacherous storms and spar regardless of the rain, snow, or blistering heat. They were quite proud to relay that they had gripped swords in frigid temperatures. They had sprinted through lightning and thunder. They had battled it out in hand-to-hand combat in gale-force winds. The reevers had been hardened against the elements not because they were any tougher than the average man or fae but through years of sheer exposure and utter desensitization to misery.

"Good for you," she'd muttered, "but I'm not a reever."

✦

Malik frowned down at the tiny ball of wet shadow, dripping tendrils of hair barely escaping from the hood, before he returned to scouring the valley. He and Ash peered through the rain at the boys who finished packing as they hoisted the banners of the north and began their march from the small canyon.

"Nox, let's go." Malik extended a hand to her where she remained curled into a ball sitting upright against a tree and sheltering her face from the rain with her hood.

"Can we wait? Until the rain lets up a little bit?"

Malik made a sympathetic face, so it was Ash who rolled his eyes and responded, "Tell me you're joking so I don't kick you off the team."

She mumbled as she made her way to her feet, saying something under her breath about never asking to be on the team in the first place.

Rather than angle for the road or head into the forest, the imposter war band followed the river. It was challenging to gauge the passage of time throughout the day, as the gloom and utter discomfort of the weather made every minute feel like a century. The three kept to the forest and hilltops that lined the river. This allowed them to trail the party while remaining undetected. The wet, splashing sounds of the deluge covered any noise they may have made while tracking the crew.

He knew from the report that Nox had given that the war party aimed for nightfall. When was nightfall if the entire day was the exact same shade of gray? The pocket watch was their salvation in these moments. They repeatedly held it under their cloaks, protecting it from the damaging effects of water while they checked the time. It had been spelled for magical properties, but the mundanity of its everyday use proved far more important today. They only paused to glance at it a few times throughout the day, terrified of drenching their precious treasure. By three past the noon hour, Nox had become unbearable.

Nox was many things. She had been tenacious and amiable for days. She was lovely, she was clever, and she was resilient. Nox had saved Malik's life and shown unparalleled bravery in the face of a demon. She was definitely a more pleasant sight to behold than either of them, which was a wonderful break from traveling with the brotherhood of assassins. Unfortunately, her good qualities were irrelevant in the midst of a torrential downpour. Regardless of how many positive attributes she possessed, she made it clear that she hated the rain and was ready to make it everyone else's problem. Her questions, moans, and protestations interjected every time they felt their shoulders relax from her last grating question. It was incredible that someone so charming and lovely could make them want to push her into the ravine.

"Can't we stop under a rock?"

"No, we cannot," Ash responded.

"What if you two continue and I find a cave?"

Ash looked at Malik. "Honestly, I say we let her go find a cave so she can live in these woods."

"Leave her alone."

"Fine, then you deal with her," Ash grumbled.

"Is that a yes?" Nox had to raise her voice to be heard over the pounding rain as she trailed behind them, foot slipping on a rock as she stumbled to maintain her footing.

"There are no caves, and you'd never find us again." Malik attempted patience. He didn't look over his shoulder at where she struggled to keep up.

"I'm cold."

"Keep moving and you'll warm up."

"You dismissed it so quickly before, but the rain is only increasing. I feel as though we just haven't looked for caves. What if we look for a cave and light a fire and then later, we can ask the pocket watch to show us where the soldiers went?"

"These aren't the kinds of hills that give way to caves. It's not the right topography."

"What if you two go and I can ask the watch to show me where you are later, once I find a cave?"

"Nox, there are no caves. These hills do not possess the rocks necessary for caves."

"My feet are so wet. I'm so uncomfortable."

"Everyone is uncomfortable."

"I miss my axe."

"We'll find you a new axe."

"I'm miserable."

"Everyone is miserable."

"I'm so hungry. Can't we stop to hunt and cook something?"

"We can't light a fire in the rain."

"The water is making my shoes rub on my feet."

"Your shoes will dry."

"I want—"

Malik had suspected for days now that he might be in some abstract form of love with the black-haired beauty, whether or not it was just his human blood yielding to her charm. He thanked the goddess for her heavenly goodness that she would send this rainy day upon them so that he could regain his senses and break whatever spell Nox had unintentionally cast on him. The others often forgot that Malik was their senior, several years older than either of them, and he knew it. It had been a long time since he'd flexed any sort of authority that seniority lent him. After hours of attempting to patiently withstand her complaints, the golden-haired man finally spun on the woman who had been dragging her feet in an intentional protest of her displeasure. Malik didn't possess a drop of malice or violence anywhere in his body. His training as a reever was the fury and power of peace and justice. Right now, the greatest injustice standing between him and his dispatch was their stubborn, whining companion.

Jerking his hands up from where they had been clutched in too-tight firsts for nearly an hour as he battled his irritation, he stared at her through the curtain of rain. He whipped her hood back so that she had to regard him, her mouth parted in startled protest. Nox squinted her eyes against the thundering droplets as she looked into his face. She looked equal parts surprised and bewildered at his motion. Perhaps it was her confidence or swagger, but he'd always felt she was far taller than she was. He'd never towered over her like this before. He was practically inches from her face, glowering down with the anger of a disappointed father.

"If you don't stop bitching, Ash and I will leave you to live out the rest of your days in the woods. Is that what you want?"

She gasped, playing the part of the scolded child. Her nose crinkled in a headstrong frown. If it weren't for the rain punishing her face, she probably would have let the moment stretch on much longer. If she wanted to spare her eyes the sting of water, she couldn't continue to look up at him. She looked to her feet, rain-soaked hair plastering itself to her neck and shoulders. "No."

"No one likes the rain, Nox!" he continued with a borderline paternal anger. "Ash doesn't like being wet, I don't like walking through the forest with puddles in my boots, and none of the soldiers down there are living their best lives in this blasted storm. You are not having a unique experience. Either you stop bellyaching, or you grow up and learn that being soaked in this storm on a never-ending mission is not fun for anyone."

He waited in smoldering silence until she looked back up at him, water running off his hair, his jaw, his shoulders as his eyes burned. She lifted her eyes to meet his and her mouth parted with her ongoing state of shock until she snapped it closed, lest she drown. If he were a betting man, he'd guess from her expression that she'd never been spoken to this way. He turned around and continued walking.

The reevers continued forward, but it took Nox a full moment to gather her bearings from where she remained in stunned silence.

Beside Malik, Ash fought off a smile. He nearly choked on his surprise as rainwater splashed against his face, concealing his laugh. Malik was confident Ash had never seen him whip out his authoritative energy either.

Malik plowed forward, his shoulders rounded with his irritation at the stubborn companion behind them. He was confident that if he looked over his shoulder, Nox would still be wearing her angry, chided expression. But by the All Mother's blessing, she kept from complaining as she stalked behind them for nearly four more hours through a blasted deluge.

The heavens opened up even further, blinding them with its downpour. Every gasp of air was sputtered as if drowning in buckets of water. They could barely see their outstretched arms, let alone the war party in the valley below. The trees were invisible through the sheet of rain. The valley may as well have disappeared through the gray wall of water. They kept the hill's edge to one side so they knew they continued to follow the river, even if visibility was damned impossible.

Sometimes for the better and sometimes for the worse, be it storms, journeys, or lives, all things must come to an end.

The rain began to slow after the six o'clock hour, and by the seventh hour, it was down to a consistent drizzle. Their clothes were soddened and their spirits were as soaked as the shoes on their feet, but they had made it through a full day's travel in horrid weather. By the time the sprinkles had reduced to mist, the storm had fully passed and they were able to see the forest and world around them. As the weather had hampered their visibility for more than twelve hours and the sounds of the storm had impeded other senses, none of them had a clue as to where they were currently nor had they any indication as to where they had been headed. Now that night was falling and the forest had stilled, the three could hear the distant sound of something like thunder.

The longer they listened and closer they drew, the more clearly the thunder had given way to a telling consistency. It was no longer raining, yet the sound continued. This was no thunder. They were not approaching a storm; they were nearing a waterfall.

Malik realized what they were hearing just as he knew he would not have the time to explain it to Nox. She had never been to these woods, and she would not realize its significance, but in the last gray moments of solemn daylight, Malik understood with a chilling horror in the pit of his stomach exactly where they were.

The war camp was headed for the Temple of the All Mother.

Twenty–Two

T HEY WERE SO MUCH FARTHER BEHIND THE WARBAND THAN they'd realized.

Precious seconds, minutes, even an hour had withered away, time dying in their fingers, lost to the rainstorm that had kept them from realizing the warband had put so much distance between themselves and their pursuers. Perhaps it was the valley that had given the soldiers a direct advantage, or it may have been Nox's being a petulant child in the rain slowing them to such a pace while the war band marched a mile ahead of them. By the time the three understood the sounds of the waterfall, they were already hearing the metallic clang of swords in the far-off distance. The moment the noise reached their ears, they knew they would not make it in time.

They were too late.

Nox didn't have to ask questions. Ash and Malik took off in a dead sprint, weaving and maneuvering between the branches and soggy, fallen logs. She followed as fast as her feet would carry her. For the first time, she was glad her axe had been left behind as she pumped her arms, struggling to keep up with them. A protruding root tripped her onto the slippery earth. She slid across the wet ground, black mud caking her arms and cheek. Ash and Malik shot through the woods like rabbits with a fox at their heels, disappearing amidst the distant trunks as they blinked out of her sight. She'd have to take care of herself this time.

Nox looked at her hands, wiping them on her sopping cloak as she gathered her bearings. She didn't have to know what was happening to understand something was very wrong, and she didn't have the luxury of acclimating herself to the emergency.

She pushed herself into a run once more, forcing her legs to move. Her hood had fallen and clung to her back. Her hair had glued itself to her face, now mingled with the mud that adhered to her. Adrenaline coursed through her as she bounded through the trees.

It grew darker and darker with every moment. Even with her adeptness for nighttime and shadows, losing the final lights of the gray day made her footing exceedingly difficult. It was all she could do to dodge tree trunks and jump over rocks as they poised themselves in dangerous positions throughout the forest. She failed. A bough hit her sharply in the shoulder, knocking her from her run. Nox fell again, stars coloring her vision with pain as her shin collided with a jutting stone. She gasped in a silent scream at her wound, knowing a welt the size of a goose's egg would purple its way onto her leg. She clutched at her lower leg, grunting as she rolled onto her backside.

The waterfall's thunder and the sharp, metallic sounds of steel only grew louder with every limping step. Now was not the time to let her shortcomings win. She had been the weakest link all day long as she'd stomped through the rain. In this moment, strength was required of her, and she would answer its call.

The darkness vanished the moment she burst from the tree line. Her eyes widened at the loud, horrible, blindingly bright pandemonium.

Chaos.

This was not the happy crackle of a campfire but the angry threat of a tragedy. The red flames were the only illumination on this cloud-covered night. Silhouettes darted around, and angry cries filled the glen. There was a building—a magnificent, stone building—in the clearing. She searched for clues to figure out where they were. It was no town, no home. Whatever rested within it was ablaze, flames lighting those within the glen as if a chasm in the earth had broken through to the angry red lights of the underworld.

This was hell.

Nox advanced toward the palatial building, the haze of shock too thick to understand anything she was seeing. Several children in northern colors were scattered in mounds of severed flesh and shredded fabric. Water thundered as it tumbled over a cliff and roared to its place in a pool. The sound joined the yells of men, the crackles of flame, the clash of metal. The aspens that lined the clearing stood in the sentry shape of a perfect circle sealing in the madness from the world around it.

Her companions were nowhere to be seen.

She couldn't look away. She couldn't stop. Her feet pulled her forward, closer to the madness, closer to the fire on instinct alone.

Before she realized what she was doing, she'd mounted several marble steps, her feet heavy against the polished white stone of the building. A scream bubbled from somewhere within. The broken body of a boy slumped against a marble pillar just outside the building. Blood pooled from a slain child, dripping down the steps, adding a red trickle in mimicry of the river and its waterfall. Her confusion had lulled her into a deadened calm. The numb wall encompassing her mind protected her from feeling, from reacting.

She heard a reever then.

"Stop!" The sound was accompanied by the clash of a sword.

Nox raised her dull, glazed eyes to where two men fought

in the stone building. She spotted Ash, his red hair matted to his face with the heat of the fire behind him. She knew she was meant to feel something. She was meant to feel urgency, to feel panic, but she felt nothing at all.

The sound of thumping and hacking rose from within the building. She recognized the man in Raascot colors who advanced. It may have been sweat or rain, but the freckled boy looked like he had been crying. Ash was crossing swords with Achard.

"I can't" was all Achard said, swinging his sword again.

The darkness wrapped itself around her like a protective swaddle, but a voice beyond it fought back. *No*, said the voice within her. *This is too important. You have to be present. You have to feel.*

She was standing on the threshold of a sacred space; she knew it to be so. The white marble glinted with gold, etched with brilliance and magic. Bodies of children and their life forces escaping in red pools littered the ground as her friends battled for their lives. She knew that while the reevers were immensely skilled, the sheer number of would-be soldiers was enough to overpower even the heartiest of warriors. Ash continued shouting while he fought. He was not attempting to kill or maim; he was merely countering each strike in preventative measure after preventative measure, making it clear he did not want to end the young man's life.

"I'm begging you to stand down!"

Behind the men was the source of the fire so powerful it had lit the entire glen. Animated by all-consuming oranges, reds, and yellows was an enormous tree. The twisted trunk and its outstretched branches were alive with the fire that devoured it. The heat was scorching, as if she were walking directly toward a furnace, and she began to feel herself bake from within her dampened cloak. Nox had willingly walked into an oven.

"Please," a woman's voice croaked.

Nox swung to the first word that had broken her daze. If

time had been at a standstill, all the moments she had lost to its slowness sped up at once. Urgency slammed down on her as her awareness shifted.

A woman was on the floor.

Nox dropped to her knees, scrambling to the stranger's aid. The woman was bloodied, her abdomen colored against her silver gown betraying her wound. Nox realized from the gown and the setting that she had to be looking at a priestess. They were two women in a kiln awaiting their cremation. The heat gobbled up all the air in the room.

"What...?" Nox had no words. Time was still catching up; understanding was battling to find purchase in her mind. She had to do something. Something was required of her. She didn't know where she was or what tragedy had befallen them.

"Tell me what to do," Nox pleaded.

The fallen priestess looked up at Nox while black smoke hung over them like a thick cloud. Flames licked at her features, setting her aglow with their light. Nox looked at the wounded woman and faintly recalled something she knew to be true: only women were allowed in the Temple of the All Mother. This holy space had been sacked by men, and the Tree of Life was ablaze with their destructive force. Men had done this.

Nox's hands hovered above the woman with no idea what to do. She had no medical training. She had no healer's hands. She grabbed for the woman's abdomen as if to put pressure on the wound but felt so worthless as the world crumbled around her.

"I'll carry you out!" She moved as if to drag the woman.

"No," the priestess gasped, pained by the effort.

The loud, grunting sound of a boy no more than fifteen tore through the temple as he advanced, his sword overhead like a child merely playing the role of a knight. He charged for them, but the priestess raised her palm from where she lay on the ground. She barely looked at the child as a light, as red and angry as the flames that licked at the tree, was sent slicing from her fingertips. Her magic tore through the boy, stopping him in his tracks. His body hovered for a moment as if trapped in its forward motion before a slash through his midsection leached blood, her fire cutting through him like the sharpest blade. The wetness of his exposed soft innards refracted in the light of the fire as he toppled, cauterized like cooked meat slapping onto a plate. The priestess lowered her outstretched hand but did not look at Nox. The woman's head bobbed to the side, her cheek pressed against the scalding temple floor. Too much blood had been lost for her to maintain her hold on the world. She was slipping.

"Hold on! Hold on. I'll get you out!"

The priestess whispered a single word: "Yggdrasil."

Nox followed the woman's gaze to where it had landed on the tree. Vermilions, oranges, and yellows so bright that they were nearly white engulfed the trunk. The hungry fire was spreading to its limbs. Nox sputtered for air as the inferno pressed down on her. Every inhalation felt like breathing into the sweltering sun itself. She began to cough as smoke filled her lungs. The priestess closed her eyes against the heat and rapidly filling smoke.

"What should I do? Tell me what to do!"

The priestess had closed her eyes for the last time and would not open them again. The fallen holy woman managed only two words from her cracked and bloodied lips. The firelight continued to illuminate her skin with a deathly beauty—the beauty of the afterlife.

"The apple."

Nox's eyes stung from the smoke that billowed off the burning tree. Her tongue was thick with the taste of its ash when she opened her mouth as if to respond. The boys in Raascot colors were still in the temple, mere child soldiers smashing and hacking at things unseen. There were rooms beyond the great hall she was now in, but she did not look at them. Their destruction had been so complete, so absolute.

Everyone within the marble temple walls was going to cook if they did not exit immediately.

Nox gaped down at the priestess. The woman's eyes did not reopen.

Then she looked to the tree again, scouring what remained of its wood as the fire's fervor crackled. She followed an outstretched branch and saw one single piece of fruit hanging from a lengthened finger of the tree's limb, the fire gobbling the limb without mercy. To reach the apple, she'd practically need to step inside the fire. The fruit's tender flesh wouldn't last much longer in the blaze. If she was going to get it, it would have to be now.

She rallied for one insane moment of courage to dive into the fire, but the inferno was so loud, so hot. She felt as if her skin were melting, pulling away from her muscle and bones with the scalding intensity of the hell that swallowed the temple. She coughed again, sucking at the air as her eyes fixed on the object of the priestess's dying words. The skin of the apple reflected golden and crimson with the dance of the flames as they swallowed the remaining parts of the ancient tree around it. The sounds of metal died as crackling flames and coughing filled the temple. The soldiers weren't fighting anyone. There had been no enemy. They were there for one reason only: to destroy everyone and everything.

Her blood would boil if she didn't rise from her knees and start moving. She looked to the priestess one final time, but the woman had crossed over to be with the All Mother.

She had to go now.

Nox rose to her feet, ignoring the carnage, blocking out the men and their destruction, ignoring the madness that engulfed this holy place. She'd been given a dying command. Her face began to blister as her skin roasted like the flesh of a skewered pig over a campfire. Burning hair and black smoke mixed with the smells of the cooking flesh of the fallen. She couldn't let herself see it. She couldn't let herself smell it. She had to move faster—to do what had been asked of her.

She pressed the heels of her palms into her eyes as they reddened and stung with smoke.

Someone called her name, but she ignored them. They didn't know that she had a mission. She couldn't find the reevers now. She needed the apple.

Nox stepped closer and closer to the tree, listening to it shudder and crackle as limbs began to fall. She protected her eyes with the hot, still-wet sleeve of her cloaked forearm. Sparks popped from the jolt. The sizzle of her leather shoes against the marble reached her ears. Old, wizened, knotted limbs burned white and gray from the embers that ate them from the inside out as the tree had abandoned any semblance of a living thing, revealing only the burnt logs of something dead.

The apple. She had to get the apple. If she could just get a little closer, a little farther into the fire... The single piece of fruit still clung to the tree at the end of a branch. The crook of the tree shuddered and the apple quivered, threatening to fall to the marble floor where it would surely fry against the scalding marble surface. She was so close, squinting to protect her eyes from melting like runny eggs within their very sockets.

She heard her name again but pushed forward, possessed with the focus of singular purpose.

As she reached her hands toward the apple, red-hot, angry pain tore through her. If her hair and cloak had not been drenched from a day in the rain, they would have surely caught fire just by sheer proximity to its source. The tree trembled again as another branch fell. The limb that held the fruit jolted, lowering slightly as the trunk began to fold in on itself. She stretched out her hands to cup the fruit, eyes fixed solely on its metallic glint against the flames. Her feet scalded in their wet leather shoes against the heated marble.

With one more tremble of earthbound momentum, the apple was within her grasp. Her fingers closed around the fruit. The apple was cool to the touch—much colder than anything else in the room. Her hands felt whole as she clung to the object. Now that she'd collected the fruit, she was terribly aware of how close she stood to the fire. Nox was yanked backward by angry hands.

Ash.

She coughed, gasping at him while she clutched the fruit close to her. Nox was not numb. She was alive, awake, and ready. She was doing what needed to be done. Her blood pumped through her veins, slowly boiling with the rising heat, seasoned with smoke, fear, and adrenaline.

"The temple's gone!" Ash shouted over the fire's roar. "You have to get out of here!"

The marble would not crumble with the heat from the charred, burning tree, but the stone would heat until it cooked all those who stayed within its walls. Her ears rang in some horrible melody as the fire began to bake her brain within her skull.

A dark spot of night revealed the exit to the temple.

She turned to run, grabbing for Ash where Achard had fallen.

"Where's Malik?"

"I'll find him!" Ash coughed through the words. His face was black with smoke, his clothes clinging to him with sweat. He summoned the strength to give her one final, choked command. "Nox! Go!"

Ash darted off to the left, hugging the edge of the temple.

No, she wouldn't go. Nox could not sprint into the safety of the night. There were too many rooms for Ash to search them all on his own before joining the dead in what was rapidly becoming a mass tomb. Her feet took her to the side rooms on the temple's right. The smoke was trapped within its smaller rooms with nowhere to go as it filled the confined marble spaces. She jumped over a fallen soldier, pushing past northmen colors as she searched. She recognized the singular, powerful bisection that had blasted from the priestess's power among many of the littered bodies and their gore.

Nox looked to one room, then the next, skidding with her speed as she ran from room to room. She was practically perpendicular to the red-hot tree when she found him. Nox tucked the apple into her pocket and felt its cooling weight against herself as she stopped to grab Malik. Though stained with smoke, he was not unconscious. He had been trying to pull a young, collapsed boy of no more than twelve from where he'd fallen.

"He's gone," Nox choked. She wasn't sure if her words were discernible above the crackle and through the strangulation hold that the smoke had on her throat.

Malik wheezed, his lungs desperate for air. He released his hold on the boy, but his eyes did not leave the child. Malik got to his feet as she swung his arm around her shoulders and rushed them into the main hall of the temple. The entirety of the tree had ignited, not a single branch or twig or stem spared from the red-hot fiery destruction befalling the sacred space. Malik tried to draw breath, but his sounds came out as asphyxiated sputters, unable to find oxygen.

The cooking temperature ate through her shoes as she guided the man more than twice her weight and a whole head and shoulders taller. His arm remained draped around her neck as they moved. Ash spotted them and was under Malik's free arm in a second. The three burst from the temple entrance, tumbling down the stairs as the Tree of Life collapsed into blazing embers behind them, unleashing a singular, powerful explosion as it toppled. The combustion was a sound that could have been heard for miles around, the force of its fire kicking them from their unsteady feet with a blast of heat so powerful it may as well have been sets of rough hands at their backs throwing them from where they stood. The smoke that poured from the temple was so dense it would undoubtedly be spotted from every surrounding village within three days' travel.

They did not get up from where the force had knocked them to the wet grass of the glen, coughing and sooty as the world around them crumbled.

The slain bodies of Farehold men in Raascot colors were scattered about the clearing. Shredded banners with the wing-and-shield sigil were scattered to the trees. A bronze-and-black-clad body floated in the pool where the waterfall crashed. Nox and Ash tugged at whatever fae parts of them had allowed them to hold on to air, to call on strength for one minute longer, to stay conscious. The regenerative parts of their cells had led them to safety and had allowed them to rescue their human friend from the smoke inhalation that had nearly suffocated him.

Nox wanted to run, to put hours and miles and days and kingdoms of space between her, her friends, and the nightmare behind them. But they were immobilized, pressed into the soft bluish grass of the sullied glen while orange and white embers flew in the night sky like fire sprites, leaving them in the valley of the fallen.

Twenty-Three

I T WAS A MORNING SHE WISHED SHE COULD FORGET.

Nox was alive, but that was the extent of it.

Her mind was working, however slowly. Her eyes didn't open. Her body didn't move.

Her traumas were so numerous, she could fill tomes with her tales. She had analyzed and intellectualized and detached herself from pain after pain. She didn't allow herself to think about how her parents had abandoned her to a mill, as she knew despair was not a useful emotion. She had only thought of Amaris in ways that fueled her sense of justice and longing for reunion. Anger protected her from thoughts of the greedy hands of men and the poisonous evil of Millicent.

Nox could have been strong and healthy and resilient without her tragedies. Instead, she thought of a broken vase. She had taken the shattered pieces of herself and forged them with precious metals, holding herself together with a renewed strength that she had built herself. The metallic cracks in her pottery did not eliminate her pain. The gilded lines that slit through the vase of her life did not rewrite her story or pretend that she had not been broken. These cracks did not imply that it was her pain that made her strong, nor did they claim it was the trauma that made her beautiful. The gilded, broken parts of her simply spoke of defiance. Her slashes and scars, as their gilt refracted against the light of her journey, merely gave voice to a truth: "You can be both broken and rebuilt. You can endure trauma and in the midst of pain discover strength. Your wounds have not defined you; it is you who have re-created yourself despite them."

Heroes and their ballads glamorized torment in a way she had always found both insensitive and tone-deaf to the world around them. The glorification of pain didn't interest Nox. She was not tougher because of her wounds, nor was she tenacious because of her horrors, but the fire had been a part of her path nonetheless, and she had proven herself a survivor, as had those before her. These wounds had become a part of her, and she would make these broken parts beautiful.

Her eyes remained closed, nose still lined with soot, body aching with the smoke's poison as it continued to coat her lungs and the blisters that covered her. This would be just another memory in a long line of scars as permanent and cruel as the thin stripes that marred her back.

The bodies that littered the temple of the All Mother were not those of warriors who had fallen for their country nor soldiers who had died for love of their queen. These had been villagers whose poverty had conscripted them. Bronze-colored cloth was ruddy brown with dried blood. Crests had been torn across the shield and compass and angelic wings of the northern kingdom, leaving only scrapped fabric in its wake. Money was every bit as responsible for this atrocity as Moirai. The boy soldiers had been promised that if they sacked the temple adorned with Raascot colors, they'd be rewarded. Their words made sense to her now.

The goddess will forgive us.

Her mind was still working, even if she considered herself dead to the world. She knew she was alive. She could hear the waterfall. She could hear the strained sounds of breathing beside her. She could feel grass against her cheek. As thick and tar-like as the smoke-filled temple, her thoughts filled with the strategies and games of power.

She wasn't ready to face the day. Not yet.

Instead, she pictured Farehold's queen.

Had Moirai known that the priestess possessed such gifts of power to slaughter her army? Nox knew enough of games and manipulation to suspect that yes, this way, it was a loose end that Moirai would not have to tie up. Northern flags and banners and bodies would remain scattered about the glen, two vulnerable parties in opposition, pitted against each other in a war that wasn't their own.

She couldn't hate the boys for what they'd done. After all, judgment was an armchair luxury for those who had never known suffering. Anyone who'd gone hungry, who'd been marginalized, who'd found themselves beneath the boot of those in power would empathize with the atrocities that had happened here. There were no bishops, no rooks, no knights or pieces with agency in this game of chess. There was only the queen and her pawns. No lives. Only a game.

Nox couldn't keep her eyes closed forever. She couldn't dwell on these thoughts for much longer. She wasn't sure how long she'd been awake as her head throbbed with anger. She hadn't opened her eyes. She wasn't sure if she could handle what she saw once she did. The sleep that had gripped them had been the hissing, gasping unconsciousness of three people clinging to the edges of life.

By morning's gloomy light, Ash had been the first to sit.

Nox could hear him moving off to her side. She could almost discern his distinct scent of autumn over the bonfire smells that coated the glen.

Instead, she remained in her state of near awareness, not quite asleep, nor quite conscious. Her body had never under-gone training. Her limbs knew no skills; her heart and lungs and muscles had no resilience to exertion. She was aware of Ash's movements as he saw to Malik, then she felt a rough and sudden movement as his fingers pressed into her jugular, checking her pulse for signs of life.

Eyes still closed, she attempted to speak to him, but her throat was coated in the sooty remnants of smoke. She merely croaked.

"Are you awake?" he asked, his voice sounding equally coated with soot.

"Yes," she choked out.

"Are you okay?"

She knew she was far from okay. Nox's eyes opened slowly, adjusting to the overcast lights of morning.

"I'll be right back."

Ash stumbled away, returning an unknown span of time later with a waterskin presumably filled from the pool. He lifted her head and dribbled a few healing drops over her tongue and into her burning throat. Once she was able to grip the skin, Nox drank deeply. Ash helped her to a sitting position as he left her to tend to their human companion.

As soon as Malik showed signs of consciousness, Ash left his side to search for survivors. She watched as he knelt beside the fallen, then frowned as he peeled the shirt from the boy. She didn't understand what he was doing until he carried the Raascot colors to the remnants of a fire and tossed it into the flame. Ash continued moving around the glen, plucking fallen flags and turning the evidence of Moirai's unconscionable efforts into cinders and smoke.

None of these boys deserved to die.

The priestess had every right to defend herself and her temple. Her power had been an incredible, slicing fire. Her swords of scalding flame had eviscerated her enemies as she protected the Tree of Life. She had undoubtedly been brave as she'd stood her ground against the horde that had descended on the Tree of Life with their swords aloft. She was simply outnumbered, one hundred children with swords to one.

And the boys had every right to take an assignment from the crown and trust that it would save their families from a life of starvation. The imposter soldiers had followed the orders given to them by their queen.

The only blame lay at the feet of goddess-damned Queen Moirai. The monarchy. A society that kept her in power. Ten thousand years of tradition that allowed a single woman to wave her hand and swat at others like they were little more than gnats.

Nox's heart hurt. She was horrified. But mostly, she was angry.

Perhaps this was why she kept turning it over in her head again and again and again. She couldn't tear her mind from the game. How could one play if the queen had a full set of pieces and she'd given her opponent a single pawn, tied their hands behind their back, and blindfolded them? It was no true game if it had been rigged for its winners and losers long before both players sat at the table.

It wasn't fair.

She'd pocket this hatred like a still-burning coal from the collapsed temple, allowing it to fester within her as they did whatever they needed to do to end Moirai and her reign. Right now, her thirst for vengeance would not serve her. She needed to move.

Nox felt her body for injuries. Her hands were swollen. Her face and neck were hot to the touch as if she'd been scorched by a dreadful sunburn. Her hair was still stuck to her face, but not with the water from the previous day's storm. Mud from her tumble in the woods and dried salt had stiffened her strands into a hardened shell against her head. So much of it had protected her from the inferno.

It took a long time to get to her knees, then to her feet.

Her eyes burned against the remnants of ashes and soot that clung to her innermost lids. Nox moved forward on unsteady feet, stumbling past bloodied corpses toward the pool where a single body bobbed facedown like a fallen tree floating in its waters. She didn't possess the fortitude to address anything around her as she knelt by the pool and began to wash the

231

mud from her face and hair, cooling her blistered hands in its waters. Mud clouded the clear waters of the pool around her as it released its grip on her hair and the places it had dried on her skin. She dipped her entire scalp into the pool, cooling herself and willing the waters to take the soot along with her memories. She wanted to be cleansed of the night. She wanted its unspeakable traumas to be put behind her. She submerged her head, hoping she would emerge baptized as someone made new.

Unfortunately, the same horrors awaited her when her face broke the water's surface.

The waterfall continued its unyielding tumble, not bothered by the ways of men and the passage of time. The river above continued its path as if it had for one thousand years and would for one thousand years more, no matter what tree did or didn't grow in the temple or who served as its priestess. The glen was lined with quaking aspens, vibrantly blue green from the soaking rain of the previous day. The dark sky overhead bubbled in thunderheads of pewter and slate, but its clouds did not release their moisture as they had the day prior.

Nox returned to the reevers. Malik was finally moving, exhibiting comforting signs of life, though his energy had not returned. Ash came back to them, shaking his head. His movements were so stilted, so leaden. He had found no survivors.

"We need somewhere we can recover for a while."

Nox closed her burning, bloodshot eyes. She blinked against the pain, the memory, the horrors that still littered the glen.

"I have a place."

"The one you visited in Priory? We can't risk returning so close to the royal city right now."

"No, I know a place where we can be safe about a day's trek from here—two if we're slow on foot. We only need to make it to Henares."

Horses met them on the regency's road.

It had taken every drop of strength they possessed to follow the pocket watch, cut through the forest, and find the path that connected the kingdoms. Nox flagged down the first man she saw. She gave what remained of the coin she'd taken from Millicent's office and begged him to beseech the Duke of Henares to return for them. One runner could not collect Nox and the reevers, but if the duke sent reinforcements, they had a chance.

"How do you know he isn't going to take your money and never return?" Ash asked.

Malik sighed, voice weary as he said, "You underestimate the sway she has over men."

Thanks to her scrub in the pool, her face and hair were free of mud. The stranger could see just how beautiful she was. Yes, the runner could have robbed Nox and never faced consequences. Maybe he would have under other circumstances, but there is a privilege afforded to the beautiful that did not show its kindness to others. Her beauty was currency as valuable as any coin she could offer. She knew it as she'd looked up at him, softening her eyes with innocence. When the runner had looked upon Nox's face, her glossy hair, her perfect skin, and her large, dark eyes, she knew he would not let her suffer. He'd ride his horse hard the rest of the way to Henares, from trot to canter to gallop.

It would have been a day or two on foot. By horse, they could be there by sundown.

The three slumped lifelessly to the side of the road, dead to the world around them as they waited. Nox leaned against Malik, needing the comfort every bit as much as he did. They did not speak. They did not sleep. They sat, they blocked out horrors, and they waited.

At first, it sounded like a storm was approaching, as if the bubbling clouds had decided to drench them once more. A thunderous cacophony of noise bubbled up from the distance before they realized they were hearing hooves.

The duke had sent carriages and horses and armed guards and water and juices and bandages and tonics for healing and pain alike, all sprinting from his estate the very moment word from her had arrived. They'd come so much more quickly than anyone could have anticipated—each horse pushed nearly to the brink to save her.

Nox had known with every fiber of her being that they would survive if they could only cling to their strength long enough for the duke's reinforcements to arrive. The reevers didn't have the energy for questions as the carriage jostled them along the road. The young men didn't care who had received them or where they were going. It had taken reserves of strength that they were hardly aware they possessed to simply stay alive. The smoke's poison had not only leaked into their lungs but had saturated their very tissues, weakening them completely.

Instead of meeting their fate and crossing over to be with the All Mother, Nox was crowded with attendants that very night. The cold forest was replaced with opulent rooms. The smells of ashes and death were doused out with bubble baths and delicious foods. Nightmarish memories contrasted against silks and woods and golds of an estate with more wealth than one man could ever need. A healer had her hands on Nox while servants bathed her. She remained too weak to fight the women who scrubbed at her skin or protest the hot water. The perfumes were too strong, their exfoliating rags too rough for how truly fragile she felt. Too many tonics were dribbled down her throat, again for healing, then more for pain, others of a somewhat mysterious nature. There were so many people in the room.

"I'm fine," she snapped when they tried to help her out of the bath.

"My lady—"

She stood, hair wet, naked, and dripping in soap bubbles,

and pointed a commanding finger toward the door. Nox summoned her strength and ordered the healers and servants to attend to Ash and Malik. The duke was her puppet and probably had little care for what happened to the men in her company. While the enchantment that had enthralled the duke would focus him on Nox's needs, she knew she'd have to massage his graces a bit to ensure her friends received similar treatment.

She was toweling the water from her damp tendrils of hair when the devil himself paid a visit. The Duke of Henares burst into the room without bothering to knock. He was still handsome, she supposed, but his roguish charm had long since evaporated. His lovelorn face was stricken with worry. She tried to remember she was grateful to have him, but she was too tired to feel anything apart from irritation.

"Nox! I sent everything I had the moment I received your message. I'm so glad you're here. I've missed you so—"

"Leave me be," she said, waving him away. "And don't bother my companions either."

"Yes, of course," he said hurriedly, needing no elaboration. He stepped aside so an attendant could navigate around him and disappeared into the hall. She pressed her lips together and tried not to take too much delight from his subservience.

Servants bustled in and out with plates and cups and pitchers of all sorts of soups from a cold pumpkin puree to an aromatic chicken and dumpling soup, red and white wines from every region along the southern coasts of Farehold, brie and goat cheese and soft mozzarella, thinly shaved and cured meats arranged into roses, an endless supply of chilled, exotic fruits and berries, and breads. So, so, so much bread. Sourdough bread and white sliced bread and sweet rolls and cracked barley and pretzel twists and honey-glazed rolls and brown loaves were piled high. She attempted to nibble at a fig, but her stomach cramped at the effort.

"Please, no more food. It's going to go to waste. It smells like a dining hall in this bedroom. I need all this food moved out of my room. Except for this." She grabbed for one of the sweet rolls, deciding she may regret the decision later.

"The cook is still hard at it, I'm afraid. We have our orders."

"Then can you bring these to the others? My friends? Will you ensure the meals are delivered to their rooms?"

"M'lady, the duke—"

"The duke will be happy with whatever makes *me* happy."

"Would you like me to open a window for fresh air?"

"Please, goddess, yes."

A single servant had remained with her to help her step into a clean nightdress and brush her long, black hair. The servant gasped at the scars that lined Nox's back, but Nox was too deadened to flinch at the sound. The healer who had been sent to her rooms had absorbed the remnants of the smoke's poison from her lungs and muscles and had tended to all active wounds and bruises but could not touch the remnants of the whip that had broken her helpless flesh again and again those many years ago.

She felt like an entirely new—albeit exhausted—person after the healer's hands, the tonics, the gallons of water she'd consumed, and the hot bath. It was by the goddess's good fortune that Nox was feeling fully refreshed, for as the servant was bundling her muddied, fire-scented clothes into her arms, a thud sounded from the collection.

Nox's sleepy gaze followed the sound to where an apple rolled on the ground. Her eyes widened. The servant reached for the fruit, but Nox found a surge of adrenaline and was on her feet. "Don't touch it!"

The servant froze, arm outstretched. The woman straightened, doubtlessly confused, but took the bizarre exchange as a good excuse to leave the room with Nox's filthy things.

Nox didn't bother to consider what the people of Henares had been going through for the months and months that had followed the duke's enchantment. The dazed lordling had perhaps been a spot more pleasant now that he'd been stripped of his mind and consumed by a singular, obedient love. Now that the object of his affection was under his roof, she could only imagine the pandemonium that must have besieged the estate.

She focused her attention on the fruit.

Nox picked up the apple and examined it properly now that she was in the bright light of a safe space. For all the world, it looked like an ordinary apple that could have been plucked from any orchard. When she turned it in the light this way and that, it seemed to catch a gilded glint as if precious secrets were stitched within its skin.

It had to be special. Whatever had been worth saving as one's dying wish demanded care and secrecy. She poked around her room for a sufficient spot to hide her treasure, choosing a drawer beneath several items, certain that it would not be disturbed.

She had been meant to take it and save it from the fires that had consumed the tree, but that was the extent of her knowledge. Now she had no clue whether she was meant to plant it so that another might grow in its place or if she was meant to store it, treasure it, or bake it into a pie.

If she sat on the bed, she was confident she'd fall asleep and never get up again. If she wanted to speak to her friends, it would have to be now.

Nox opened the door to her chambers and tiptoed her way through the hall lined with tapestries and oil paintings and lively lanterns and lounging chaises. She knew she was not a prisoner, nor was secrecy required of her, but she couldn't quell the instinct. She supposed if she wanted to parade through Henares like its new duchess, she would be very well received. There was a comfort in the knowledge that she held a seat of power here, even if it was one that she had no interest in having.

She hadn't knocked when she'd pushed open the first door. Servants had been scrubbing at a weakly protesting Malik while the healer stood over him. He'd gone positively pink while Nox stood in the doorway, and he did his best to cover himself. Nox's hand flew to her mouth in an attempt to stifle her giggle of apologetic surprise. She felt perplexingly shy to have caught him in such a vulnerable moment.

"I'm sorry!" she squeaked, averting her gaze. "I'll be back in a bit!"

She closed the doors and fought her laugh at the walking contradiction of a man. He was burly and sweet. He was masculine and innocent. He was handsome and kind. He was strong and timid. He was a man, and yet she did not hate him one bit. Nox shook her head, if only to herself, willing the smile away from her lips She continued picking her way down the hall, this time knocking before she opened another door.

"Yes?"

She recognized Ash's voice and pushed the door open. His hair was wet, his clothes clean. Ash was much easier to understand. He was strong and diligent and honorable and predictable. She could count on his consistency. She let herself in and closed the door behind her. The familiarity was comforting.

"Do I want to ask how you know this lord?"

"Oh, the Duke of Henares? We go way back." She brushed it away with the wave of her hand.

The reevers were no fools. She was confident they'd known for a while that they traveled with a creature who refused to relinquish her secrets. They also respected her too much to demand any information that she was unwilling to surrender on her own, which she'd greatly appreciated.

Ash breathed out a sigh. "Thank you," he said. He made a half-hearted gesture to the room around him, his clothes, the bathing room adjoining his chamber. She was sure this was quite the courtly suite for him. It was grand by anyone's standards, let alone a reever's. The healer had sealed Ash's wounds, and the tub had washed away the dirt and blood that had clung to him. His red hair was slicked back by the cleansing water of the bath, creating a dampness on the back of his clean shirt. She wasn't sure if she'd ever seen him fully washed before.

She sat on the bed next to him without waiting for an invitation. "What the hell happened?"

Ash's face paled. He shook his head, dropping his voice. It was the kind of moment that lent itself to appropriate pauses—for disbelief, for mourning, for tragedy. "I'm not a religious person," he began. "I had never worshiped at the church; I had never tithed for the goddess. As a man, I knew I wasn't welcome in the Temple of the All Mother, but when Amaris visited the temple—"

Ash stopped briefly as Nox's voice hitched with her question.

"Amaris was there?"

His tone changed. His face softened a bit. "Nox...I haven't asked. I haven't pressed. And even now, I'll ask you only once and then never again if you don't wish to tell me. What is your relationship to Amaris?"

She had not expected this question. They'd been together for weeks and he'd never mentioned a thing. She'd expected him to elaborate on the situation at the temple; instead, this pivot caught her fully off guard. Ash and Malik had been there in the dungeon and watched the girls embrace, saw how they'd sobbed, how they'd kissed through the iron bars. Her eyes were hot with the threat of tears at the memory. It was easy to think of how she felt when she was alone, but to say it out loud...

"I don't know," she answered honestly. She was surprised at the single tear that escaped before she had the time to register its presence. She wiped at it as she whispered, "I know that I've loved her for a very long time."

Ash stayed very still, not daring to speak. She sat with her emotions as his eyes busied themselves examining the gaudy art over her shoulder, gaze politely averted. The only sound was the cheery fire in its perfectly contained enclosure, its safety a mockery of the wildfire that had consumed the world only a night before. The logs in his fire popped and cracked. Enough time had passed that he dared a question. "You two grew up together. I'm sure you were friends—everything to each other, even—but you were more than that, weren't you?"

Nox nearly laughed. She tilted her head back as if hoping the motion would prevent any treacherous tears from spilling downward. Instead, the pools were caught by her eyelids, preventing gravity's siren song. "Yes? No? Does it matter?"

His voice was gentle. "Of course it matters."

She shook her head. "The world is so easy when it's split into its dichotomies, isn't it? If you're from Farehold, you can find peace in knowing the south is good and the north is evil. If you're born without magic, there's a comfort in the belief that witches are nefarious, and humans are pure. Even as fae, it's so enticing to categorize one as dark or light. It makes the world so simple, don't you think? Isn't it tempting?"

She looked at Ash, but her friend was wise enough to know that she was not looking for an answer. He eyed her contemplatively. His amber gaze glistened with both patience and willingness to listen. Nox was brimming with some long unspoken thoughts. Her heart was torn by whatever she wrestled.

"I blame you two for a lot of this, you know."

His forehead creased as his brows collected. "Blame us?"

"There was a safety in knowing men as my enemy." Nox nearly choked on the statement. "Hate is a luxury. Do you understand what I mean?"

He shook his head to tell her he didn't understand.

"The world is simple when you can bisect it." She was no longer speaking to him. She was talking to the room, to the fire that popped within the safety of the hearth, and to herself. "Everything is so much more painful when it's gray."

She had meant to ask him what had happened in the temple, but she knew that if she stayed in here a moment longer, she would start to cry, and she would not be able to catch herself with a single graceful tear. Ash and his answers would still be there in the morning. She would ask him then.

"I'm sorry," she said hastily, getting to her feet.

"No, don't be."

It was a small wonder to feel the soft, plush carpeting of a rug under her bare toes. She wiggled them slightly and enjoyed the tiny moment of peace. Nox didn't want to stay in this room with her thoughts. This wasn't his fault, and she was confident he wouldn't hold it against her. She glanced over her shoulder, and Ash merely looked after her. She opened his door and closed it behind herself without a second glance.

✦

Assuming Malik's bath had ended and the healer had left, Nox needed to check on her remaining friend. He'd been in such a rough state at the temple and barely clung to consciousness as they'd waited for the duke's forces. She found herself worrying about Malik more often than she should.

Nox knocked this time before opening his door and waited longer than necessary for him to stutter a greeting. She dipped her head as she entered. "I've just returned to apologize. I should have knocked before. I wanted to make sure they'd brought the food to your room, that you had something to eat, that the healer had stopped by...all those sorts of things."

Whether the pink had never left his cheeks or if he had found entirely new ways to redden, she didn't know. He was freshly bathed and in clean, comfortable clothes. He was fully dressed but still shifted with a remnant of bashfulness. "It's okay. And yes." He gestured to two empty plates with little more than crumbs to show evidence that he'd dined only moments before. "It was delicious. Thank your friend for me."

"I just wanted to check on you. You were in rough shape."

He looked frustrated at that. "I was also in rough shape after the fight with the spider. Perhaps you and Ash should pair up with someone better matched to your skill sets."

Her entire being recoiled at the absurdity of the statement. She hadn't expected the conversation to take this turn.
Nox's brows knit together. "Malik, how can you say that?"

He shook his head. "This isn't self-pity, I promise. I'm a
good reever, I am. But I do feel like I hold back the mission.
I am so honored to fight alongside Ash, and Amaris was a
marvel to behold in the sparring ring. You've had no training with the sword, and you've still come out of the temple
at twice the recovery that I could have hoped. If only every
village were blessed with the money that Henares has at its
disposal, so its duke could throw his weight toward our cause
and send healers across the land."

Nox's mouth twitched. "The duke is a…friend. He
owes me."

Malik nodded. "I'm glad of that. Can I ask you a question?"

She frowned. Something in his tone told her that she
would not like his question. She joined him on the bed. "You
may."

His question revealed his cleverness. Whatever it was, she
knew from the weight of his words that Malik saw through
Nox and her enchantments. "Is the duke a friend…because
he is human?"

She understood what he was asking. Perhaps he didn't
know the specifics, but he knew that the duke was under
a power that could be neither dissected nor explained by
anything short of magic.

She thought of the disparity between her knowledge and his.

In her upbringing, Nox had heard of fae. She had known
that there were immortal beings with pointed ears and beautiful features. She had heard of the demonic northern fae and
their wings. She knew of witches and their spells. The citizens
of Farehold did not have the encyclopedic knowledge of the
creatures that might allow for a term as horrible as *succubus* to
have found its way into most of their minds, but Malik was a
reever. He had studied the beasts of the land. She wondered
how much he'd guessed.

Nox had spent months hating herself for her gift. She had spent nights crying over the fate of her immortal soul. Then, on a day as ordinary as any other, something had clicked. She had been making notes, as she often did to sort through her thoughts. She had been sketching and writing and creating diagrams of names, faces, and commonalities. She hadn't seen their connection at the time, but she saw them now.

"Would you believe me if I told you that his enchantment was not because he was human but because he was wicked?"

His verdant eyes fixed on hers.

Nox didn't herself quite know where her words were going, but she spoke from the heart as Malik eyed her. "Do you know I've met many humans throughout my life? I've known more humans than I ever have fae. Perhaps one in ninety-nine is nonhuman. I've been fairly exposed to mankind, to say the least. None of them act the way the duke does now. None of them fawn, fuss, or obey with this sort of compulsion. It is not his humanity that has demanded obedience of him. It is what he had chosen to do with that humanity and how that choice brought him to me."

Malik's voice was breathless, not sure if wanted to know the answer. "What did he choose to do?"

She wasn't sure why she did it, but she touched the side of his face with her hand. What she knew was that she wanted to comfort him. She did not want him to fear her. She cared for this man. His features softened under her silken touch. His green eyes bubbled with questions as he waited on bated breath.

"He took." She held his eyes for a moment. "He felt entitled to that which did not belong to him. From his people, from his kingdom, from his friends, from his family, from women, and his final act of taking was when he met me."

Malik leaned imperceptibly into her hand.

"You do not take, Malik. You give."

"You sound like an avenging angel."

She relaxed her hand, dropping it from his face. What

pretty words. He found her open palm and squeezed her hand gently in acknowledgment.

She had accomplished what she'd set into the hall to do. She merely needed to know that the reevers were okay, that her friends were alive and cared for. She left Malik sitting on his bed amidst comforts he'd perhaps never encountered in his life between his humble village, his training at the reev, and his encampments on forest floors, and she stole back into her own room. Nox called to the servant who had been attending her and requested that the woman ensure she be left in absolute privacy for the night, no matter who called upon her. She was very specific that no servant, no reever, and no duke were to knock at her door until morning.

What she was about to do couldn't risk disturbance.

Nox dug through her drawer until her fingers wrapped around the flesh of the apple that had been the final offering of the Tree of Life. She had no answers, no handbook to follow as she sat on her bed. She arranged the blankets comfortably around herself. She drank deeply from the water that rested in the ostentatiously beautiful goblet beside her bed. And then she bit into the apple.

Twenty-Four

PRESSED AGAINST GADRIEL, HELD IN HIS WARM ARMS WHILE
they pierced the clouds under the ten thousand diamonds
of a star-drenched sky wasn't the *worst* thing Amaris had ever
experienced.

Traveling by foot was tedious and miserable. Every time
she walked or ran, she'd developed blisters, moved slowly,
and arrived with aching feet. Traveling by horse was faster,
of course. Their legs may burn and their mounts may need
to rest, but a horse can cover triple the distance, if not more,
in a single day. If forced to choose between the two, she'd
always claim horseback as preferable. A carriage might have
provided coverage from the elements, but it would slow the
traveler's ability to cover ground. Amaris had never been on
a ship, so she could not speak to the experience of traveling
by sea. Amidst the galaxies, she thought that if one had never
flown, then one had never truly experienced the potential
for joy, speed, and awe at the goddess's lighted kingdom.

Gadriel had scooped her into his arms and flown them
for nearly five hours as they'd bolted from the university. He
claimed he would have liked to have gone farther, but carrying an entire person complicated his travel plans.

"I'll just go ahead and lose a few pounds," Amaris joked through pale lips and chattering teeth. While the sky was a beautiful, endless expanse for open travel, she had felt quite certain she was going to freeze to death. She had pressed herself into Gadriel for warmth, but her fingers had gone numb and her body had felt drained of its blood before they'd made it far. She wasn't sure how, but she'd warmed rather inexplicably just as her lips had begun to turn blue, as wholly as if she had curled up on a hearth. She'd thought maybe she was losing her nerve endings to the early warning signs of frostbite, but she felt her body relax into the warmth. Her shivering ceased as she allowed herself to enjoy the night.

"Sure, then you'll have no muscle mass and be of even less use to me."

"You always know just what to say."

The night, lit only by a crescent moon, provided enough darkness for them to fly undetected. They didn't land until they neared the outskirts of a village. If they had hopes of continuing, they had to get provisions beyond the few tonics and wrappings Amaris had stuffed into a pillowcase in their great escape. They needed food, she needed a cloak, and they both needed weapons. Unfortunately, they had neither money nor the connections necessary to gather supplies.

"Reevers are supported by the church. I should be able to ask—"

"It's after nightfall, and we need weapons just as badly as we need food, water, or cloaks. We need something a little more substantial than whatever coin the church has collected for its sword arm. Plus, they'd give you a few silvers, but I doubt it would be enough to get us a weapon. And they certainly wouldn't be inclined to help out your ag'imni."

He didn't mean to chide her, but his knowledge of the way the world worked frequently felt grating. "Then what's the point of the church supporting Uaimh Reev? Also, *my* ag'imni? Yes, they did think you were my pet, didn't they?" She smirked.

246

"Excellent question, and equally terrible observation. Do your best to forget whatever you were told at the university. While you're pondering those, go into the town and see where we are. I have outposts in several cities and towns throughout Farehold, but we need to gather our bearings before we can find anyone or anything helpful."

"First off, don't tell me what to do. Also, you had mentioned an outpost in Yelagin once upon a time. Is that where we're going?"

He laughed at what she assumed was her ignorance of geography. "Goddess, no. We've been flying as directly east as possible. The sooner we cross out of Farehold, the better we'll be. Yelagin would be several days southward."

Perhaps he was trying to piss her off. Amaris called on the mental image of a map and drew an eastward line from the university toward the border. "We can get provisions at Uaimh Reev! It's directly in our flight path."

He denied her proposal with one quick move of his head to the side. "We're still three night's travel from your reev as the crow flies. Do you think you can go three more days and nights without food, water, or a cloak? We're already going to have to light a fire tonight just so that you can warm up."

"As the crow flies," she repeated dryly.

He shot her a look.

"I'm fine," she insisted, though she trembled. Gadriel extended a wing, offering his body heat. She took a backward step, refusing his gesture as she kept several arms' lengths between them. She preferred instead to chafe her arms for body heat.

"To be clear, you're fine being close to me all night while we're in the air and using me for heat, but as soon as we land, that's where you draw the line?" Gadriel had begun his sentence with an attempt at wry amusement but was unable to keep the frustration from his voice. As a general, she knew his men had depended on him, fought with him, and respected him. As the king's cousin, he was loved and

247

trusted. Unfortunately for him, he'd been paired with the most ungrateful, disagreeable witch in the kingdoms.

She ignored his antagonizing, choosing instead to continue to fight for friction as she rubbed her hands rapidly on her sleeves. She couldn't get her muscles to relax from their frigid, stiffened positions. "I'm going to go into town and try my luck. Stay here and look menacing, or whatever it is you do."

"What do you have to barter?" he yelled after her as she disappeared amidst the pines, but she merely waved a hand above her head in some indiscernible gesture that may as well have said *don't bother me.*

Amaris wasn't exactly sure what she could trade. A healing tonic would be an acceptable trade for food and a waterskin, but what of swords, daggers, or cloaks? Gadriel wanted her to simply inquire as to their location so he could ascertain where the nearest Raascot outpost was hidden, but her stomach grumbled and she had made it perfectly clear that she didn't like being bossed around. He was a general, just not her general.

They had landed relatively close to town. The woods here were different from the oaks and box elders that tangled their way around Farleigh, interlocking so that the boughs had created an impenetrable fence around the orphanage. These woods were filled with the bright scent of pine and littered with a soft carpet of fallen, reddish needles. Amaris had seen conifers before, as the matrons would often have one cut for winter solstice, but they were not native to her upbringing. The reev had been a wonderful place to train, but its granite walls and sheer rock faces offered few opportunities for vegetation, save for the tenacious little plants that burrowed out from the fissures in the rocks. She couldn't quite name what it was about the crisp scent of evergreen, but there was something distinctly enchanted about the thick pines that surrounded her.

It had taken her less than half an hour to free herself from the forest and step into town. Her ears were pink with chill, and her fingers had become difficult to flex against the numbing air. The trees had been cut to leave ample space for villagers to spot any wolves or unsavory characters who might be approaching them from the alpine trees. She felt appropriately exposed, just as the town intended for anyone emerging from the woods. She made her way toward the lone building that was still alive with light as its yellow-orange glow spilled out from its windows. There may have been others around corners and out of sight, but she wasn't interested in the nuances of this nameless village. The only people awake at this hour would be the town's baker, who rose before daylight to set his rolls to rise, and the seedy underbellies of gamblers and drinkers who haunted the tavern. The homey scent of stew wafted past the closed doors of the inn and demanded attention over the fresh smell of pine.

She approached the door and paused, experiencing a moment of déjà vu. She'd been particularly self-conscious the first time she'd entered a tavern after escaping Farleigh, as it had been her first exposure to the outside world. Years had gone by, but had she acclimated to society? She'd spent her time isolated in Uaimh Reev, and any time apart from the keep had been either with her brothers or with Gadriel.

The loneliness of social anxiety was not a comfortable sensation.

The small, common sounds of folksy commotion traveled through the night air as she advanced. It was too late into the night for any musician to have continued their jolly alehouse tunes, but those married to their pint glasses knew no concept of time. Amaris closed her hand around the inn's iron handle and could scarcely find the strength in her fingers necessary to twist and open the door. She was so blasted stiff. It hadn't been too terribly long since her frozen night in the forest outside the university after they'd fallen from the ag'drurath, and while they'd traveled, they had gone no farther south. The night's temperatures dropped with every moment they traveled, and her blood was markedly colder in response.

There was no reason to feel so afraid of something as mundane as an unfamiliar tavern. Odds were the establishment would be full of humans. If things went terribly, she could always just *tell* them to believe she wasn't a peculiar oddity and that they should hand her a satchel full of food. She could probably tell them that she was in fact the most interesting and charming and normal person they'd ever met. It was a morally questionable tactic, and she wasn't sure she was ready to cross that particular bridge with her gift.

If it weren't for the cold, she might have stayed frozen on the doorstep. Instead, her need for warmth overruled her fear of missteps, rejection, and the unknown. Somehow, new people and unfamiliar social situations were more terrifying than the ag'drurath. She reminded herself with some wavering pep talk that she had indeed survived a demonic dragon as she pushed open the door.

The blast of warmth that washed over her as she opened the door to the tavern was glorious. The town she'd entered was large enough to possess probably three or more inns, but she'd selected the one that seemed from its outpouring noise to have the most active patrons—that, or because it had been the first one she'd seen, and she was cold. The delicious heat from its enormous hearth only warmed her topmost layer of skin. Her chill was too permeated through her body to have any quick or easy solutions. Still, she savored the feeling as she crossed the threshold and advanced toward the bar.

She was already self-conscious of the stares she drew, though she knew they were inevitable. It was probably her white hair and prominent scar that drew their attention, but some part of her told her that it was also because her skin had frozen blue. She remained aware of the eyes on her as she approached the innkeeper.

People did their best to keep up polite conversation as they watched her. The innkeeper, serving as bartender among the other hats he doubtlessly donned, offered a hospitable though cautious smile as she stepped up to the bar.

Amaris wasted no time. "Would you be willing to trade healing tonics for food that travels well? Breads, cheeses, salted meats, and the like?"

The middle-aged man was portly and thin of hair, save for the halo that clung to the crown above his ears. He had been cleaning a glass with a rag as she'd entered the tavern, but he set it down to give her his attention. His body language communicated enough. The twist of his mouth told her both that he wasn't typically one for trading and that good healing tonics were rare and valuable. His face was transparent, and that quality alone was likable enough.

She liked the strange man more for not questioning her presence as a female, nor inquiring as to the lateness of her hour. A white-haired, pale, scarred, purple-eyed girl in the middle of the night? No problem, as long as she came with purpose. The man went straight to business. "These tonics of yours are genuine?"

She stifled her sigh of relief. "They are indeed. I'm traveling from the university. These bottles came directly from the healers' hall."

"And you've come by them honestly?" His voice had a rather thick, rural curvature to his vowels, clipping the ends of his words in a way that made comprehension a tad challenging, but she managed.

This would be a lie she'd have to tell. She had gone into the university honestly. She had been treated honestly by the healer. She had stuffed tonics into a pillowcase and left in the night in a less virtuous departure. "I have."

He set down his glass and approached her. "Let me see your tonics."

While she and Gadriel did need food, a good healing tonic meant the difference between life and death given their propensity for trouble. When she'd slashed her body outside Farleigh, a healing tonic had closed her wounds without any risk of infection at nearly triple the speed of a typical wound. Perhaps if she'd been offered them right away instead of hours

251

after the fact, she wouldn't have any scars at all. Gadriel had lain motionless on the table in the healers' hall until they'd administered the tonics. Reevers were never to leave the keep without a few of the brown glass bottles in hand, should they find themselves poisoned, bitten, or maimed. A single authentic bottle of tonic was worth at least five silvers.

She pulled out only one. "I'd like to barter for a few loaves of bread, whatever dried meats you may have, and any dehydrated fruits. What do you have in your pantry?"

He moved his mouth into a tight, sideways line again once. His eyes wandered up and off to the side as if reading off an inventory list. "I do have a number of dried apricots, and we made an awful lot of sausage and jerky out of a buck if you like deer meat. I can cut up a few wedges of hard white cheddar and a rather large block of three-year aged sheep's milk cheese, though it's awfully crumbly. Let's see... There's apples, lots 'a those, and we have a few barley loaves fresh from this morning, and day-old sourdough rolls the missus made yesterday. I'd like at least two tonics for that."

She understood why he wanted them, and she also knew their value. "Ah, I understand. I'll try the other innkeeper." She pushed away from the bar and offered him a friendly smile as she rotated her body toward the door.

"Wait!" His tone stopped her in her tracks. She turned to eye him skeptically, playing the role of the disinterested traveler. The key to a good negotiation was the believable willingness to walk away. Amaris hadn't wanted to go to any other inn. She had no desire to search one step further. With a small relief, she approached again, maintaining the slow air of uncertainty.

"You swear it's genuine?"

"I'd slit my wrists and test it for you, but I feel like that would be an awful waste of tonic."

She could have commanded him to trade with her. She could have persuaded him to sign over the deed to the tavern if she'd desired. That wasn't the kind of person Amaris

252

wanted to be. He was a man running a business; as long as he treated her fairly, the least she could do was extend him the same courtesy. It did comfort her to know that there was an exceptionally powerful trick up her sleeve that she could use should she need it.

He nodded and extended a large hand to examine the tonic. Amaris knew that he'd find nothing dissatisfactory, but she was curious if the innkeeper would attempt any further bartering tactics. He could always pretend to find a flaw or feign doubt to try to keep the tonic while parting with fewer traveling foods.

He finally asked, "Do you have more than one tonic?"

She nodded. "I won't lie to you. I do have more, but not that I'm willing to trade for. I need your bread, but loaves will do little good if I meet a wolf on my travels."

He frowned, though she knew the argument was finished. "Would you like any pickled beets, eggs, or cucumbers? Jars with salt and vinegar last for a long time."

They did preserve, but such delicacies were meant for a traveler in a caravan. She couldn't imagine the horror of reaching her hand into her pack only to discover that a pickled jar had shattered and soaked her clothes, bread, and weapons. Not only would she come up smelling of vinegar and having ruined her food, but she'd undoubtedly slice her palm on pickle juice and glass shards. She shook her head. All she'd be able to take were the dried fruits, a few apples, venison jerky, loaves, and whatever aged sheep's milk cheese the innkeeper had mentioned.

Her stomach grumbled again. Fortunately, the chattering din of late-night patrons covered the sound. She didn't want the innkeeper using her obvious hunger as an excuse to cheat her from her food, though the country man did seem honest enough. He dipped his head in a nod and began to fill a burlap root vegetable sack with a variety of foods. The innkeeper tossed in hardened cheese that didn't require chill in order to keep, and the pumpernickels and ryes would maintain their flavor in spite of any staleness—even if it wasn't a flavor she particularly liked. She fought an unintentional twitch of the lip as she thought of how disgusting rye bread was if it hadn't been prepared with hot, corned beef, tangy cream, and shredded, pickled vegetables. The reev had made such wonderful sandwiches.

Maybe if her persuasion worked on fae, she could have sweet-talked Gadriel into diverting to Uaimh Reev just for a few delicious meals. After blanched vegetables and boiled meat at the university, coupled with the cold, boring traveling foods, she was owed a lovely meal. Brel would undoubtedly be thrilled to see her, and he loved his work in the kitchen. She missed her younger, almost reever brother more than she missed sandwiches.

Now was not the time to think of sad things.

Another emotion slipped inside the box.

Amaris abandoned the tonic atop the bar for his retrieval and advanced toward the fire.

"Girl," a gruff voice grunted from behind her.

The sharp stab of agitation pierced her. Amaris stopped herself short of rolling her eyes as she turned to assess the gentleman. "I don't suppose there's any chance this is a nickname for your drinking companion, as I can't imagine you'd dare to be so rude to a stranger. Or perhaps are you mistaking me with a friend of yours whose mother gave her such an unfortunate name?"

"Huh?"

The speaker wasn't the slovenly, fiftysomething drunkard she'd initially assumed had barked at her. A man in his thirties with a cropped beard and the rosy, burst capillaries of a wind-chafed complexion was eyeing her from where he sat with two other companions. The three were dressed and armed as if they too were travelers. She suspected from their weapons that they were mercenaries in various states of drink and disarray. Swords for hire were common across the continent and could be found in nearly any alehouse.

The thirtysomething man jerked his chin as if to summon her over, but she didn't move. Amaris had no energy for their games when she responded with dry disinterest, "I'm sure you're fine company, but I prefer the fire. Thank you."

Maybe it was the few beers in his belly or the entitlement he felt as a man with a sword, but he had no interest in dropping the conversation. He pressed, "What's a snow fox like you doing out at this late hour?"

She turned to face them fully, giving the fire an opportunity to warm her backside. Her lower back seemed to melt, muscles unraveling from how it had tensed against the cold. She eyed the men at the table but felt no particular threat from them apart from mild annoyance. She idly wondered how Gadriel would have responded in a situation like this. She answered, "I'm traveling east and was hungry. I figured it would be easier to buy my dinner than hunt it myself. The roads have been a bit treacherous, after all. You wouldn't imagine what's in these woods."

He laughed at that. "I've never seen a woman hunt in my life. What are you really doing on the roads?"

Amaris seriously doubted his assertion. Women were nearly as likely to be conscripted as mercenaries as men across Gyrradin. Not a speck of the goddess's lighted kingdom was spared from the need for battle-ready warriors. Even conservative farmer's wives knew how to snare a hare and bring down a deer. Wielding a weapon was both a part of country life and a reality of the continent's violence, regardless of gender. It was certainly easier to imagine women as helpless damsels if one needed to narrow their worldview into binaries, but it wouldn't serve him well on the road to underestimate opponents for their gender.

Amaris enjoyed the fire's comforting glow as it heated her thighs, her buttocks, her shoulder blades, but she knew she'd be better off if she wanted to find a way to prevent the cold from biting her so deeply again. An idea warmed her nearly as brightly as the fire in its hearth.

"I'll tell you what," Amaris began, eyeing the man. "I'm cold, and you're rude. I'd like to relieve you of your cloak."

The mercenary laughed with his companions at that, but Amaris's face remained sincere with her challenge. From across the room, the bartender called to her to indicate that her sack was filled with foodstuffs, but she merely gave a curt, smiling nod in acknowledgment. He left the tavern folk to their discussion, tucked the healing tonic into his pocket, and resumed cleaning glasses with his rag.

"I mean it," Amaris pressed. "I will fight you for your cloak. If I win the fight, you hand it over. What do you say?"

"Three against one? We'll have you in a second, girl."

"Amaris," she corrected. "And it's one against one for the cloak. If I take all three of you, you help me beat the ag'imni residing just outside town."

Twenty-Five

AMARIS HAD KICKED MANY ASSES AND SETTLED MANY scores in her time, but this had to be among the most satisfying. Not only had been the pleasantly buzzed men been good sports about their thorough and humiliating defeat, but she now possessed a new cloak and the wounded egos of a band of three too proud to back down from the challenge to face the demon in the woods.

Following their somewhat humiliating, though mostly amicable defeat, the mercenaries settled their tab with the innkeeper and followed Amaris beyond the comforting walls of the inn as she led them through the forest. The crescent moon provided little light even in the open clearing and absolutely none in the heavy-hanging limbs of the canopy once they left the safety of the town for the thick pine trees. While Amaris was never foolish enough to light a fire at night, these mercenaries had no such rule. They soaked a rag in oil and set a torch ablaze as she led them through the trees. Her body was warm with the comfort of the woolen cloak she'd won, and her pockets were heavy with the weight of the goods she carried. With the men carrying her intended weapons directly to her camp for her, she decided she'd allow them their woefully unwise torch. It wasn't worth arguing the point.

They had been walking for nearly twenty minutes before she started speaking a bit too loudly for the men's comfort.

"We're close. I was right around here when I saw the ag'imni," she explained.

One hushed her, but she continued pressing forward in both volume and spirit. Amaris felt their tangible tension over her shoulder. Gone was the merriment of the fight. The joy and escapism that alcohol brought had evaporated from their bellies. Nothing was more sobering than picking through the woods with eyes screwed against the dark for a demon. The men may have thought her story foolish when hearing it in the warmth of the tavern, but after learning of her exceeding capabilities, they did not underestimate her ability to spy a demon against the dark of the night. Everyone was rigid against the smallest sound in the crushing dark of the pine forest.

"He was asleep when I saw him, and I didn't have any weaponry. I'm sure he slumbers still," she responded, feigning reassurance.

The bearded leader placed a hand on her shoulder, urging her to be quiet.

She nodded as if realizing for the first time that she was perhaps being too loud. "You're right. We don't want it to hear us," she said without adjusting her volume.

The flicker of their torch illuminated not only their displeasure but their genuine fear as Amaris's words drew attention to their approaching party in the thick woods. Every rabbit, deer, wolf, and demon would undoubtedly hear her chatter, and they'd be little more than sitting ducks. There was nothing to conceal them. The canopy of the conifers allowed for no growth, no bushes, and no bramble. Sunlight did not reach this forest floor even in the warmest light of day. There was naught but the large circle of torchlight reaching as far as it could past the rigid trunks of sappy trees until its luminous sphere gave way to the gloom of the woods around them. The pine trees cast long, ominous shadows wherever the torch failed to reach.

"I'm pretty sure it was just ahead in this glen," she said in a whisper meant only for the stage. Her voice carried too far. The men's shoulders tensed, eyes widening as they begged with silent desperation for her to be quiet. "As soon as we crest this next hill, we'll see him."

"Girl!" one of the mercenaries hissed, his terror betraying him.

"Amaris," she corrected.

They slowed to nearly a crawl as the forest floor tilted upward. Their feet slipped every few steps against the slick, fallen pine needles as they ascended. A mercenary smothered the torchlight before they reached the top of the hill so as not to give them away. She beckoned them forward as their eyes struggled to adjust to the sudden dark. The crescent moon was worthless in a forest so dense. There was no starlight, no break in the trees, no differentiation between one spot of black and its counterparts. She gestured downward to where a small clearing had opened up at the bottom of the hill.

"The demon was here? You're sure of it?"

Slightly too loud, she responded, "I was walking just here on this hill when I saw it down there. Keep looking. It has to be around here somewhere."

The men were on edge as the knelt on hands and knees to peer into the clearing. If she didn't know better, she thought their weapons may be rattling slightly with the sound of their tremors. She fought from rolling her eyes at the bravado they'd attempted to establish in the bar. If a small girl of eighteen could pick her way through the woods, then surely, they could accompany her. Pride was one's own worst enemy in that way. Even still, they were rigid with apprehension.

The men could see nothing in the clearing below. A stump may have been a demon, but no—further examination revealed that it was only a broken branch. Another tree could have been the shape of a man, but it was merely the blackened, charcoal husk of a fallen pine that had most probably been twisted and hollowed by a bolt of lightning. A boulder may have been a beast of the night, but as the rock did not move, they tore their eyes from the shape and continued scanning for the ag'imni.

She heard a flap, a flutter, and the snap of a branch the moment before it happened. A loud crack broke the silence as a sound like a boulder hitting the earth cut through the air just behind them.

Gadriel had dropped from the sky, slamming into the ground with a flare of his wings. He shot her an annoyed look, and she fought the urge to grin as the men scrambled. The blood drained from their faces in an instant. They kicked up a cloud of pine needles in their haste to get to their feet. The smell of piss mingled with that of the pines around them as one of the mercenaries wet himself. A strangled cry of unbridled fear tore its way from the throat of one of the others.

"Drop your weapons!" Amaris commanded, looking at them with widened eyes. Her flex of persuasion seemed like nothing more than a harried plea for them to escape.

The swords clattered from the trembling hands of the mercenaries.

"Run! Save yourselves!" she cried, moving as if she might run with them. Scrambling on all fours, hands and knees scraping and pierced by the fallen needles, the three tore through the forest with the rabid speed and strength that was only offered to cornered animals with a desperate need for survival. The sounds of clanging and a distinct thump as one man hit a tree, fell to the ground, and scuttled to his feet again rang through the forest. She giggled to herself as their footsteps padded into the distance.

Gadriel glared at her after the men had left. "That was your plan?"

She shrugged, failing to conceal her impish smile. "I got us weapons, didn't I?"

He looked like he might kill her himself. By now, the mercenaries had run far enough into the forest that she could no longer hear the iron sounds of armor or the choked cries of the terrified. The forest was nearly quiet again. She dipped to gather the swords they'd relinquished. Gadriel grabbed one, face still set to ensure that she knew he did not agree with her methods.

"If you could order them to hand over their weapons, why the theatrics?"

She feigned innocence, bringing a hand to her breast. "Me? Theatrics?"

His voice practically dripped with his disapproval. "That was cruel."

"Hey, I won these things fair and square. Besides, swords are heavy, and they were rude to me in the bar. This way, they carried them to us. Work smarter, not harder."

"So you're both a brat *and* lazy."

"Not a brat. A witchling, remember?"

"They were rude to you?" His voice dropped a bit. "What did they say to you?"

"They didn't hurt me. Haven't you seen me fight a dragon? I'm basically untouchable. They acted boorish and deserved what they got."

"You're right." He raised a scrutinizing brow. "Sometimes people need to be disciplined. Especially those who need a lesson in humility."

She crossed her arms. "I don't like your tone when you say that."

"You'd benefit from a firm hand."

She couldn't keep the shock that cast her brows into her hairline. "What's that, General?"

His eyes twinkled a bit at her use of the formal title. "See? How hard would it be to show a little respect?"

"Unbearable."

"Sure." He smiled. "You tell yourself that."

"What are you implying?"

261

Gadriel's wicked grin had scarcely registered when a new sound curled through the forest, cutting their conversation short. They'd relaxed with their victory, enjoying the disarming cat-and-mouse chatter of a disapproving general with a disobedient subject, when a malevolent sound silenced them.

The world changed in an instant.

It chilled Amaris's blood, freezing her to the ground like ice over oil.

She'd done exactly what the mercenaries had feared. This was why you didn't hoist torches at night. This was why you were meant to keep your voice low, not scream, to disappear amidst the shadows. All their noise had drawn the attention of something that no one in the goddess's lighted kingdom ever wanted to encounter.

The sound was unlike anything she'd ever heard before, utterly terrible as it pierced the night. There was a smoke-like crawl to the noise as it slithered across the darkened forest floor and wrapped around her ears, dripping into her soul. They remained tense, frozen, each half bent inward as they clutched their stolen weapons. The sound continued to writhe through the woods, working its way over their feet, twisting up their legs, slinking around them until they could understand what it said.

A single word. A name. The cold, cruel, terrifying sound of *her* name.

"Amarisss," hissed the voice.

She stopped breathing. The dense wood was too dark for her to see much, but she could tell Gadriel still hadn't moved so much as a muscle. How long had it been since she'd taken a breath? Her legs were wooden. Her blood ran cold. Any warmth she'd gained from the inn leached from her body as cold dread replaced it.

Gadriel took three silent steps sideways toward the clearing, extending his hand to beckon Amaris to follow. The crescent moon offered little light, but perhaps if they could get behind the tree coverage of the forest, they'd have a chance at whatever illumination the dull sliver of moon might offer them. The sound was as slick as grease as it slid in the air around her. The thing was speaking.

She couldn't stay exposed. She had to do something.

She looked at Gadriel again, seeing his outstretched hand.

Amaris mimicked his movements, picking her footing carefully. She mirrored him as she moved one foot after the other, slowly relocating herself from the crest of the hill to the opening below. Her heart flitted arrhythmically as it forgot how to properly push blood in and out of her veins. It stuttered and skipped each time the oily sound of the voice snaked through the forest.

Amaris had no idea what was coming, but it knew her. It called her by name.

She fought the urge to run. Running would expose her. She didn't know what she was facing. She needed to see her enemy in order to know how to fight it. Everything within her begged her to turn, to sprint, to put as much space between herself and the voice as possible.

She resisted.

Amaris trained her wide eyes on Gadriel. His face was not fixed in a posture of fear but set with the stoicism of someone who understood exactly what they faced. He knew. She continued her silent, sidelong steps as she moved over the hill and toward the clearing. One of her shoes caught on a particularly loose patch of pine needles, and she felt her foot slip slightly, the sound causing her to jolt. Despite her noise, the creature did not seem to be advancing. It was everywhere and nowhere. If Gadriel told her to run, she would run. Goddess, she wanted to run. She continued to stare at him, waiting for a sign, waiting for a signal. They continued their crouched movements toward the glen, each of them tightly clinging to a sword that had been left by a mercenary.

She heard her name again, the *s* stretched into something serpentine. What horrible creature could know and speak her name? She'd said it too many times in the town and in

263

the woods to the mercenaries who'd accompanied her. She'd practically been shouting her true name into the darkness.

Amaris tried to clear her panicked thoughts. She knew beasts. She had studied demons. Still, her mind went blank. She had no memory of her lessons or tomes. All she could think about was picking her steps and pushing breath in and out of her lungs. Her memory flashed to the fear casters that the Master of Magics had mentioned. Her mind paged through the bestiary that had sat on the shelf in Uaimh Reev. What among the demons could speak? She shoved the thoughts down time and time again, focusing on breathing. She needed to relax. Her life depended on it. If she was caught distracted, it may just be the death of her.

Gadriel extended his hand again, urging her closer. She was only a few steps away from him in the gloom's nearly indistinguishable depths of shadow. She took one step, then another toward him.

A sound like the compression of air thudded from somewhere behind her. Before she knew what was happening, Gadriel crashed into her, wings and arms and chest and the hard wood of a tree trunk slamming into her from front and back. The noise had reached her ears before the force of his hard body pushed against her own. He shoved her torso into the twisted hollow of a lightning-struck tree, crushing her tightly into the dark space as he all but smothered her. Her back cracked into the charcoal of the tree trunk while the shelter of his black wings completed the trunk, tucking them into its crevice. She had no room to move. She tried to wriggle against him, but he pinned her more tightly to stifle her movements. The smallest hiss escaped his lips to shush her, and for once, she obeyed. For all she knew, this sorry hiding spot was the difference between life and death.

Another sound like the cracking of early-winter ice over a fragile lake, the sweep of winter air, and the slithering of serpents swept over them. Gadriel drove himself into the log more tightly, flattening his chest against hers. She hadn't even realized there was any room left between them until this final shove. Every curve of his body, every muscle, every dip of his stomach, his hip bones, his chest, even the space between his legs forced her as flatly into the trunk of the tree as he could. His size pressed down on her small frame. The black shadow of his dark wings shielded them from whatever was approaching. The snakelike hiss of her name filled her ears again. Gooseflesh budded across her arms and the back of her neck. She could feel Gadriel's hot breath on her as she stayed pressed beneath him. Adrenaline and confusion had her heart thudding against its ribbed cage, pressing against him in rapid flutter.

"Gad—"

"Shh." He swallowed the sound, chin tilted in alertness from where she remained tucked against him. She could feel both of his hands. One held the broad side of a sword flat against her. Its metal would have been cold had she not been wrapped in her newly acquired cloak. His free hand pinned her body as he used his full size to force her into the tree's trunk, stilling any movement. He pushed in more closely, forcing whatever remaining air she'd been able to keep in her lungs from her chest. There was scarcely a hair's breadth between them. His lips moved against her ears as he urged the information into a hushed whisper.

"It's an ag'imni."

The knowledge stole whatever reserves of air she'd maintained. Light-headedness claimed her. Amaris had known the Raascot men for so long that she'd begun to think of ag'imni as a fiction. They were merely a name invented by southerners for the dark fae they saw on their borders. While Farehold's citizens had seen ag'imni any time they'd encountered a northerner by happenstance, Amaris had never truly lain eyes on the gargoyle terror. She had never seen the too-long arms, the outstretched talons, the jagged, blackened teeth, the sunken, gaping holes in the humanoid faces of the demons that others had witnessed. She had only encountered the dark fae, lovely and intelligent, never the shadows and horns and membranes of a true demon.

Ag'imni weren't real. She had convinced herself of this simple falsehood. As far as Amaris was concerned, these demons were folklore. They were a curse, an illusion, a nightmare, a misunderstanding. They were the immortal fair folk of Raascot who'd had the misfortune of crossing the border. It couldn't be more than a title prescribed to those who hailed from the northern kingdom and suffered under a perception curse. Real ag'imni—true demons—didn't exist. Not like this.

She was suddenly unable to catch a single breath as confusion and fear pushed whatever remained in her lungs. She was trapped. She needed to get out. She tried to buckle against him to free herself, but Gadriel forced her into stillness. She jolted with more ferocity, and he brought his forearm to her throat, thighs to her legs with immobilizing resolve. His forearm pressed up in a way that forced her to her tiptoes. It was all she could do to stay on the ground, chin shoved upward, head against the trunk of the tree as she struggled for air.

It was effective.

His voice was so quiet, it could only be heard as his lips brushed her ears. "If we're going to make it out of this, you're going to have to listen to me. Nod if you understand."

He was neither her friend nor her traveling companion. He was a general focused on obedience and survival. This was war. She attempted to swallow.

She bobbed her head slightly against the pressure of his forearm. "This is a one-way conversation, Amaris. There is no room for power trips." He never used her proper name unless things were terribly serious. His words were scarcely more than wind over the fallen pine needles as his voice remained so low, so close against her ear that only she could hear. "I know you're strong. I know you can fight. But what I need from you now is to do as I say."

The panic flitted in her chest like a caged bird unable to perch.

She didn't know what to do, but he did. Gadriel knew.

She wanted to nod but struggled to find air. She couldn't breathe. If he didn't provide her with oxygen soon, she'd panic all over again. There wasn't enough space. She wiggled her body, nearly releasing a groan in protest. She knew he was pressing into her a defensive, protective stance. His wings sheltered them. She dug within herself to find a sense of relief, but none came.

"Breathe," he said in her ear. His words were softer and so much more comforting than she understood. "Relax and breathe."

"I can't—" she choked through tearful suffocation.

"Breathe," he repeated against her ear, lowering his forearm so that she was flat on her feet once more. The relief was instant. Perhaps it had been intentional. Maybe he'd given her something fixable to dread so that once the pressing threat of his arm on her throat had passed, she could feel a stilling, steadying power that accompanied her newfound calm.

Over his shoulder, beyond his wings, another sound like claws against stone rippled through the forest. The sound was getting close. The creature hissed her name.

"It knows my name," was the first thing she said. She regained control of her breathing, but her muscles were still tight with fear. The demon was speaking directly to her as it moved through the darkness. The charcoal of the burned tree trunk bit into her back, and Gadriel's wings blocked out all hope for light. He was too close. His body was too hot. She felt her ears ring with the high sound of bells. She attempted to swallow again and again.

His voice held no fear. "You know ag'imni, reever."

He never called her Amaris, and he never called her a reever. This was a specific summons to remember her training. She closed her eyes as his mouth moved against the skin of her ear and cheek.

"You know that they lie. They're agents of fear. Focus.

267

We're going to make it out of this. When I say so, we're going to split the glen like we did with the beseul. Keep as much distance between you and the creature as possible, but never turn your back to it. When I come for you, be ready to grab me. Nod if you understand."

She did her best to dip her head as she had before. The beseul had been a challenging battle, but it hadn't scared her more than any worthy opponent. She knew it might eat her, she knew she might fall to its terror, but she had been prepared. Reevers knew that beseuls were afraid of sunlight and that their heads could be severed. She challenged her memory for what she knew of true demons. She felt as though she'd shaken her knowledge of them from her head once she'd met the dark fae. They were the familiars of the ag'drurath; they knew no death. The terror that gripped her now was unlike anything she'd ever felt. But the question rang through her: How did the monster know her name?

She understood the sound of compressed air now. The creature was flapping its wings as it circled them. The true, batlike wings of an ag'imni—not the angelic, feathered wings of her Raascot fae. The demon closed in on them. She struggled to picture how they must look in the darkness, begging Gadriel's wings to be enough to conceal them against the hollowed tree trunk.

"Come out, Amarisss."

"It knows my name," she whispered to him again, choking on her fear.

His nod was almost imperceptible. Surely, he could hear everything the creature uttered.

The ag'imni's greasy voice wove through the trees as it sought them out. It continued to speak, not caring whether its eyes found them where they hid. With a bloodcurdling vitriol, it said, "The general who holds you now would sooner destroy you than save you, reever." It stretched the final word, elongating her title with its smokelike voice.

She tensed, but Gadriel did not move from where he had

pressed her into the tree. He remained impassive against its assertions.

The demon continued circling. "He knows what you are." Once again, its final word was like hot tar, slowly dripping, extending the single assertion to expand and fill the glen.

She wanted to ask him what it was saying, what it meant, but now was not the time for conversation.

"Are you ready?" Gadriel asked her, his voice low. They could hear the beating wings of the creature tighten as the demon descended.

"What do I do?" She didn't mean to sound so strangled. Now that the time to run had come, air left her once more.

"Once we leave this tree, don't open your mouth. Do you understand?"

She shook her head in wan agreement, sealing her lips, unwilling to let the misty tendrils emanating from the creature slither down her throat.

"No matter what it says, keep your mouth closed."

"How can we win?" She parted her lips long enough to ask the question.

He shook his head, his hair against her face. His heat overwhelmed her, but she trusted him. He'd lived more lifetimes than she could number, and he wouldn't let them die now. "We don't. We distract it, and we escape."

She attempted one final swallow.

"Are you ready?"

She nodded.

"Keep your mouth closed," he emphasized.

Gadriel shouted for them to go as he sprang backward. They jumped into action, releasing themselves from the hold of the hollowed tree. Amaris took a ragged breath through her nose, inhaling the rotten scent of sulfur and spoiled meat. She ran to position herself opposite Gadriel.

The ag'imni seemed delighted. It beat its wings downward, slowing its descent to come level with the ground. Her jaw nearly dropped at the sight. Nausea roiled through her, but she forced her mouth to stay shut. These were not the strong, feathered wings of the dark fae. These were the pocked, spiderweb wings of the undead. This was not the face of a person but the unhinged slick of carrion, decay, and spoiled blood. This was every dripping nightmare, every terror that spilled over from one's sleeping mind into a horrible, twisted consciousness. This was a demon.

Its lips pulled back in what might have been a mammalian smile. Its wings continued to beat, not fully allowing it to plant its feet on the ground. The demon did not seem interested in Gadriel as its obsidian eyes fixed on Amaris.

"Amarisss," it hissed. "I wondered when we'd meet."

She held her stolen weapon in front guard, glad for the mercenary's blade. She adjusted her grip on the hilt of the sword, refusing to look away from the monster. A memory of the white, membranous webs knitting the ag'drurath's limbs together with every slice assaulted her. This was not a beast that would be felled by her blade.

Very little moonlight filtered through the dense pine canopy to illuminate the beast's silhouette. Its wet skin seemed to peel away from the very bones beneath. She continued to pull breath stained with rotten eggs and decay through her nostrils, refusing to open her mouth. She didn't understand the instruction but wasn't ready to take risks.

She recognized the nearly human emotion on the ag'imni's face.

The demon glinted with something like delight. Somehow its eyes were too sunken, too black, and too large all at once. Its mouth was soaked with the viscosity of whatever black moisture dripped from its slackened lips. Its thin arms with their wicked claws seemed to be the length of its entire torso and legs combined, too long for this world. This was not the senseless, drooling pursuit of a beseul. This was the calculating, intelligent examination of a hell-born predator.

The ag'imni flapped again, moving slightly to one side as it eyed her. "The shadows have spoken of you for yearsss.

Your whispers fill the continent, moon chiiild. Do you knooow what you arrrre?" The monster tasted each sadistic word. Its oil-slick hisses sparkled with its own dark pleasure. It continued to prolong its sentences in an ominous threat. Its claws seemed to flex as it continued to flap its spider-web wings, their many holes paying no mind to the air that carried it.

It moved casually around the glen with only a few beats of its wings, moving deftly to the side as it eyed her. It continued its hellish glimmer of unholy joy as it spoke. Her eyes darted to Gadriel, waiting for a signal, for a sign to move, to run, *anything*.

"Has the general told you that he knowsss how you will die? Or is this one of the many secrets he keepsss?" Black teeth glinted in the scant moonlight.

Amaris held her sword in an unflinching show of strength. She didn't know its trick, whether it was baiting her to respond or just open her mouth for its smoke.

It flitted to the other side of the glen, circling them. What was Gadriel doing? She couldn't see him from where he stood on the opposite side of the clearing. He had not said they were going to attack the creature, merely that they were going to escape. If the ag'imni was anything like the ag'dru-rath, it too would have fibrous white tissue that knit together its wounds and regenerated its limbs. She wanted to scan the glen for Gadriel, but she didn't dare take her eyes from the demon. Her ears rang. She wasn't getting enough air. She wasn't breathing enough. She was going to pass out. Why was it so hard to breathe?

She saw him the moment he spoke.

"Speak to her again, ag'imni, and lose your head." Gadriel's voice was unwavering behind the monster.

Amaris was taken aback. Hadn't her lone instruction been to keep her mouth shut?

The demon flicked its neck with serpentine speed. It turned to address the Raascot fae. "One more word and she'll learn your game, generaaal." The demon gleamed with its wet glee, taking satisfaction from every word.

That was all he needed.

Gadriel dove for the ag'imni and it lunged in response, screeching the sounds of snapping bones and whetstones as it struck. The demon reached for Gadriel, but his strike had been an intentional distraction. He had lunged for the left, and as soon as he saw the creature dive to intercept him, he rolled for the right. With two powerful beats of his wings, he had Amaris in his arms. She hadn't comprehended the time or space of their escape from the glen before they were moving. They climbed higher, higher, and higher with the serpentine movements of the monster closing in. They crashed through the trees, pushing past the pines and exploding from the canopy. Pine branches and thorny boughs slapped her in the face, reminding her far too much of how they'd fallen through the air together and hit the ground, motionless and bloodied.

No, this was different.

Gadriel had his wings. He had the advantage. They were not falling; they were flying.

The demon was on their heels, but Gadriel dove for the forest again, plummeting through the canopy toward the forest floor.

Amaris squeezed her eyes tightly and tucked her head against Gadriel's chest as they flew into the top row of branches, prepared to crash. She buried her face against him the moment she realized they were going to dive for the ground.

"We're okay!" he promised through gritted teeth.

Before he fully committed to their descent, they were aloft once more. The demon continued its downward plummet, careening toward the pine-carpeted forest floor. They shot eastward, Gadriel's powerful wings beating with every drop of his strength to where daylight's first moments began to purple into twilight.

The ag'imni had recovered from the evasive maneuver and emerged from the canopy, but Gadriel was climbing. Higher, higher, and higher once more. She could have sworn a sparkly, snow-like frost clung to his wings. The stars were so bright, so piercing in the sharp, clear, cloudless air. He soared upward as if trying to touch the crescent moon until Amaris's ears rang and her toes felt frostbitten. A warming sensation filled her, convincing her that her brain had begun to die with her cells as the cold claimed her. There wasn't enough oxygen to compensate for whatever death of nerves and tissue battled the chill. She couldn't catch her breath. The demon followed their ascent until Gadriel dove again. The sudden descent caused her ears to pop with painful force. She recognized this maneuver from the birds that chased each other through the sky.

"Gad!"

"Hold on!"

The punishing sound of his dark, angelic wings bit through the early morning light, painful against the red sting of her frostbitten ears. When the fae dove this time, he followed through in his descent beyond the canopy and nearly crashed into the bedrock of the earth. He pulled upright just in time to begin to dodge and weave through the trunks of mighty pines in what would have surely been a plunging death for anyone else attempting the maneuver, particularly while carrying the weight of an extra body. His arms did not waver as they held her, clutching her as if his life depended on it.

Gadriel curved like a coiling arrow, threading through the forest with absolute speed and precision. Every time he pulled up, the ag'imni matched his upward motion. When he dropped, the ag'imni threw itself toward the earth. Gadriel continued his forceful braid through the trunks until he saw what he'd been searching for.

"There," was all he said.

She saw it. Her fingers tightened against his clothes, fabric and leather balled within the viselike grip of her fists as she prepared for their maneuver.

273

The earth dropped off below him where the hillside fell into a valley. Gadriel plunged into the canyon. Amaris felt her stomach catch in her throat as gravity worked its way against her body like a powerful, nauseating tide. The very moment he saw the demon plunge after them, Gadriel pulled up against the sheer, vertical climb of stone. He had been prepared to abort the move and roll away from the gorge. The ag'imni, which had committed too completely to the descent, crashed into the stone wall of the cliff on the valley's opposite side as soon as it attempted to ascend.

The moment they heard it hit the cliff, they knew they'd won.

Amaris choked out a laugh. The relief came out as a strangled thing, somewhere between a cry of joy and a sob. Gadriel's surprised, breathy chuckle told her that he was just as relieved as she was.

He'd succeeded—however temporarily. This was their only chance to put as much space between themselves and the monster as possible.

Gadriel did not look back. It would recover, and if they weren't long gone by the time it found them, it could very well continue its pursuit. When he cleared the canopy this time, he did not twist but continued the frenzied beat of his powerful wings as he chased the rising sun. Gadriel clutched Amaris to him, and she returned the embrace.

The flight was no longer one of terror but of determination.

Gadriel didn't dare slow until the first rays of daylight began to burst from where the horizon had hidden them in vibrant yellows and oranges. Though the dark fae generally sought to be well hidden by sunrise, he flew and flew and flew, and Amaris prayed he would be perceived as little more than a large bird against the pink gradient of the morning sky until the forest began to change shape below him. The pine trees grew fewer and farther between. The conifers dotted the landscape in clusters around what Amaris supposed might have been ponds, streams, or farmsteads. Twisted deciduous trees and their expansive canopies rose from hilltops and stood alone in fields.

Amaris dared to speak against the exhausting length of their escape. They'd been sprinting through the sky against death itself for what felt like hours. "Gad, we can't keep going. We have to hide."

"I'm looking," he growled into the wind that rushed around him.

There'd been no sign of the ag'imni since its impact against the gorge, but assumption was the downfall of the proud. No matter how successful his evasion maneuver had appeared, they needed to create certainty before they could safely land.

In the distance, a grayish, dilapidated building slumped into sight. While the base appeared to be stone, the structure had once been a wooden barn. It had long since collapsed against practical use, a few unloved trees dotting the space around it. There were no houses, towns, or farmsteads in sight. Gadriel angled for the crumbling barn, stopping their speed with a few powerful backward beats of his wings. He slowed them just in time for their feet to touch the ground. His wings continued their strong, successive beats as he stilled their fall before he released Amaris.

He'd probably meant to set her down gently, but she rolled from his grasp and tumbled to the mess of stone, moss, fallen timber, and filth on the floor as he collapsed. She twisted to a stop and pushed herself to her knees, covered in dust.

Her eyes widened as she saw Gadriel.

She'd known he'd given everything he had, but the man was truly spent. He did not land on his feet but collapsed to his knees with his exhaustion, fists pressed into the ground to keep him upright. The escape had taken more out of them than she realized, physically and mentally. He stared at the ground, hands and knees planted firmly on the earth. Golden rays of sunlight cut through the cracks of rotten wood just as they'd landed. The true ag'imni would not risk traveling during the day. They were safe.

Amaris tried to swallow but found her mouth had gone

completely dry. She grappled for her pockets and found where she had strapped the sack against herself, unleashing a waterskin from the bag. She drank greedily, beads of water dribbling down her chin. She gasped through her swallow and extended the water to Gadriel, who accepted it with an outstretched hand but did not look at her. He pushed himself off his remaining hand and stayed on his knees, drinking just as deeply from the waterskin. He returned it to her without making eye contact. Why was he avoiding her like this?

"Did we almost die?" Her question was little more than a rasp.

He nodded.

"Gad." She waited for him to look at her before she continued. The sweat that clung to his forehead beaded like little droplets of the sun itself. "The ag'imni... What was it talking about?"

His dark eyes held her piercing, lavender intensity then. The sunbeam struck from his brow to the middle of his nose, lighting his eyes as he waited just a few moments too long before he said, "What do you mean?"

Her heart stopped.

He could have said anything.

He could have told her anything.

He could have given her any excuse, and she would have swallowed it whole. Instead, his deflection told her more than any answer could have. The ag'imni had hurled accusation after accusation at the dark fae on Amaris's behalf. Gadriel had to know exactly what she had asked with her question. Ag'imni had an ability to deceive—this much she knew. And the best deceptions were parasites that sucked their blood out of a plump, singular truth. She didn't know how or why, but she was certain Gadriel was hiding something.

Twenty-Six

W RONG. NOX KNEW THIS WAS WRONG.
    This wasn't what it looked like. This wasn't what it smelled like. There was no smoke, no fire, no screaming or anger or pain. It was familiar, but nothing about it was accurate. She had been here before. The textures of the glossy floors and walls, the smells of the quaking aspens and waterfall, and the polished sheen of the marble all rang with familiarity. But she'd never seen it like this.

Was this a dream?

Nox scrambled within herself to remember what she knew to be true. She was Nox. She was twenty-one. She'd grown up in Farleigh. She no longer lived or worked at the Selkie. She was traveling with two reevers. Amaris was gone. She was asleep in Henares. She had taken a bite of an apple. An apple?

But this...

She had visited this place just yesterday.

It was the Temple of the All Mother, except when she'd seen it, everything had been on fire. The tree had been consumed with the grotesque twist of ash and embers, its bark up in flames. The white and gilded marble of the temple had been a kiln, every touch against its stone a painful, punishing scorch. There had been blood, bodies, and cinders. Smoke had been thicker than air. The sounds were those of men, metal, and pain. Any clouds above had been too thick to reveal a moon. All the light that colored her memory had been red and angry. It had been so, so hot.

As she looked around, everything was cool—not just the temperature but the energy, the moonlight, the gentle rubbing of the blue-green leaves in the glen beyond the temple.

She peered down on the room as if witnessing everything from a vantage point overhead. She was a bird, a phantom, a fly on the ceiling. The marble room was motionless and utterly peaceful, bathed in night-quiet shades of silver and shadow. The gilded flecks in the white stone caught not only the outside light of a vibrant full moon but the irides-cent luminescence of the tree growing from the center of the room. The tree—the focal point of the temple—seemed to be somehow both below her and all around her. It was healthy, twisted, ancient, and wise, with no sign of flame or char or ruin. The tree, as old as time itself, bore no fruit. A gentle breeze rustled its limbs, and its branches swished along with the wind as if moving to music. She felt the air as if it were brushing her hair along her cheek.

Then she saw someone.

She recognized the Tarkhany priestess before her immediately.

Nox had seen the holy woman just yesterday, and it had been one of the most horrible moments of her life. The fallen woman's tragic state was not one Nox would soon forget. Tonight, the temple's priestess wore a rich, blue gown that contrasted beautifully against the deep color of her skin. The dress appeared to have been soaked in the celestial glimmer of starlight. It shimmered with her every elegant movement, the fabrics flowing noiselessly behind her as if made from things as fine as wind and water and thought. The woman was one with the stars, twinkling like a living heavenly body. Silvery pins held back her rope-like braids, adding another gleam of light in the calm, palatial temple.

The priestess had been tending to the tree while she prayed. These were not conversational prayers but the beautiful, familiar melodies taught to the people who worshipped, sung in haunting, slow progression. Her song was quiet but strong, its minor chords rising and falling as the notes wound through the marble walls of the temple in acoustic a cappella. Its echoes reverberated so that her voice sounded from everywhere at once.

Nox was acutely aware of the fresh scent of life. It was like the smell of water and the subtle flowers that only opened for the moon. Everything about this temple hummed with beauty and holiness. She should have felt awe; she should have felt peace. But she didn't.

Somehow, she knew this was not a good dream.

Nox couldn't see a perceptible change. Nothing looked obviously wrong, and nothing smelled amiss. There were no noises, but her heart stuttered within her chest, missing beats in irregular patterns. Dread washed over her as it only can when a dream becomes a nightmare.

The priestess seemed to sense something too.

Her prayers stopped and the last notes of the song echoed off the walls. The priestess's soft touches left the tree as she wandered on bare feet toward the center of the temple, peering past the smooth pillars that held up the enormous marble structure. Nox tried to ask what was happening but found she could not speak. Instead, she watched as the priestess cocked her head, ears turned to listen. Nox's vantage point was not a fixed position, and her view seemed to gravitate overhead to better observe what the priestess saw, as if her eyes traveled down the limbs of the tree's mighty branches to where they remained overhanging.

Nox heard it then.

It was small, but it was there.

Whatever sound the holy woman had caught finally

reached Nox's ears. The noises were the rough sounds of rustling from a distance far outside the temple, as if a large animal were moving through the underbrush. These were not the angry, crashing noises of an advance but the careful sounds of gradual approach. Things were not breaking or cracking. This was not the sound of carriages and parties. Whatever was arriving was not coming upon the temple with ill intent, but Nox still hummed with nervous anticipation. The priestess walked to the edge of the temple and stood atop the stairs until she saw what she was looking for.

Nox strained her eyes, but she could get no closer. She couldn't move or talk or shift around the dream the way she had so many other times as she'd wandered lucidly through people, places, and ideas in her slumber. This was different.

Trouble clutched at her as she watched the woman's bare back in the moonlight just like the shine of her night-blue dress. She stood with statuesque stillness at the temple's entrance for a long while. The sounds continued to draw nearer, but they muted as the underbrush gave way to the clear spaces between the aspens that neared the glen. Only the heavy compression of approaching footsteps as they pressed into lush, mossy grass punctuated the quiet.

Finally, Nox saw a shape. Something appeared through her doorless window to the outside world. Though she remained fixed near the top of the temple, she could still see beyond the pillars, over the grass, and toward the aspens and willows that lined the sacred glen.

A light-colored horse stepped out from the aspens, its gray mane and tail shaking against the night. The horse bore the slouching silhouette of a rider.

Nox's sense of anxiety spiked as if her heart knew what was going to happen before her mind or eyes were made aware.

A body tumbled from the back of the mount, hitting the blue-green grass of the earth with a soft thump. The rider had been slumped awkwardly over the saddle, barely clinging to it, and was not able to dismount with any sort of grace afforded to the healthy.

Nox had a sense that it was not common for the holy woman to step foot on the grass. Filled with whatever sense of importance this night carried, something had pushed the Tarkhany woman forward. The priestess left the safety of her temple for the moss-soft grass of the glen. She held her gown up with two hands as she hurried across to the fallen figure. The body that had tumbled to the earth was too cloaked in shadow for Nox to discern much. The priestess stooped and began to help the rider toward the temple's steps. Every movement was a challenging struggle. Every step was labored and halted as odd shapes emerged from the glen.

This wasn't right. None of this was right.

The feeling of dread spread from Nox's stomach to her throat and into her fingertips. She didn't know what there was left to fear. The temple had already been sacked. She had seen the worst. She had lived through hell itself on these very grounds. What could possibly happen on this silver-mooned night in such a peaceful place?

The feeling persisted as if sickening, icy stones rested in her belly. She wanted to vomit, but her roiling stomach had no purchase in this disembodied dream. She was left with the weight of her nauseating dread without understanding why.

While the priestess had moved with the silence of a cat, the person accompanying her could barely stand on two feet. The stranger seemed too bulky, too angular to move properly. Something was terribly odd with whatever Nox was witnessing. She didn't know what she was seeing. She couldn't make sense of it.

The stranger's feet hit the marble steps with wet, slapping sounds. The footsteps sounded wrong. Everything looked off-kilter, as though a distorted mirror reflected silhouettes of the otherworldly.

Nox found herself floating closer to the priestess and the stranger as the dream carried her nearer to the shapes. If she could have spoken, she would have gasped. No sound came from her, as she did not exist.

It dawned on her slowly, then all at once.

This was not her dream.

She was in a memory.

The priestess escorted a badly wounded woman into the temple. She spoke in hurried tones as she brought the woman closer and closer to the tree. Its ethereal glow illuminated the woman as well as the odd bundle she carried. While her face was swollen and bloodied, Nox could see through the bruises, the puckered red areas, the dribble of blood that ran down from the woman's brow. Nox recognized the face immediately.

It wasn't someone she'd met, not really, but Nox knew her. She had seen this face nearly every day for seventeen years and would have been able to pick her out in a crowd of ten thousand. This woman's portrait had hung in Farleigh along with those of the other members of the royal family for her seventeen years at the orphanage. Nox was looking down at the battered face of Princess Daphne.

The portrait in Farleigh had shown the stunning, vibrant princess in her tiara with her parents, standing just in front of the late king and reigning Queen Moirai. While the young monarch had passed to be with the All Mother long before Nox was old enough to learn of such things, the portrait had remained a testament to Farleigh's fealty to the crown.

This was a very old memory.

That knowledge did not comfort her.

Princess Daphne stumbled across the white marble as she drew nearer and nearer to the tree. The priestess gripped her, not to stop her but to help her complete her journey. Everything about her movements was too stilted—too lumbering. It was not the nature of the dream but the difficulty of her steps, of her movements, of her breaths. As the princess collapsed to her knees, it became clear why she had seemed too angular and encumbered. Her arms released what she had been holding. A small child rolled to the ground, and Princess Daphne joined him, kneeling over him. She cried over the tiny, broken boy. She touched his hair, shushing him lovingly as if it might bring him back to life.

The priestess allowed an unhurried space for their grief, lowering herself to kneel beside Daphne, hand resting comfortingly on the princess's back as she mourned.

"He knows," the princess sobbed to everyone and no one. "He knows."

The priestess was every bit as calm as Daphne was shattered.

The priestess seemed to know her role in this moment in history. Daphne had come to have her words heard, and the priestess was ready. Her voice was serene but not pitiless. The woman's words were heavy with the importance of the moment. "The All Mother is ready to receive your prayers, Princess."

Daphne coughed, and a small gurgle of blood splashed from her lips.

She was wounded.

Nox hadn't understood the extent of the princess's injuries, as she'd been too focused on the crumpled body of the boy. Daphne tried to wipe the blood away with the back of her hand, but she merely smeared it further across her face. Princess Daphne had been so beautiful in the oil portrait that had hung in the orphanage. She'd had golden-brown hair that had hung to the small of her back, golden-brown eyes nearly the color of honey, pink cheeks full of life, and the kind of honest, wonderful smile that was only lit from within. There were elements of her features that resembled Moirai, like the color of their hair or the shape of their chins, but the ruling queen regent had never been the beauty that her daughter was. Between the swelling, the blood, and the bruises, it was hard to see any of those lovely features now.

The princess continued looking down at the small, lifeless boy.

"He knows it's not his son." Every sob prompted a new cough, more terrible than the one before. Small droplets of blood scattered to the marble floor. This was not the time for stories or elaboration or horrors. This was no moment to relive the terrors that had brought her here tonight. Instead, she could only choke out the lone reiteration, "He knows."

The priestess continued stroking the princess's back. "Tell the All Mother. I am here with you, and the goddess is here with you now."

Daphne attempted to nod, but it only led to another cough, another gurgle of blood. This time when she went to wipe it away, her hand did not lower to her side. She reached her crimson-stained fingers for the holy woman.

The princess was struggling to breathe. Between the blood and the strangled, labored inhalations, Nox felt with a sickening certainty this was the night Daphne died.

Their hands remained interlaced in silence until the broken, bloodied royal was ready.

There was a tradition of prayer familiar within the circle of true believers. The faithful knew what to do when prostrating before the All Mother. With a small nod, the two women raised their palms together. Princess Daphne tried to speak, but each word came out as if she were speaking from underwater. Whatever damage she had sustained was too great for her mortal body.

"It is too late for me," the princess said through her smothering injuries. Nox heard no trace of self-pity in the woman's voice. If she had wanted a healer or solutions to her wounds, Nox knew the princess would have gone to the city. This young royal had not come to the temple to seek a miraculous healing. She was not here for shelter or even for vengeance. She arrived consumed with a singular intent. Nox listened for whatever purpose lifted Princess Daphne's chin as she rallied what remained of her strength to beseech the goddess.

"I would ask that the All Mother—" Daphne coughed again. A hand hit the floor, scarcely keeping her up as blood dripped from her lips onto the ground. It took several long moments before she could continue her prayer. Her eyes were squeezed shut when she lifted her face toward the tree. "I would ask the All Mother to show mercy on this land and on my baby. I would beg the goddess not to let the hate that consumes my mother allow her to win her battle for our lands. I beg the goddess to turn this tide. Please, All Mother, send someone. Please, goddess, I beg you." Her voice broke against the jagged sob of her tears. "Please, send someone."

The priestess swayed in reverent fervor as her lips moved in intercession. Nox watched the two women pray before the Tree of Life, and a new wind rustled its branches. All around her, Yggdrasil's glow seemed to intensify, imperceptibly at first, then in a way that thrummed throughout the room. The temple pulsed with energy. Another bloodied cough gurgled from the princess's lips as she gagged against her internal wounds. Nox felt the humming energy as if it consumed her as well. The buzz of life and power drowned out the sounds of coughing, of pain, of languid death.

Daphne hadn't finished. She no longer had the strength to wipe the blood that pooled against her chin, allowing it to drip to the marble floor. Her head dropped, facing the roots of the tree as she could no longer keep herself upright. Her life was rapidly waning as she continued her prayer. "Please, All Mother, have mercy on this kingdom. Do not let her hate win. Do not let her curse consume us. Please send your grace across this land. Please protect our child, I beg you."

There was a change, an expansion, a throb of life and power as Yggdrasil answered.

The priestess's hands had begun to shine with the same light that had shone from the tree itself as the woman prayed above the broken body of the child. The glow was slowly consuming her body, setting all her features to reflect the light of the tree. The princess's fingers began to slip from the priestess's grip. Daphne coughed again, her mutilated face collapsing to the marble floor of the temple. Her prayers

285

became more forceful, growing in strength and volume. She was singing to the tree, but this time the tree appeared to be singing back.

A wave of light flooded the temple, consuming the tree, the holy woman, the princess, and the child. The light burned, not hot and red like the fire but intense and sharp and white like heaven's stars had filled the space, overwhelming every sense. It rang with a high, vibrant energy. It was everywhere. It was everything.

And then it was gone.

Darkness. Silence. Stillness.

Nox felt as if she were holding her breath, but she had no lungs with which to breathe.

When the light disappeared, the temple was empty. The bodies of both the living and the dead had left. There was no priestess, no princess, and no child. All that remained was the tree and its strange glow—now muted, nearly imperceptible once more. Nox had the sense of the passage of time, though she could not tell from the aspens beyond the temple's entrance if the seasons had changed. It may have been months; it may have been years. She felt colder somehow, though she did not exist and should have felt nothing.

Nox slowly began to realize whose memories she was seeing. She was not looking through the eyes of the priestess or that of the fallen princess. This was not the memory of any human or fae. These memories belonged to the tree. Everything she overheard in the temple was because she was able to see from the outstretched branches as they sprawled and knotted their way across the sacred palace, the Tree of Life's consciousness seeing and knowing everything that went on in its home.

A small sound drew Nox's attention.

She looked anxiously for its source, scanning the vacant space. Distress over her helplessness filled her as she waited for the priestess to go to the sound, but the holy woman was nowhere to be found. Nox's sense of worried urgency grew with each passing moment. It was too soft for her to distinguish anything about it, save that she needed it. It was valuable. It couldn't be ignored. Someone needed to attend to the disturbance. What was the noise? What was she hearing?

It was important. The sound was very, very important.

A tether pulled her toward it. She needed to see it, to go to it, to be with it.

She began to fight against the limitations of the tree, desperate to see what was making the noise. It called to her. It needed her. It demanded her presence. The sound, the very important sound…

At the steps of the temple, a figure moved. Nox did not see the gown nor the braided hair of the onyx woman that she had hoped to see. The dread that had consumed her while she looked down on Daphne filled her once more. It was stronger. It was more potent. This was a nightmare. The silhouette of a man was approaching the temple, his black shape encased within the dark of the night. Men were not allowed in the Temple of the All Mother. What was this man doing? Why would he dare come here?

She wanted to scream out, to tell him he was forbidden, to cry for him to leave, but she had no mouth. She had no air. She was bound and useless, a captive bystander to the nightmare.

The hooded figure did not enter. He stopped at the steps, drawn to its entrance by the small sound that had called to Nox. Its tether stretched as she felt herself drawn to it, wishing she could chase the man from the temple. She didn't want him here. She wanted the priestess. She wanted to go to the sound. Instead, a second, newer disturbance entered her awareness as rain began to fall. The soaking resonance of the deluge drowned out any other noises as the man stooped to pick up something at the entrance of the temple. He was taking whatever it was that had made the noise. He tucked it under his cloak and took off into the night.

This wasn't supposed to happen. The man wasn't supposed

to steal into the night with something that didn't belong to him. He was running with something intended for the tree. What had he stolen? What belonged to the tree? Nox opened her mouth to cry after him, but she made no sound. She called to the man, but her words were stolen by the wind. She was screaming for the man to come back. She needed to see what he had taken.› She was desperate for him to return it. She called for him again and again, but he did not hear. She yelled with everything in her, but the tree had no mouth.

No one could hear her screams.

Twenty–Seven

N ox!"
  "Come back!" she wailed. Her cries tore through the manor, clanging off the stones and filling the spaces until no shadow was safe. Her throat was raw with the brutal scrapes of glass shards over flesh as they clawed. "Come back! Come back!" She thrashed at her blankets as she tore after the man and his stolen bundle, reaching for the object, grasping to stop the man.

"This is a dream, Nox! Wake up! This is a dream!"

"Come back." Her voice was hoarse against the cry. It hurt. Everything hurt.

She trembled, every inch of her body racked with the force of her sobs. She tried to make sense of the pain, of the noise, of the darkness as she no longer saw the temple, the man, the rain. She was being held. She was not in the temple. She was not the tree. This was her room. People were in her room. The knowledge reached her one lifeline at a time but couldn't stop her free fall. She shook with the desperate need to see what the man had stolen. She knew it had been so vitally important. She needed him to return. As if under a compulsion, she let out one final choked sob, quieted as she cried into someone's shoulder. "Come back."

"This is a dream." The strong arms that held her rocked her slightly. She felt her body buckle with her hysteria. She released her grasp on the pillows and blankets and returned the hug. Her arms folded against his chest, her fingers against the bare, shirtless torso of whoever held her. He shushed her, stroking her hair while she cried. "You're safe, Nox. It was a dream."

She realized she had her face buried against the skin of Malik's bare shoulder. Her tears burned hot against his skin. She blinked her eyes open and drew in several ragged breaths, but he did not let go. Her face shifted through her several states of confusion as she absorbed her surroundings. She was a lucid dreamer—she did not have night terrors. This had never happened. She'd never cried out in her sleep. She'd never...

Nox tried to catch her breath. Her sobs slowed, each ragged, teary breath met with a small intake of air, a hiccup, and a blush of embarrassment as she saw that they were not alone. The room was dark against the late hour as she distinguished their shapes from the light of the hall. Ash remained at the door holding a candlestick as a makeshift weapon, ready to spring on whatever attacker had assaulted her in the night. The duke appeared to also be loitering in the hallway with the worried, barely intelligent eyes of a lovesick hound dog that heard his master cry and came running.

Nox swallowed, wiping at her eyes. She couldn't explain the shame she felt, save for the intense vulnerability as the men witnessed her tears.

She wondered how loud she'd been that everyone had sprinted into her room in the middle of the night. Perhaps if she were someone else, she would have felt self-conscious about how thin and sheer her thigh-length nightdress was amid these men. The duke had seen her entirely naked once while he'd still had his wits about him, and the reevers had spent their first day in the forest with her in a tattered silk gown, so she supposed this couldn't be much worse. No, it was not her clothes, not her body, nor the various state of the men's undress that sent her into an uncomfortable squirm.

The rawness, the honesty made her feel weak.

She'd never cried out for help in the night, not even as a child. She did not scream. Her armor was silence. Her protection was her stoicism, her control. Now she was a woman with no shield, no barrier, utterly defenseless against a dream. She was the one who did the holding. She was the pillar who'd protected Amaris at Farleigh, who comforted the new recruits at the Selkie, who was never rattled or shaken or bested by terror. When anything did become too big, she didn't cry but simply slipped into silence.

She blinked herself into a groggy state of lucidity. She slowed her breathing and wiped her tears. "I'm sorry," she whispered. Her words came out ragged. She had the sensation of being a child once more. Losing one's breath from the force of one's tears was something she'd seen in so many toddlers, as the orphans would often cry themselves out of a tantrum until there was no more air left in their lungs. Her breath hitched in a hiccup once more and she rubbed the last of the salty water from her face with the back of her hand.

Malik slowly relinquished his hold on her, moving back slightly to give her room to breathe. She hadn't realized how good the human touch had felt until he moved away. She didn't understand the urge, but she wanted him near her again. She wished he hadn't let go.

It had felt like an eternity, but only a few excruciatingly long moments had passed.

Realizing there was no imminent danger, Ash made an awkward gesture of acknowledgment to Nox and saw himself out of the room, shooing the duke away as he did so. The Duke of Henares needed his fingers pried from the wood of her doorframe, but eventually Ash succeeded. The door to her room clicked as he shut it behind them.

Malik stayed.

"I thought something terrible was happening," he admitted. She was suddenly very aware that he'd come running in only night shorts. He seemed to also become aware of his state of undress and hedged uncomfortably, fidgeting against the awareness. "Do you want to talk about it?"

She wiped the dried salt from her cheeks with the heels of her hands, sniffing as she did so. "It wasn't a dream."

Malik offered her a supportive, pitiful frown. His face told her that he didn't want to correct her, but the evidence was stacked against her. Perhaps now wasn't the time for logic or reason. If she needed to grieve, he was good enough to listen.

She sensed the implication of his silence and reiterated, "It wasn't a dream. It was a memory."

She understood something in that moment with profound clarity. Nox could count the number of people she'd loved and trusted on roughly two fingers, and Malik was one of them. It didn't matter if he'd seen her at her worst. She'd been insufferable in the rain, a smart-ass in the forest, and a killjoy to all their excitable plans to hack and slash. He'd met her in the dungeon when her heart had fractured into a million pieces at the sight of Amaris bound and gagged. Though she was embarrassed that she'd woken the estate with her screams, she didn't feel judged by the man who'd comforted her against the vulnerability of a nightmare. Some part of her knew that if she let him in, he would believe her.

And so she did. She told him everything.

She explained that during the sacking of the temple, the priestess's dying words had been for her to retrieve the apple. Everything had all happened so fast between helping the reevers out of the blistering oven to barely surviving the smoke inhalation that she had completely forgotten the fruit until she'd bathed and gotten ready for bed in Henares. She'd taken a bite before bed and fallen into the tree's memories.

Despite the dim candlelight in the room, she saw his reaction clearly. The blood drained from Malik's face.

"You ate from the Tree of Life? Without anyone knowing? Nox..." He shook his head. "We have no idea what kind of power that has! It could have been poison! Why wouldn't you have told one of us before doing it? Who knows what could have happened? The apple could have killed you! It could have turned you into the next tree for all we knew! Why would you eat it?"

She had wanted to interrupt him but allowed him to run through his lists of fears. Nox was out of salt. There were no more tears to cry. She still sniffed with the residual efforts of her sorrow, but she was empty. Her face remained red and puffy. Her throat ached, still painfully raw. Malik was right, of course. She honestly didn't know why she had done it. He had every reason to be mad, worried, or disappointed. It had been terribly irresponsible, and she probably would have been just as angry if she'd learned he'd been this reckless with his safety. Anything could have happened. She could have grown roots and buried herself in the earth of Henares, rupturing forth from the roof as a mighty, twisted oak. But she'd trusted her intuition. She had felt intrinsically that she was supposed to eat the fruit.

The fact remained, she hadn't died. She hadn't been poisoned or shape-shifted or sprouted branches to replace the now-lost Tree of Life. She'd lived a memory.

"What did you see?"

Nox looked away, not wanting to make him feel more immodest than he surely already felt. His shoulder glistened slightly where the evidence of her tears remained. "Malik, I'm embarrassed over waking you. Go back to bed. I can tell you about it in the morning."

He laughed and stood, but he made no move to leave. He merely created space to rest against the carved post of her bed. "My sense of fight or flight won't settle down for another hour at least. Why not humor me with a bedtime story?"

She smiled at the man, wishing once again that he hadn't

moved away. A similar thought tugged at her in the moment it took to recognize the emotion—the one that wanted him closer. It was the same thought she'd had over and over again, almost like a songbird had whistled its tune outside her window and she'd never been able to get the chirp out of her head. Here she was, thinking it again: he was so unlike anyone she'd met. He was sunshine and kindness and patience in human form. She believed him when he told her he was in no hurry to leave. She believed that he had no ulterior motive or agenda for being in her room at such a late hour.

He asked her to tell him, so she did. She described the marble, the moonlight, the temperature, the colors and textures and scents. She described the horse, the tumble to the ground, and the priestess who'd run to aid the stranger. She explained how she'd seen Princess Daphne at the Temple of the All Mother, beaten within an inch of her life. She told him about the lifeless child, the glowing light, and the passage of time. She told him about the man at the end and that he had stolen something terribly important from the temple.

Malik was frowning. "There's one thing I don't understand."

She laughed at that, tucking a stray bit of her hair that had muddled her vision behind her ears. "One thing? I was seeing the memories of a tree. There's plenty I don't understand."

He shook his head, gold-brown brows knit in a frown. "Well sure, that part is a mystery for another day, but there's something about the princess's prayer I don't understand."

Her sniffling had stopped. Nox was breathing normally again. She pulled her knees to her chest and hugged them to herself. Once again, she wished she was still being held. She wanted to feel safe. "Daphne was asking the goddess to intervene against her mother."

"No," he said, still dissatisfied. "It's not that. It's what she said about her child. Can you say that part to me again?"

Nox nodded. "There were a few things. She said, 'He knows it's not his son.' Do you think Princess Daphne had a lover?"

294

He considered this. "That would make sense. If her husband was violent and realized the boy was not his natural-born heir, that the boy was Daphne's lover's child, it may have driven him to whatever murders he committed. If he were a terrible man, and clearly, he was, this could have driven him violent or insane, but that isn't the part that's troubling me."

"The savage domestic murder of a wife and child doesn't trouble you?"

He gave her a tired look. It was exceptionally late and they were both too exhausted for games, witty though she was. "It's not that. I just don't understand why she would pray for the goddess to protect her child if her son were already dead."

"Maybe it was a prayer for the afterlife? Perhaps she was asking the goddess to grant her son safety as he goes to live with the All Mother?"

He twisted his mouth. "I'm not particularly religious, but I did go to church with my mother on each of the solstices. We were never intercessors for those who had already passed on. Were you?"

Nox shrugged. He no longer held her, but he remained close enough for her to rest her head against him. The contact made them both relax, and he draped his arm behind her, supporting her back as his hand pressed into the mattress. That part of her dream hadn't resonated with her as it had with him. She spoke into his shoulder once more. "The mill was a sham of a religious institution. I don't consider myself well versed in the church's teachings. But no, we didn't say prayers for the dead. If we had, I suppose all the orphans would have been praying for their parents in the afterlife. I suppose a more pious person would be a better resource than me for this sort of question. I wasn't really interested in religion, but now I'm wondering how much I've missed out on...like maybe I was the blind man and the dragon. Do you know that one?"

"Tell me."

"It's a proverb about everyone being correct and no one being correct at the same time. It's a bit about how everyone can be perfectly right and perfectly wrong. You have three men who've lost their sight, and they all stumble on a dragon. One touches its tail, and he feels its scales and cylindrical quality and announces that the dragon must be a snake. The second man happened to be at the dragon's leg, and as he feels its width and girth, he decides that the dragon must be a tree. The third man is at the dragon's mouth—"

"And he gets eaten?"

"Shush, I'm the one telling the tale. Anyway, he touches the horns and teeth of the dragon and believes the dragon is a stag."

"I don't think he's seen a stag."

"Well, he's blind."

"That explains why he doesn't know what a stag looks like."

She gave him a look. "I'm not finished. The point is, none of the men were wrong. It's a proverb on perspective. They aren't lying. They aren't unintelligent. They are using the information they're given and funneling it through everything they have available to understand it. Their knowledge is just incomplete. They can't understand what they lack, because there's no frame of reference for what's missing."

"Did any of them touch the wings?"

"Malik, no, that's not the story."

"Did they come together and discuss their information?"

"It's a proverb. They didn't…" She wound up her fists with frustration before she caught his look. He was trying to make her smile. It worked. "You're difficult."

"If you feel like a blind man touching a dragon, we can always get you more theological texts so you can study the All Mother. But maybe we do that in the morning? And in the meantime, we avoid eating magical fruit?"

She sighed, but her heart felt lighter. "Maybe I'll save religious studies for my second life. And luckily for us both, I'm not feeling particularly hungry."

He gave her a squeeze. Malik stood then and started for the door, the blanket still wrapped around him. "If you have any more bad dreams, you can come find me, you know?"

She nodded, but she wasn't sure what she was agreeing to. She would not come find him—or anyone—if she had a nightmare. She didn't want to bring others into her suffering. There was something on the tip of her tongue. She felt so close to an answer. If she dreamed again, it would be her cross to bear, not that of the reevers.

The apple sat on the bedside table precisely where she'd left it. It had not begun to brown or wilt the way she had suspected a normal fruit might. She wasn't sure if taking a second bite would offer her more memories, but she decided it was unwise to try again tonight. Besides, she'd told Malik she wouldn't, and she didn't feel like being a liar. Instead, she closed her eyes and tried to fall back asleep, but she couldn't stop thinking of the way Princess Daphne had looked with her once-lovely face so swollen and bruised.

The beautiful, angelic Princess Daphne and her accompanying royal parents had watched over the children of Farleigh from their gilded frame above the balcony for the first seventeen years of Nox's life. The oil painting that had hung in Farleigh had been saturated with vitality. The princess had been so lovely, so genteel. Her rosy cheeks and kind face had practically vibrated with her goodness and her joy for life. When Nox saw her in the memory of the temple, she hadn't looked anything like her painting. Nothing had remained of her gold-brown hair or her sparkling eyes.

Nox had known men and monsters, but to think of even someone as powerful and untouchable as the princess of Farehold subject to such monstrosities... Nox had seen the evidence. Daphne had brushed the small, lifeless child's hair from his face. She had hushed him with such love and comfort, though he'd long since passed. Nox thought of the woman in the village who had stroked her hair and shushed her after they'd fought the spider. She thought of Amaris and how she'd sat with her day after day following the whipping. She thought of Malik and how he'd held her as she cried. The world was terrible, but it had moments of beauty that could only be seen when contrasted against their pain. The same beauty of the sun illuminating the silver outlines of storm clouds showed the loveliness of splendor against the cruelties of pain.

Though she tried for hours, sleep would not find Nox again that night.

Twenty-Eight

NOX FOUND HERSELF IN A TERRIBLE IN-BETWEEN, CAUGHT in the miserable loop of sleeplessness and the inexplicable inability to get out of bed that insomniacs know all too well. Her rooms in Henares reminded her very much of the silks and ornate decorative objects at the Selkie. She hadn't shut the curtains before going to bed that night, and now the sun filtered through the window, changing the sky's colors from dusty pink with orange-lit clouds to the cheery, clean light of day. She remained beneath her sheets, staring at the wall and hugging a pillow between her knees, tucking it to her chest. She had to remind herself to blink every now and then to soothe her stinging eyes.

She heard the duke's house come to life in the early hours. She knew it would be in full swing before long, but still, she didn't feel like getting up. She didn't see the furniture and wallpaper and trinkets that belonged to her suite in Henares. The only things that danced in her vision were the memories that the tree had revealed to her and the swollen face of a dying princess.

Her door opened and Ash let himself in rather unceremoniously. He hadn't knocked, nor did he apologize for the interruption. He was a man of irreverence, which was something she appreciated about him. He appeared to be carrying a small tray of food.

"Guess who I had breakfast with?" he asked.

Nox finally sat up for the day and propped two pillows behind her back. Ash set the tray of food on the bed next to her. "I'm guessing you're going to tell me," she mused, picking at a strawberry.

"Why, your beloved, of course."

She suppressed the urge to stiffen as her mind shot self-consciously to how Malik had held her. She thought of how Ash had left them behind to give them privacy, allowing his shirtless friend to keep his arms around her. Had the reevers already shared such personal details? Would there be no privacy amongst them?

Ash went on. "The Duke of Henares is quite love drunk, you know. He can speak of nothing else. Did you know he's written poetry about your breasts?"

Nox blanched.

"Oh yes, everyone at the breakfast table was subjected to a very graphic bit of original literature where he rhymed nipples with—"

"Goddess, please stop."

Ash's eyes were positively sparkling. "See, I'd always fancied myself to be a good lay, but I've never had anyone offer me their home, write me poetry, send horses and armed guards to my aid at the drop of a hat, and take in my ragtag band of friends without asking questions before. You'll have to give me some pointers before I take my next maiden to bed."

Nox laughed him away, though her chuckle contained a bit of a sinister edge. "Believe me, you'd never be able to accomplish what I can after a night's tumble."

Ash feigned offense. "Do you really consider yourself peerless in such acts? Or are you referring to your witch powers?"

300

She shook her head, swallowing her food. "You'll never find the upper hand that I've found. Your problem is that we have sex for two vastly different reasons."

"Oh, do tell."

"Over breakfast? How indecent."

He shrugged, helping himself to one of the muffins that had been intended for her.

She nibbled at another strawberry as she leveled her gaze. "Sex is for one of two things. You either have sex for passion or for power. As long as you're making love to maidens with goodness in your heart, you will never find the leverage that I hold."

She knew from the surprised lift of his brows that this had been far more telling than anything he'd expected her to say. She wasn't sure why she'd said it. She continued to nibble at her food, picking at a few bites of everything without committing to any one pastry or fruit or meat altogether. Ash had alluded to being no saint, but the look on his face said this little riddle had given him a bit more to consider than he could sort through in one morning.

"I did come in with ulterior motives, so don't start expecting breakfast service."

She narrowed her eyes, though her humor remained. "What motives could you possibly have while talking about sex? Do you want me to try to kill you again?"

He chuckled. "I asked your duke for a favor between his limericks, and he was more than happy to oblige."

"Is he giving us a puppy?"

Ash clapped his hands together. "Are you going to stay in your nightdress all day, or do you want to see what I have for you?"

Nox frowned and pulled away from the tart she'd been nibbling.

"Oh no. This is much better than breakfast. Get dressed, raven. You're going to love it."

Ash left without a word more.

She put on a set of clothes that the personal attendants had laid. She descended the stairs and burst into the bright, clear day only to learn that she did, in fact, love what Ash had found for her.

Nox erupted with unspeakable glee as she eyed the gift. Her squeals were as loud and unbridled as her night terrors had been. She swept Ash into a hug so tight that he acted like a trapped cat in his attempt to claw his way from her affection. After freeing himself, it took him a moment to smooth out his clothes and realize he owed a few quick pats on the back in return.

He politely grimaced, regaining his composure as he said, "Come on. Are you just going to fuss, or do you want to learn how to use it?"

They stood on a long stretch of grass behind the duke's stables on what appeared to be an archery range. The sky was both crisper and clearer after the cleansing rain that had soaked the southern regions for days. Ash held the beautiful, varnished wooden handle of a shiny, silver axe. This weapon was no farmer's wood-chopping hatchet but the threatening cleaver of something forged for battle. She reached both of her hands out in front of her and clasped them together like an eager child on winter solstice.

Ash beamed. "You got really lucky with the spider. If you want a chance at landing a blow like that again, you're going to have to practice your aim. Since this weapon is quite a bit heavier than your farmer's axe, we're going to use two hands when we throw it. Come here."

Nox danced from foot to foot.

"Stand still."

"I'm excited!"

Ash put a firm hand against her back and urged her closer to the target, lining her up with her mark. He tried somewhat unsuccessfully to steady her bouncing. "Okay, now stack your hands one on top of the other and keep your thumbs lined up. You don't want to hold it too tightly, or else when you release it, you might struggle with its arc and send it right into the ground. Plant your feet. Good. Now when we release, we're not going to worry about flicking your wrists or think about the rotation. As you take a step, your axe is overhead— yes, good, like that—and you're going to release as you step forward. Are you ready?"

Nox eyed her target. She checked her hands and kept her left one on the bottom of the axe's handle, her right hand stacked just on top. Her thumbs were in a straight line. She practiced the motion of stepping and hoisting a few times before she was ready to release. With her eyes on the bull's-eye, Nox took a step forward and flung the axe from where she stood. It hit the edge of the target but did not bite into the wood. The weapon clanged against the wood and clattered to the ground.

Ash jogged up to where it had tumbled to the grass in front of the target and returned to her. She accepted it in her palms, her face twisted in a small frustration.

"That wasn't bad!" he said reassuringly.

She squinted against the sun while regarding him. She'd unintentionally convinced herself that she had an undiscovered, natural talent for axe throwing and was rather disappointed that the axe she now possessed hadn't been informed about her secret special skill.

"So in that one, you were forcing it forward with a strong throw, but you need to trust that the axe will have its own momentum. Don't thrust it with your own power. Just hoist it overhead, and as you step forward, release. Trust that the axe knows where it's going. Don't force it."

She looked at her weapon. "The axe knows?"

He nodded. "Axes are weighted specifically for this sort of gravitational advantage. The axe will do most of the work if you trust it. All the blade needs from you is for you to make eye contact with your target, take a step, and release. Your weapon will take it from there."

"Ash?"

"Yes?"

"Why are you doing this?"

He frowned at her.

"The axe, teaching me to throw it, helping me out... Is it because of Amaris?"

His frown deepened. "What about Amaris?"

"Oh." She shifted her weight with a bit more discomfort, adjusting her hold on the axe's handle. "Is it...is it something else?"

He seemed to realize her implication as if a bucket of water had been doused over his head. "Goddess, Nox, no! You're my friend! Holy hell, woman, I'm not sure what sort of friends you've had in the past, but I'm glad you have new ones now." He shuddered as if he needed to physically shake what he'd inferred. "Honestly, the way you look at the world is a whole box to unpack on its own, but maybe that's best saved for another day. Now, do you want to learn how to throw your axe, or should we continue with truly the bleakest outlook on the world I've ever heard?"

Her lips parted as she blinked rapidly. Ash was indelicate but correct. She hadn't had good friends. She'd never known people who didn't want something from her. The best-case scenario she'd been able to fathom was that he'd been kind to her because he knew that she and Amaris cared for each other. She had suspected they'd become friendly, but each new twist and turn of companionship was strange and utterly unexplored territory. Did she know how to just be friends with someone?

"I'm...sorry."

"No, goddess, *I'm* sorry at whatever sort of life led to... Never mind. Now's not the time. Anyway, don't be sorry. Just stack your hands. Come on. Plant your feet like I showed you. We've got this."

"We?"

He shrugged slightly. "You're not as alone as you think you are."

Nox planted her feet again, and once more, she practiced hoisting and stepping forward without letting go. She twisted her mouth in concentration, eyeing her target. She repeated the motion again and again without committing to the toss.

Ash watched her go through the motion a few times before stopping her. "I appreciate your thoroughness, but throwing an axe is not like swordplay, and it's not like archery. Swords can be disarmed, defended, parried, and used in a number of different ways. One needs to think through a number of complex steps and moves when they use a sword. Bows require a lot of strength, stillness, forethought, and breathing. We are not using either of those weapons at the moment. This little masterpiece needs you to *not* overthink it. These steps you're taking, the practices you're making are fine, but it's not the science that you're making it out to be. Just step, release, and trust."

Trust was not her strong suit.

She chewed on her bottom lip and looked at the weapon in her hands. The axe was truly a thing of beauty. Unlike the farmer's small, rusted hatchet, this was an invention meant for war. The haft was made of a single, solid cherry-brown piece of wood with runes etched into it. She didn't know what the runes said or who had written them, but if she had to guess, she assumed that whoever forged this blade believed in the old ways. The metal butt of the axe had another beautiful rune carved into its steel. The pommel had been cleverly wrapped for gripping and secured leather, but it was not the sloppy wrapping of somebody who chopped wood. No, this creation had never tasted fireplace wood; it was intended to eat flesh, muscle, and bone. The most beautiful element of the axe was how the blade curved into two hooks on each end, creating a dramatic scooping effect that nearly made it appear as though the blade were smiling. She ran her thumb lightly against the axe's edge and let out a small sound at the drop of blood it drew. This was truly a thing of beauty.

"You're mine," she said to it with grave appreciation.

305

Nox took a breath and forgot about Ash. She let go of the world around her and allowed her eyes to see only the target—except it was not a bull's-eye staring back at her but the snarling face of the she-spider. Nox took a step and released the handle at its apex. The axe flew through the air, embedding itself in the center of the target.

Her mind whirled with joy and gratitude and celebration. At long last, she was right. She had an amazing, secret, special skill. She was a natural. She had a spectacular gift for the axe. It was perfect and flawless and empowering! She was on top of the world.

Ash made an excited noise to her left, and off to her right, she turned to see the Duke of Henares practically dancing with delight while clapping his hands together as if he had never seen anything so spectacular in the goddess's lighted kingdom. A smiling Malik was sitting on the ground next to the duke and made an encouraging gesture with his thumb. She had been so focused on her beautiful weapon that she'd failed to realize she'd gained an audience.

Unfortunately, the axe reminded her on more than one occasion as she continued to practice that, *no*, despite the lies she wanted to tell herself, she had no inborn gift for the axe. Sometimes it ate earth and grass. Sometimes it clattered against the wood before flopping to the ground. Sometimes she threw it too wide, and then Ash would jog behind the target to fetch it while she burned with frustration. Nox ran the gamut of emotions, going from thinking she was an axe goddess to thinking the axe hated her to thinking it was an absolute fluke requiring no skill, only luck.

She hated cheery weather when she was frustrated. Frustration and irritation and sorrow demanded cloudy skies. The audacity of the sun to continue beaming happily down on them in the crisp, clean day was aggravating, but blaming the sun probably wouldn't help her get any better.

Ash was patient, her audience was supportive, and she was too proud to give up.

Trust. She had to line up her steps, relax, and trust.

The world slipped away as she focused on the single word, the thought, the meditation that stood between herself and success.

It worked.

Nox repeated the motion time and time again, each time landing its mark. She, of course, did the appropriate celebratory dances and squeals and thrusting her fist into the air the first few times, but as it became more replicable, she found her confidence. She trusted the axe, and the weapon did not fail her.

Nox threw the axe for nearly two hours until Ash made her stop so that she didn't get blisters. He taught her about whetstones for sharpening and how to properly clean and store her weapon. Nox gave a vaguely worded order for the duke to have his leather smith craft a holster so that she might strap the powerful object to herself, and the lordling set off with the utmost urgency to complete her request.

That night, the three ate their dinners together in the duke's dining room. The lordling continued to oversee the careful creation of Nox's leather holster and was blissfully absent from the meal. The servants bustled around, serving assorted roasted meats from tender lamb to salted fish, a variety of green and purple and orange vegetables, some fried, some steamed, some grilled, decadent pastries, and apple juice to accompany their dinner if they weren't in the mood for the fine, vintage wine, all on ornately gilded plates and cups. She could tell the reevers wanted to focus on their meals, but Nox couldn't stop talking about her axe.

"I just let it go! I just pretended I saw the spider, took a step, and trusted the axe! Just like Ash said!"

"I know. I was there."

"And did you see how it embedded itself? It would have killed the spider all over again!"

"Technically, I think I killed the spider," Ash amended.

"You're both wrong," Malik said through a mouthful of

food. "The spider is incapacitated, shredded, and buried, but demons don't really die."

"Does that make you feel good about yourself?" Ash chuckled at Malik.

"Yeah, maybe," Nox mumbled while chewing her meat pie, ignoring Malik entirely, "but I helped."

They promised her that tomorrow they'd work on a few short-range swings and techniques. She still had the small knife that Malik had given her at their first campfire, and though she had never used it, she kept it securely tucked against her everywhere she went. She knew exactly what grip and thrust she'd need to land a killing blow with the dagger.

"Axes aren't really made for close combat, so we'll only do a few swings. If your enemy gets close enough that you can't throw your axe, you'll need to switch to your knife. Still, it would be useful to practice."

Malik asked, "Have you considered naming it?"

Nox looked positively gleeful. "I can give my axe a name?"

The men nodded and said they had named their reevers' swords—the very weapons being held hostage somewhere in Castle Aubade—and that all good weapons had names.

She considered it for a moment but was relatively quick to answer. "What about Chandra?"

They both frowned.

Ash spoke first, asking, "Why would you choose that name?"

She shrugged. "It's from the Tarkhany dialect. I don't speak their language, but one of my clients left a book for me once at the Selkie. It was one of my favorites, so I wrote the whole thing down after he…" She stopped herself from informing the men that she had, in fact, murdered the teller of this tale. "Anyway, it was a beautiful little story where the hero needed to bring his lover the moon! He set out to grab it when it was full and chased it night after night, climbing the tallest mountains to fetch his prize. By the time he reached it, there was scarcely a sliver left to return to her. The axe's edge is so dramatically curved, and with those open spaces on either side, it looks like the smiling mouth of a crescent moon. The hero in the story had called his beloved Chandra after the very test she'd requested of him to prove his love. I thought it would be appropriate to name it as such."

"Because it's a crescent?" Malik clarified, looking from Nox to Ash.

Ash's frown deepened. "You're naming your axe 'moon'?"

Twenty-Nine

S HE'S RIGHT, YOU KNOW—MASTER FEHU, THAT IS. I AM relying on powers I discovered by accident." Waking nightmares had filled Amaris's mind over the days and nights following their escape.

Gadriel had not pushed her to talk to him beyond idle chatter, which had been uncharacteristic. This, of course, only deepened her wariness. Particularly in the wake of the demon's ominous threats, Amaris hadn't stopped thinking about what the Master of Magics had said. Powers could be unlocked if intentionally explored.

She knew so little of the fae or magic. Amaris wasn't thinking solely of herself as she eyed the unknown threat before her. Did she truly know the man with whom she traveled?

"Is that something you want? To see if you might have any underlying powers?" Gadriel sat on a log some distance away as he sliced up an apple, voice low as he spoke.

It wouldn't serve her if he knew she was harboring suspicion. So she said simply, "Doesn't it seem important? Aren't my powers something I should be able to knowingly access?"

He chewed on an apple slice as his eyes unfocused, looking

into a memory. "In Raascot, we go through pretty excruciating trials to get our powers to manifest. Those of us in the
military do, at least. I don't have too many civilian friends,
but not all make an effort to see what abilities they can access.
Plenty of fae live long, full lives without bothering."

They had slept well into the evening under a makeshift
shelter. She had been adjusting her sleep schedule to match
Gadriel's nocturnal hours, the challenging transition yielding little rest. The sun had proved an awfully cruel bedtime
companion. The pink of the late afternoon lit the man's
features. She eyed him groggily as he ate his fruit.

"Is sleep deprivation one of the trials? Because if so, we're
well on our way."

"Eat something," he said without looking up.

"I'm not hungry."

He threw an apple directly toward her face, and she
snatched it out of the air. "You're not good at taking no for
an answer."

"I'm excellent at taking no for an answer if the person
speaking to me is genuinely saying no. You, witchling, are
just obstinate for its own sake, which I'm sure everyone else
finds spectacularly charming. I'm not going to let you starve
yourself because you like being disagreeable."

She bit into the fruit and immediately regretted it. It gave
him too much satisfaction to see her do what she was told.
She wanted to slap the smirk off his face. The tart, sour rush
of apple was unpleasant, which solidified her irritation at
having listened to him.

The forest was warm with the last lights of day, and he'd
only been awake for an hour or so. Having recently woken,
he was not yet particularly chatty. Once night was fully upon
them, they'd resume their travel for the northern kingdom.

He spoke with a matter-of-fact tone when he answered.
"Many of the exercises involve pain or fear. There's a primal
part of ourselves that wraps itself tightly around our magic.
In those moments of survival, our abilities unleash as a means

of salvation. Discovering them is challenging, but mastering them is the most difficult of all."

She was unbothered by his assertion. "Training as a reever was challenging. If I could spend years running up and down a mountain and sparring with men twice my weight and head and shoulders taller than me, I think I can handle whatever trials are needed to figure out whether I have access to other gifts."

He finished chewing his apple and cleaned the small knife on his shirt. "If it's really something you want, it's something we can do. I don't think you'll like it."

"I didn't like running up the mountain, but it was good for me. Medicine rarely tastes sweet going down."

Gadriel went uncharacteristically stony. "Amaris, look at me for a moment."

She never understood his shifts in mood. One moment, he was gnawing on a sour breakfast and talking about military training, and the next, the air was solemn and filled with an unseen question. "What?"

"Do you want this?"

"Do I want what?"

His dark eyes were unmoving. "Do you want to be tested to see if you have other underlying powers?"

Amaris shifted uncomfortably. She was the first to drop her gaze, shrugging off his sullen attitude with lowered eyes. "It's wise, isn't it?"

His sober energy contained none of the taunting levity he often possessed. "If this is something you want, you need to say so."

"You get so intense sometimes. It's unnerving."

"So I've been told. Answer the question."

She folded her arms across her chest as if to protect herself from the discomfort. "Why are you being so peculiar about it? Yes, of course I want to know if I have any other gift. Who wouldn't want to know?"

"I just need you to understand what you're getting into.

312

Training is…not pleasant. It would need to be something to which you knowingly agree."

"You weren't under duress when you unlocked that door in the tower. How did you discover that ability?"

He grinned, stoicism melting from his face. Gadriel's ability to shift from one emotion to the next was unmatched. "That one was much like your own: uncovered by accident, some time ago. It turns out I have an aptitude for locks. My mother could never keep sweets stashed behind lock and key. Many of us find the edges of our gifts by accident, as have you."

Amaris had a small smile on her lips. "You never speak of your family. Are your parents alive?"

Gadriel nodded, perfectly normal once more. "They do live, but they're no longer in Raascot. They left nearly two centuries ago after I had fully become a young man and Ceres's newly appointed general. They went to live among other fae in the Sulgrave Mountains. That journey is quite the feat, but they're not the type to back down from something just because it's difficult. Maybe perseverance and the love of a good challenge is a trait I inherited from them."

"Do you have any way of knowing if they made it?" She regretted asking it as soon as the question left her lips. Why had she prompted Gadriel to picture his parents dying on the Frozen Straits?

"Few have attempted the journey successfully, though geography might be a conversation for another day. I haven't seen my mother or father in a very long time."

"Were you close?"

He smiled. "They're good people and good parents. They were, however, parents. Educators, mentors, disciplinarians, but not friends. I respect them, and my mother makes an excellent apple pie, which I do miss, but no, we weren't close. Not in the way you mean."

His body language told her that he wanted to be done talking about them, and she obliged. She respected any choice to deflect from speaking about one's family, hoping that others would do the same for her. "So other than fly and pick locks, do you have anything that sets you apart from a bat and a street urchin?"

He mock scowled at her, and she returned it. She was relieved that his stoic energy had left him and much preferred the comfort of glaring. Amaris was too proud to back down from an occasion to be surly.

After the ag'imni had spoken its tar-like words in the woods, her heart had not known true peace. She had already been irritated by Gadriel for his dismissal of her friendship at the university, but she'd thought they'd healed that wound between them. Every time one hole was patched, a new leak seemed to spring up. Now in addition to holding on to her hurt over his comment, she'd become distrustful as well.

Anger was a comfortable, preferable emotion. She vastly preferred anger to pain or suspicion. She wished she could return to the way things had been before they'd fought the ag'drurath, when his worst quality was how he irritated her. She would have traded every present emotion for anger in a heartbeat.

While it had made sense that Gadriel would see her skill with discerning enchantments as a tool to be put to use, it still wounded her to perceive herself through the eyes with which he viewed her. Leaders used their men as pawns. Militaries would crumble if their commanders had to recognize the humanity in every soldier beneath them. The rational part of her mind understood why he was not—nor could he ever be—her friend. She'd found him presumptuous and intrusive, but until the true ag'imni had spoken those words, she had never considered him a potential enemy.

"Show me what you can do, then," she prodded the dark fae.

She'd come to accept that he wasn't her friend. However, if Gadriel was truly her enemy, she needed to understand both who and what she was facing.

Her eyes flitted to her weapon as she considered what it might be like to fight him in one-on-one battle. The sword she'd taken as the mercenaries had dropped their weapons rested against the same tree, but knowledge was an asset more valuable than steel.

He eyed her skeptically. "I don't think you want to see what I can do."

She dismissed his hesitation. "I can assure you: I do."

Gadriel made a face. His expression was conflicted as he seemed to be tugging against an inner battle. The burly, intimidating man stashed the knife he'd been using for his apple and returned the rest of the traveling food to the sack. "What do you know of the fae in the north? What have you heard of their abilities?"

She'd always enjoyed reading, particularly works of nonfiction. Books had been an escape from the walls of her child mill or the fortress of the reev. She'd consumed tomes on the dark fae. She was no expert, but she knew enough.

"I'm aware that those north of the border were forced to relocate from elsewhere on the continent long ago because their abilities aligned with powers of darkness. Even the humans born in the north are more often predisposed to the dark small magics, like voice mimicry, astral projection, communicating with the dead, things like that. The books make it sound like traits of the dark fae don't just stop at your wings but that your people are like magnets for the dark abilities. Fae are conduits of power throughout the continent; northerners just seem to manifest in more terrible ways."

Gadriel looked sad at her answer, which confused her. She wasn't sure what he'd expected, but her explanation had been precisely in line with everything citizens of Farehold had told themselves for centuries.

"Do you think your queen is a good queen?"

Amaris was surprised at the direction he took the conversation. She blinked at his response. "Moirai? No, of course not."

"Because our king is a good king—was a good king. He's troubled, but Ceres is a good man with a good heart. I would have stood behind him for ten thousand years. He is extremely powerful and possesses numerous gifts, but he has used them for the good of his people and to help those he can." Gadriel's face softened as he spoke. "King Ceres can speak to animals. Do you know how terrifying it would be to have a king who could conscript bears, foxes, falcons, and the beasts of the earth to do his bidding? Yet the wolves of our forests love him and have protected the people in our cities for the hundreds of years he's served on the throne."

"He can command animals? Can he call the demons?"

Gadriel shook his head. "No, demons aren't animals. They bleed black, not red. But he has a more impressive ability—at least we've all found it exceptionally impressive."

"More important than making a bear do your bidding? That's hard to believe."

"Ceres is a dream walker."

She looked at him, not fully comprehending his statement nor what was extraordinary about it.

"It's a rather rare but spectacularly useful gift," Gadriel said. "He can visit others in their sleep. While southerners have horror tales dedicated to the murders and nightmares of those who can kill you while you slumber, our king used dreams to hold council and bring wisdom to his people no matter where they were. He's sought council with advisors, soothed fears, met commanders on the battlefield—all while asleep. It's been of extreme comfort and use to everyone in Raascot. Do those sound like they are evil things?"

She looked at her feet as she said, "I guess not." Then her brows puckered. "Have you been able to meet with Ceres while you've been on your southern mission? Has he visited you, I mean?"

He shook his head. "We're still on the topic of morality, reever. This is important, especially for someone in your station. You can't serve as a true neutral from Uaimh Reev and continue thinking this way—using the words you do. Do you think the humans you've met in Farehold have all been good people?"

Amaris twitched at his use of her title. He used her names—whether her true name, her station, or the irritating pet name—with intentionality given his message. Her mind went directly to the flawed human matrons of Farleigh. "No. I know they aren't."

Thoughts passed his lips as if they'd been the sorts of things that had haunted his conscience for years. "Good and bad can lie on either side of the border, but only people on one side of the border confidently label themselves as the heroes and everyone else as the villains. They insist on it even when the evidence is stacked against them. Think about lighted gifts for a moment, will you? Even magics considered good can be used for evil. If you are born with the ability to heal, what if you use your power to bring a wicked monarch regeneration time and time again, leaving them to reign in terror for hundreds of years? What if you're born with the ability to make things grow, but your vines crawl down the throats of people who displeased you and your mushrooms poison all who touch them so you could steal whatever delighted you? Why are those powers considered light and ours dark?"

She wasn't comfortable with this line of questioning. He'd turned a very simple question about his abilities into a lesson on the gray areas of morality. "Are you trying to avoid telling me what you can do?"

He sighed.

She felt a little guilty with the way she'd handled their conversation. "I'm sorry," she said, and she was. "You're right. It's not fair to your people."

"Life is rarely fair."

She waited for as long as she possibly could before pressing the issue once more. "Gadriel, are you intentionally not answering my question about your gifts?"

His expression informed her that she was getting under

his skin. Whether that was a good thing remained to be seen. He scanned her again, almost as if searching for an answer to an unasked question. Finally, he began, "You know the fae to heal more quickly, be stronger and more agile, show more stamina, correct?"

She nodded.

"What of primary and secondary powers, things like that?"

Her eyes tightened with her frown. "I'm not sure what you mean."

Gadriel rubbed at his chin, considering his words. "It's easy to forget how little you know of the fae. I don't mean that as an insult. It's not your fault. There are just so many things we take for granted in Raascot that I wouldn't have imagined myself explaining."

He may not have been trying to insult her, but it felt that way. She fought the urge to cross her arms, suspecting it would lower his opinion of her even further if she went out of her way to look childish. The Gray Matron had made a point of discouraging lessons on magic or stories of fae.

"Primary powers," he began a bit delicately, "are the ones that manifest naturally. They don't expend energy from their user. Just like how we don't have to think about our heart beating or consciously make our lungs breathe in and out, there are some innate things that give rather than take. It's almost like the body of the fae who wields it is a natural conduit for such a power."

"So for you, that's locks?"

He chuckled, and it was an honest laugh. She so rarely saw him flash his full teeth in such a disarming way. "Like I said, that's a knack, not a power."

"I think locksmiths would disagree."

This elicited the same warm chuckle.

"You might be right about that. Plenty of us have fun knacks up our sleeves, but primary powers are the ones we're born to use. Secondary powers are the ones that some fae can access, though they often come at great personal risk."

"And flight? That's not a primary power?"

"You ask a lot of questions for someone who's barely said more than a few words to me for the last three days."

"And you always want to be right about everything, so now's your time to teach me while I'm a willing participant. Make up for lost time. Educate me, oh great one."

"I'd like to do more than educate you," he murmured.

"What was that?"

"Flight. We were talking about flight." He flared his wings, the lovely, reinforced fabric glinting in what remained of the light for emphasis. "Our wings are genetic, like hair color or height. We've been fortunate to have wings become a commonality among the fae north of the border if both of their parents are also Raascot fae. Our wings are a dominant trait."

"Why don't you call yourselves dark fae?"

"Because it's racist, witchling."

She balked a bit at this. Darkness had been an attribute ascribed to them for centuries. It had been the norm. She had accepted it as truth. Never for one moment had she considered how it had made the fae on the receiving end of the descriptor feel. Her eyes widened. Her lips parted, but she was too stunned to understand whether she should apologize.

Gadriel didn't seem willing to press the issue. He brushed her off and continued, "You know of my wings, and you know of my convenient—and accidental—proficiency with locks. You're sure you want to see what I can do?"

"Will you stop dragging this out? Yes, I've asked several times—" She bit off her sentence right before calling him "demon." It seemed a little less tasteful after he'd informed her rather matter-of-factly that "dark fae" had certain connotations.

"It's your funeral, witchling," he said with a sigh, coming to his feet. "Do you still have your healing tonics?"

She frowned at the question but found herself slowly dipping her chin in a nod. "Do you need them?"

"Not yet, but you will in a moment."

Amaris stiffened. "Why? Are you going to hurt me?"

His eyes twinkled mischievously. "Touch me."

Uncertainty flooded her. "What?"

"Yes, I'm going to hurt you, since it's what you want. But it'll be quick, and I'll take care of you afterward. Now, grab me," he commanded. His voice invited little argument.

Hearing him admit he intended to inflict pain on her was jarring. She blinked several times, wondering why in the goddess's lighted earth she was even considering complying. He'd *told* her he was going to hurt her, and yet...

"Just touch you?" Her voice dropped to a whisper.

Gadriel folded his arms. The last light of day streamed through the branches overhead in beams of red and orange as she eyed him. She wasn't sure if it made the sight ominous or poetic. Inflicting pain at sundown felt reminiscent of the scar she bore on her palm from her reever's oath. Soon, it would be time for them to travel once more. She was still confused as her emotions roiled within her chest but reached out a tentative—though obedient—hand to touch the exposed skin of his forearm.

She yanked it back instantly, crying out as his skin burned her. Touching him had been like touching a glowing-hot branding iron. It was as if she'd stuck her hand in the fire, dunked her fist in boiling stew, or picked up red embers by the fistful. A second, horrified sound escaped her lips as she felt her flesh sizzle. Blisters rose on her hand, her entire palm filling with angry, hot fluid. She looked at him in horror as she gripped her wrist, holding her swollen hand away from her as if it were a venomous snake.

Gadriel moved from where he stood and fished in her bag for a healing tonic. He reached for her arm, but she winced away from him, unwilling to be touched again. With no sense of decorum or patience, he grabbed her wrist firmly. He yanked her to him, rubbing a bit of the tonic into her swelling hand with more gentleness than she'd expected. She cringed, but he was once again cool to the touch.

The tonic felt wonderful. She hated to admit it to herself, but the slow trace of his fingers felt just as lovely. She stopped resisting his touch as he tended to her wound.

"That hurt," she said, the tone of her voice every bit as wounded as her palm.

"I said it would."

She opened her eyes to watch his hands rub the tonic against her palm. "You can burn?"

"Like the sun," he said, almost smiling. "It's also useful on cold nights, though I have had nightmares end with my sheets reduced to ashes. These things come with their pros and cons. I've used it on you before, you know. A few times, actually."

"You've what?"

She suspected he'd start to believe she was hard of hearing if she had to constantly force him to reiterate all his statements, but she couldn't hide her confusion.

"Do you remember how cold you were on the back of the ag'drurath? Or as we've traveled? Every time we're in the sky, your teeth begin to chatter, and I don't have it in me to let you suffer...for that reason, anyway. I couldn't very well let you battle your way out of a coliseum just to freeze. Flight is an arctic mistress."

Amaris did remember, though she'd assumed she'd just gone numb from the cold. She hadn't realized he was capable of compassion. Her mind turned to battle. "That ability must make you almost invincible in hand-to-hand combat. No one could grab you."

"You don't know the half of it." He laughed quietly to himself as he finished rubbing the healing tonic into her hand. The swelling was dissipating, her blisters almost completely gone. She watched as his thumb traced circles on her palm. She may have been imagining it, but his finger seemed to be moving with a bit of idle slowness as it brushed against her wrist. Her hand tingled. The sensation ran up her arm, through her shoulder, and filled her with gooseflesh that ran the length of her spine. With a bit of rushed, nervous energy, she prompted the conversation forward.

"That's why I'm asking. I want to know more than half of it."

He exhaled through his nose, resigned to her persistence. "Do you know why I am a general?"

"Yes, because King Ceres is your cousin and nepotism is alive and well in Gyrradin."

He let out a dark chuckle. "I'm sure that doesn't hurt, but no, that's not all of it. And it's also not just because I'm the toughest, strongest, and most handsome. Though I do think those should be the qualifying features when selecting your general. This is where my secondary power comes into play. And for this one, yes, I will need you to keep a tonic on hand—for me, this time."

He waited for her to smile, but she didn't take the bait. She realized with a flash of vulnerable embarrassment that he was still tracing a circle, holding on to her.

"Amaris, I don't think you really want—"

"Stop making assumptions about what I want."

"You're right." He shrugged, and she was surprised. "I shouldn't be making judgment calls about what you do and don't want. Okay..." He breathed out again, watching her hand return to her side. "I'm going to tell you to do something, and I need you to obey without questioning me."

"Absolutely not."

"Then you don't get to see it."

She glowered. "I don't like that word—*obey*. It's not in my blood."

A twinkle she didn't quite understand sparked behind his eyes as he said, "Believe me, I know."

Instantly, she regretted asking him. "I'm not a troop you can order around, Gad. I let you tell me what to do with the ag'imni, but I don't blindly follow orders. Reevers don't have the hierarchy you seem to have. We're equals."

"You're not with the reevers right now, are you? I'm

going to need you to do your best to stop being a brat long enough to listen to me."

"I don't like where this is going. And also, that's not something I've ever been called."

"A brat? Just because no one's called you by the proper title doesn't mean it isn't accurate. You want to see my abilities, don't you? Didn't you demand it?"

"Gad, I—"

"We have more healing tonics? Correct?"

"Gad—"

"Break my neck," he said with a cool, controlled command. He made a come-hither motion with his fingers, egging her onward. She would have thought he was joking with the odd playfulness that joined his words and the beckoning of his hands, but nothing about this moment had true levity.

Her eyes widened. Her fingers flared out in a protective reflex. She didn't understand his sense of humor, but it didn't feel funny.

"Are you crazy?"

"Unless you're not brave enough to take on a general?" he taunted.

Her back remained stiff. "Listen, I'd love to kill you, but—"

"Then do it. Here's your chance."

"You've lost your mind." She made a face, unable to conceal her displeasure.

"You pushed the issue, witchling. You're the one who wouldn't let this rest. Do you need me to goad you into it? I'd love nothing more. Come on, reever. Haven't you been waiting for a chance to work out that aggression? I know you've thought of snapping my neck more than once already."

He was right. She would have thought nothing of it if he weren't so intentional with the way he used his words. She knew from the way he called on both her title and her pet name that he wanted her to think of her training while remaining antagonized.

323

Amaris took a half step backward, confused anxiety building against his energy. "Nice try, but that isn't going to work, no matter how satisfying it would feel to be the one to end your life."

Gadriel didn't allow her the opportunity to retreat. She attempted to brush him off, but he grabbed her a bit too roughly. Her eyes shot from where his fingers dug into her arm to the gleam in his eye. He was enjoying himself.

"I can do this all day. You're going to do it, one way or another."

"I'm not."

"You said you wanted this."

"I *do* want you to share your ability! I deserve your honesty. I deserve to know. I shouldn't be asked to blindly trust someone who's hiding huge things like literal powers from me. But this—"

"You want it?"

"Yes! But—" She tried to twist away from him, but he tightened his hold. Adrenaline spiked through her as she had the very distinct sensation of feeling like a rabbit looking into the eyes of a wolf. Only this wolf already had her in his teeth. "You're hurting me."

"Then stop me." He advanced on her, adjusting his hold on her arm so she couldn't turn away. When she tried to shake him loose, he threw a punch directly toward her. She ducked and missed his blow, freeing herself from his grasp with a competent twist. Amaris stumbled backward with her surprise. He drew his feet back, lifting his fists in a familiar combat stance. He swung at her again, and this time when she ducked from his blow, he was ready with a counterstrike. He anticipated her movement and kicked at her. Amaris went flying to the ground. She jumped to her feet.

"Are you fucking serious?" She gaped.

"Serious as death."

"You think I can't take you?" she asked, anger building.

Her adrenaline sizzled into fury. "I've bested every reever at the keep, *General*."

"Good."

Once again, she was acutely aware of how large he was. Gone were the warm reds and oranges of sunset. In the purpling light of the rapidly fading day, Gadriel looked enormous. His wings flared behind him to cloud anything beyond them from her vision. She was tense and confused. She didn't know if she should run or if she should pounce for a weapon. She raised her fists but needed plans for both offense and defense. She began scanning for her best escape routes.

He folded his fingers in twice to beckon her forward for the second time, but she did not advance. With a shrug, he lunged for her, throwing fists and beating his wings to knock her off her feet when he made contact. While Amaris was excellent in the ring, the only time she'd fought with wind as an enemy had been against the beating wings of the queen's dragon. With a powerful backward beat, Gadriel knocked her from her footing just as the beast had. She might have had a chance of recovering, but he was quick to act. Amaris hit the ground as his fist connected with the flesh of her cheekbone. She saw stars—bright lights that blinded her against the gloom of the gray and purple trees around them. She gasped, but her body went into fight or flight. Her reever training overpowered her.

She was ready to fight.

"You think I won't cut you down where you stand?" she snarled.

"Finally, she listens."

This time when he threw a fist, she grabbed onto his outstretched hand, using his arm as leverage. She needed the momentum of his punch to twist as she pulled his arm downward, flinging her body up in what may have been an anchored cartwheel had the goddess been looking down at them. She rotated in a near-perfect circular arc so that her legs could find his head. Her thighs wrapped around his neck in a scissor hold, squeezing as they both toppled to the ground. As they fell, Amaris angled her body upward so that he absorbed the impact and she could free herself from the tumble. She intended to twist to get on top of him again, but he rolled to his back and grabbed her foot as it descended to connect with his throat.

Gadriel wrenched her leg mid stomp to protect his throat, but she allowed the movement to rotate her. Resisting motions was how one got their bones broken. Instead, it propelled her backward until she landed on her back. A whoosh of air escaped her lungs, and before she could get to her feet, he was on top of her. He pinned her to the ground, holding each of her hands to the side as he weighed her down, crushing her beneath him. "Are you angry yet? Come on. Let it out."

She grunted, "I don't think you could handle it."

He was positively glowing. "Oh, believe me, I want nothing more."

She pulled up her knee in the small space between them and twisted it to the side to create leverage. Her opposite leg pushed off while she created a cross tear on his opposite wrist and rolled to the side. She was panting a bit too wildly. Exertion was only half of the drain. The rest was the spiral she felt at the insanity of the event itself.

Gadriel made a laughing sound as if he were enjoying himself far too much. He made another motion for her to advance, which only infuriated her further. She accepted the bid, turning into a side kick.

He grabbed her leg and gave it a twist to send her spinning away from him.

She landed and couldn't hold in the enraged sound that came from her.

"Cute try, witchling," he grunted with his twisting motion. "You're going to have to do better than that."

Her muscle memory had trained her to flow with the battle as if it were a river. Her opponents and their punches were merely logs and boulders that she must glide around, never forcing her way through and risking them breaking her. The flutter of his wings gave him an unfair advantage as she jumped to make an incapacitating blow to his throat, and the force of their backward beat sent her from her sure footing once again. She narrowly missed planting herself in a tree behind her. The force would have knocked the air from her lungs completely.

Instead, she skidded onto the ground beside the towering tree trunk, tripping on one of its protruding roots. Amaris slid in the pine needles and dirt, panting as she wasted no time getting to her feet.

"One of us is going down," he growled, baring his teeth in a wicked grin. "Which one is it going to be?"

She'd kick his teeth in just to get the delight off his face. Now she had to kill him out of pure fucking spite. Amaris had never seen him look so primal. Gadriel was more beast than man, the powerful spirit of an enormous cave cat ready to spring on her. He looked feral, bloodthirsty, delighted all at once. The hungry glint in his eye was terrifying.

Amaris felt the real thrill of threat tingle through her.

This did not feel like sparring. Something predatory in his eyes sent her adrenaline coursing. Her gut was torn, conflicted between confusion and the fear that she was in true danger. Gadriel advanced again and she used the leverage of a tree to throw her feet backward against its trunk and then push off it, using its height and force to jump over him while he missed his grab for her. She landed on her feet, but the motion put her at a disadvantage as her back was to him. She was too slow as he twisted for her, grabbing her from behind with both of his arms. He had her in a tight grasp, but rather than try to twist within his viselike grip, she threw her body weight down, sinking into the space between his legs and forcing them both toward the earth. As she sank, she rotated her shoulders so that he rolled off her, the weight of his muscular body working against him as he stumbled forward on uneven footing, slipping on the pine needles. His groans were absolutely animalistic and unmistakably pleased. She gasped for breath, her lungs screaming at the exertion.

"Gad!"

"It's over when it's over."

There was no room to argue.

Anger, panic, fear, and fight coursed through her.

She was ready for him this time as he turned, and when he charged for her again, she used the moment to close the space between them. She pushed off on both feet and jumped toward him. She was going to use his size against him. Small and nimble enough to leap through the air, Amaris wrapped her legs tightly around his waist, clinching herself to him as she faced him. His mouth was inches from hers. She squeezed her thighs together with every drop of her power, holding him in too close to her torso to grab her. In the same motion, she used the split second of advantage and seized her moment as the palm of her right hand went to his chin, encompassing the lower part of his face, and her left hand went to the crown of his head on its back side. With a quick thrust, she shoved his chin upward at an angle until she heard a loud, sickening crunch.

Amaris realized what she had done the moment the motion was too late.

Gadriel's body crumpled. She barely had time to untangle her legs and release herself so that she could push back from him and land on her feet. She stumbled backward in slack-jawed horror. Amaris couldn't blink or breathe as he fell. She was too stunned to move. His neck and head were set at an unnatural angle.

Then she heard the thud.

When Gadriel hit the ground, she knew she had killed him.

She was going to be sick.

The world spun. Stars filled her eyes as the tree trunks began to waver, ground rippling like the surface of a pond. She reached for a tree and missed, struggling to find something to stabilize her as she doubled over against the bark.

She'd killed him. She'd murdered the general. She'd broken Gadriel's neck.

One word banged through her mind.

Shit, shit, *shit*.

She had no idea what she was supposed to do. She gaped at him as her equilibrium floated.

Amaris continued to stare. She didn't know what to do. He had made her do this, yet she was now responsible for his death. Gadriel's blood was on her hands. Their mission was in jeopardy because of some sick, psychotic break of Raascot's mad general. She couldn't think of her dispatch. She couldn't think of the curse, King Ceres, or how she was supposed to get to the north.

"Fuck." The single word escaped his throat in a groan.

Her lips opened and closed like a fish as she continued to gape. The shock of hearing him speak reverberated through her.

He didn't stay down for long after that. Though his movements were slow and anguished, his hands came up and he grabbed his chin and head, creating a counterforce to her motion. His neck snapped back into place. He groaned again, sweat shimmering on his brow against the clear signs of pain. He took a long while steadying his breathing as he extended a hand. "Those tonics would be great about now," he rasped.

She stared blankly between his fallen form and the place where he'd left the brown glass bottles after helping her heal from her blisters.

"Please." He did his best to sound polite. His normally bronze skin had taken on a chalky pallor. Sweat formed solid beads across his forehead as he weakly lifted a hand. There was nothing but pain, illness, and death on his face.

Amaris had no idea what carried her forward. She walked with numb, unseeing footsteps from where she'd stood above his fallen corpse to where the healing medicine lay and back again. She pushed the glass bottle into his hand and backed away from him as if he were a spider. It took him a while to fidget with the bottle against the clammy sweat that had formed on his upper lip and the glaze that had begun to cloud his eyes. She stared in ongoing horror as he parted his lips and emptied the container into his throat.

This was impossible.

Gadriel moved with phantasmal slowness on the ground, righting himself until he leaned against a tree. He attempted a smile, but it was not the warm, happy smile he'd used when laughing about his knack with locks. He popped his neck by rolling it from one side to the other, sighing in relief as his spine realigned.

He did still look terribly ill, which logically tracked, as she'd seen him die.

"Come on. That was supposed to be fun for you. Haven't you wanted to kill me for some time?"

Aghast, her single word came out in a hoarse whisper. "What?"

Gadriel shrugged with feigned nonchalance despite the cold sweat that gripped him, soaking his tunic to his body. He must know exactly how this ability looked. His voice attempted to capture all the ease in the world when he spoke. He arched a brow and said, "Have I ever complimented you on your combat? You're quite a formidable force, witchling. I didn't have the opportunity to appreciate it in the coliseum like I should have. Now seeing you in action, I would have no qualms putting you in charge of a training ring."

She hadn't realized how long her mouth had stayed open. Her tongue was dry. She didn't remember the last time she had blinked. There was a buzzing in her ears as if a hornets' nest had been built around her, their angry wings making it difficult to hear what he was saying.

"You died."

Gadriel had provoked her into something unspeakable. She had sparred and then panicked. She hadn't even realized what was happening before she found herself fighting for her very life. He was the living dead. The world saw him as a demon because that was exactly what he was.

He grunted again, still looking pale.

"I'm not unkillable, if that's what you're wondering. This would have taken me down for a lot longer if you hadn't had medicine ready. Sometime in the future, remind me to tell you about the battle where I lay in a field for four days before I found the strength to move." He swallowed with both humor and pain as he recalled the memory. "This isn't like my ability to warm. That's something I do freely. With this, I'm just invulnerable. But it costs me." He attempted to shrug, though the motion seemed to agitate his neck. "My strategizing and military advice aside, between the heat I summon and my ability to put myself back together if they manage to make contact, I make a great general. No matter how many times I'm brought down, I can rally and stay with my men. Of course, I do try my best not to be taken down in the first place. I think I handle myself quite well, but damn, you put up a fight."

Amaris couldn't move. She couldn't speak.

"That was a great tactic, reever." He kept his voice level, doing his best to sound conversational. Perhaps he was attempting to reestablish normalcy. "You're quite the murderous little thing, which gives me an idea as to how difficult it's going to be to train you when it comes to eliciting any powers that might be locked up in that furious body of yours. You have combat skill far beyond what I'd estimated, and for that I apologize." He rubbed at his neck and winced.

Gadriel was clearly in pain. He seemed as if he were recovering from a common flu. Other than that, he sounded *happy* as he talked. Everything he said came out with such commonplace ease, as if he were discussing morning strolls or how best to trim rhododendron bushes. His chalky pallor would undoubtedly ease as the healing tonic worked itself through his blood, but for now, he managed to chat like the living dead.

"Your reevers' training hardened you against those sorts of tactics, which is wonderful for a warrior but makes it a challenge for you when it comes to magic. I'll have to tell Samael the next time I see him that he hasn't lost his touch. He'd be proud of you."

Her feet remained glued to the ground. She was aware that Gadriel was speaking, but she'd long since tuned out his cool, collected words. She couldn't hear anything he said. How could he be acting as if nothing had changed between them?

"Pick your mouth up off the earth, witchling. If you want to choose a safe word before we fight again, just say so."

She could barely breathe, nor could she understand how he was speaking so casually. She caught the last bit of his sentence, playing it over in her head to try to make sense of it.

"A safe word?"

He scanned her hair, then her face, as if examining features he hadn't seen one thousand times before. "How's 'snowbird'? That will be our safe word. Anyway, as with most things on this earth, if I'm beheaded, I will fall. So if I genuinely piss you off, I'd recommend using the sword if I were you. You can also put plenty of space between us from the time you snap my neck and the time it takes me to heal if you aren't feeling quite so benevolent. You know, if you're mad enough to kill me but not quite angry enough to keep me dead."

"You're…you're okay?"

With painstaking effort, he stood from his sitting position and scooped up the brown glass bottle of tonic that he had used on her palm.

He dropped his voice as if talking to a startled kitten. "Come here."

She couldn't move.

Gadriel crossed the space between them, his posture still far too relaxed. She was frozen. She knew that fear was supposed to result in a fight-or-flight response, but she couldn't move. He dipped his thumb into the tonic and

332

rubbed it gently across her cheek where he had punched her, the rest of his hand holding her face in place with a tenderness that felt borderline cruel in contrast with what she had just done and seen.

"I'm sorry about that," he muttered, tracing his thumb across the small hurt and watching it knit the wound together beneath her milky skin. His touch was so confusing. It sent chills of comfort and fear in equal proportions down her spine as her skin rippled into gooseflesh.

"I killed you," she finally sputtered. Her voice felt detached from her body. It was someone else's voice entirely.

He shrugged appreciatively. "You came close, I'll give you that much." His face had softened substantially. "It would bring down most men, fae, and even beasts. It's a bit of a funny story. This particular power of mine was also discovered by accident. My commander kicked me off a cliff with my wings bound to see if I would manifest anything. When I landed, my spine broke my fall."

Despite how profoundly numb she felt, she managed to discover yet another way to be horrified. "You fell to your death?"

"Do I look dead?" He dropped his hand from where he had been resting it against her face and returned the remainder of the tonic to his satchel.

She swallowed hard. "You said you had other talents, didn't you? What are the other ones?"

"I'm afraid they're not something I'll be demonstrating for you today." He winked.

"Do you plan to kill me too?" Her voice was so low she wasn't sure if he could hear her at all.

His eyebrows gathered as he frowned, genuinely troubled by her question. "Our training camps in Raascot never performed violent tasks like that unless we had our healers and proper medicines on hand. I'm not going to push you off a cliff to see what powers you manifest—probably." He smiled fleetingly to see if she would take the bait, but she did not.

333

"You did say that finding your powers was something you wanted. Is that still something you want? After this?"

She seemed to have lost the ability to speak as she stared in response.

"Is that a yes or a no?"

"I... You're asking me?"

"Of course I'm asking. I'm not a monster. Though it might not feel that way during training. Like I've said and like you've seen, it's not particularly pleasant. Do I have your permission to help you find your abilities?"

Gadriel offered yet another crooked smile, but she did not return it. His joke felt so hollow to her ears. Instead, she shrugged with scarcely one lift of a shoulder, refusing to meet his eyes. She still felt speechless at the entirety of their exchange.

"I need a verbal confirmation."

Amaris sat in a state of shock as stars began to populate the sky. It was hard to know how much time had passed before she found her voice.

"Yes," she said finally, mind and body still whirling with disconnect. "I guess if it's going to help me live through broken necks and become the walking undead. But, Gad, that power is horrible, and you're wrong—you are a monster. You didn't exactly get my permission when you said you were going to wrap your hands around my neck."

"That's because I was never going to hurt you."

"How was I supposed to know that?"

"You weren't, but I'm a good actor."

"Is that supposed to make me feel better? That you deceive well?"

"Amaris—"

"You never call me by my right name when it's something good."

His expression collapsed in displeasure. "Listen, I was only egging you on because you insisted on having me show my abilities to you. It's not an easy power for me, and not one

I use lightly. Would you have believed me if I had just told you I can put myself back together after attempted murder? That snapping my spine wouldn't take me down? Would you have taken my word for it?"

She considered the question before answering. Her faith in him ebbed and flowed, perhaps because he was unlike anyone she'd ever met. Every time she doubted him, he proved himself to her. She didn't understand Raascot fae or military life or half of Gadriel's choices, but he had yet to let her down.

She vividly remembered the sincerity on his face as he'd extended his hand to her in the Tower of Magics.

Jump, and trust that I will catch you.

Her life had been in his hands, and he had not failed her.

Still, their exchange with the ag'imni left her with a gnawing uncertainty. She'd worn her skepticism on her sleeve ever since the encounter.

Amaris finally settled on, "No fae has that ability."

"I do. And you did exactly what you were supposed to do. Now, granted, you may not have fully understood what it was that you were asking for, but you did demand it of me. Repeatedly. I was never going to hurt you. I just didn't think you'd give my neck the crack it needed if you weren't ready to fight."

"Did you let me win?"

"Yes and no. I certainly didn't go down without a fight. I like a little struggle now and then."

"You're a sick fuck."

He smirked. "You're not the first to think so. Besides, there are plenty of reasons I don't go around talking about this gift. It's saved my neck a time or two." His eyes sparkled at his dark joke. She could see the flash of his teeth at he chuckled at his own sense of humor, paying particular attention to the subtle points of his canines.

"You're not funny."

"I beg to differ."

She knew from their conversations that Gadriel frequently felt the weight of why the kingdoms had forced his kind beyond the border. Dark gifts like this were precisely what the people of Farehold feared. She was sure part of him wished he had never shown her, but the milk had already been spilled.

"At the university? The ag'drurath?"

He looked at her, not understanding her fragmented question.

"You would have been okay? When we fell from the ag'drurath, did you jump knowing you'd be fine?"

He made a contemplative face. "No, I don't think I would have been fine. I certainly didn't jump counting on that gamble, though we could have gotten lucky. What happened there was an issue of blood loss and, for all goddess knows, possible internal bleeding. I wasn't just faced with broken bones or tissue that needed mending. I really do owe you my life on that one. Though maybe we're even, since you did just kill me. Now, are you ready to go?"

"As if none of that happened?"

"What? You don't want to remember that I can keep you perfectly warm in the air or that I proved I wouldn't do anything to you without immediately being able to take care of you after?" With that, he scooped her up before she could respond, holding her by her back and the crook of her bent knees as he got ready to take to the sky. If the mountains were any indication, this would be one of two more nights remaining in which they flew over Farehold.

"Just remember, little witch: 'snowbird.' Say it and we stop—no matter what."

Gadriel took off into the night with his wings spread like a great, dark bird and continued their eastbound journey for Raascot.

Thirty

G ADRIEL DIDN'T WANT TO TOUCH DOWN. HE STRUGGLED against whatever it was that urged him to stay in the air. It wasn't like him to delay the inevitable, but reluctance fought him like a chain tethering him to the sky.

None of it had gone the way he'd hoped, but then again, how could it?

The whipping wind and air above left little opportunity for verbal communication, and the silence was a welcome relief after what had passed between them. The wind would blow her hair into his face from time to time, but he didn't particularly mind. Each time, he was hit with the scent he'd noticed every time they'd flown together. He wondered if anyone had ever told her that she smelled distinctly of juniper. It was a smell that reminded him of winters in the forests beyond Gwydir. It smelled like home.

The clear night was scattered with white, vibrant stars, but he struggled to enjoy the sky. There was nothing easy about any of this. Amaris was frequently unhappy with him, which he probably deserved more than even she realized. It wasn't what he wanted, but her reaction was justified. He was confident things were going to get worse before they got better.

The moment Amaris's teeth began to chatter, he warmed himself with the inner light that allowed him to burn. It was tricky to strike the balance between warming and scalding, but she relaxed from her shivers after a moment. After their day, he knew she was now conscious of exactly who she had to thank for her warmth.

As the sky had begun to show its first hints of gray, jagged mountains could be seen silhouetted in the distance. There was nothing like the feel of coming home after a long journey. Seeing the Raasay Mountains was like salve to a wound. Yet as excited as he was to get back into his kingdom, a nagging dread tugged at him. After only one more night of travel, they'd reach Raascot's border. He'd no longer have to live in fear of being spied as an ag'imni.

He had to land. It was going to be light, and he'd already stayed in the air too long. He couldn't keep putting it off. He spotted a place where the trees parted enough to allow him to maneuver carefully to the forest floor.

He concealed his pained expression, struggling to keep his face neutral as he fluttered his wings and set his feet to the earth. Amaris wasn't one to linger when their feet touched down. She always shoved away and created space as soon as she was able. She wasn't particularly grateful for the flight or the warmth, but she also hadn't asked for any of this. She'd been sent by Samael to make her plea before Moirai, not to join Raascot in its efforts in the south. Gadriel empathized with her fears and frustrations, but that didn't make it any easier. Oh well, he thought. If she already hated him, it couldn't get much worse.

Still, he wasn't looking forward to this.

Well, maybe a little bit.

A small, vindictive part of him would take a morsel of pleasure. She had broken his neck, after all. She could handle it. Hell, there was a chance she'd hate it and enjoy it in equal proportion. It would certainly make things a lot nicer if she did show certain predilections. She was quite the peculiar little monster. And there had been times when he'd thought...

She already had her back to him. Amaris wrapped her cloak tightly around her, though the air was not particularly chilly. She'd curled up into a tiny ball within herself. She'd declined any offers to eat, opting instead for immediate slumber. It frustrated him that she so often refused to eat out of sheer obstinance. If he hadn't offered it to her, she probably would have sought out a loaf of bread on her own. Instead, she was too stubborn and proud to accept the hand that fed her—literally.

His eyes had narrowed slightly as he dropped the bread back into the bag. Okay, maybe he would enjoy it a little bit more than he should.

Since it was nearly daybreak, Gadriel told her that if she slept, he would take the first watch. He knew she hadn't been sleeping well during the day. Traveling by night and sleeping in the heat of day wasn't easy on anyone, especially if it was unfamiliar. He'd had centuries to perfect his craft. She wordlessly agreed, putting as much space between them as possible before lying down. Gadriel rested against a tree and watched the sun come up, appreciating the golden rays that punctured the forest.

Warm daylight soon filled the forest with a beautiful blue sky overhead. They were far enough north that, though the sun was cheery, it did not heat the ground as it might in the southern half of the kingdom. Sleep would claim her any moment. He was meant to be keeping an eye on the woods, but instead he watched the tiny bundle that had rolled herself onto her side. Small, threadlike strands of silver peeked out from the hood that she'd kept up over her head. Her body moved ever so slightly as her chest rose and fell with slumber. She seemed too small, too vulnerable for the tasks the world was laying at her feet.

There it was. She was asleep.

It seemed cruel that the All Mother would choose

someone so small to take on a mission so big. He frowned at the unfairness of it all. Even if she was excellent in combat, she'd need every drop of strength she could summon. He truly hoped for all their sakes that there were other abilities within the little, moonlit package.

Some things had to get done. If they were going to reach Raascot tomorrow, there was no time like the present.

Gadriel slowly took his weapons off and placed them noiselessly to the ground beside him where he sat. He took his time getting to his feet, ensuring he made no sound. One step at a time, he crept nearer and nearer to Amaris. She didn't stir, dead to the world in her sleep. The day around them was happy and peaceful. Birds chirped distantly, but not loudly enough to wake her in her much-needed unconsciousness. There was no wind in the trees today, and the sun was not hot enough to bother her as she slept in the shade beneath the canopies of the trees.

He'd chosen every step carefully, moving with catlike silence. She'd have to stay asleep until it was already too late. He lifted one foot carefully and planted it on her far side so that her sleeping shape was trapped beneath him.

The small, ivory lines of her profile poked out from the hood. He could see the gentle curve of her forehead as it gave way to the slope of her nose, and he followed the curve down over her pink lips and the hill of her chin. He had known her features to be white, but the thickness of her bright white eyelashes surprised him every time he saw them, whether she was yelling at him from across the room or trying to snap his neck in the woods. Staying as silent as possible, he stretched his hands out and readied himself to strangle her.

Thirty-One

P ANIC.
          Amaris had been hit by an avalanche.

Pain lanced through her body, and panic gripped her. Every cell, tendon, bone, fingertip, toe, joint, muscle, and fiber of her being within her jolted awake. She was being crushed. She was drowning. She was trapped. She was thrashing, flailing in confusion. Her eyes flew open as she searched for the terror that overpowered her. She was so wild, so feral with incomprehension that she was clawing and scratching at the shackles that bound her neck long before she realized what was happening.

Adrenaline flooded her with such intensity that she could taste it on her tongue like hot copper. She dug her fingernails into his skin and drew deep, bloodied lines across his forearms, reaching for his face. If she could get to his eyes, his ears, his weak points.

No, no, this was taking too long.

No time to plan. No time to think. Only fight.

Gadriel—it was Gadriel.

He stood over her, his dark hands in a viselike grip over her throat, fingers on her jugular so no blood reached her brain. He tightened his grip, pressing into her windpipe. She choked. She gasped for air, but none came. She beat her hands and feet against him anywhere she could land a blow, kicking, scratching, bucking like an animal with its leg in a snare. She was too panicked to call on training, too terrified to remember anything. She had no defensive maneuvers. She had no skills. She had nothing. She was going to die while looking into the cold, dark soul of the general.

How to disarm him? How to free herself? How? *How?*

Her eyes bulged from the exertion as she tried desperately to claw for breath. Her knee couldn't reach him. Her feet found nothing. She tried to squirm, tried to fight, but she could feel the blood pounding as it was trapped in her head and neck with nowhere to go. She had no oxygen. She had no blood flow. She had no access to words or any way to scream.

All she knew was terror.

She was going to die.

A low snarl escaped from his lips as he tightened his choke hold.

This was it.

Amaris's nails abandoned his arms, taking bloodied stripes from his face, digging her claws across his cheek. She lanced for his eyes, pulled at his ears with what she had hoped would be the force necessary to rip them from his scalp and catch him unaware. Somehow it had been only seconds and it had been days and weeks and months all at once. She kicked once more, but her leg could not locate the sensitive space between his legs. This would never end. It would be the last thing she felt on this earth. Pain, fear, betrayal, and the suffocation of shock were to be her final emotions.

In a herculean feat of strength and desperation, she flung her hands to the ground in tight fists on either side of her, hoping to push herself up into a new position.

The blast connected.

The world shook beneath her.

A sonic boom shattered through the woods as her fists made their impact. The invisible force of wind and sound and battering rams collided with his chest and sent her winged enemy flying away from her, hurled back as if he were nothing more than a piece of driftwood in a tidal wave. The trunks of the very forest bent and bowed in response to her exertion of power, bark and boughs and earth rippling away with her at their epicenter. The shock wave was still shaking the trees around them, their leaves trembling and branches colliding with the blow.

Birds abandoned their perches with squawks and cries as they rose from the canopy and took to the safety of the skies in a thick cloud of sparrows and blue jays and crows and robins. Rabbits, squirrels, and forest creatures were sprinting from where they had hidden in dens and hollows of trees, escaping the terrible, unknown disaster at the center of the forest.

The only sound aside from the startled cawing of birds had been the thud of Gadriel as he struck a tree. He had collided with the trunk of a nearby oak from the backward blow and stayed where he struck.

Amaris sat up and scrambled backward on her hands, desperate to put as much space between herself and the villain as she could. She grasped with one hand for her sword while simultaneously trying to pull air into her lungs. Her throat felt so bruised. Her chest was hollow and empty. She reached from where she stayed on the ground and made contact with steel. She wrapped her hands around the hilt of the sword, pulling it close to continue the battle for her life. She knew she'd need to get to her feet, to start running, but she needed to breathe. She needed a plan.

Gadriel pushed himself into a sitting position against the trunk he'd crashed into. He didn't move, though he was grinning, his elbows resting on his knees as he smiled at her proudly.

"That was amazing!"

Amaris stayed in the defensive position. Terror and fury chafed her on the arms, gripping her with the smoky, liquid tendrils of death's fingers.

His face was delighted as he said, "I've never seen a shock wave! I've never even heard of this gift! Really, really impressive, Amaris. Bet you didn't know you could do that, did you?"

Her grip on the hilt slackened as he spoke. Her ears began ringing. She felt the bile as it left her stomach and burned its way through her reddened throat. She turned and threw up onto the ground, unleashing whatever small morsels had remained in her stomach, though the acids that hit the forest floor were mostly liquid and bile. The acrid, bitter taste was like fire against her bruised throat. Her muscles ached, abdomen clenching.

Gadriel stood from where he'd been recovering from the blow. He approached her to offer a waterskin, but she skidded away from him like a wounded animal into the corner of its cage.

"Hang on there, reever. Are you okay?" His brows knit with more concern than she understood. Yesterday he had shown her he could not be killed. Today he showed her that he would do the killing.

"Stop," she tried to say. Amaris held her hand out flat. Her voice croaked, words barely making it over her lips.

He shook the waterskin with a bit more insistence, continuing to hold it out to her. His face twitched with something like agitation as he watched her.

"Oh my goddess, you can't be serious. *Snowbird*, witchling! *Snowbird!* You didn't even try the safe word! Besides, I did get a verbal yes from you yesterday before even considering exercises that might help unlock your powers. If you want to stop, you have to say so."

She blinked from where she remained on the ground, half propped with her elbows from where she'd scurried. She was aware of him speaking but her ears felt as if they had been stuffed with cotton. Battling with Gadriel was not like sparring with the reevers where she knew they were all equal. It was not like fighting the ag'drurath, which was not evil, just a creature doing the only thing it knew how to do. Living and fighting with Gadriel was like nothing her training had prepared her for. She didn't understand him, nor did she know if she could trust him.

He offered a crooked, apologetic half smile. "Here. Wash your mouth out."

She refused his outstretched offer, feeling made of ice and stone.

He dipped his head as if in acknowledgment and set the waterskin down on the ground between them and took several steps backward, open palms showing he meant no harm. Her eyes remained wild, breath scarcely coming in ragged pants. The day was too happy, too clear and cheerful and bright for such a monstrosity to have occurred. Her hand went to her throat to feel the tender parts where he had attempted to kill her while he collected a brown glass bottle from the bag.

"I'm going to come over there now."

She shook her head from where she remained looking up at him on the ground, but the motion pained her.

Gadriel sighed, ignoring her silent protests so that he could help her whether she wanted it or not. "Stop it. You can't very well be left to suffer just because you're too proud to accept help," he muttered more to himself than to her. "The bruises will be gone in a moment. We have plenty of tonic left."

Amaris couldn't even protest. She couldn't believe what he had done. He hadn't been her friend. He may have been using her to further his northern agenda, but to actively try to murder her in her sleep? Every muscle in Amaris's back and shoulders ached from the tension as she refused to relax. Her heart was alive like the savage beat of a drum, thrumming uncontrollably within her.

"Hey, at least I didn't push you off a cliff."

The cotton fell away from her ears then. Her lips parted

as she fully understood what he was saying. "This was a test? This was... You did this as...as a training exercise?" She tried to speak but her throat was so bruised, so tender that she could barely rasp through the words.

He winced at the rough sound of her voice. She was too shocked to resist as he helped her to a sitting position.

"Amaris," he said quietly, "I'm trying to help you. I'm *still* trying to help you. Now, stay still."

He was exceptionally gentle with her while restraining her enough to prevent her from fighting his efforts. He cupped the back of her neck in one large hand, supporting her head gently. He dribbled a bit of water into her mouth. She flinched against the pain as she swallowed. He raised the medicine to her lips and poured half the bottle of tonic down her throat. It burned as it went down, but she could feel its healing effects as it knit her together with its medicinal waters. The tonic cooled whatever inflammation and swelling had been threatening to close off her air passage altogether.

She swallowed again and found that the saliva was able to flow more easily down her throat this time. She made another attempt to back away, but Gadriel kept a calming, kind hand on the back of her neck. He was no longer proudly smiling as he had been. Instead, his voice was compassionate and understanding.

"That wasn't intended to hurt you, witchling." His voice was low and reassuring. "I did it as a general might to his troop in training—a training I was sure you had agreed to. If you had calmed yourself for a moment to cease your panic, you could have stopped at any time by even mouthing the word. You can't let fear consume you when it counts, Amaris, or it won't matter what gifts you possess."

She blinked at him several times, feeling the hate burst from wherever it had been contained within her. "I am not your soldier, demon." There wasn't a lot of room between the two of them, but she had the space to bring her hand around with the fast, stinging arc of a single, powerful slap.

346

His cheek was red with the imprint of her fingers. The high, sharp sound of its impact hung between them.

A thick tension rang like a bell, the sound echoing. She wasn't sure if she had made things much worse by provoking a monster. He made a small warning face as he looked into her eyes. The moment passed, and it was clear there would be no further retaliation.

Gadriel carefully released his hold on the back of her neck and took a few steps backward before reaching the opposite side of their camp. She created distance and was relieved when he respected her need for space. It was clear he wasn't thrilled with her response. She had expressly said she wanted to learn. She had agreed to training. She had been given a magic word to stop. What seemed to bother him most was that she hadn't even attempted their word, as if she hadn't believed that he would stop, as if she had no trust for him at all.

"You can hate me for now, but you'll understand why I did what I did in time. I won't touch you again."

"You're sadistic."

"That's true, but also entirely unrelated to what happened here."

"How can you say that?"

He sounded both confused and disappointed when he spoke. "I had thought we were on the same page from yesterday's conversation. Fear can be a really useful tool in unlocking powers and was absolutely effective for you today. Look what you achieved, witchling. Look at what you uncovered. This is how all the fae are conditioned in the north. The element of surprise is an unmatchable force."

She stayed utterly silent.

A small, pained look flickered behind his eyes, and he lowered his voice as if speaking to a wounded creature. "What do you need?"

With the tonic soothing her injured throat, she was able to shake her head once again. "What do I need?"

"From me. What do you need from me in order to feel safe?"

"How can you ask that? You just tried to kill me."

He looked distinctly frustrated. "I didn't. I helped you find a power—*your* power. But that was then, and now we're here and you're looking at me like I'm going to slice open your belly the next time you let your guard down. Now I'm asking you, because it's the right thing to do: What would make you feel safe right now? Do you need me to put my weapons somewhere else? Do you want to talk through the training? Do you want me to camp somewhere else?"

"I can't believe you're asking me this. Nothing. There's nothing I want from you. There's nothing you can do to make this better."

His face softened to a gentleness she'd never seen from him. His voice was quiet. "I am sorry. It seems I'm on something of a losing streak with you. It's better for a troop to hate their general than to be coddled and undertrained and die in battle."

"I'm *not* your troop," she said, this time with a cold, low whisper. Her words were a firm end to their conversation.

After an extended, unbroken silence, Gadriel gave her the space and silence she desired. He smothered the fire. After a time, he rolled onto his side, putting his back to both the smoke and to her.

Amaris stayed where she had been sitting, weapon still loosely held in her hand. As she pressed on her throat, she could no longer feel the pressure of the damaging injuries that had been there only moments before. Betrayal heated her, burning her up from the inside out. She thought of how she had trusted him in the tower, how she had put her life in his hands. She thought of how he had looked standing over her with his grip around her small throat, merely a single flex away from snuffing out her life force altogether.

Then her mind flitted to the shock wave that had sent him flying from her. It was a power so great it had sent the

348

very trees shaking as it tore through the forest. The shock wave and its force had belonged to her. They were a part of her. She had possessed whatever ability necessary to shake the very earth. She had weaponized the air around her and thrown him from her.

The earthquake was hers to command.

The thing she hated herself most for was a horrible thought that gnawed at her uncomfortably from somewhere unspeakable at the apex of her thighs. She thought of the smug way he'd waved it away as if it had all been the matter of some safe word. She thought of how he'd cupped the back of her head while he'd dripped tonic down her throat. She could still feel the idle circle of his thumb as he'd traced it against her palm, her wrist, her face. No matter how many times he caused her injuries, he was there to care for her. She couldn't stop the creeping heat as she thought of how powerful he was, how strong he'd been as he stood over her, and how it had felt to have his hands wrapped around the tender flesh of her throat with her life, quite literally, in his hands. And the deep, gnawing conviction that she wanted him to do it again—she hated that most of all.

✦

Clouds dotted the sky overhead in the waning hours of daylight. There was no beautiful golden sunset as Gadriel stirred. The moment she looked at him, it was clear to her how little he'd rested. His eyes were red and underlined with the purple bruises of sleeplessness. She wondered if he'd merely lain there with his back to her for the better part of eight hours.

Amaris had managed to fall asleep, though it had taken a while. She had expended enough energy in shock, anger, and hate. Once her fury ebbed, whatever survival instinct dwelled inside her had told her that regardless of what she'd said to Gadriel, she was fine. Exhaustion had lulled her to sleep.

He began to strap his weapons to himself while Amaris

349

pulled out two small loaves of brown bread and handed one to him. He took it and frowned, turning the stale offering over in his hand.

"About what happened—"

She cut him off. "You were training me. You said it yourself: I had verbally agreed to allow you to train me."

"I know, but..." His voice was thick with an unrecognizable emotion. "Growing up in Raascot, we know exactly what we're getting ourselves into when we go to training camps. Of course, we don't know the specifics of how our individualized education might go, but all our cousins and brothers and fathers and friends tell stories of someone throwing knives near their head, holding them underneath ice water until they think they're about to drown, or unleashing a barrel of venomous snakes and closing the door to the room. You had never heard any of these tales. You didn't even grow up around fae, magic, or any part of our culture. I *did* intend to scare you and surprise you, which I did. You *were* meant to fight for your life, which you did. But it's not the same."

Amaris closed her eyes. This was the very thought that had reached her in the wake of her anger. She understood training. She had accepted the rigors of exercise. She had come to know submission to torture in the name of progress.

"It is the same."

"It's not. You should never have felt like you were in real danger with me. If you had been one of my men, no matter what lengths I went to or what extremes I had taken in training, they would know that regardless of how frightened they were or how dire the situation, I am for them—not against them. You need to know that you're the one with true power when we're training. You can stop it at any time."

"I know. Gad, I do want this. I wanted...I *want* you to train me." She refused to reflect on the other, more confusing reasons she didn't want it to stop. How hard he'd worked to ensure she felt safe and reassured wasn't lost on her. She appreciated his protectiveness. She loved and hated his strength and power in equal proportions. Perhaps these complex feelings, as with all that were too uncomfortable to examine, would be ones she'd need to suppress. For now, what she needed was access to her abilities.

He said her name slowly. "Amaris, I have wondered since the day you met me whether you know I'm not your enemy."

There it was again. Her name. She chewed on her lip and picked away the stale crust on her bread. The action offered her an element of distraction. "I know I'm not your enemy. I'm just someone you fought with in Aubade."

His brows collected as he looked at her. Gadriel's gaze darkened as it prodded hers for further explanation. His eyes seemed to move as if reading through scripts as he searched his memories. She saw the moment the memory struck him.

"The masters? The healers' hall?"

She was still picking at the crust of her bread. "When they asked what I was to you, you said that I was someone you fought with in Aubade."

He nodded slowly and took a tentative step forward. She did not shrink away. She had been emotional over the memory and how stupid it had made her feel. Her mind's eye conjured a vision of how she'd sung to him in the forest. She remembered her desperation as she'd begged the healer to save him and pleaded with the masters to free him. Then she thought of how he'd tricked her into the horrors of snapping his neck and repaid the favor the following morning by latching on to hers.

"I know what I am to you, and I understand. I do. I was mad—scared, even, at least for a minute while I processed everything. It was frustrating. But I've come to terms with it, and I get it. I'm an incredibly useful tool to Raascot. I'm not mad at you anymore for doing what you need to do for your people."

It was said with empathetic intentions. She'd made peace with her reality.

She tried again. "I also understand why it's important for me to have access to my powers. If I'm going to be of use to you and your king, you need me at my full potential. I want you to do it again. Help me train, that is," she amended.

Gadriel's face was painted with his speechlessness. He raked a hand through his hair, shaking his head slightly, but he had no words for her. He only muttered her name, "Amaris," as if the name was meant to rebuke her words and set things straight, but it did not. After it became clear that neither of them would speak of this further, he collected her into his arms to set off toward the mountains. Before they abandoned the earth for the sky, he said, "You're so much more than someone I fought with in Aubade."

Thirty-Two

N OX WAS DROWNING IN GOLD, JEWELS, AND SILKS. SHE WAS having trouble breathing through the choking swirl of perfume and floral bouquets. After dinner, several personal attendants were sent to her room with gifts of handmade gowns and elaborate, customized jewelry along with a bouquet of sickeningly perfumed flowers. A three-page love letter that seemed to be using her breasts as their anchoring theme accompanied the flowers, though honorable mention was also made of her hair, her eyes, and her toes. She had thanked the attendants but informed them that she would be unable to travel with such finery when she and her friends did eventually leave Henares. Nox would, however, accept a few new, clean tunics and tailored riding pants if the duke were feeling generous. A seamstress was sent to her quarters within the hour to take her measurements. She requested that the reevers also have a few shirts and a set of britches made for each of them as well. The seamstress, who was doubtlessly under orders from the duke to give Nox whatever she asked, hastily agreed.

"Wait!" she called after the seamstress.

"Yes?" The woman turned, concern coloring her face.

"Take a few things with you. What do you like? Necklaces? Dresses?"

"M'lady, I couldn't—"

"I'm no lady. I will, however, take it as a personal insult if you don't leave this room with at least three items. I need all these things gone. Tell your friends as well."

It took a bit more persuading, but the seamstress eventually left with a cashmere shawl, an emerald ring, and three bottles of perfume. The perfume had less to do with the woman's wants and more to do with Nox needing the overpowering odors gone. She opened the window, desperate to escape the duke's suffocating mist of noxious affection. Other servants continued to file in and out of the room—some to drop off new gifts, others to follow her bidding and remove the odds and ends from the bedchamber.

It was while the estate's attendants were bustling about her room that she noticed the apple still remained—no signs of wilting or browning—on her bedside table. She took a careful step in front of the table to conceal it with her body and smiled at them as they filed out. She wished there were someone she could talk to about everything going through her mind, but she knew exactly what Ash or Malik would say. The duke was about as intelligent as a bowl of marmalade. She had no friends or confidantes. She could really use the unbiased opinion of a stranger.

Nox sat at the desk in her room for a while and strummed her fingers against its surface. She missed music. No part of her missed the Selkie, save for the gentle sounds of the lutist strumming up from the lounge night after night. Silence was an uncomfortable companion in its stead as it left her alone with her thoughts, particularly as her mind had never been her favorite companion.

An idea came to her, though she didn't know how foolish or clever the thought might be. She chewed on her lip and bounced her foot as she reflected on the potential consequences. She hadn't touched any of her spelled objects ever since the pocket watch had taken them successfully from the Temple of the All Mother back to the main road. With one sharp inhalation, she decided to take the plunge and write to her phantom pen pal.

Nox retrieved the elaborate black quill from her bag and took a piece of parchment from the desk. A lovely crystal container filled with fresh ink sat ready at the desk for anyone who might need it. There was also a secondary, far more mundane quill that the duke and his estate had provided, but it was precisely for its magic that she had decided to use this spelled object.

She anxiously tapped the spelled quill against the paper several times before writing one word.

Hello?

Nox stared at her pages for a long time, but no mystical answer came in return. She was not a patient person. She stood and paced the room, looking at the paper with every passage by the desk. If she stayed in the room much longer, she'd asphyxiate on impatience and perfume.

She stepped out of her clothes and allowed an attendant to draw her a bath.

Nox soaked amidst the clouds of popping bubbles, scrubbing the day from her body and using mild scents and lathers in her hair. She needed a break from the florals and musks and opted instead for a bar of soap that smelled faintly of cream and almonds. She had intended to relax in the tub for far longer, but after less than ten minutes of soaking, curiosity drove her from the tub. She took sopping wet steps from the bathing room into the bedroom, leaving tiny lakes of sudsy water in her footprints. Water dripped from her hair, her limbs, her fingertips, but she had crossed to the desk for nothing.

No message awaited her.

Nox toweled herself dry and took a brush through her

long, damp locks. She slid into one of the many risqué night-dresses the duke had provided, keeping an eye on the paper all the while. She continued to stare at it, empathizing with why so many clients at the Selkie would pour out their hearts and share their likes, their dislikes, their most controversial opinions, and their life stories with the women who worked the salon floor. It was often easier to speak to a stranger.

When still no message came, she decided to write again.

I don't know who you are, but I'd like to speak with you.

An eternity passed before Nox gave up entirely, simmering with frustrated excuses, from assumptions to the quill being broken to the death of its owner. Perhaps she'd imagined their initial correspondence. Maybe it had never been real.

With an agitated flourish, she hid what remained of the apple, tucking it into the same drawer as she had on her first night in Henares. She crawled under the covers and began her fitful night. Ever the light sleeper, her problem was exacerbated by the nagging curiosity that refused to leave her in peace. She roused several times throughout the night, glancing at the starry sky out her suite's windows. The night was moonless, which gave her no indication of the passage of time.

Though she was no stranger to insomnia and often stayed up late and woke even later, the sounds of the rooster stirred her around dawn. Normally, Nox would ignore it as a pleasant sign that she had five more hours of sleep ahead of her, but this time, eagerness tugged at her from a cord to her belly button. She sat up and peered over to the desk where she could see in perfectly neat handwriting, a response had been written.

I have been in the same hands for forty years and in the same home for one hundred years prior. It is you who is the stranger.

Nox nearly leapt from her bed, tripping on the tangle of blankets that wrapped around her legs as she fell to the desk. The loud thump of her forehead hitting the wood with her exuberance was one of the only sounds throughout the otherwise silent grounds of the estate. She cursed against the sharp pain as a hand flew to what would surely become a big, purple lump above her eyebrow, but the pain didn't distract her for long. Only she and the rooster were moving at this hour. She pulled herself into the chair and hastily wrote back.

Then may we, as two strangers, discuss something?

She stared at the paper anxiously. She wasn't sure when the message had been written, but she didn't have the patience to wait another full night's sleep. Between poor sleep and a self-inflicted blow to the skull, the dull throb of a headache began to beat in her temple. Much to her relief, black letters began to bleed into the paper before her.

What would you like to discuss?

She nearly choked on her excitement. Where to start? Nox was long past debating the wisdom of revealing anything personal or important. She wanted to talk, consequences be damned.

I would like to pose a hypothetical scenario and gain the neutral perspective of an impartial judge.

The phantom said nothing.
After a pause, Nox continued to write in the space below her sentence.

If you were in possession of an object that offered you knowledge, but you did not understand the risks affiliated with the object, would you seek knowledge at any cost?

Ink began to blot onto her paper as the response came.

And why, hypothetically, am I in need of knowledge?

Nox considered this. She didn't feel particularly inclined to offer her life story. She didn't think it was necessary to describe her life as an orphan or her years in a brothel. She didn't want to mention their mission, the Temple of the All Mother, the apple, or the broken princess. How could she ask for advice without giving anything away? A familiar agitated fidget filled her as she bounced her knee, tapping the quill rapidly against the paper. Small flecks of ink splattered across her parchment. She wondered if the marks of her haste and irresponsibility manifested on the paper of the quill's twin. Finally, she decided on two statements, followed by a question.

I am on a mission, but in order to understand the task ahead of me, I am missing vital pieces of information. I do not know that this object will offer me the precise knowledge that I need. Is it worth a try?

Her question felt so foolishly worded. How could she possibly ask for advice when she wasn't even giving the barest outlines of the task at hand? It was a profoundly empty hypothetical unless she could be honest with the stranger. She was frustrated with herself. Her face scrunched in irritation with her inability to convey what she truly needed to ask.

The paper relayed a message.

I have found that some secrets are best left buried. Some missions are worth abandoning.

Nox realized there was a fundamental flaw in her communication. While there was comfort in speaking with an unnamed person, she had no way of knowing if the owner of

358

the other quill was good or if they were wicked. Furthermore, she could think of no way of dividing the world with such clarity as to discern friend or foe.

The rooster crowed again outside her window at the first light of dawn and stirred her from her contemplation. Perhaps, she thought, it was not about whether the person was good or bad but whether the owner of the quill's twin had a worldview that aligned with her own.

I need to ask your opinions on three things.

Ask them.

She wasn't sure why she had chosen the number three, other than knowing that fairy tales usually held some significance with this number. She moved her lips into a tight, sideways twist and then wrote,

Men. Money. Morality.

Nox didn't elaborate. Whatever the owner of the quill's spelled partner had to say about these subjects as well as how they chose to interpret her brevity would divulge plenty. After several minutes of hopeful anticipation, the paper revealed nothing. Her skin positively crawled with restlessness as she tried—and failed—to wait. She remembered being told that a watched kettle never whistled, but she'd always found the saying trite and stupid. Of course it would still boil. Water heated at the same rate whether eyes were on it or not. As she stared at the page, she decided that the saying should have read, "The person watching a pot will go insane before it boils."

Nox stood and began to dress for the day. She braided her hair into one long, single braid down her back. Just as quickly, she combed out the braid and attempted a variety of different paints, hair clips, and hand creams for distraction.

The moment she saw her parchment blot with color, she abandoned her attempts at charcoal and rouge and ran for the desk.

I've never found a use for men, though I have found use of money. Perhaps money clouds my morality, but I've long suspected it's those who wish to divide the world into good versus evil who create the continent's problems.

Nox's face spread into a slow, appreciative grin.
There she had it.
She was speaking to a morally flexible misandrist who neither idealized the church nor the continent. If this had been a religious individual, their stance on morality would have been clean-cut. If this had been someone beholden to the crown, they would never have taken the opportunity to slander the state of the continent. She smiled as she read the message a second time and then a third. This could be a friend after all. She wrote one commiserating sentence in return.

I've found men's primary use to be their money.

Nox felt as though she were bonding with another courtesan at the Selkie in the lounge over a glass of red wine and obnoxious stories of foolhardy patrons. Given the nature of the stranger's response, Nox was nearly positive she was writing with a woman. While she smiled at her own clever sentence, she wondered if she still believed it to be true.

Before her fateful encounter in the coliseum's dungeons, she would have said yes, absolutely.

Her exposure to men had for so many years been filtered through a very specific lens. At the orphanage, she had grown to despise the bishop. The boys who'd hated her and Amaris had been reacting to the cards stacked against them as the two girls had been given privileges and advantages not afforded to the others. She'd loathed the Selkie's patrons more often than not.

It wasn't until fate had united her with Ash and Malik that she began to wonder at the humanity of the men around her. The reevers were…whole.

While her sample of men had given her absolute certainty that men were horrid, they had been a particular subset of humanity. She'd been exposed exclusively to those who disliked or attempted to exploit her, whether it be the church, her young peers, or her clients. The reevers were teaching her that perhaps in the past, she'd only met the same man over and over and over again, though he'd had different names, different origins, and different faces. Her disdain for men and willingness to feed had been fostered under this unwavering truth she'd held so tightly.

Nox read her sentence again a few more times and decided she didn't need to amend her statement to the stranger, but she would amend it in her own heart. Ash and Malik had no coin, but they were worth more than their weight in crowns.

Surely if two were capable of integrity and kindness, there could be more.

The paper began to reveal the dark markings of another message.

You must tell me one thing if we are to continue speaking, and if you do not answer honestly, then I do not wish to continue our conversation.

Her pulse quickened.

Yes?

After a few tense heartbeats, the next message came into clarity.

What is your name?

The question was so intimate, so personal. She had expected a question about loyalties to the crown, religion, or how she had come to possess this spelled object. Nox debated abandoning the quill altogether and forgetting that she'd ever trifled with something enchanted. She chewed on her lip and thought through the consequences. What power could there possibly be in a name?

With only a name, they could not locate her, they could not discern her allegiances or intentions, nor could they learn of her mission. Nox had fostered a reputation for her renown as a courtesan in Priory that had stretched into Aubade, but if the phantom penman was a woman, she almost definitely would not have been running in the same circles as the gossips who spoke in hushed tones of Nox's beauty and skill in the bedroom.

If she didn't answer honestly, how would the recipient know? She could write any name on this page and no one would be the wiser. She could be Anna or Fae or Theresa, and she was quite sure that whoever she spoke to would never know. Still, if she wanted genuine responses from the person who held the quill on the other end, shouldn't she offer the same?

The rooster crowed again, urging her to make a decision.

This wasn't a game. There was no right or wrong answer. There was only whether to move forward. For no justifiable reason at all, she opted for honesty.

Nox.

Hello, Nox. It's nice to speak with you.

Her heart stuttered and she feared she may have played with fire for a bit too long. After her hasty introduction, she wrote a quick message about how she needed to leave for breakfast but promised she would write again later that night. It was a lie. She could have corresponded from the first light of morning until the waning hours of the night if she had wanted.

She couldn't shake the vulnerable feeling that she had

done something terribly foolish. She crumpled the pages that contained the evidence of their correspondence and burned the conversation in the crackling fire. The paper itself held no magic; it merely looked to any prying eye as if she were conversing with herself. She hid the quill in her bag and took several calming breaths before she went downstairs for breakfast.

Her heart was still beating quickly when she stepped into the dining room, only to come upon a lone individual chewing on a piece of jam-covered toast. She could tell from Malik's raised brows that he was surprised to see her awake so early. She understood, as he was normally the first one up, followed by Ash and the duke, and then Nox several hours later. He gestured for her to take a seat as if this were his house to offer. He had not yet finished his morning tea and wasn't particularly chatty, though he always managed to find a smile for her.

After a few bites, she decided to inquire about her axe. "Will you be helping me practice any short-range combat today?"

He perked up at this. "Would you like me to be there with you?"

"Of course I want you there!" And she meant it.

He reddened slightly, and she wondered if she had been too enthusiastic. There were a few things she knew and a few things she didn't. The first thing she knew was that, irrespective of how much time had passed, she loved the reevers deeply and they cared for her in return. The second thing she knew was that Malik, perhaps because he was purely human and she had the blood of a succubus in her veins, had a fondness for her that surpassed whatever amiability Ash felt. The third thing she knew was that she liked the way he made her feel. What she didn't understand was why. She wasn't prepared to examine her feelings too carefully on the subject. She hadn't even finished her morning tea, after all.

Playing with Chandra made the morning fly by.

She was delighted that both Ash and Malik joined her on the grassy archer's range in what appeared to be new tunics.

She was less delighted to see the duke lurking behind them, but she ignored him to eye their shirts. She clapped her hands together with excitement. "Do you love them?"

Malik tugged at the fabric of his shirt while he mumbled something or other. "Ash's is black. Why can't I have a black one?"

"Forest green is a perfectly lovely color, and it matches your eyes."

"I still want a black one."

Nox promised she'd have all the colors of the rainbow sent to their rooms.

The reevers looked at the duke, perhaps to thank him for his endless generosity, but it was quite clear from his affectionate dithering that he wasn't cognizant of his own philanthropy. He was too busy watching Nox with wide, puppy eyes to bother looking at Ash or Malik. She pointedly ignored him so she might fully enjoy time with her axe.

While they practiced combat maneuvers, Nox felt both pleased and heartsick that they continued to bring up Amaris. She learned more about her white-haired love that day on the grass than she had in a long time. She hadn't dared speak about Amaris, as she was never sure what would come out of her mouth if she did. She learned that Amaris was the most nimble and tenacious of all the reevers and one of their most formidable assassins, perhaps solely for what she stood to prove. They didn't gloss over her months of strife, failure, and softness. They mentioned every bet placed against her that she'd quit or die or run away in the night. Their faces beamed with pride when the tide of their tales began to turn, waxing poetic about their favorite brother. They wholeheartedly agreed that Nox already showed more grace and aptitude with movement in days than Amaris had in her first six months of lessons.

Nox smiled in earnest, thriving on the compliments. She had grown accustomed to feeding on a daily supply of external validation and had begun to feel a bit starved. If performing well in combat gained her more praise, it would only motivate her to work harder. Plus, she really, really loved her axe.

They practiced swinging Chandra but emphasized that if someone came in closely, she needed to switch to her dagger. She and Malik went over a few more defensive maneuvers, and Nox was acutely aware of each touch when he'd correct her, whether it be adjusting her grip with his hands, straightening her arm, or widening her stance. Eventually, the reevers abandoned Nox to allow her to practice throwing Chandra over her head at the target while they wandered off to busy themselves elsewhere on the estate. There was still plenty of day left for them to get into some trouble.

She busied herself with her deadly best friend for some time, cleaning the axe carefully when she finished. It was one of the loveliest evenings she'd had in a long time. Her high spirits buoyed her as she entered the manor with a smile on her face. Nox was taking her leisurely time as she walked up to her rooms, arms tired from the day and heart overflowing with her success.

She'd just crested the stairs when she heard something. From the space in the corridor, she could just make out the men talking rather conspiratorially in Malik's room. Nox paused in the middle of the hallway and her smile flickered. Her joy was little more than a candle caught in a breeze that threatened to extinguish it altogether. She couldn't tell what they were arguing about as their tones remained hushed. She hadn't intended to eavesdrop, but curiosity forced her forward. She crept closer to the door and debated interrupting. If she didn't make herself known, she'd be spying, and that didn't feel right. Nox knocked on the frame of the door and poked her head in, summoning her smile once more, though it was a shadow of what it had been moments before.

"Hey." She let her eyes flit between the reevers. "I heard you chatting."

Both men tensed where they sat. "You did?"

Her face fell, though she did her best to contain whatever complicated emotion had a downward gravitational pull on her heart. This was unlike them. Nox used her years of acting to keep herself from frowning, resisting the urge to cross her arms as if to protect her heart from a physical wound. "I didn't hear what you were chatting *about*. I just heard you speaking. Does it involve me?"

The reevers exchanged looks.

With a stab of anxiety, she pressed, "Only good things, I hope?"

Ash stood and clapped his hands together. He made an excuse to leave the room, saying something about needing to bond with his good pal, the duke. His exit had not been subtle. He brushed past Nox, not making direct eye contact with her as he left.

"Is everything okay?" She looked after the blank space in the hall and then to Malik.

Nox fidgeted uncomfortably in the doorway before Malik invited her fully into the room. He made a gesture for her to join him for conversation. This was not a pleasurable tension. She felt like she was somehow in trouble or about to be excommunicated from their group. Despite years of swagger and confidence, an intense insecurity pushed down on her.

She forced herself to stay both present and calm. She needed to hear what had to be said. Maybe she was imagining things. Maybe nothing was amiss. Maybe everything was all right. Maybe.

"I'd like to talk to you," Malik said quietly.

Thirty-Three

H IS EYES DIDN'T MEET HERS. THE SAME SICKNESS COURSED through her. They had never treated her like this—whatever *this* was.

These were not words one used to begin a pleasant conversation. Nox took a few steps into the room and opted to sit at the chair intended for the writing desk, angling it to face Malik where he rested on the edge of his bed. She tried to swallow against the knot swelling in her throat.

She continued looking at him, prodding him with her worried gaze.

Her fingers twisted in her lap. "Did I do something wrong?"

Malik's eyebrows lifted as he shook his head, wide eyes locking on hers intently for the first time. The eye contact was a relief compared to avoidance but didn't make the situation any easier to understand. He spoke a bit too quickly, struggling to select the proper volume and cadence of his voice. At first it was too loud. Then it was too quiet. "No! No, not at all. It's me who has done something wrong."

His answer was so unexpected that she felt as if she may have misheard him. Nox's face rearranged itself with surprised, expressive brows pulling together, forcing him to look away once more.

While she'd known him to be shy from time to time, it had always accompanied a charming sort of blush. Though she sincerely doubted it, she hoped it was just about him disliking his green shirt. If that were the case, she'd be sure to get him a black one posthaste.

"I like you," he said. He raised his lily-pad-green eyes to meet hers, then pressed them shut as if humiliated at the three words.

She curved her mouth upward a little unhelpfully at that. The fire from his hearth licked its oranges and reds against her attempt at a reassuring smile. "I like you too, Malik."

He exhaled through his nose, his mouth pressing into a line. He shook his head. "No, I mean, I like you more than has been appropriate. I want to—no, I need to ask for your forgiveness. I owe you an apology."

A distressing heat crept up her neck. Conflicting emotions battled within her as blood colored her chest and cheeks, betraying her feelings. Nox felt a bit like she'd been kicked in the stomach, though she couldn't articulate why. She looked down at her hands, continuing to twist her fingers. Her words came out quietly.

"You have nothing to apologize for."

He was still disagreeing. "No, I do. How long have you been with us now, Nox? You've traveled with us, slept beside us, and been through the fires of hell and back with us. We believe in you, and you trust us to protect you all the same. And we will—I will. You shouldn't have to worry about any intentions other than being a brother in arms."

Nox's frown became more pronounced, revealing her tangle of feeling and confusion. "Do reevers have some code for celibacy?"

This took him by surprise. "No! No. It's not that." Malik cleared his throat and tried to steady himself. "I'm not a virgin." He blushed deeply at the word in a way that almost made the statement feel like a lie. He made a face, clearly hating every single second of the conversation. Still, his honor prompted him to continue. "Regardless, if I were to court someone, I would want to make my intentions known. I would want her to accept my gestures of her own volition. It's not honorable to show any other intentions toward you, Nox." He began to reiterate his convictions, "You trust us, and we believe in you. Ash and I care about you. I…care about you."

Nox had always thought herself to be an emotionally intelligent person, but it had generally applied to reading the room and understanding those around her. She was having some sort of epiphany as she realized that very little of that emotional intelligence extended to inward reflection. At present, she was baffled at the storm she felt within herself. Her heart wrenched, and though she hadn't yet named the reason, she was starting to develop a suspicion. She wanted to stop him from speaking, explaining himself, apologizing, or whatever it was he was doing. She wanted to counter his arguments, but she wasn't sure how. She felt quite confident that she'd be sick if he cut her off from whatever well of affection he'd been offering.

"There's another thing," Malik said quietly. He'd done his best to hold her eyes for as long as he could, but they drifted to his lap as he continued his humble apology. "Ash is a good friend to both of us, and he was right to call me into accountability. He's a good man. I was there in the dungeon when you were with Amaris. I heard what was said and I saw what was shared. I want you to know, I honor whatever your relationship to her may be. Amaris is a reever, but she's more than that. She's our family."

Nox felt her eyes prick with the familiar sensation of impending tears. The room suddenly felt too hot. She was terribly uncomfortable. There wasn't enough air in the room. "Malik, it's so complicated…"

He smiled, but it didn't reach his eyes. His voice was so kind, so tender in its sadness. "It doesn't have to be complicated. I've liked you, Nox, and I will still continue to like you in ways that value you—but not selfishly."

His message didn't resonate with her. It was wrong. She felt the honor in his words. She was touched by the sacrifice. It was noble. She felt gratitude, upset, loss, and…something else.

"Malik." She said his name again, tasting the word and willing him to look at her. His emerald eyes met her dark, cautious gaze. The uncertainty was disquieting. The spirit of the room felt like the weight of a rain-sodden blanket that desperately needed to be wrung out. Nox didn't know if she could squeeze every drop of water from the fabric between them, but she had to try. "Can I say something?"

"Of course." It was an automatic response, delivered with as much discomfort as every other bit of the conversation.

"Even Amaris doesn't know how I feel about her, not truly. She and I have never spoken about it beyond three words shouted in a jail cell. I spent fifteen years with her and never had the conversation you and I are having right now—not an honest one, not one that would allow me to be vulnerable like you're being." She looked at him with kindness and was grateful that he looked back. "Perhaps my views on love and life are skewed from my…*profession*…but the thing I've come to believe about love is that it has never been a finite resource. People seem to understand this so clearly in settings like a typical family: a mother does not have to continue to divide her love between each of her children, with each son and daughter getting a smaller percentage as the siblings grow and her love dilutes. Her love infinitely expands, doesn't it? Yet when people think of affections in their romantic capacities, they suddenly lose grasp of the concept of what a bottomless well love can be. Time is finite, and perhaps you can only give so much time to each individual. Resources are finite, so perhaps you can only give so much or spend so much or offer so much to someone. But in matters of the heart, why should it be any less so with me and my capacities for feeling?"

The look on his face told her that he had no idea where

she was going with this or what she was saying. Honestly, neither did she.

"You have romantic feelings for women." He said the words carefully, reiterating what he had stated above. His sentence was not one of judgment but of cautious fact. It seemed as though neither of them were breathing.

"I do," she affirmed. "I like women, and I love Amaris. That said, I have been with both men and women, to varying degrees of success." Nox laughed humorlessly at her own dark, private joke before proceeding. "I will always love her, whether or not she returns my affection. Perhaps I don't need her to care for me for me to love her. Love isn't ownership, after all."

He tilted his chin to one side, unable to complete the shake of his head that he undoubtedly wanted to make. "I'm not sure I understand."

She nearly laughed. "And is that so bad?"

He looked at her, waiting for her to elaborate. Some of the unease left the room as a new type of tension replaced it. They were entering unfamiliar territory, but they were doing it together.

"Why do we need to understand everything?" Nox grew a bit bolder. She dropped the twist of her fingers, cocking her head as she held his stare. She continued, "Truth be told, I don't believe in dichotomies. I know that the world is very comfortably split into one thing or the other, but I think that some of the best things belong in the gray."

Nox had been speaking for such a long time. She bit her tongue to stop herself from rambling further. She wasn't sure where any of this was coming from, as she hadn't truly voiced the convictions bubbling from her. Though she believed everything she'd said, and she supposed she and the lovely Emily had discussed the outlines of these philosophies while wrapped up in the rumpled silken sheets at the Selkie, these weren't thoughts she'd often spoken aloud.

Malik's eyes were so bright as he tried to piece together

what she was saying. Nox felt the impulse to close the space between them and gave in to the urge. She abandoned her chair and crossed the room to sit on the bed beside him. He didn't pull away from her as she sat down, mere inches away. She placed her fingers on top of his, squeezing his hand gently. Her expression softened. She lowered her voice as she implored him to listen. "What I know is this: whatever it is you're trying to say or do to be noble, whatever this conversation was meant to be at its onset, I don't want it."

Nox continued lightly holding her hand over his. She could sense his pulse as it began to increase. She had heard everything he had to say and had rejected his apology. She'd drawn nearer. She'd opened herself up. She knew that if she wanted anything, she would have to be the one to make a move. He was too gallant to even hold affections for her when it was inappropriate, let alone touch her without her permission. He was too honorable to pull her to him with their lines so blurry. His respect, his boundaries, his decency wouldn't move him forward. This was her dance to lead.

Nox leaned in close enough to feel the heat of his body, consequences be damned. Rationale was unimportant. Labels and identities and the world that spun around her didn't seem as consequential as the individual in front of her.

She heard Malik's audible swallow as he choked back his nervous energy. He'd gone from the humility of apology to the spark of affection in a matter of a few short minutes as everything shifted. There was electricity between them, and while she felt it thrum, she was certain he felt it with the strength of a lightning storm. Her face was terribly near to his. It could be nearer. She could be closer.

"I do have to warn you." Her voice was barely a murmur, her lips just a hairsbreadth above his own. She lowered her lashes and let him feel the heat of her breath, tasting plums and dark spice on his mouth. "You wouldn't survive a night with me—and I do mean that literally. But for now? Between you and me? Let's forget about black and white."

He answered in something that was scarcely more than a whisper, lips nearly brushing hers as he spoke. His voice was husky with the longing to close the small gap between them. "Well, in that case, I respect your right to stand firmly in the gray."

She sucked in a final breath, warm air exchanged between them before she sealed the gap.

His mouth touched hers, lips parting as they connected. This was no kiss of life as it had been with the spider. This was not perfunctory; this was not for work or coin or power. This was composed of two people sharing the forbidden chemistry of a single moment.

The energy pulsed into life like a candle erupting into a bonfire. The moment throbbed into passion as he put one hand to the back of her neck and the other on the small of her back, holding her against him. Gone was the gallantry. This was something they both wanted.

Malik pressed her body into his own. She wrapped her arms around his neck and kissed him deeply, tongue drinking in his goodness, flicking against his words, his care, tasting his compassion as it moved. She kissed with an intensity and fervor that she'd never been afforded with a man. While she had embraced Amaris with all the love in her heart, she had no idea whether the young woman on the other side of those iron bars had felt the same or merely returned the kiss out of reunion and fear of death.

But this moment was not about Amaris.

This was a need, but not one of the thirst she'd come to know so well.

In that moment, she moved on Malik knowing that he wanted her as badly as she wanted him. The complex flavors of longing and plums and confusion moved between them, exchanging with each breath, each touch, each press of hand against skin. She pushed herself into him fully, relishing the feeling of the firm outline of his muscles beneath her touch. Their mouths and lips and tongues and hands tangled and moved for several heated seconds, gasping air sparkling between them, until Nox pulled away.

She could feel herself getting hungry.

Malik was dazed. He caught his breath while she struggled to pull herself together for an entirely separate reason.

Damn. Damn it all.

Nox was not hungry. Her vision had started to grow glazed with want, and she recognized the feeling from the times she'd drunk too deeply at the brothel. Malik's eyes were still crystal clear and terribly sharp. The longing in those verdant eyes had not been satiated. If anything, his appetite had merely been whetted. As she'd broken the kiss, he waited in anticipation of her next move.

They couldn't, for so many reasons.

There was so much she was unwilling to say. She didn't want to shatter the goodness in him that held her in such high regard. She couldn't bear to see the way his eyes would dim, the way his shoulders would slump when he realized what she was. Even if she could, she wasn't sure if she was ready to examine how she could possibly have stumbled into this beautiful, quasi-romantic mess with a man.

She didn't like men. In fact, she hated men.

But she didn't hate Malik.

Nox pressed her forehead to his and put a hand to the side of his face, willing both of them to calm down. She wanted to kiss him again. She wanted him to raise his strong arms above his head as she took off his tunic. Her mind clouded with visions of allowing her hands to trace the ripples of his pectorals and abdominals, kissing the divide that demarcated the center of his stomach. She could taste the heat and salt of his skin as the wild burn of thirst ached for her mouth to travel across the curves of his body. Her fingers twitched against the impulse to feel his calloused hands on her soft skin while he undressed her, to feel his mouth on her neck, his hands in her hair. It would be so easy, so welcome, so wanted. She throbbed with the temptation. The picture of their clothes crumbled on the ground, her legs on either side of his as she straddled him, the look in his eyes as he felt her with every inch of his being was all she could see. She was already wet with the longing to slip him inside her. She wanted, for the first time in her life, to *want* the man she was with.

Goddess, she was hungry.

Nox forced herself to picture mundane things. She tore her vision from naked tangled bodies, her back arched, toes curled, gasps and moans and growls, to images of kitchen sinks, scrub buckets, horses and clouds and vegetables. She forced herself to stop thinking of how it would feel to have his mouth on her breasts, struggling to remember the rough scratch of burlap, the cold feeling of walking to the washing room with bare feet in the middle of the night, the taste of boiled cabbage. She had to think of something—*anything*—else.

Nox released a ragged breath, tightening her grip on the collar of his tunic. It was a steadying move, a denial of self. She needed to check in with him, to ask him how he was, to talk, but she was still struggling to rein herself in. He seemed content to linger in the pulsing afterglow of their exchange, which allowed time for her internal battle.

She could have him if she wanted. She knew she could take.

If she did, Malik would no longer be the man she knew once she released him. He would not continue to be the clever, charming, sweet man she'd grown so bafflingly fond of. He wouldn't fight, wouldn't think, wouldn't love or grow or live. He would become another shell, a husk, as was the duke who flitted about his manor now writing poetry about her tits, sending her gowns, and showering her with gifts. If she were to sleep with him, she would be the one responsible for his death certificate.

She wondered if she should tell him, asking herself if she owed it to him to explain why she could never consummate their electric energy. She did, in fact, prefer women. She loved women. She loved the softness of their bodies, the gentleness of their curves, the hitches of their breaths, the taste of their sweetness on her tongue. She loved that she could roll into the throws of passion with a woman and know that her partner would be safe, that her dark powers would not steal any life from the women with whom she lay. All that was true. And the truth of it had no bearing on what she felt for this man now, in whatever capacity.

She felt his hand tense and relax against her lower back. It had been an involuntary moment as he'd controlled himself, but goddess, it had been sexy. Her body responded a number of ways. Her hips rolled involuntarily. Her breath caught. Her shirt betrayed the peaks of her breasts. A similar movement happened as his hand twitched against the back of her neck, their foreheads still connected. Chills trickled down her spine from his fingers near the base of her hair all the way to her tailbone. It was delicious to be desired. The urge to give herself over to that thirst…

Stop it, she cursed herself again and again.

She didn't want to tell the reever what she truly was. Nox didn't want either of the men to know, but especially not Malik. However, he had attempted honesty with her even when it had nearly broken his heart. She should try and do the same…to whatever extent she was able.

"I want you to know that I do like you, and…" Nox swallowed, ensuring that he felt the weight of her next four words as she ran a hand along his chest. "I *do* want you. And this. I want this. And…" She had to stop again, feeling the way his callous fingers had brushed her neck, her hair, her lower-most back as she'd confessed her wants. She wasn't done. She needed him to listen. "And I want you to remember that as I tell you what I'm about to tell you now." Nox removed her forehead from where it had rested against his while they'd steadied themselves and caught their breaths. When their eyes met again, it was with comfort, affection, and lingering, unquenched longing. "I do possess abilities, and please don't ask me about them."

His lips parted in a question as his golden brows furrowed, then closed once more.

She continued, "Whether it's a gift or a curse, only the goddess knows."

"You saved me, Nox. The spider—"

"Please." She stopped him, fingers bunching in the fabric of his shirt once more. Yes. They'd seen a facet of her abilities that she didn't even know she had. She'd taken souls on so many occasions. After a year of corpses and carrion, she'd learned she could breathe a bit of their lives back into their bodies. Instead, she'd given Malik what she'd stolen from Eramus—the piece he needed to make it out alive. "My abilities made me an excellent courtesan. And they're also precisely why we can never be together, Malik. I'm not ashamed of who I am or the life I've lived, but *what* I am… well, when I tell you that we can't do everything we want to do… When I tell you I can't spend the night in your bed, that we can't take off our clothes, that I can't press myself into you, that I can't taste you or feel you inside me or—"

"Please stop." He closed his eyes as he inhaled sharply through his nose to stay connected to reality.

"Right, sorry. My imagination got a little carried away. It's just… It's not because I don't want to. Quite the opposite, in fact. It's because I care too much about you to allow you to become like the shed snakeskin of a man that the duke is. You've seen how hollow he is, haven't you? I did that to him. That's because of me. I don't want that to happen to you."

He tried to swallow. "But, Amaris—"

This wasn't a logical flaw she was willing to pursue. She cut him off swiftly. "Nothing I do or have shared with you or have done detracts from how my heart also beats for Amaris. This moment isn't about her. This is about you, me, what we feel, and what I'm going to do to keep you alive."

His fingers tensed against the tender space where he'd continued to hold the back of her neck. Malik's hands gripped more tightly, pulling her nearly to the point of another kiss.

Their lips were so near. Their mouths wanted to meet again. He allowed the static to tingle between them, resisting the lure of closing the gap.

He made it clear: he wanted her badly.

Goddess damn it.

The barest distance he left between them was a pause for permission. The temptation and its denial were better and worse all at the same time. Dangling forbidden fruit was a delicious brand of torture. Once more, she would need to close the remaining distance if she wanted it. Once more, he allowed her the steps of their dance while making his intentions exceptionally clear as his fingers continued to dig firmly into her flesh. The air passed between them, hot and damp on each other's lips. Nox felt the hunger claw at her belly. She felt the craving peak against her breasts and the innermost parts where her thighs met. The succubus banged against its cage, howling to be released. It scratched and clawed until she felt bloodied from within. If only he knew what she was denying herself to keep him alive…

No.

She was no monster, nor a hopeless addict.

Nox blinked under heavy, lowered eyelashes several times and pulled away. The motion took the restraint of a shark tearing itself away from blood in the water. She battled for her own sense of self control, confident that her human half was fighting her fae half with whatever goodness and decency it possessed. She pictured her demon half with wings and fangs and talons, but her human half had responsibility, love, and consent.

Nox broke their hold, and he relinquished his grasp.

The puddle of longing from her own water as it moved against her inner thighs. She had less than a minute of self-restraint within her. It took her a moment to get to her feet, stars dancing in her head as her blood pulsed in her lower-most parts.

She smoothed her hair and her clothes, exhaling noisily in frustration.

He looked after her with the half-dazed look of a deeply smitten man. It took them a long time with her swaying on unsteady feet before he spoke. "What should I tell Ash?"

She almost laughed at the abrupt confrontation with reality. So normal. So human. Such an appropriate, honest question. Nox quirked her lips into a smile. She chuckled lightly as she reached the door, looking over her shoulder at him. "Tell him that I appreciate him looking out for me and that he's a good friend to Amaris but that life is complicated and it's none of his damn business."

Nox made it into her own room and closed and locked the door behind her. She was in a hurry to accomplish the release she so desperately needed. With several quick tugs of her hands, she freed herself from the clothes that bound her and crawled naked onto the bed, alone with the water that was saturating her, starving for the filling sensation of oxytocin. If she genuinely cared to keep Malik alive, then the only place they'd be able to be together would be here, with her hand, alone in her bed in the safety of her mind, where she let him touch and taste and feel everything she wanted but would never be able to have.

Thirty–Four

NOX HAD FALLEN INTO A BLISSFUL, COMFORTABLE NAP ATOP her sheets. It was nearly dinnertime when she awoke and realized she was still fully nude. She redressed, blushing to herself as she thought of her complicated afternoon. A man! A human man. It was the most ridiculous thing she'd ever considered. She brushed her hair and began to braid it once more from where strong, calloused fingers had tugged it loose only hours before. Her fingers moved nimbly against the back of her head when she noticed a fresh sheet of paper begin to show dark, inky markings.

Have you made your decision about your pursuit of knowledge, Nox?

Now was not the time for thoughts of sex and hunger. She'd satiated herself, to whatever dissatisfying end. It would have to suffice. Nox cleared her throat to sober herself. Between the haze of her sleep and the complicated exchange from her moments with the reever, she needed a clearer mind before she was to respond to her phantom.

Focus on the phantom penman. The question. The problem.

She sat down at the desk and stared at the paper. She hadn't had the time to consider if she would eat the apple and risk dreaming once again. Truthfully, the spelled quill and mysterious fruit had been the furthest things from her mind over the last few hours. She felt a twinge of discomfort that the stranger was addressing her by name.

She contemplated her predicament and her need for knowledge. She thought of the stranger who owned her quill's twin and how they might help her without her revealing anything about the tree, what she saw, or her mission. She decided to offer the penman one more element of information in the form of a question.

What do you know of the princess?

The paper did not reveal any further responses.

Dinner was ripe with the potential to have been terribly awkward. Malik seemed to spend the entire meal unsure as to whether he should look at the food or his friends or into his goblet, which didn't help things. He was too pure-hearted to be truly blessed with the ability to conceal his emotions. Fortunately, the duke accompanied them for the meal with a small team of minstrels and attempted to serenade Nox while she ate her potatoes. Ash was too busy laughing aloud to notice how his friend blushed any time Nox looked in his direction. The minstrels did their best to remain professional, but it was clear it was the most uncomfortable hired performance of their lives. Nox hoped they were being fairly compensated for this exercise in torture. She chewed on a charred vegetable while wondering if she should use her influence to steer the course of the duke's finances more directly. She could ensure the musicians were well paid, help his staff, see that the people of Henares were given breaks from unfair taxation… Yes, perhaps her powers didn't have to be used for evil. She could make sure some good was done in the land before her time in Henares ended.

After dinner, the duke presented Nox with not one but three intricately crafted leather holsters for her to strap Chandra and her knives close to her body. The holsters were adjustable enough that she was able to gift the reevers with the remaining two as they could slide the clasps and buckles to fit their broader bodies and hold their own swords tightly against their backs and chests. Rather than continue using their stolen sentinel swords, the duke had unlocked his personal armory and allowed the three to raid his weapons. Both Malik and Ash picked out beautiful, balanced broadswords, a collection of knives, and reinforced hunting bows with their complementary quivers of arrows.

Nox made an offhand comment about being impressed by archery, which devolved into an archery competition that no longer interested her. Malik had said with some certainty that he'd hit the bull's-eye even in the dark. Ash had countered that he would split Malik's arrow in half and pierce his bull's-eye. The duke had said the men were free to shoot their arrows and spend their evenings however they wished.

Eventually, all three were matched with horses from the duke's extensive stables and each horse fitted with saddlebags necessary for their travels, including blankets, whetstones, waterskins, and an entire bag dedicated to their newly tailored clothes. While staying in Henares had been vital to recuperate their strength and supplies, their time was nearing its close. They wanted another full night's sleep on comfortable beds with down pillows and silk sheets before they became forest rats once more.

Nox returned to her room and readied herself to pack what remained of the apple, carefully wrapping it in a scarf and stashing it in her bag. It was then that she noticed her phantom had responded with two words.

Which princess?

Nox blinked a number of times at the question.

"What?" she whispered to the room.

She thought through all she knew of politics. Queen Moirai ruled alone in Farehold, with the crown prince next in line for succession—a prince who, if the reevers were to be believed, did not exist. The north held only King Ceres on the throne in Gwydir. The Etal Isles were said to have had the same benevolent fae imperatress reigning for hundreds of years with no information about heirs filtering through. Beyond the Frozen Straits, Sulgrave was said to be ruled through their individual territories with comtes overseeing each of their seven lands. She could think of no princess aside from the late Daphne.

How could she prompt the phantom to respond without giving away her ignorance? Chewing on her lip, she debated what fabrication she might spin to elicit elaboration. She finally wrote one word.

Both.

The response came almost instantly.

You know, then.

Nox's pulse quickened. She felt as though she stood on the precipice of something, though she had no idea what. This was important. She closed her eyes and practiced inhaling through her nose and exhaling through her mouth before finally responding with a sentence.

Tell me everything.

She swallowed but found her mouth too dry to alleviate the nerves she felt. She still had no idea whether she was speaking to a helpful friend or a dangerous foe, but there was information at her fingertips that she couldn't quite grasp. The object of her knowledge was too slippery, too oil-slick for her to find a hold. The Tree of Life had wanted her to know about Princess Daphne and her final plea before she collapsed to the temple floor. The apple had fed her memories of the princess only known to Daphne, the priestess, and the Tree. That knowledge now rested in her belly like a rock, her stomach acids roiling around it while she struggled to understand what it was trying to tell her.

Somewhere in the world, whoever held the other quill wrote a response, and Nox knew exactly what she had to do.

I'll grant your answers where your journey began.

Her fingers wrapped around the slippery thought in that moment. Whatever word had been at the tip of her tongue snapped into place. It all became so clear as she remembered exactly where she had once been wandering through an office when she'd seen an elaborate black quill.

Revelation. Realization. Disbelief. Shock. Horror.

Nox left her room immediately and knocked on the reevers' respective doors, summoning them to the hall. Her eyes were wide. Her tone was grave.

"We have to leave in the morning."

They nodded immediately, both tensed against her expression. "Are we ready to go back to Aubade?"

She shook her head. "No, we're heading north. To Farleigh."

Thirty–Five

IF SHE WERE GOING TO TAKE ANOTHER BITE OF THE APPLE, IT should be now. She was in a safe, warm environment far from the terrors of the forest and perils of enemies beyond these four walls. If she was to ride for the mill in the morning, she might as well set off armed with every bit of insight available to her. Perhaps the tree had already bequeathed the entirety of its gifts and she would drift off into a dreamless, uneventful sleep. Perhaps it would show her interesting though irrelevant memories of how it had been planted and grown through the millennia. Maybe it would do nothing. Maybe another bite truly would kill her.

Ash had returned to his room, but Nox grabbed Malik lightly by the arm before he could turn away.

"Will you sleep with me tonight?"

He looked like she had hit him in the face with the broad side of a sword.

Nox nearly choked on her own spit as she stumbled over her correction, "I'm sorry, that was misleading. Goddess, sorry. I'm about to do something potentially unwise—my mind's made up, I'm doing it—and it might be helpful to have someone beside me in case I stop breathing."

Understandably, this didn't console him. "What are you talking about?"

"Come with me." She pulled Malik into her room with her and closed the door. "I'm going to take another bite of the apple."

His face paled. "You still have the apple? Why would you do that? Last time, it had shaken you so thoroughly that your screams woke the entire estate."

She didn't disagree. "I know, but if I could possibly learn anything more, I feel like I need to try. If it seems to be going poorly or if I look like I'm in trouble, you could just shake me awake and pull me out."

"Nox…"

This wasn't up for discussion. She was going to eat from the fruit whether or not he stayed.

Nox stepped into the bathing room to change into her nightdress while Malik remained fully clothed. She gave him a disapproving look. "You know I'm not going to try to ravish you in the night, right?"

Malik fidgeted. "I think I'll just stay awake for a while and let you sleep."

She frowned. "You should be able to get some sleep too. We're traveling tomorrow, and I don't want you to be exhausted."

He shrugged. "I won't be able to fall asleep knowing there's a chance you may die in the night." Malik helped himself onto the bed, sitting on top of the covers. He patted the space next to him.

"No. I won't be able to sleep knowing you're being peculiar and watching me, fully clothed. Can you do your best to pretend it's a normal night? Prepare for bed? Just…lie next to me?"

He opened his mouth to protest but couldn't think of an argument. "If I fall asleep, I can't help you. It's better if I stay ready for action, don't you think?"

"I don't think whatever I might face can be stopped by

swords or reever apparel. I do think that I have trouble sleeping and that if you're staring at me, it won't make it any better. However, I have often slept better if someone I trusted was sound asleep beside me."

Once again, he opened his mouth, then closed it. She stood in the doorway to the bathing room in one of the silken nightdresses that barely grazed the tops of her thighs, leaving little to the imagination. The duke had provided almost nothing by way of modest attire, but she preferred it that way. She'd rather sleep naked, but it may have caused Malik's heart to seize if she disrobed completely. Standing before him in a paper-thin slip probably wasn't much kinder.

Eventually, he stood from the bed and excused himself to wash and change into night shorts. When he reemerged, she was already tucked beneath the covers with a small bundle in one hand. It was her turn to pat the open space beside her.

"Can I just say one more time, for the record, that this is a bad idea?" he asked while sliding into the sheets beside her. Her dark eyes grazed his shoulders, his chest, but stopped before dipping below his stomach. It would serve neither of them if she let her mind wander. She wasn't known for self-control.

Nox tilted her head. "Does it help if I tell you I feel safe with you?"

He made a defeated sigh. The only thing it accomplished was to mollify him, as there was no way for him to protest such a lovely sentiment.

Nox unwrapped what remained of the apple from where she had stashed it in a handkerchief.

"Here goes nothing," she said as she bit into its flesh.

She probably rested her head against the pillow. She probably cuddled into the sheets. Malik's presence had most likely comforted her, allowing her to settle into her dreams. But she didn't recall any of it. Her lips had tasted the sweet, sour flesh of the apple, and then she was somewhere else entirely.

Nox didn't remember falling asleep. She had no recollection of how her eyes had closed or how Malik had taken the apple from where it had plopped from her hand onto the bed. She didn't know how much time had or hadn't passed with her eyes rapidly moving beneath closed eyelids. She didn't know that he remained fully seated, perched above her, carefully monitoring as she slept.

She was the tree once more.

When Nox had first visited the temple, the world had been on fire.

In her first dream, the air was peaceful, with only the priestess tending to it until Daphne rode in on her horse.

This was different. The energy, the people, the hazy, frantic words of those near its roots were charged with an unfamiliar anticipation. Nox watched from above as a circle of women clustered on the temple floor. The normally clean, empty marble floors were littered with sweet-smelling moon flowers and soft, silk pillows. Women surrounded a central figure while she howled in pain. The night throbbed with magic. This didn't have the dread of a nightmare, despite the woman's anguish. There was an importance and excitement to the air. The power coursing through this moment was all-consuming.

The other women wore gowns and cuffs like the ones she had seen on the priestess both in person and in her previous dream. She knew instinctively that these women, human and fae alike, must also serve in temples across the continent. Their sounds chilled Nox as the cacophony of music and cries washed over her. She didn't know enough of theology to speculate as to why so many holy women might gather in one temple.

The temple glowed as the full moon poured its luminous, milk-white light into the palatial space. The tree hummed in magical incandescence. Shadows and shimmery, silvery reflections like ethereal ocean water rippling and reflecting throughout the room cast the holy women as unworldly, goddess-like creatures.

The central figure was someone Nox had seen before. It was the beautiful, onyx priestess she had held the night the temple was sacked. She had watched the priestess as two women beseeched the Tree on the night of Daphne's prayer. She had witnessed how their hands glowed, how the temple filled with light. Now the priestess lay on the ground once more as she had the night of the fire, her wails of pain joining the songs of the holy women gathered around her. One rubbed her back. Others were at her sides. One knelt before her. All these spiritual creatures sang their prayers as they comforted, supported, and chanted for the priestess.

A loud, agonizing sound came from her again. It was the high, divine pain of something sacred. Nox understood what she was seeing. The priestess was giving birth.

"Goddess, give her strength!" one woman yelled, bowing before the tree.

Another cried, tears staining her face and falling in hot rivers onto her shimmering gown.

"The All Mother has chosen you," said the eldest priestess at her back, her words hurried, "and the All Mother will see you through this. Look to her!"

The pregnant priestess screamed again as a contraction tore through her. The sounds rang through the marble of the temple, screams reverberating in echoes as they mingled with the haunting melodies of the prayers. Her body relaxed as the moment passed, exhaustion consuming her. Her words came out in broken, excruciating sobs. "I have been devout all my life," she cried. "Please, goddess, help me now."

Nox wished she could gasp. She wished she could turn away. The women at the Selkie had taken extreme precautions to prevent pregnancy, and her aversion to men had driven the horrors of impregnation to the furthest reaches of her mind. She didn't want to see a birth. Yet this was important. This was happening before the Tree of Life.

"Push!" the woman at her back said again, and the priestess cried out in agony.

"I see its head!" called the woman who was kneeling before her.

"Focus! Bring the All Mother's blessing into the world! You must push!"

From where Nox looked down, she could see how sweat covered the priestess, drenching what remained of her gown as most of it was pushed up to her belly to give the kneeling woman access to the birth. Nox had no eyes, or else she would have closed them. She was Bodhi, Genesis, Yggdrasil. She was the branches and leaves and life and memory at the temple's core. She was there for it all.

Nox could not see the baby from her place along the tree as the kneeling woman blocked her view. She felt as if the eerie music of their prayers was filling her like pails upon pails of rainwater. She was drowning in their songs, overwhelmed with the chaos of the cries of pain and prayer.

"You're almost finished! Push!" The command was filled with urgency.

The priestess screamed again with one, final push before collapsing to the floor of the temple. Half of the holy women ran to tend to the priestess, dabbing at her forehead and comforting her. The one at her back was preparing her for another push to expel the afterbirth from her body. The one who had been kneeling now clutched a tiny, bloodied bundle. From Nox's place among the branches, it appeared to be nothing more than the wiggling filling of a strawberry pie until the freshly birthed baby let out a wail. Someone snipped the cord.

The collective sigh as joy and celebration flooded the room was infectious. Nox felt it in her nerves, her bones, her branches and twigs and buds.

Someone began washing the crying baby in a basin and wrapping it in clean, delicate fabrics.

"What do I do now?" The priestess's voice was so riddled with her exhaustion that her words were barely intelligible.

Nox wanted to see. She looked among the branches,

wondering if there was a different angle that would allow her access. No, until the priestess turned, her view would remain obscured.

The older woman was comforting the priestess. "Your part is done, beloved. Your devotion allowed you to be the vessel for the All Mother's blessing."

The cleaned babe was put into the tired priestess's arms. "Am I to raise it?"

"The child belongs to everyone and no one, beloved. We will keep it safe, fed and cared for in the temple until the goddess determines where it must go to fulfill its destiny. The babe is the manifestation of the prayers of the faithful."

As the path to her view cleared, Nox felt a new, puzzling wave wash over her. The priestess was the beautiful obsidian of the people of Tarkhany. The pearly babe in her arms was as starkly contrasted as the silver moon outside.

Nox didn't understand what she was seeing. How could this baby be born to this woman? She thought of the priestess again, how she'd been so overcome with the goddess's light while she'd prayed with the princess in her final moments. The princess had begged the goddess to send someone to break the curse on the land. Daphne had implored the goddess to save them.

"It looks so human," the exhausted priestess murmured as she held the bundle, sleep nearly consuming her. Sweat beaded down her brow as her eyes began to close.

"For it is, and it isn't."

"Do we tell it what it is?" another asked.

"Who are we to interfere with fate by steering it with our own hands? The All Mother made Daphne's final prayer flesh, and it is the goddess who will guide it."

The baby had stopped crying now, and Nox looked down at it, joining the priestesses as they all peered into the tiny bundle of snow.

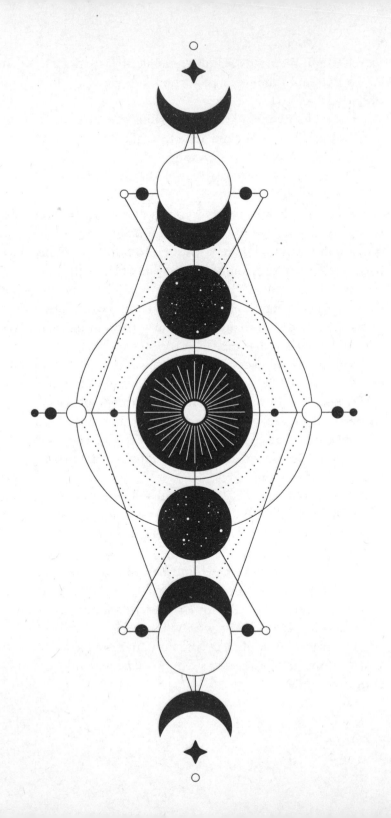

PART THREE

Everything You've Ever Wanted

Thirty-Six

I T WAS AS IF GADRIEL HAD DIED AND BEEN REBORN THE
moment they crossed the border. So much of his edge left
him when they touched northern soil, like a heavy layer of
snow sloughing off a peaked roof. He was quick to smile as
he set her down. He was free.

"Welcome to Raascot, witchling." He gestured broadly
to the woods around them. The forest did feel different
here. It had thin, alpine air. Each breath had a bright, pine
flavor. Between the indigo hour and the evergreens bending
overhead, Raascot's mountainous region had a distinctly
magical feeling.

"I'm not a witch," Amaris grumbled good-naturedly,
having left her annoyance in Farehold. She grabbed what
remained of their salted meat and passed him a piece.

"So you say," he said, voice light with his own amusement. Gadriel wasn't worried about reaching the end of their
supplies, as he'd be able to enter the first village they found
in northern territory, finally seen for his true form by the
people once again.

"How long to Gwydir?"

"Only a few days," he continued, smiling. "Raascot is

smaller than Farehold, but we're also continuing directly east, and we're traveling as the crow flies."

"Do people normally laugh at your jokes?"

"They do."

The plan was to transition once more from nightlife to travel by the light of day, but these things happened gradually. It was their first morning on Raascot soil, and all they needed to accomplish was to set up camp and allow Gadriel some time to regroup his strength.

Amaris eyed him from where she stood across their makeshift camp. His relaxed energy was infectious. He might be cocky and violent, but she was surly and murderous in equal proportion. She continued to study him while his back remained to her, wings tucked comfortably against his broad muscles as he gathered wood, considering the camaraderie they'd cultivated.

She couldn't relate to his reactions or rationale half the time, but even if she didn't find them intuitive, she did understand. She'd had no exposure to military life before meeting him. She understood the elite training undergone at Uaimh Reev was nothing like the hierarchy, secrecy, or blind obedience required in a kingdom's ranks under a superior. She was sure he found her every bit as difficult as she found him. Perhaps it made them well matched in more ways than one.

They were still settling in, starting their fire, and unstrapping the mercenaries' weapons when they heard a snap. Gadriel's head shot up to where twilight moments before dawn colored the forest. They'd suffered at the hands of too many demons. Of course, the moment they crossed into Raascot, their joy would be cut short.

A hesitant voice came from the trees. "Gad?"

The relief and elation that washed through his features may as well have been a bucket of water. He beamed with excitement as he shouted into the woods, "Yaz?"

The young woman who burst from the tree line was a blur of curled auburn hair and black wings as she jumped into Gadriel's arms. He hugged her and gave her a spin.

Amaris's thinly veiled reaction was immediate, deep, and borderline feral. A territorial tug of jealousy yanked the corners of her mouth downward as the two winged fae embraced. Possessiveness was an unfamiliar emotion, and not one she knew how to deal with. She fought the feeling, pressing it into the box where all her unpleasant thoughts were stored. Fortunately, the pair were too distracted by each other to have caught her expression. In fact, they seemed to forget about Amaris completely for a moment until Gadriel released the winged woman from the hug.

Gadriel turned excitedly back to her. "Amaris, this is Yazlyn! She's one of my best sergeants. Yaz, this is a sour witch who's going to help us save Raascot."

Amaris blinked once at the surprising face of an entirely all too lovely woman in fitted fighting leathers. Her black, angelic feathers were glossy and unmarred by tragedy. Her face was full of expression and life. Her too-large eyes were a complex weave of vibrant hazel. She was stunning, and Amaris didn't know why, but she found the woman's beauty infuriating.

Yazlyn didn't bother with the formality of extending her hand. She bundled Amaris into a hug, filling the embrace with warmth as if they were long-lost family members. "It's so nice to meet you!" She looked to Gadriel, eyes widening slightly, then back to Amaris, still clutching her in her arms. "Holy shit! Oh my goddess, this is amazing!"

"Nice to meet you," Amaris coughed through the cloud of auburn. The woman smelled pleasantly of walnuts and blackberries. Her friendliness made it challenging to hate her, even if the jealousy Amaris felt hadn't fully subsided.

Yazlyn whirled, hands still loosely on Amaris's arms. "What the hell are you doing at the border, General?" She used his title as a form of endearment.

He grinned. "Barely making it out of Farehold alive is what I'm doing. We need to get to Gwydir and see Ceres as soon as possible, but remind me to tell you about how this one got me into a fight with an ag'drurath."

Amaris held up a hand, which served two purposes. She was able to stop Gadriel in the middle of his arrogance and create a modicum of personal space between herself and Yazlyn. "I think you mean how this one got you *out* of a fight with an ag'drurath."

Yazlyn's mouth dropped open. "An ag'drurath? You're fucking with me. No goddess damned way. I absolutely refuse to wait on such a story."

Amaris's mouth quirked against a smile. She'd known the stranger for all of three minutes, and she was already the most foul-mouthed person Amaris had ever met. She tried to run a tally of the curses that had already spun out of her mouth, but she wasn't sure if she had enough fingers.

Yazlyn sat down and urged Gadriel into a rather embellished retelling wherein he came across as a bit cleverer and stronger than Amaris recalled him being at the time. Gadriel went on to show off his iridescent wings and gave the barest rundown of their time at the university, which brought their newest addition up to speed. He seemed to be conveniently leaving out the parts about how he'd made Amaris snap his neck or then promptly tried to murder her in her sleep to unleash an ability.

"And what are *you* doing all the way at the border? Isn't lookout duty a little below your rank? Or did you manage to get in trouble while I was gone and lose all your stripes?" Gadriel finally demanded of Yazlyn, playfulness coloring his voice.

She shrugged, returning the grin. "I wish I had the opportunity to get up to no good. No, we can't leave border patrol to the shithead privates any longer. With our best and brightest in Farehold on mission, we've shuffled posts entirely. The entire second army now lines Raascot's border. It isn't just about keeping people out, you know. It's also in case…"

"I understand."

They shook their heads in shared, unspoken disappointment at their king's delusion. Amaris assumed there was some collective fantasy that the king's son might come to Raascot to try to find him.

Yazlyn's eyes brightened with a question. "What about the demons? Have you seen them in the wild? Are the beasts showing up in the south as well?"

He nodded. "Since I've met the witchling alone, we've taken on a beseul and an ag'imni. The queen had been holding the dragon, so I don't suppose it counts toward the creatures flooding the woods."

"An ag'imni?" She looked to Gadriel, then to Amaris, face paling. "Did it..."

"They speak."

"It talked to me," Amaris clarified. "It spoke specifically of Gadriel. It said things about him and about me."

"Oh." Yazlyn's face paled. "How...ominous. How fucking creepy that it would try to get under your skin like that." Her voice was strained. "They're creatures of manipulation and pain. What did it say?"

"Nothing worth mentioning," Gadriel answered.

Amaris pressed her mouth into a thin line.

"Now." He turned his attention to Yazlyn once more. "Yaz, the demons? Are they in Raascot? Have they made it to Gwydir?"

The color returned to Yazlyn's cheeks. She winced against the pain of her answer. "They're everywhere, Gad. With so many of you in the south and considering the king has lost his damned mind with his search and rescue effort..." Her eyes flitted to Amaris, perhaps to see how she would react to monarch slander. "Ceres doesn't have anyone keeping the creatures from the land. No one understands what's making them come down from the mountains."

He sucked on his teeth. "Have you been in contact with the reever?"

Amaris perked at this. They must be speaking of Ash's father, Elil.

"Last I heard, two more had joined him in Gwydir. It's a regular beehive of reever action at the moment."

Gadriel gestured to Amaris. "Soon to be three more."

Yazlyn's face lit again. She had a mouth that was made for smiling and cursing in equal proportions. "You're a reever? Holy shit!" She looked at Amaris for a bit too long, soaking in her hair, her scars, her eyes, her muscles, and her weapons. Finally she asked, "Why does he keep calling you a witch?"

Amaris made a face at that, glowering at Gadriel. "Yeah, Gad, why *do* you keep calling me a witch?" She returned her eyes as politely as possible to Yazlyn. "Yes, I'm a reever. I've trained under Samael. Is Odrin in Gwydir right now?"

Amaris's voice was hopeful as she thought of her surrogate father.

Yazlyn shook her loose curls. "I've been at the border too long to have met them. Word has just passed through the ranks. We believe they're amassing in response to the beasts. Every time you think it can't get worse, it does." Her eyes returned to Gadriel. "Whatever you're thinking, multiply it by ten or twenty or fifty. Honestly, I have no concept of your capacity for imagination, so maybe multiplication wasn't my best strategy. It's not good, Gad."

Gadriel nodded. "If Ceres isn't going to do anything about the imbalance in the land, that's where the reevers come in." He looked to Amaris. "You might want to consider boosting your numbers over at the keep."

"I'll get right on that."

Amaris felt an ember of pride at this. She remembered how she'd called Odrin an assassin the first time they'd met and how he'd laughed. The reevers were more closely aligned with the All Mother than they were with any mercenary. They were the weapon-clenching arm of the goddess, established to help the continent maintain balance.

Maybe it was his excitement over being reunited with Yazlyn, but Gadriel decided that they could skip a night's rest and fly through the day if Yazlyn could carry Amaris. He was up for twenty-four hours of flight but wasn't sure if he could do it while holding on to his passenger. Yazlyn had flexed her biceps at the prospect and grinned. Any fear of lack of food supplies dissipated, as their newest addition was stocked to the gills with her own crackers and dried foods. If they flew all day, they'd be able to catch up on sleep overnight in a mountain town on the far side of the Raasay Forest.

Yazlyn was happy to scoop Amaris against herself and take her into the sky. The sergeant was kind, irreverent, and objectively funny, all of which Amaris found profoundly irritating.

She expected things to be uncomfortable in the sergeant's arms, but Yazlyn had a way of making things perfectly pleasant. She tried to chat with Amaris on and off throughout the flight, but the wind and air made conversation nearly impossible. Still, she'd give her arm a squeeze anytime she wanted to point out a particularly pretty mountain ridge, the rapids of a snaking river, or a large bird worth seeing. Flying in daylight was an entirely new experience and one Amaris would never forget.

Every element of travel was substantially colder when flying with Yazlyn, even in the light of day. Though the summer sun shone down on them, Amaris hadn't realized how much she'd taken Gadriel's gift for granted until her fingers turned a burning shade of pink against the frigid air of their elevation. Yazlyn seemed to notice, tucking Amaris more tightly against her. The sergeant was also chilled, her nose and the tips of her ears blooming into similar shades of red. Still, the view was incredible. Amaris felt like she'd tripped and tumbled into the illustration of a fairy story from the children's books at Farleigh. The mountains were sheer and snow-capped. The pines scraped the very sky. It wasn't the thick, foggy region of the university but a clean, bright mountain air both familiar and separate entirely from her life at the reev. Everything was greener, more vibrant, and fascinatingly new.

They flew until early afternoon. Once they reached the nearest mountain town, they stopped at an inn using Yazlyn's coin and spent the night resting on the soft beds of three modest bedrooms. The innkeeper was a human man but positively jolly in welcoming the soldiers and their guest under his roof. He didn't bother to conceal his open stares at Amaris's silver-white hair, pale skin, and purple eyes, which was nothing new. She'd be an oddity wherever she went. Amaris had thought she'd be too anxious to properly rest after all they'd been through, but the moment she touched the mattress, she slept like the dead.

The bed could have been stuffed with a pile of shoes and leather belts for all she cared; she drifted off as if it were made of the softest down feathers. Her exhaustion consumed her fully, pulling her into its deep and bottomless trenches.

It was a good dream.

It had been a while since she'd dreamt of Nox's supple curves or the way her lips parted. The familiar scent filled the air, as if the girl was stitched together by the same violet fruit and spice in every encounter. The soft, contouring press of their bodies had been a recurrent dream. Amaris knew how her beautiful friend's hands would slide along her sides, tantalizing her nerves. She knew how her eyes would hook on her own until she shied away under the intensity of the stare. She knew the powerful force of the energy that passed between them as their bodies pressed into each other with a convoluted confusion of hope and longing. She knew that in this recurrent dream, their lips never met. Such a familiar dream. Such a beautiful, constant want, such an ongoing thirst. It was one that locked them in the eternally suspended moment before a promised kiss, lingering between the urge to close the gap and whatever hesitancy or denial might rip one away.

She knew how this dream ended.

She missed Nox.

Amaris swallowed against the pain, hating how her dreams didn't respect the painstaking effort it took to maintain her box. The dreams took the emotions out, let them roam around freely, allowing them to dance and play and explore beyond the cage that she worked so hard to keep shut.

Her first moments awake were spent gathering the feelings like scattered sheep and corralling them back into the pen, slamming the gate behind them.

After collecting herself from the wounds left by her dreams, she realized she'd fallen asleep in her clothes, leaving the bed smudged in dirt from her days of travel. She wasn't sure of the hour, but morning light was already showcasing a snowy peak so breathtaking that her window looked like it might have been an oil painting. Amaris rose and crept down the quiet hall toward a communal bathing room. She allowed herself the indulgence of a long, hot bath while the inn remained asleep. She was about to towel herself off and redress in her filthy road clothes when a gentle knock sounded at the door.

It was Yazlyn's voice.

"Amaris?" She spoke the name through the door, voice respectfully quiet for the early hour. "I heard you wake up and I thought you might not have anything else to wear. Can I set some things inside for you?"

Amaris cracked open the bathing room door, towel still clutched in front of her.

"I'm sorry all my shirts have slots in the back, but I don't have anything else."

"I'll try to grow wings and meet you downstairs." Amaris smiled sleepily at her weak joke. She left her hair in wet, silvery coils that dampened the tunic at her shoulders. Once she'd dressed in new, clean things, she found her way down to the common hall of the inn. The warm, homey smells of breakfast were so comforting contrasted against her days of camping and travel.

Yazlyn sat in front of a particularly large plate of pastries and meat at a table against the lavender morning window. The view beyond the inn's windows was breathtaking, littered with greenery and mountains alike. She hadn't noticed Amaris walk in as she continued chewing, staring out the glass window-panes at the indulgently beautiful mountain range.

"Are these all for you?" Amaris asked as she approached.

Yazlyn perked as she turned toward her. "Yes, but I am willing to share, as I'm particularly benevolent."

Amaris took a seat, bit into a buttery, chocolate pastry, and felt her eyes roll into the back of her head.

"Good, right? No one makes chocolate like the mountain towns."

"Are you not from here?"

Yazlyn smiled. "No, no. Gad and I are both from Gwydir—or I am. He's from just outside it."

Amaris didn't love the familiarity with which Yazlyn used his name. She felt the same unpleasant pinch of emotion she had the day before and wondered at their history together. The sergeant was too beautiful for Amaris to enjoy the image of the two of them sharing extended company.

Through a mouth full of food, Yazlyn began asking Amaris about her life. She asked about where she was from, how she was raised, how she'd met Gadriel, and her plans for the future. Her hazel eyes sparkled with genuine interest. Her irises alone were enough reason to find her interesting, with their darkened, exterior-most rings melding into golds and greens before they met her pupils. Yazlyn was a bottomless well of enthusiastic questions. Her charisma was infectious.

"What about you?" Amaris asked. "What's your life story?"

Yazlyn nodded at that and spoke without swallowing, continuing to eat and chew while she talked. She raised a hand in a half-hearted attempt to cover her mouth so she could tell her story without spitting pastry. "Born and raised in the capital to two perfectly charming parents who were and remain military. I began training as soon as I was able to hold a sword! That's where I met Gad. Well, sorta. We met at a military bar when I was newly enlisted."

"I don't know if this is impolite, but I don't know many fae. Do you mind if I ask how old you are?"

Yazlyn smiled. "No! I'm a baby by fae standards. I'm only

404

sixty-three, which is pretty much the equivalent of whatever you are in your human years."

Amaris frowned. "I don't think I'm fully human."

Yazlyn agreed with that. "No, I don't suppose you are." She let her eyes wander for a bit too long before amending, "You certainly don't look like any human I've met. Such a curiosity."

Amaris twisted her mouth at her next question. "And you and Gadriel...?"

Yazlyn nearly choked on her pastry. Her eyes bulged at the shock of the question, as if it were the single most absurd thing she'd ever heard. It took her a while to clear her passageway as her coughing consumed her. "What!" She banged on her chest as if she couldn't quite absorb the thought. "Goddess, no. I'd sooner bed a beseul than a man. Gad is practically family. He's my boss, my friend, my drinking buddy, and the person I want at my back in wartime. He even introduced me to my first partner."

Amaris's eyes widened at this, though she tried not to let the shock be too obvious. She wasn't sure if all northerners were so open about their sexuality or if Yazlyn was just particularly chatty. Since the fae had asked her a number of questions, Amaris felt like she could do the same. "You say first partner, so I assume..."

Yazlyn's voice was something like a reminiscent sigh. She'd finished her pastry and pushed her fingers among the crumbs as if she were a seer lost in the tea leaves of prophecy. Instead, she was a quietly reminiscent fae who hadn't healed from whatever memories plagued her. "Not all love is meant to last, you know. She was a bird who couldn't be caged. Married to travel and the pursuit of knowledge before all else." She plucked another flaky, buttery roll from the platter. Every broken thought was interrupted by a mouthful of crumbs, pastry, and nostalgia. She looked at Amaris just as often as she looked at the pile of food, the fireplace, and the mountains beyond the window. "She wanted to see the world. I needed to go where Ceres sent me, and she needed to go see the merfolk of the Etal Isles and the sand snakes of Tarkhany and whatever furry white snow creatures live beyond the Frozen Straits. There's no bad blood between us. Things don't always have to end in disaster...but that doesn't make them less sad." Yazlyn picked a third pastry—a sticky, cinnamon spiral—and pulled it slowly apart with her fingers. "What about you? Do you have any love in your life?"

In Amaris's years on this earth, no one had ever been as frank and straightforward as the fae with loosely curled hair currently gobbling breakfast food before her. Amaris was uncomfortable, and Yazlyn could tell.

"Oh, I'm sorry. I shouldn't pry."

Amaris shook her head in apology. "It isn't prying. It's just complicated. I guess I don't fully understand the answer to the question myself."

Yazlyn smiled at that. "What's there to understand? Like what you like, don't what you don't. For what it's worth, Gad seems to like you a hell of a lot, though don't tell him I told you so."

Amaris battled the involuntary response her body made at the implication. She silently scolded herself for feeling silly, girlish, and irrational. She wasn't sure how to respond, though despite her best efforts to remain silent, she said, "That's what liking someone looks like?"

Yazlyn laughed, tilting her head slightly to the side, letting her curls fall in one downward direction. "With him?" She chuckled darkly. "Indeed, it is. Though if you're looking for more obvious displays... When was the last time someone told you that you have absolutely stunning lilac eyes?"

Amaris heated to what had to be a shade of true crimson—one she couldn't conceal. Her eyes shot to the baked goods, but through her peripheral vision, she could see the winged fae's eyes still twinkling with amusement under flirtatiously lowered lashes. Fortunately, Yazlyn was distracted by something on the other side of the room.

"He lives!" she said, beaming as she snapped her head up.

If Amaris had thought Gadriel to be a new man after landing in Raascot, that was entirely before seeming him freshly bathed and with a good night's sleep on a bed big enough to fit his wings. She had always found him wickedly handsome, but the way he looked this morning was positively disrespectful to her sense of decency.

He ate twice Yazlyn's portion of breakfast foods, chatting all the while in the magic of being reunited with his country, his people, and the joy of a good friend. He waved away the second cup of tea and turned to Amaris.

"Shall we, witchling?"

Yazlyn laughed, her speculative gaze flitting between the two. "Again with the witch thing? Aren't we on more respectable terms with Uaimh Reev? Witch? That's what you're sticking with for your little moonlit find?"

His lips curved into an indecent smirk as he said, "You haven't seen what she can do."

Amaris deliberately ignored them both. She had more serious business than whatever dance the Raascot fae liked to perform around pertinence. "Next stop, King Ceres?"

The Raascot fae exchanged sidelong glances. Gadriel's low voice was cautionary as he spoke. "Next stop, Gwydir. I'm not so sure Ceres will be happy to see us. Are you ready?"

"Ten minutes?" Maybe it was the contagious nature of their joy, or maybe it was being in a new kingdom that she'd only heard about in hushed whispers, but she was excited. Maybe a part of her was looking forward to getting to know these happier parts of Gadriel.

Amaris gathered her few earthly things and met them outside while gnawing on the meaning of Gadriel's words regarding his king. They took off into the sky, grazing past mountains and high over the Raasay Forest. Anytime Amaris started to shiver, Gadriel would warm himself until she relaxed against him. It was her first time traveling with him by daylight, and the landscape below was a glory to behold.

In the glow of his warmth, she was able to truly appreciate it. Raascot had a rugged, wild beauty unlike anything she'd ever beheld. She could have sworn Gadriel grinned at her gasp as they flew over the bridal-veil mist of a particularly magnificent waterfall.

Usually, the sky was black and empty as they flew, but it was by the orange evening light that Amaris was able to see the outline of Gwydir silhouetted in the distance. They had another two hours in the sky before they touched down on the outskirts of town. She stretched her limbs from the flight while examining their surroundings. They didn't appear to be stopping at an inn, and she wasn't quite sure where they'd gone or why they were there.

Amaris felt profoundly out of her element now that two skyborne fae led the way before her, as if she were little more than a passenger on their quest. They crossed a wide yard into a midsize home on the edge of the city with two horses tethered outside. There was something vaguely familiar about the mounts, but her eyes didn't catch on the horses for too long before trailing after the fae. The first thing she noticed was the fire crackling on the hearth as they pushed the door open. The second thing she noticed was the shocked, overjoyed face of Odrin as he opened his arms for her.

Thirty–Seven

MALIK AWOKE TO WARM, GENTLE CURVES BESIDE HIM, TO morning light streaming in through the windows, to a subtle, feminine scent that reminded him of plum pie, and into the rapid awareness that something was wrong. Any hope for a sleepy, happy smile faltered when he turned to see Nox sitting up, listlessly staring at the wall as she hugged her knees to her chest. He'd touched her back once, then stopped, not knowing what she wanted or needed and unable to get any answers from her.

"Nox? Are you okay?"

The unmoving wall behind her eyes answered him. It suggested there were consequences to answering his question.

"Is there anything I can do?" he asked.

She shook her head, though not directly at him. His unease grew as he watched her. Malik struggled not to pester her for responses. He told himself that it would be selfish to make her speak when it was a desired outcome that would soothe his anxiety rather than what might be best for her.

With that, he dressed, he watched, and he waited.

Malik muttered what little he could to Ash before the departed. The reevers did their best to respect the distance she was intentionally creating as they departed Henares at long last.

Surely, it would end after the first few hours.

Surely, she would speak again by the end of the first day.

Surely, two days of silence would be enough.

"Is she sick?" Ash asked in a stressed whisper.

Malik didn't know how to answer. He'd seen this expression once before. Their village tailor had been returning from a neighboring city's market when their caravan had been ambushed by vageth. The man had returned, but his wife and children had not. If it hadn't been for the citizens who found him pinned beneath his tarp on the road, no one would have known what had happened. The man had become little more than a shell, and while he eventually reopened the shop, spoke to others, and carried on with the wreckage of his life, he was never the same. Witnessing the horrors that unholy demons brought to the continent had driven Malik to become a reever.

He'd been beside Nox all night. She hadn't encountered a vageth, but whatever she had encountered had shaken her to her core. All he could do was ask Ash to be patient.

They continued their northeasterly trip in eerie silence as they followed the road that had connected Aubade to Gwydir for centuries. They were on horses that had once been the duke's, in shirts and pants that had been sewn by his tailors, and with weapons that had been forged by his bladesmiths. Nox rode several paces behind them on a fawn-colored horse with the axe that had been such a source of joy strapped to her back.

The men were disquieted after the first day, worried after the second. It had taken three days of having the once-witty Nox as a despondent travel mate before Malik told Ash what had happened on their final night in Henares. Ash was angry to have been left out of the initial plans, but time softened his irritation into concern as neither of the men could get her to speak.

410

"Nox, come on," Malik pleaded with her. She looked at him, but she wasn't there. Her eyes made contact and then floated away. "Please, talk to me. Talk to me about anything. Tell me about your favorite color. Tell me what food you hate. Tell me about the Duke of Henares or Priory or Amaris—"

Her eyes revisited his at the mention of the girl's name.

"Amaris? Do you want to talk about Amaris?"

He watched the flicker of attention darken, then snuff out entirely. He sensed his misstep and didn't say her name again. Though he couldn't fathom how or why, he suspected Amaris had something to do with the despondency that had joined them like a fourth party in their camp.

After one week on horseback, the reevers were beside themselves.

Malik let his anxiety fester like an infection, pacing and breathing as if he were fighting off a terrible urge to scratch an unseen itch. He didn't know how to bring Nox back to life after whatever she'd seen or experienced after eating the apple, and no matter what he said, she didn't open her mouth to help him. He hated himself for letting her bite into that fruit and hated himself even more intensely for falling asleep next to her rather than staying awake and shaking her from her slumber. If he had kept his eyes open, perhaps he could have stirred her and spared her from whatever she'd seen.

Malik sat across the fire and watched Nox's attentiveness float through the void like a speck of dust in the dark until Ash broke the silence.

"It's two fucking weeks to the border, Malik! Two weeks, and she hasn't even told us why we're going to Farleigh! Since when do we take our orders from a stranger? Since when do we—"

"It was from the temple, Ash. This isn't a command from Nox. We aren't taking orders from her. It was knowledge from the Temple of the All Mother. We were in the glen with Amaris when she entered the temple so long ago. We were there with the demons—or whatever they are—when they

411

told us there was knowledge within those walls inaccessible to men. Nox received it. Nox got her hands around what you and I could not. She learned from the apple, and she told us we need to go to Farleigh."

"What sense does that make? She gained forbidden knowledge and we have to go back to *her* orphanage?"

Malik spun on his friend. "I'm sorry. Did I miss the part where you were the one who ate the fruit? Weren't you also seeking this knowledge? Isn't this your mission as well?"

The men settled into a moody, uncomfortable silence.

Each night, they'd offer Nox food and ensure she had water. Malik watched her pick at it listlessly, chewing a few bites here and there while staring into the fire. Malik slept close to her, worried that if something happened in the night, no one would hear her if she needed help. Ash showed signs of helpless concern, though his appeared to be equal parts worry for Nox and uneasiness over what it was doing to Malik. They kept telling themselves her shock would wear off, but night after night would give way to morning and she was still as absent as if her mind had been lost entirely. The Duke of Henares had been a shell of a man, drunk on his love for her. Nox was a phantom in a woman's body while her mind remained lost to her thoughts.

The reevers had been on the road for more than a week when the tension building between them finally erupted. Nox had curled her knees to her chest while they fought in the distance, either unaware or uncaring of their exchange.

"We have to do something!"

"What do you expect me to do? We've fed her, and we've tried talking to her! Do you want me to slap her?"

Malik was horrified at Ash's willingness to bring corporal solutions into the equation. "No! No, of course not."

"You said she ate from some apple, right? The fruit from the Tree of Life? Could she be poisoned?"

Malik held his head in his hands. "It doesn't seem like that at all. It feels like she's seen something and never left her

412

state of shock. The first time she ate it—well, you were there. You saw the effects of her nightmare! This time... I don't know how to help her. I don't know what to do."

"Her heart rate is normal. She's eating and drinking, even if just barely. She's not at risk of dying."

"But she's not herself!"

"It's not physical, Malik."

He looked like he was about to burst into flames. "I don't know what you're implying, but it being psychological doesn't make it *any* less real."

Ash looked at him sadly. "I know you have feelings for her. We talked about this. I thought we'd agreed."

Malik stood and began pacing again. Nox was only feet away, lost to their conversation as if she wasn't present at all. "This isn't about that. This is about what's right. At the very least, she's our friend. We have a responsibility to help her."

With frustrated helplessness, Ash said, "We are helping. The last thing she said to us was to go to Farleigh. Every day, she gets up on her horse and she moves forward. She eats. She sleeps. She's still in there. She's still with us."

"Is she?"

Ash balled his first against his chin. "I don't have any ideas, Malik. If you won't let me slap her or throw her in the river, I say we just keep our horses pointed toward Farleigh and give her time. She's functioning. She's just...dealing with whatever happened in her dream. You're forcing her process on to your timeline. Maybe this just takes...time."

"She's strong, Ash. We know her. The things she's seen and done and been through... She isn't some fragile person who would..." His voice hit a sharp note as he glanced at the quiet shell of a woman who'd been accompanying them. "She's stronger than some dream breaking her."

Ash shook the copper hair that had remained tied behind him. "But it wasn't you, was it?"

"What?" Malik turned in preemptive offense.

"You can't say what can and cannot break a person. You

413

don't know their threshold for violence or tolerance before they snap. She could be made of steel, Malik. She could be the strongest person in the world. You can't be certain without knowing what she saw. Even then, you don't know anyone's limit for what will or won't break them, because it's not you. It's her experience. She's the only one who knows what she can and can't handle."

Ash was right, and Malik knew it. He'd known they could do little save for have patience and empathy since the moment he'd awoken beside her. He should have been grateful that Ash had finally joined the chorus as a voice of reason, but he felt only helplessness.

It was another in a long string of disagreeable conversations and tense nights.

✦

Somewhere past the edge of the fire, Nox was vaguely aware that the men were speaking. She could hear them. She knew they were there. She knew they cared about her and that they were trying their best. She knew that each day they rode, and each day they ate, and each day they slept. She knew that Malik would ensure a blanket was over her and her knives and axe were carefully unstrapped before she fell asleep. She would mount her fawn-colored horse and follow them for hours and hours until the warmth of the daylight ebbed and the chill set in. They would ride over well-trodden roads, over green hills, past thick forests, passing modest thatch-roofed villages. She would dismount and repeat the process day in and day out.

Nox spent hour after hour staring down from where she had been in the tree's memory and seeing the tiny, frosted face of a baby as white as snow. She had known that face. She had gasped in awe the first time she had seen it on the stormy doorsteps of Farleigh. She had loved it for many, many years.

Days stretched into nearly two weeks without Nox speaking.

Malik took a knee and rested a hand against her face. "Nox, I need you to look at me."

She did not. It was not for lack of ability. Nox knew where she was. She knew who accompanied her. She hadn't been lost to the world as the men might have suspected, though her understanding of it had shifted beneath her. Maybe it was difficult for anyone who hadn't needed the true safety of a shell crafted within their own body to understand. She didn't expect Malik to understand. As long as she was safe and quiet, she could remain shielded from processing how the information would shift the very fabric of her being. Her eyes did not meet his, nor did they look into the darkening forest beyond. They stared into the Tree of Life's memory as it had peered down at the priestess who had given birth to its tiny miracle made flesh.

"Listen," he emphasized. "Look at me, Nox."

She tilted her chin toward his. She was aware. She was listening. And she wasn't.

"Nox, we're going to reach your orphanage tomorrow. You wanted us to go to Farleigh, right? To your orphanage? The villagers said it's one day's ride east of where we are now. Are you ready to see whoever it was you needed to see at the orphanage?"

Her eyes traveled from the space beyond him to the place behind him, gliding over him. She tried again. Her gaze struggled to stick to his eyes as if her line of sight was composed of mere water droplets over glass windows. "Farleigh?"

Ash went rigid from where he'd been fussing with weapons across the fire. She noted how their breathing caught in mutual shock and excitement, which only helped to reel her closer to the present.

Malik's face brightened where he had taken a knee before her. "Yes, Nox. We're almost there. Are you ready?"

"We're in Farleigh?"

He nodded, perhaps too eagerly, in agreement. The green of the leaves around him matched his eyes. She liked those eyes. They were kind. They were good.

"We'll get there tomorrow, Nox. You were quite determined that we needed to get there the night we left Henares. Do you want to tell us what we need to do at Farleigh?"

She had trouble keeping her eyes focused on his. It had been so long since she'd forced herself to stay present. This was the longest she'd ever remained within the darkness. The dream clouded her every waking thought. She was the tree. Princess Daphne was dying before it. A moonlit girl was born. A prayer. A bundle. A stolen object of great importance. A baby made of snow. A princess and her crumpled boy. A tree, a priestess, a temple. Her mind began to churn again, its cogs rusty with disuse.

Malik seemed to sense her whirring thoughts and gripped her arms kindly. "Nox, what's in Farleigh?"

She blinked and raised a loosely gesturing hand to her velvet bag. She could see the men. She could see the fire, the trees, and the bag. She could also see the temple, the princess, and the tree's memories.

Ash grabbed the bag from where it sat and brought it over to her. He procured the pocket watch, which elicited no reaction. He showed her the candle, and she once again failed to respond. When he pulled the black quill from her bag, she closed her eyes.

"They're going to tell us about the princess."

"We're going to Farleigh to learn about Princess Daphne?"

Nox felt her soul fully reenter her body for the first time in two weeks. She was here. She was in the woods, near the fire, with the reevers. She had allowed herself the peace of retreat. There had been no wine to drown herself in, no sex to lose herself in. She had been alone with what she had seen. She had watched a priestess give birth to a child who had not belonged to her. A vessel, the women had called her—a surrogate to whatever had grown within her womb. A prayer.

Nox moved her head to the side slowly, as if hoping she could avert her gaze from the memory. She saw the priestess holding the baby as she asked the other holy women what they should do with it or how they would raise it. The women had said they wouldn't interfere with the hands of fate. It had been the goddess who had willed this life into its birth through the prayers of the believer, and it would be the goddess who would guide destiny as this child came into the world. Some child of immaculate conception by the glowing of the Tree of Life and a dying princess's wish had been born into this world.

Nox had heard other children, like Emily and her younger sister, talk about their parents abandoning them for need of food or money. She had known several of the orphans to have been left on the threshold of the mill, never knowing their heritage. Nox had been small when she had heard the thuds against the front door of Farleigh in the middle of the night. It had been one of her first memories.

Thoughts of the dream dissolved into the memory of that night.

Her first memory.

The storm had howled throughout the night, and Nox hadn't slept. She'd been too excited by the wind and the thunder and trees. She stayed awake as the rain pounded against the windows of her dorm. Other children had wiggled in their beds when they'd heard the knock against the manor door, but she'd been the only one to leave the warmth of her sheets and wander into the hall. The Gray Matron had spied her and admonished her, but Nox had merely followed in the dark. Her curiosity had propelled her forward that night.

She remembered how it had felt to kneel in the shadows, shielded by her black curtain of hair while she listened to them talk about the secret bundle.

"No one is going to come looking for her."

That was what the man had said to Agnes as he'd collected fifty crowns. The matron hadn't questioned him, but nearly two decades later, Nox understood why. Amaris had not been stolen from the crib of a loving mother and father. She had not been taken from a nursery or snatched from the hands of

417

a nanny. The man had been the one who had snatched the bundle from where it was in the temple. No one was going to come looking for a baby who had been left alone without parents at the Temple of the All Mother.

"Stay with me," Malik's voice said from the distance. He watched her eyes begin to slip as she retreated into her memories.

"It's Amaris."

Ash crossed from where he stood and joined Malik on the ground. Nox didn't miss the thinly suppressed frustration in his voice as he clarified, "What's Amaris?"

Amaris was the girl she'd loved and protected and fought for. She'd murdered, manipulated, stolen, and changed her life for the girl. She'd taken her place at the Selkie, amassed forces, and plotted to march north. She'd gulped from the goblets of souls. She'd taken beatings, been sold like a commodity to the highest bidder, done and thought and endured unspeakable things for the love that burned more intensely in her heart than the light of the sun. That was Amaris.

"The baby."

Their brows were mutually furrowed. "What baby?"

Nox blinked several times and seemed to realize her mouth was exceptionally dry. "Do you have any water?"

One of them scrambled for the skin before producing it for her. She drank deeply until water dripped down her chin. She wiped it with the backs of her hands as she began to speak. Her story was slow, and large sections of it felt disjointed or made no sense at all. Nox told them about how she had seen the priestess give birth to the goddess's baby and how that baby had been stolen from the temple and sold to their orphanage. That orphan had grown up to be the one she loved and the reever with whom they fought.

"What are you saying?" Ash's features were knit with more lines and creases than she'd ever seen on his lovely faeling face.

Nox could barely shrug. She had spent so many days

without moving or speaking that the movement felt utterly foreign. "Amaris was the answer to Princess Daphne's prayers. The princess prayed for the goddess to break the curse on this land, and the All Mother heard her prayer and sent a child. She's not..." Nox couldn't bring herself to finish the sentence. Amaris wasn't a person? Amaris wasn't fae? What was she?

"That doesn't make sense."

She didn't bother shaking her head. "It doesn't need to make sense. A prayer was made on the princess's deathbed, and the All Mother answered."

Malik clutched her hand, desperate not to lose her to her thoughts again now that they'd regained her. "This knowledge has shaken you to your core, Nox. Why?"

Nox tried to smile at him.

His good, green eyes implored hers for answers.

"You wouldn't understand."

"Try," Malik prodded gently. Another silence passed between them.

"Because I love her."

It was all she could say.

He smiled at Nox. "We love her too. And if this information could help us, then we're going to use it and find out whatever we need to know. Now, are you ready to meet whoever it is you need to meet at Farleigh tomorrow to tell you about Princess Daphne?"

"Both princesses."

"What?"

"We're going to Farleigh to learn about another princess." She looked to her bag again, then back to the men, regretting not telling them sooner. "This feather I've been carrying is an enchanted quill. When I write on parchment, the message is seen by whoever holds its twin. The other quill—the person who has been writing to me—is in Farleigh."

The reevers had plenty of questions, and she had no will to resist answering them. They wanted to know how she'd acquired such an object, when she'd written to a phantom

419

penman, and most importantly, why she had never mentioned this to them. Objectively, she knew they'd done what they could to bite their tongues lest they scare her back into her shell.

Ash and Malik discussed as much as they could in hushed voices out of earshot while the day departed and night fell on their campsite. No one slept well on their final night. The next day, around midday, they would arrive at the child mill that Nox had called home for seventeen years.

Thirty-Eight

IT WAS LIKE SLIPPING BACK INTO SHOES THAT HAD BEEN SOAKED in the rain and then dried in a way that no longer molded to your feet. Nox knew her body fit, but it didn't feel right. It was dreadfully uncomfortable to return to the present. The darkness had done its job. It had provided a shield of protection when she had been too delicate to defend herself. The darkness wasn't her enemy. It wasn't bad or wrong or immoral to detach. It was safe. It was kind. It was armor against a cruel, sharp, cutting reality.

She was certain it wasn't wrong to safeguard oneself, but sometimes, she needed to endure life's agonizing, jagged edges.

"How involved do you want us to be?" Malik asked.

She shook her head. "I think you should stay in the foyer," she said. She wasn't quite herself, but she was trying. "Entertain the children with stories of a world beyond their walls. I know it was terribly exciting when an assassin—sorry, a reever—spent the night in our orphanage."

"Spare them the monster talk?" Ash asked.

"No, talk exclusively of monsters. Traumatize them." She rolled her eyes as they approached the door.

She didn't miss the buoyant relief on their faces at her sarcasm. It must have been such a welcome change to her despondency. They crossed the courtyard, passing the area where she had knelt while taking lashes as the bishop watched. The reevers behind her, Nox knocked three times on the manor's front door.

Her knuckles were sore from the bruising force of her raps when someone answered.

Apparently, she would not be easing gently into reality.

Matron Agnes opened the door. Her expression was not one of surprise. She remained as stoic and unimpressed as ever, even as her eyes lifted from Nox to drag over the armed men flanking her on either side. "I was wondering how long it would take you to get here."

It was not exactly the greeting she'd been expecting, but then again, Agnes had never been a warm woman. She turned and retreated into the manor.

Nox looked over her shoulder and offered a half shrug to the reevers. They crossed the threshold, remaining on the carpet near the door while Nox walked up the stairs after Agnes.

"Be nice," she mouthed to Ash. Malik would have no trouble being kind to the orphans, but some part of her was convinced that her faeling friend was about to scar a handful of impressionable young minds.

A mix of dread and nostalgia stirred within Nox. The rugs were the same. The outdated oil painting of Queen Moirai, her late husband, and the angelic face of long-dead Princess Daphne hadn't changed. The sounds of children in scattered dormitories were familiar, though the voices were not ones she recognized. She was confident that if she took the back staircase down to the kitchen, she'd find Matron Mable kneading dough while covered in a thin sheen of flour. The faint smell of baking bread gave credence to her suspicions.

Agnes took out a key and unlocked the latched door to her office. Nox followed.

She had been here many times. Though she realized it had been just under four years ago, it had felt more like a decade had passed. She'd departed Farleigh with her maiden-hood intact, naive and terrified, mere hours after holding Amaris. She returned now an empowered creature of the night, a fully realized woman darkening the mill's doorstep. She'd slayed men and demons. She had titles and estates at her feet. She'd done more and seen more and conquered more than the matron could ever imagine.

Nox tilted her head slightly, feeling her hair cascade to the side as she eyed the older woman. Agnes had always seemed so much bigger, so much more powerful. Now Nox realized she stood several inches taller and a great deal straighter in posture. Agnes was hunched slightly, her salt-and-pepper hair pulled into a familiar bun.

"Sit, sit." Agnes motioned Nox into a chair as if she were any client or prospective buyer here to negotiate terms of purchase.

Nox sank slowly into the chair. The office looked more or less the same, cluttered with shelves and armoires and trinkets. It reminded her greatly of Millicent's office, and she noted how both women seemed to hoard their treasures behind locked doors like wicked dragons sitting atop their jewels and gold. A sinister thought within her wondered if children were part of the dragon hoard at Farleigh in a way she'd never considered. Perhaps material possessions hadn't been all the Gray Matron had amassed.

Agnes wore her fatigue and anxiety in deep, etched lines across her face—nothing like the pillar of intimidation and strength Nox had remembered. Bruised crescents of age and sleeplessness were prominent below her eyes. Meanwhile, lords crumbled at Nox's feet. She had brought men to their knees. If she wanted, she was sure very kingdoms would bow before her. This matron held no power over her.

"How did you find out?" Agnes broke their silence.

Nox had come too far to back down. "How do you think?"

Agnes shook her head. "I thought that she, her handmaiden, and I were the only three in the kingdom who knew. Her secret died with her, and mine has never left my lips."

Nox dared a question. "By her, of course, you mean Princess Daphne?"

Agnes's eyes narrowed with a nearly imperceptible assessment. She examined Nox then—truly studied her. Nox could almost see herself through Agnes's eyes, witnessing the glossy black hair and how it hung loosely around her face, the glow of her skin, and the depth of her eyes. She was not the young woman who had departed Farleigh.

"You're clever," Agnes said at last.

Nox refused to budge. She offered nothing.

"I don't mean that as an insult. You deserve to know," Agnes said.

Once more, Nox kept her face blank. She was nothing if not an artist at controlling facial expressions to garner responses.

Agnes sighed. "I suppose it will be me who tells the tale after years of silence after all. You are twenty-one now, Nox?"

Her lips moved as if to frown, but she fought it. "I am."

"Seven and three are both magic numbers. Did you know that?" Agnes waited for a beat as she continued eyeing her. "It seems appropriate that you would seek your destiny at their multiplication. It's almost as if fate waited for such a moment." Agnes was speaking as if to herself. She sighed with the world-weary sound of a woman who had done and seen far too much.

Agnes stood from her desk and crossed to a dresser encased with frosted glass. She opened the doors and pulled a small piece of jewelry from the head of a velvet bust. Nox was struck with a memory of how she and Amaris had looked through the office, laughing at the tiara as if it might be some small treasure Agnes wore atop her head after the children had gone to sleep. Agnes returned to the desk and sat, holding the tiara out to Nox.

Nox frowned at the extended jewelry.

"Take it."

Her frown deepened as she accepted the small crown with its black jewels, turning the metallic ring in her hand. She studied it but understood nothing. She responded with a confused, "Thank you?"

Agnes shook her head, ignoring Nox's questioning words. "Twenty-one years ago, I heard a knock at my door. It wasn't a dark and stormy night. It wasn't winter. It was nothing remarkable or dramatic or special, except..." Agnes's words drifted quietly. "I'd opened the doors of Farleigh to peasants and thieves and whores for decades, but never before had I seen a princess."

The air was sucked from the room at the words.

"She clutched you so tightly, she did. I'd seen so many at that threshold. I'd seen the poor, the needy, the sick, the sad. I was a pitiless woman. I didn't have room for the emotion. Sympathy had never served me. But this...this broke my heart. She didn't look like her portrait after the hands he'd laid on her, but I knew it was her. And Daphne...well, she knew that if her husband saw you, with your copper skin and black hair, he'd kill you sooner than he'd spare you. So there she was, asking for a boy who matched the man's coloring."

No.

Her ears were mishearing. Agnes was mistaken. Lies. Inaccuracies. There was no way. For the briefest of moments, Nox felt herself slipping away before she used an invisible hand to slap herself into the moment. She slammed the door on the darkness and bit back the ringing in her ears.

"You were to be named for the night, she said, so you'd always feel connected to the north. She left you the crown that rightly belongs to you."

Nox's gaze lifted from the tiara she had been eyeing while Agnes spoke.

"Daphne?"

She'd never seen Agnes look kind before. The hard mask

425

she wore ebbed, if only for a moment. Her face relaxed as she looked into Nox's eyes. "Yes. Your mother gave you your name and your crown and brought you as far north as she could."

Nox's gaze remained on the matron who had raised her. She thought of the seventeen years of preferential treatment and favoritism. She thought of how she'd been sent away each market day and every time the bishop visited, supposedly to hide Amaris.

"You weren't hiding Amaris, were you?" Nox's voice was so low, it was scarcely more than a whisper.

Agnes shrugged at that, doing her best to regain whatever aura of bitter nonchalance she'd spent decades cultivating. "Two birds, one stone, my dear. Amaris knew she was for sale. It was better for all of us if you believed you were merely helping her than to begin questioning why you were similarly set apart."

Nox had spent too many days in shock to truly feel the emotion now. Instead, she merely looked at Agnes. "You knew who my mother was for all this time?"

"I did."

"And you didn't tell me?"

Agnes scoffed at that. The woman had no time for coddling. "What safety would it have been to tell you? How could I keep the secret the princess had given me if you knew? If the children had known, if the other matrons or villagers had learned…or worse, if your mother's wretched, filthy excuse of a husband had learned…"

"I spent years thinking I was unloved. I have spent twenty-one years thinking I was abandoned."

Agnes had spent so many years playing the role of the strict matron, the cruel mother, the callous housemaster. For once, her face was not unkind. "All Princess Daphne knew was that Farleigh was the closest orphanage to the northern border. I think some part of her had hoped your father might find you."

"My father?" A dizzying airlessness continued to suck at Nox.

Agnes nodded. "If you had been the natural-born heir to the princess and her brute of a husband, what need would she have had to swap you for a changeling? I don't know much about your conception, girl, but look at yourself. Your face is northern, and Princess Daphne was as southern as they come."

Nox was doing her best to breathe normally. The colors and jewels and paintings of the office swam in her vision while she forced her eyes to focus. "When you asked me which princess I was talking about, you were referring to my mother and to me."

It was not a question.

"You are the only natural-born heir to the throne in Farehold. Queen Moirai had one daughter, and her daughter had you. The queen believes the crown prince—"

"There is no prince."

Agnes eyed her skeptically at that, and Nox merely shook her head. She couldn't allow herself to get into it now. She had seen the crumpled, lifeless body of the boy as Daphne laid the child before the tree.

"He knows it's not his son."

"You mean because he's your changeling? Yes, I bought—" Agnes cleared her throat. "I took him in myself. I've known for more than twenty years that the crown prince was little more than a half-starved, lowborn infant from a neighboring village. I did so many things before her...before you. After Daphne came to my door, things changed, Nox. I stopped. My life—"

"You still bought Amaris."

Agnes exhaled through her nose. "I did. Amaris was... exceptional."

Princess Daphne had been using her dying breath to explain her trick had not worked. The changeling had not passed for a natural-born heir. The reevers said that Amaris had screamed to the throne room that there was no crown prince, and now Nox understood. The queen had been expending her energy to maintain the illusion so that no

427

one knew the child had been murdered upon the father's discovery.

Years ago, when Nox was small, the children had loved to spread rumors about a princess and a changeling. They had all reveled in the fairy tale that perhaps one day, they could be snatched from the orphanage, taken from their life of poverty, and elevated to royalty. No one had truly considered the rumor to hold any weight. If it had, they definitely wouldn't have considered the price it would have cost the princess to leave her natural-born child to the care of those she believed to be pious women while she took a small, golden-brown baby boy home to Aubade.

Nox found her voice. "You let Millicent take me."

Agnes deflated. She was both defensive and defeated in a single motion. "She was never meant to take you, Nox. Never in one hundred years could I have foreseen how that morning would transpire. She had put a deposit on the silver-haired girl. You were meant to stay among the matrons. I had been grooming you to take a matron's role so that you could seamlessly become one of us and remain safely hidden. When Amaris escaped on the day she was meant to leave with Millicent, I didn't know how to tell the Madame she couldn't have you without giving away your secret."

"Agnes, I've spent the last three years as a courtesan."

Agnes did not meet her eyes.

"You have no idea what I've become."

Agnes found both strength and anger at those words. The woman seemed to grow three times her size. Her energy swelled to fit her passion. This was the matron Nox remembered. She knew no weakness. She was not moved by plights or tragedies or the realities of this life. She was the morally flexible pillar of strength who guided the home. She had spent Nox's life successfully shielding her from an unknowable truth.

"So? Who among us hasn't done things? I swear to you, the one with the most pious exterior has the darkest secrets.

Your exterior is less saintly so that your interior isn't chock-full of deceit. You wear your badges with honesty. If I had to examine two souls, I'd take the honest whore over the lying bishop every day, and that's speaking from someone who's built her career on her empire of bartering in human lives. I know what I am, Nox. I know where my soul is destined when I'm six feet beneath the earth. But this isn't about me or others or anyone but you. What you have been does not matter. All that matters is what you will be. Now you know everything. What will you do with this information?"

Nox caught herself in the midst of her spiral like grabbing a swirling stick out of the air. She'd been given so much. She'd been told more, learned more, gained more than she could begin to absorb.

They didn't bother themselves with the pleasantries of departures. Nox had her crown, her title, and her knowledge. Agnes stood unceremoniously, gesturing for the exit.

"Just like that?" Nox asked.

Agnes gave her an unimpressed look. "There's nothing more for you here, and you know it. Now go. It's your life. Decide what you'll do with your fate."

Thirty-Nine

THE REEVERS WERE STILL STANDING ON THE THRESHOLD AS Nox made her way down the stairs. She vaguely recognized the faces of some of the children. Others sparked no familiarity as they congregated around the excitement brought by the strangers, faces changed by time and distance. Malik had a toddler on his hip and three others surrounding him from where he'd taken a knee to talk to them. Ash was standing with far more discomfort as the small army of curious children encroached on him. Orphans clung to the balcony and clutched against doorways to gawk at the reevers. Nox paid them no mind as she set her feet on the landing, brushing past where Ash and Malik remained on the rug. She was still clutching the black-jeweled tiara as she abandoned the gates of Farleigh, vowing to never return.

Her horrible dreams crashed through her once more. This time, there was no threat of darkness but the sharp, furious sting of realization.

"Please protect our child," Daphne had begged. *"Please send someone."*

Nox's mother had begged the All Mother to send Amaris...to her.

Nox heard Malik say his hasty goodbyes to the children as they came out after her.

She mounted her tawny horse while the men were still approaching their horses.

"Nox, what happened?" Malik shouted up to her, gripping his saddle as he flung himself onto the horse.

"We're going to Gwydir."

"You want to go farther north?" They gaped after her. "We're already at the edge of Farehold!"

"I have to go north." Nox stashed the crown in her saddlebag and urged her horse forward, first into a trot until its muscles warmed up, then to a canter, and finally into a gallop. They were only one day from the Raasay Forest if they headed directly northeast into the woods, two days if they took the regency's road into Raascot. She took turns between running and relaxing her horse, allowing it to catch its breath and cool its lungs before urging it forward again. She drove her fawn-colored mount into the dying light of evening as she headed north. They had already been on the road for two weeks, and yet they were nowhere near where she needed to be for an answer.

✦

They urged their mounts into an outright sprint, desperate to catch up to her as she became little more than a dot against the horizon. The sun was already setting far to their left as she dashed into the darker, deeper parts of blues and purples, headed for the kingdom of night. In the break it had taken her to cool down her horse, Malik forced his mount to a gallop and skidded to a stop, cutting her off. He held up a hand and shouted from his diaphragm. "Hold on!"

She pulled up on her reins, her tawny horse coming up on its back legs as it found a sudden halt. Nox parted her mouth in an angry gasp. She glared at the man standing between her and the northern kingdom.

Ash closed the distance between them and snatched the

reins from her hands while Malik continued blocking the road. "Nox, you are not a reever. We love you, but we were dispatched on a mission for the south. You cannot lead this party any farther than you already have, especially if you won't talk to us."

"Then leave me!" She tried to yank the reins from Ash's hand and force her horse around, but Ash held firm. The hottest parts of the day had passed, and clouds had begun to collect, threatening the gray of oncoming rain.

"Nox, talk to us!" Malik begged.

The reevers had been trained for many things. They had been trained to take on a sustron or contain a djinn before its owner made their final wish. They knew how to assassinate an agent of magic and how to bring peace to the kingdoms through a pure driving will for balance. They had learned sword play, archery, and hand-to-hand combat. They had been forced to sit through lessons on poisons, tonics, healing, and techniques. Samael would press politics upon them time after time. One of the few things they'd been left to learn on their own were the ways of women.

Nox tried again to yank the reins from Ash's grip, but two weeks of obstinance had brought them to their limits. Malik dismounted, grabbing her horse on its opposing side. "Get off."

"No!" she yelled at them. She kicked her horse, spurring it forward. The tan horse jolted, but between Ash's grip and Malik's steadying hold on its saddle, it had nowhere to go.

"Do you want us to go north with you?" Malik asked from where he stood.

"Stay or go, I don't care. I'm going to Gwydir."

He felt like he might cry through his frustration as he stared up to her. "Tell us why."

She closed her eyes against reality. Vibrant hues lit half her face as the sunset shone to one side while clouds and darkness shaded the other. "I don't know where to start."

He felt the victory, as small as it was. He was a mountain climber who had discovered the tiniest ledge on a sheer rock face. He trusted his grip strength as he latched on to it, pulling himself upward. "Why don't you start at the beginning?"

"I can't." Her words were thick.

He felt himself pulling up the rock face, foot searching for another lip to move upward.

"Just try, Nox. We're here to listen."

The mood changed like tumbling dominos. First, her face softened. For the briefest of moments, he felt confident they'd gotten through to her. He realized his mistake a second later. As soon as he let down his guard, she made her move. Nox kicked her horse and broke free from the reevers. Ash's hands were nearly burned from the friction of the reins as they ripped from his grip. Malik barely jumped from the horse's path in time to avoid being trampled. They gaped at each other in the valuable moments it took Nox to break free of their hold.

"Let's go!" Malik began mounting his horse.

"Wait." Ash's voice was cold with authority.

Malik's eyes went wild.

"You can't let the fact that you fancy her cloud your judgment, Malik. Is following the beautiful girl to the northern kingdom wise? Does it align at all with what we've been dispatched to do?"

Malik's face was ripe with emotion. "It sounds to me like you've already decided the answer to that question."

"We weren't dispatched to Raascot."

"No," he growled from his impatient posture on his horse. "We were sent to find out the queen's motives. What if those motives can't be discovered in the south? Nox seems to have been given a lot more information by the Tree than either of us have, and the answers we need don't seem to be in Farehold. We've met with Moirai. We tried barging into the castle and demanding answers. How did that work out for us last time?"

Ash's face was desperate. "We can't just follow her because she's beautiful."

Malik felt like he might throw a punch. "Her being beautiful is the least important thing about her, Ash. She rescued us from the dungeon in Aubade. She saved me from the spider. She has put her life on the line for us more than once. She gave us shelter in Henares, she has led us to answers, and she is the most important person in the world to Amaris. She knows things that she learned from the All Mother herself. I'm not going to lose faith in her just because she's struggling to speak right now. If Nox is confident that the answers we need are in the north, then I believe her."

He burned with intensity as he leveled his challenging stare.

The sound of her horse's hooves had long since disappeared against the speckled clouds of the distance as she thundered toward the northeastern forest. The only sound between them was the humming intensity of their challenge. Finally, Ash spoke.

"Then we go north."

With solemn gravity, Malik repeated, "Then we go north."

And off they set.

Forty

A MARIS!" HER NAME IN ODRIN'S RICH, DEEP VOICE WAS THE
most wonderful sound in the world. It was like the
four seasons melted together and freshly brewed tea every
morning. It was a warm fire in the winter, fresh bread in the
fall, spring grass, and the sunshine in the heat of summer.
Goddess, she'd missed him.

"Odrin!" She threw her arms around him, and he accepted
the hug fully, squeezing her in return until her back nearly
popped. Her response was the high squeak of unbridled joy.

"Now you are the last face I expected to see in these
parts!" Odrin's face crinkled with delight against her hair.

Amaris was so lost in the paternal hug, she forgot all about
the weariness of travel. He had been a bit awkward when
they'd parted ways so many moons ago, but this reunion had
no room for decorum. He held her as tightly as if she were
his natural-born daughter, overjoyed at seeing her after their
time apart. From his cropped beard to his towering height,
he was precisely as she remembered him, as if no time had
passed at all.

"And who do we have here?" Odrin turned his attention
to the fae who had escorted her into the room.

"Ah, yes. Blame this one for why I'm in the north in the first place." She jerked her thumb toward her companions. "This is Gadriel, Ceres's general. And Yazlyn, his...sergeant?"

"One of them," Yazlyn confirmed.

"Gad, Yaz, this is Odrin. He's the reason I'm a reever!" Amaris looked at Odrin fondly. "He's the reason for most of the good things that have happened to me. And where's Grem? Is he here?"

Grem was still descending the stairs when she spotted him. He joined the crowd on the main floor of the town house that served as dining room, sitting room, and kitchen all at once.

Gadriel shook hands with Grem and Odrin with the sort of respectful acknowledgment that felt so strange in light of all she'd shared with the separate parties.

Amaris felt a peculiar sensation tickle through her—a nervousness, perhaps. She watched Odrin's face as he clasped hands with the general, studying his expression to see if her mentor liked him. She wasn't sure why, but in her gut, she felt deeply that Odrin's opinion of Gadriel mattered.

It took them a moment to exchange information, but Amaris quickly learned that Gadriel and Yazlyn had brought her to the home designated for reevers—one that Elil had occupied for the past decade. Elil was usually out in the woods until dinnertime but was expected back any moment, which would finally give her a chance to meet Ash's father. Amaris was too grateful for the opportunity to reunite with family to care that they hadn't gone directly to the castle. Answers could wait.

This time, Amaris was the one to tell the story of what had happened in the south, and Yazlyn was just as enraptured in the tale as she had been while Gadriel had been the one telling it. The reevers' faces went stiff when she revealed her power of persuasion, but soon after the story advanced, even Grem gasped when she explained that Queen Moirai had not been susceptible to the command. Amaris described her horror as she and the others were dragged from the throne room, the pommel of a sword knocking her unconscious.

Odrin and Yazlyn were both leaning forward in their chairs, features lit by the firelight while Amaris lowered her voice to describe how she'd blinked into consciousness to find herself gagged and bound in the queen's dungeon with the reevers in a separate cell. A thin hand went to Yazlyn's mouth when Amaris exclaimed that Nox, her childhood best friend, had sought her out and cut her free of her gag. Amaris skipped over the more intimate details and went into the bright light that had blinded them as her cell wall rolled away to reveal the burning sun of the coliseum.

Elil returned from the woods, interrupting the story only long enough to exchange pleasantries and join the others around the fire for Amaris's story.

"Elil!" Odrin said in a hurried voice, "We're just getting to the part where Amaris was dragged into the coliseum at Castle Aubade! Go on, go on!"

Gadriel took a seat across from her, and she touched his arm for emphasis in the midst of her story as she explained how Queen Moirai had painted the reevers to be demon sympathizers and used the opportunity to spur the south against the north. Yazlyn punched Gadriel in the shoulder upon hearing for the first time that he had been ready to die for the cause, horrified at the visual of her general kneeling on the sand. Gadriel's gaze locked on to Amaris's as she described her refusal to kill him, choosing to fight the dragon rather than behead him. She met his eyes in return, feeling a charge in the way their eyes touched. Her lips twitched in a smile as she carried on. Though her gaze flitted to those around the room, they returned to Gadriel time after time. Grem's eyes bulged at the reveal of the ag'drurath. Gadriel couldn't remain silent as they took turns excitedly telling their parts of the dragon battle, including the shock of seeing the Captain of the Guard run out to begin slicing at the leg that was chained.

"I've always said you had a warrior's heart. From the day

you ran out of that orphanage, dagger in hand, and bribed me with my own money," Odrin said proudly. "My little she-bear against the world."

She sparkled back at him. She truly had spent every day doing her best. No music in the world was sweeter to her ears than knowing she'd made him proud.

No one in the town house released a single breath while they spoke of the orb and the curse they'd seen. Elil shook his head at the news, particularly upon learning the revelation that King Ceres had been kneeling before Queen Moirai as she damned the border to the perception curse. No one in the house had ever stepped foot inside the fabled university. Hearing of its masters and their powers had been just as baffling as the knowledge that a true ag'imni had loitered outside in its forests.

"A real ag'imni?" Elil tested.

Amaris nodded for emphasis. "It was terrifying! All the demons have the same smell, that smell like—"

"Like rotten eggs?" Yazlyn offered.

"Yes!" Amaris agreed emphatically. "Rancid meat and sulfur! But with the ag'imni, they have this sort of smokelike quality that emanates from them..."

"I've seen it myself," Odrin agreed. "Could you feel it?"

She nodded. "I didn't know I wasn't supposed to breathe it in! If Gadriel hadn't mentioned not to open my mouth— I'm going to have to send word for Samael to make a note in the bestiaries."

"Your mouth?" Odrin clarified, brows lowering slightly.

Gadriel put his hand in the middle of her back, warming her. "I'd take one hundred ag'imni before seeing Moirai again, whether in person or in curses."

She felt the touch from his palm radiate from where it rested on her back all the way into her stomach. "And that's why we've come," Amaris finished. "It doesn't make any sense as to why Queen Moirai would have looked into Ceres's eyes and condemned the entire kingdom unless his lover was her daughter. We need to know."

Everyone was so swept up in the story that they'd lost track of time, dissolving into murmurs to one another or clarifications for emphasis.

"We've been to hell and back together, haven't we?" Gadriel said quietly. Some at the table overheard, but it was clear he was only speaking to her.

Amaris was acutely aware he hadn't looked away from her in a long, long time. She wasn't sure why she did it, but she held his eyes. There it was again. That charge. That palpable static like the impending certainty of lightning that had taken on so many forms—irritation, loathing, concern, trust, panic, fear, and hope—in its ever-growing metamorphosis.

Odrin patted Amaris on the shoulder in response to Gadriel's statement, seeing it as nothing more than the highest praise. "She's quite the asset, isn't she? Warrior's heart, this one. Always has been."

She wasn't sure if she'd ever seen Odrin's spirits this high.

"She's more than an asset," Gadriel said in response, his thumb moving in one arc against her back before he dropped his hand from the point of contact.

Odrin nodded along happily, returning to whatever other element of the conversation he'd been having with Grem.

Yazlyn's eyebrows had collected as she'd listened to the exchange. Perhaps she had more of an ear for the nuance and underlying implications of Gadriel's words than Odrin.

Elil not only looked but also sounded so much like his faeling son. Elil was pure fae and had much sharper features than Ash, but the resemblance was unmistakable. "The king has sent all his forces and all his men to search for a child without giving them the information they need to fulfill their task. He's so consumed with his search for his child that he's completely let his lands fall to the beasts invading from the mountains. The demons are our true threat, and if he won't turn his eyes to look to Sulgrave for why the creatures are descending, his kingdom will be left in rubble."

Amaris frowned at this. "I'm afraid of the answer to this,

Elil. Perhaps King Ceres is so certain that he has a son because of how word spread throughout the kingdoms once Princess Daphne had given birth. If that's the case… Queen Moirai is using her gift of illusion to manifest a prince. I don't believe a prince exists."

Everyone deflated at this. Grem asked, "How can we tell Ceres if this is true? How could anyone tell him that he's wasted twenty-odd years on a phantom?"

Gadriel and Yazlyn weren't making eye contact. It was one of the first times he'd looked away, and Amaris found herself missing the intensity of how it felt to be the target of his gaze. She wondered how long they'd been carrying the burden of their once-great king and his utter consumption by a single obsession. This was why Ash hadn't seen his father since he was a child, even after his mother passed. The task rested on Elil's shoulders to attempt to slay and contain the monsters as they poured down from the mountains, picking up the slack while the king remained otherwise occupied.

"How long do you think the crown prince has been dead?" Odrin asked.

Everyone shook their heads. It could have been one year, it could have been ten, or perhaps there had never been a child. If Daphne was indeed his lover, Ceres would have heard no alternative to the child's fate. The boy had been his last remaining tether to the love that had eaten away at him, turning from a thing of beauty to an infection that had festered until it enveloped him. Perhaps when his spies weren't able to locate the prince in Aubade, he'd assumed that the boy had been stashed elsewhere in the kingdom. How could he have known that the reason his reconnaissance efforts could lay no hands on a prince was because the boy had been a mere illusion?

Elil sighed. "The people have hoped just as desperately that the prince would be found, though not for the same reason as their king. Perhaps if there were an heir to the throne, they might be spared from his delirium. Raascot is desperate for change."

440

Amaris understood why the winged fae remained silent. Gadriel loved his cousin, and Yazlyn remained loyal to her country. Ceres was their king, and even in his hour of madness, they would not abandon him.

They shared a hearty dinner with roast beef so tender it fell apart in their mouths, tiny potatoes that had been cooked over the fire with salt and butter, and far too many pitchers of ale. They exchanged stories and jokes, ribbed one another, and made plans for some challenge to see who could get the most knives to stick in the tree outside the town house. Eventually, the party disbanded to the various rooms of the large home. Elil had long ago been given a place of honor as ward of the magical balance, gifted his living quarters by the king as thanks for his watchful eye over the peace in the north. Grem and Odrin had doubtlessly expressed their envy that they hadn't received such cushioned placements over the last ten years, but the imbalance of magic seemed to be drawing more and more reevers northward. All the pieces were clicking into place as everything fell together. Maybe they'd all have mansions in Raascot before long.

Forty-One

GADRIEL HAD BARELY BEGUN TO SETTLE INTO THE ROOM he'd been given when Amaris knocked at his door. The ghost of a wry smile played across her features as she echoed the only revelation that mattered. "We really have been to hell and back, haven't we?"

His expression told her he was surprised to see her in his room, but he returned the smile. "Not too many get to brag about surviving an ag'drurath."

Amaris closed the door behind her and leaned against it.

Gadriel cocked an eyebrow. "What brings you to my room, witchling?"

"I'm an asset, huh?"

He twinkled at that. "I think I said you were more than an asset."

"Mmm." She nodded slowly. "That's what I thought I heard."

"And you've come to gloat?" A single eyebrow stayed up, eyes fixed on hers again just as they had while they'd exchanged tales. There it was. The charge. The tangible energy that wore its many masks as it squeezed through her. They'd done so much. They'd seen so much. They'd saved each other time and time again. And then there was what he'd done to her in the forest and the curious bloom of sensation it had triggered deep within her.

She tilted her head to the side, feeling the creeping pink of blush as she picked her words carefully. "I think we haven't properly celebrated our survival."

He stopped what he was doing, going totally still as he regarded her. "And," he began slowly, "are you implying we're due for a celebration?"

She was. She wanted to add a new memory to their list of experiences. A new emotion had asked to be explored, and after they'd laid their journey together out for the world to see, she was forced to truly appreciate the interconnectivity of their lives. They'd been interwoven through hardship, curiosity, tenacity, duty, courage and…maybe something else.

She bit her lip while she looked up at him. She was so rarely afforded the opportunity to simply want. At Farleigh, she had been set aside for the price she might fetch. At Uaimh Reev, she was focused on training. Since then, there had been travel, there had been torment, and there had been survival. Now that they were safely in Gwydir in a comfortable home, with a hot meal and a belly warm with ale, it felt like she might truly be able to take a breath. She had been through the fires and deserved a little pleasure.

She didn't budge from the door. Gadriel took a half step closer. He normally looked so self-assured, so cocky. Right now, his expression curated a single, cautious question. She had found him beautiful from the moment she had met him. She had found him arrogant, bossy, irritating, and dominant. Some part of her felt so drawn to the raw power he controlled so wholly. She hadn't stopped thinking about how hard he'd pressed himself into her when he'd shoved her into the tree to shelter her from the ag'imni. Her hands still felt the place where he had rubbed healing tonic on her palm. Her cheek remembered where he'd fixed her bruise. Her body had felt flushed at the memory of being truly bested in battle by someone she trusted.

"Well, demon." She let her eyes sparkle with the mischief she knew she tempted when she used the word. "I spent so long distrusting you. But then, retelling our story...truly seeing what we'd been through together. You and me. I don't think either of us would have made it to Gwydir alone."

"And so you've come to thank me for being such an underappreciated blessing? How very polite, witchling. I didn't know you had it in you." He smirked at his smart-ass remark, but his face still held a question.

"About that." She tested her words hesitantly. Her heart rate spiked as she battled a fear more potent than any dragon or demon or orb. "You've mentioned a time or two that I would benefit from a firm hand."

The way his face changed would have been imperceptible to anyone else, but she knew him well enough to see the fire ignite behind his eyes.

She heated as she remembered him asking repeatedly if she truly wanted him to train her, insisting on her verbal confirmation, signing her willingness over to him. A warm, curling sensation in her lowermost parts tickled at the memory of his authority. She looked at him again, her teeth still tugging at her lower lip until he fully understood why she'd come to his room.

"I've been thinking about something..."

"And what would that be?"

"I liked..." She didn't know how to say it. She swallowed, looking away. "When we were in the forest, when you..."

He was enjoying himself entirely too much. The sharp points of his teeth caught in the firelight as his lips pulled back in a wicked smile. Watching her squirm with her inability to articulate herself seemed to bring him its own brand of sadistic pleasure. "What did you like?"

She blushed deeply. "Don't make me say it."

It was the invitation he needed.

Gadriel closed the space between them, one step at a time. With tantalizing slowness, he rested his right hand beside her head on the door. He relaxed his powerful weight over her

444

until little space remained between them. This was an energy they'd never openly acknowledged. She knew herself to be powerful, she knew she was strong, and yet there was a wicked, sensual curling of the toes as she felt the sheer force of him and how, despite his power, she felt completely safe. As he leaned in closer, she allowed the leather, pepper, and black cherry scent of him to invade her blood. The house was still full of the loud sounds of laughter, music, and dining downstairs. No one would hear the noises of a white-haired reever.

"Look at me," he said in a quiet, firm command, hand still resting on the door beside her head.

She struggled to listen as the embarrassment that stemmed from admitting her wants painted itself into every droplet of her body.

"I don't know if I can," she admitted, face hot.

He used his thumb and index finger to lift her chin until her eyes touched his. The breath escaped her body. Her head swam. Adrenaline coursed through her. "Because you don't know how to listen."

She squirmed, sucking in a small gasp of air.

"Is this what you want?" he asked. Gadriel had asked something similar so many nights ago in the woods when she'd talked about unlocking her powers. There was something about his strength that was so brutal, so beautiful, and yet latched behind the doors of whatever he kept inside himself without explicit permission. His face was terribly close to hers.

She shivered. A chill of anticipation ran down her spine.

Amaris raised her chin slightly, lessening the space between their mouths. Her lips remained parted. He didn't move any closer. The hum that passed between them was a deep, low throb of sensation.

"I—"

His hand was the first thing she felt as he slid it up her body, resting on her throat as his thumb and index finger compressed her jugular, restricting her blood flow. "Or is this what you were talking about?"

Amaris closed her eyes, rolling against the flood of pleasure as her head spun with stars. She felt a flush of water in her deepest parts as his callouses firmly gripped her neck. She released a small, involuntary moan, but it was scarcely more than a vibration over his hand.

One large palm remained planted on the door, but the other slowly found her hip. He relaxed his weight into hers and she nearly moaned at the sheer pressure. He repeated himself, "Is this what you want?"

"Do you?" She swallowed. "This? Me?"

He pressed into her further, bringing his lips to brush against her ear. "I've thought of nothing else for weeks. But I'm a pillar of self-control. Unlike some of us."

"Hey." She tried to worm away again, but he held her firm.

The words unleashed a flood of slick, wet pleasure between her legs. Her hips moved involuntarily against him. She wanted it so badly that she nearly choked on her desire. She wanted him more than air. She'd never done anything like this, and that made it all the more exciting. The fear of the unknown matched the excitement of the power of the man before her. She felt his heat, his pressure. She could feel precisely how excited he was by the size of him as he pressed into her, yet still he made no move. She wanted him to tear her clothes off and throw her to the bed. She wanted to feel that crushing power she'd felt in the woods where for once, she was utterly in someone else's control. She loved the delicious temptation of handing over power completely. She attempted to nod, but a shy tug akin to shame forced her eyes downward. His hand left her hip. He used a knuckle to raise her chin to meet his gaze.

"Say it."

Her heart buckled at the words. She inhaled through her nose, feeling herself tighten. "What?"

"I want to hear you say it."

She nodded weakly.

"That's not good enough."

She barely gasped, "This is what I want."

A smile tugged at the edge of his mouth, but she couldn't see it for long. His hand moved from her chin, cupping her neck slowly, stopping just below her jaw. He allowed for a throb of anticipation, then another.

This was it.

The kiss she'd craved. The moment they'd connect, meet, taste and explore and experience each other in a new way entirely. His first kiss was slow and her mouth responded, their lips and tongues moving in tandem for a sweet, delicious moment.

Her breath caught as he pulled away, hand still on her throat.

"You know," he began, voice low, "humans, fae, witch-lings—we have something in common. We only live for two minutes." His grip tightened, and Amaris felt her world grow dizzy against the hold. Her inhalation, her very life, were both stuck in the pressure of his hands as he said, "Every time we breathe, the timer resets."

She let out a weak, half-articulate sound as her hips rolled.

"Do you remember our safe word?" He relinquished pressure just enough for her to gain the blood flow she needed to respond.

Amaris sipped the air around her, lips parting in a silent plea. She tried to press her body into his, hands gripping for his back to pull him closer.

He tsked under his breath. "Use your words."

She could barely breathe. She was so consumed with how badly she wanted to feel him. Her hips bucked against the door, rising up to meet him.

"Snowbird."

"There's a good girl."

Her fingers dug into his body through his shirt. Everything about their tempo changed. He crushed his mouth down on hers. This was not the tender, loving kiss of stories. This was the possessive, claiming kiss of domination. She swayed at how small she felt beneath him. His mouth parted her lips, his tongue circling hers. Her breath disappeared entirely as his hands explored their way up her shirt, clutching against her stomach.

She attempted to grab for him, but he growled against her effort and used one large hand to pin her wrists above her head. Amaris inhaled sharply as she raised her head, exposing her neck to him. He consumed her, his fire burning her everywhere his mouth or hand traced. She wanted him to cup her breast. She wanted him to loosen her pants. She wanted to be horizontal, pinned underneath him while he crushed her from above.

"Please," she choked out, desperate for his hand to gravitate north or south of its place on her stomach. She wanted to feel him in and on her most tender places.

"Look who's learning manners," he said, his mouth continuing to move across her throat, tasting her skin. She gave herself over so fully, wanting nothing more in this moment than to belong to him. His hand cupped her breast, thumb circling around its most sensitive part, and he made satisfied noises every time a small catch sounded from her throat.

"I know what I want."

"You think you're ready?" He released her wrists, intent on carrying her to the bed.

"Yes." She halted him with a definitive drop to her knees. His eyes flared in surprise, which filled her with a wicked delight. He'd stopped in his tracks, observing her from where she looked up at him, kneeling subserviently on the floor with a gleam in her eye.

"I want you," she repeated. She wanted it all. She wanted him over her, wanted his hands covering every part of her. A wicked part of her wanted to hold the same power over him that he held over her. She didn't know if he felt the same weakness when he looked at her that she did, but she felt that perhaps she could make him start.

Gadriel made a sound as if to object, but she both steered

448

and served with the strength of a single kneel. She loved what it did to his face, his body, the evidence of his pleasure in his pants. Even in submission, she didn't take direction from him. If she truly was a witchling, she figured she may as well live up to the name.

She ran a slow, soft finger along the topmost seam of his waistline, watching as he parted his lips. She enjoyed the shock that kept him fixed on her. It was clear from the way he stared that he wasn't used to anyone else taking control. This was meant to be his dance to lead. He knew the steps. And yet...

His eyes were hungry. She unfastened his pants with slow, intentional movements, thriving under the low growl she elicited. She released his most sensitive parts, letting out a murmur of admiration when comparing it to the size of her hands. Amaris ran appreciative movements along its length. Male anatomy hadn't exactly been covered in her studies, but living in the keep with a dozen crass brothers in arms had provided her with exceptionally graphic, if unintentional, education. She'd tucked away the information knowing that one day, every ale-washed story and obscene joke would prove useful.

His hands found the back of her head, balling with fists full of her hair. He raked his hands along her silver locks, pulling the loose strands away from her face. Holding the entirety of her hair in his hands prolonged their confusion of power. He held her, but it was in service to her act. Her mouth felt so small compared to the size of him.

"Start with your tongue," he said.

The instruction took away her uncertainty. She obliged, tracing her wet lips and tongue along his length. He groaned his approval. She didn't give him the opportunity to say more before putting as much of him as she could into her mouth. She looked up long enough to see his chin tilt toward the ceiling, eyes closed.

If it had been a contest, she felt quite certain she would be winning.

He was too big for her to swallow fully. She attempted to take him in deeper and felt herself gag, choosing him over oxygen. She enjoyed the effect it had on him far too much. There would be no stopping.

"Relax your throat." His voice was low, his words spoken through gritted teeth as he struggled to maintain control. He freed a hand from her hair and braced against the door to keep himself upright. She looked up at him from where she knelt, and his eyes were on her alone. She choked, but he did not relent. She breathed through her nose and obeyed, taking him in even more deeply. She relished the noises he made, elated at her own power. "Good girl."

She was a tingle of lust, pride, and victory. Her body hummed with how badly she wanted this. It was music. It was wine and candy and bliss. Those two words held more power than any she'd experienced.

"Let's—"

"No," she groaned, mouth still full. She was not ready to move on to any next activity. Whatever he wanted to do could wait. The way his hand pressed into the back of her head was in relinquishment of expectations. It was the pressure and thrust and entanglement of excitement as he allowed her to lead the dance.

"If you don't stop, I'm going to finish in your throat."

"Good," she gagged, word muffled as she continued to move up and down, the liquid sounds of her mouth and hands joining his attempts to control his groans of pleasure. He tensed against the door as he leaned into the full, dominating release of his hand on the back of her head, forcing her mouth up and down on his cock until she felt the palpable inevitability of his release.

"Amaris," he gasped, then gritted his teeth as he practically banged against the door with his free hand.

He was close. She knew just enough from her texts on basic anatomy and how her own body responded to approaching pleasure to understand the inevitable. She could feel it in the tension of his shaft, in the throb, in the way his hand fisted in her hair, pulling it at the roots. The painful tug on her hair was thrilling. She loved that she'd done this. She'd had this incredible, disarming, powerful effect. It was better than persuasion, better than combat, better than shock waves. This was power.

"I—" He inhaled sharply, presumably about to tell her that he was going to come, but he was unable to finish his thought before he began to fill her mouth with his flavors.

She was relentless, consuming every drop of him as she drained him wholly.

His entire body flexed against the climax, holding her mouth tightly to the base of his shaft as he finished. She drank it down, peering up at his face as she did so. Amaris grinned through the control she felt in her ability to bring the mighty general to a shell of his former self.

She'd won.

While she was grateful for the years of drunken nights with unwholesome tales that had unintentionally prepared her for what to do and expect, doing it was a new victory entirely. She was also relatively confident from what she knew of Gadriel's discipline that unlike the reevers, he was not the sort to talk about his conquests over pints.

His hand slowly unraveled from her hair. She looked up at him with the soft, twilight-purple eyes of a doe, awaiting praise.

"Was it good?" she asked.

The shock that she could ask such a question was plain on his face. He lowered his thumb to her lips, wiping the smallest remaining drop from her mouth. She could tell from the way that he looked at her that she was about to get more than praise.

Before she'd had time to process his expressions, she was being swept from where she'd knelt on the floor. Gadriel lifted her from where they'd remained by the door and carried her to the bed, treating her as if she weighed nothing. She

451

panted again, gripping herself closer to him as he laid her horizontally across the bed. She wasn't finished playing their game. She wanted more of him. She began to lift her tunic over her head, but he stopped her again. "Did I tell you that you could move?"

Amaris felt a sense of thrill and shock that he had not been exhausted but invigorated.

She nearly let out a cry of pleasure at his low growl. She fought the urge to lift her shirt but couldn't resist the temptation to move. Her hands were on him again, and the action merely spurred him on. Gadriel's bronze hand made another swift grab for hers, collecting her small wrists in his own. "Are you going to listen, or am I going to have to make you listen?"

She arched at that, her back curving off the bed. She didn't know how he was maintaining such control while she felt herself utterly losing all sense of her own. This question had an obvious answer. "Make me," she challenged.

She knew from the glint of his smile that he'd been hoping she might say that. Gadriel shifted her so that her head rested on the pillow. When she attempted to rise and straighten herself, a hand went to her throat. This was the sensation that had driven her to this moment. This was the rough, calloused, choking hand that had awoken something primal in her. It had been these hands that had allowed her to tap into whatever power had been wrapped tightly around her survival instincts. She let another small gasp escape her lips and he smiled.

"I'm curious to know how loud I can make you, witchling."

She moaned at that and reached her hands to attempt to free herself from her pants.

His laugh was low and gruff. "Goddess, you are defiant."

She smiled through the hand that was still at her throat. "But that's something you already knew about me."

His grin was wicked. His wings flared slightly behind him, enveloping her in an all-encompassing sense of his dominance.

She attempted to reach out for him again and released another sound of pleasure when he restrained her once more.

"Are you such a brat with all your lovers?"

There was a pause in the way she failed to answer that caused him to relax his grip slightly. He didn't quite frown, nor did he advance. He studied her hesitation, searching her face for the reason that had kept her quiet.

Shit.

There was no reason for her to have kept her maidenhood intact. She had no connection to her celibacy. She had even attempted to give it to Ash after the beseul had attacked, if only for the sense of closeness. She'd merely lacked opportunity. Amaris had no emotional or spiritual attachment to whatever one might have been taught they are to feel about their first time, and yet it was this pause that had assuaged whatever fire burned between them.

Gadriel relaxed his grip on her and instead used his knuckle to tug her face toward his once again. Her eyes were still glistening with need but had softened. "Your first time should be a bit softer than what I can offer you, witchling. Boundaries run in two directions."

She shook her head against a rising panic as she felt the moment begin to slip away. "I don't want soft."

He raised an eyebrow at that but said nothing. She loved how expressive his eyes were. "I still owe you," he said.

"I hope you don't want me because you owe me," she said.

"I want you because I want you," he promised, voice low as an oath.

Amaris narrowed her gaze slightly. "Good. And if you think any more or less of me for any such maidenhood, then you think less of women than I expected."

His wicked glare returned. "You truly are a brat."

"Oh, not a brat. A witchling."

She attempted to wrap her legs around his waist and pull him closer to her, demanding more of him.

"Amaris, I—"

"I want this." Her words were both a plea and a command.

"You'll get it."

He kissed her neck, his teeth grazing the tender parts of her. He was a bit slower as he progressed, moving more softly over her stomach, cupping her breast. She let out another gasp as he moved south, grazing the sensitive parts of her.

She raised her hands above her head as he stripped her of her tunic, her small, ivory breasts peaked against her excitement. She raised her lower half off the bed as he pulled her pants down over her hips. When she tried to remove his clothing, he merely smiled, delighted to restrain her. He took his shirt off but left his pants on after having tucked himself safely back into his waistband, stretching beneath the manhood that still throbbed against them. He was so warm. His body, his wings, his mouth, his teeth, his hands were all-encompassing.

Gadriel rolled her onto her side, keeping one hand on her throat to hold her in place. Her hands clutched the forearm that flexed against her as she had in the woods, but this time it was to force his grip in more tightly.

She lost her breath so fully she may as well have been drowning. It felt like being pulled under the depths of the sea while enjoying every moment of choking on the waves. If this was death, it was the most beautiful feeling in the world.

Gadriel licked his fingers and traced them from her navel downward, finding her most delicate place. She had never been touched there by any hands but her own. She wanted her hands to roam backward to feel him as well, but one hand continued to hold her wrists while the other moved from its resting place on her neck to explore her body, teasing her. His mouth stayed on her skin, on her throat, his teeth biting into her shoulder as his hand found exactly what made her gasp. The moment he made contact, his fingers were instantly soaked with her. He groaned in his own delight, his hips grinding against her as she pressed herself into him. He used a leg to pin hers together, trapping her against him.

Once he'd found what made her body taut, what made her go rigid with pleasure, he honed the action. He felt how her hips moved, how her pulse throbbed in her throat, how her eyes had closed so tightly. He increased his pace slowly, building as a song might. She was a fiddle and he plucked her strings with expert precision, feeling her grow tighter and tighter as her muscles tensed, each moment a new swelling sensation as someone else played her music. The melody within her swelled, each note growing higher and louder and more powerful until the song reached its climax.

The chord hung in the air as the song crested, holding on the verge of ecstasy, repeating its ultimate note until the melody shattered.

She cried out with her release.

She wasn't just music. She was a symphony, and he was its composer.

She bucked, shuddering against the release as the song hit its climax time and time again. He watched her as the final notes were plucked, allowing the music to fade into oblivion.

His hand slowed but stayed against where she had drenched him. He pressed a kiss into her throat from where he remained behind her. Her eyes began to lower, her lids heavy with the wave of exhaustion that followed the flood of endorphins. She could feel his teeth as he smiled, kissing her again. While she had come to the room wanting to feel the fullness of him, she felt sleep taking her as she sank into the heat of his body. She'd never felt so deeply relaxed. Every fiber of her being had melted into the sheets like butter over hot toast.

"Holy shit," she breathed into the pillow.

He ran his wet fingers over her lips. When she sucked them into her mouth, she could have sworn she felt his soul leave his body.

"Are you sure you don't want to fuck me?"

He chuckled. "I want to do so much more to you than you can even imagine. I'm in no rush, witchling. I have you now."

Her heart surged, body throbbing at the words.

I have you.

She let the words fill her as peace, pleasure, and exhaustion stole what remained of her energy.

He shifted the blankets up over her pale, naked form as his arm stayed draped around her. Months of travel had culminated in the most excellent reward, and now she could truly rest under the release of her pleasure. As sleep pulled her under, she could swear he was still smiling.

Forty-Two

A SOUND STIRRED HER FROM THE BOTTOMLESS DEPTHS OF
her perfect, dreamless rest. She had never slept so well.
She found herself pulled from the warm, comfortable trenches
of restorative depths of sleep and smiled as she eyed the arm
still around her. He'd held her through the night. The weight
of Gadriel's arm made her feel so safe.

She hated him, and she wanted him, and she respected
him, and she resented him, and she would do anything to stay
in this infuriating game of tug-of-war between heart, mind,
and body. It was complicated, delicious, and frustrating, and
she wanted to do it again and again and again.

His words rang through her just as they had in the Tower
of Magics.

Jump, and trust that I will catch you.

She'd stood at the lip of a literal chasm, but here she was at
the ledge once more. She'd jumped, and he had not let her fall.

Her eyes opened fully when someone rapped their
knuckles against the door. Sharp, staccato knocks shook the
remnants of sleep from her. She had been so comfortably
warm under his body heat, wings draped over them both like
a heavenly blanket. He roused as well at the sound. Maybe

if the knocker would leave, they could finish what had been started last night. Simply the weight of him against her and the memory of how he'd held her wrists in place had her ready for a new, more spectacular round. They had so much left to do, to touch, to taste, to explore. Her fingers wrapped around his arm as if begging him not to go to the door.

Amaris attempted to sit up, but Gadriel shushed her as he pressed a kiss to the back of her neck. She blushed, wiggling into the action with sleepy bliss. He rose from the bed, having fallen asleep with his pants still on, though the rippling muscles of his shoulders, pectorals, and abdomen had pressed against her throughout the night. When he opened the door to greet the knocker, his wings flared in such a way as to conceal her from whatever prying eyes might have stood in the hall.

"Raven came this morning," came Yazlyn's voice. "Two more reevers were met at the border and are escorting a female traveler."

Amaris shot up straight, any semblance of sleep evaporating. Though she could only see the back of Gadriel's head, she could almost hear his frown.

"That will total six reevers in the north," he said quietly. It was almost with a curse that he continued, "There have never been so many at once."

"I don't have a good feeling about this, Gad."

He nodded. "Intervene. Send word to have them come here to the town house, not to the castle."

"Gadriel, you know our mission—"

"I'm not asking, Yaz. I'm telling you as your general. Don't let them go to Ceres. Bring them here." He closed the door behind him before Yazlyn had a chance to say another word.

Amaris tugged the sheet up around her chest, still fully nude from the night before. "Did she say reevers?"

He nodded, crawling onto the bed. Something in his eyes betrayed whatever delightful hunger flickered within him.

He had not been deterred by Yazlyn's message, remaining wholly focused on her. "She did indeed."

Amaris didn't lean into him as she had the night before. She lifted a hand and pressed it against his chest to make him pause. "Did Yazlyn say there was another traveler with them?"

Gadriel stilled in his pursuit, immediately responding to her signals. His body had been angled to crawl atop her and perhaps continue the fire they'd ignited. He nodded in acknowledgment.

Amaris pressed, "When will they be here?"

He sat up on his knees from where he had been on the bed. She could see the moment his face went from lover to general as if it were a page turned within a book. "If the border already had time to write to us and send a raven, they're at least two days into their travel, if not three. Presumably they arrived on horseback, but if they're being escorted, they could be flown. Depending on where they crossed the border, they might be here by tonight. Tomorrow at the latest?"

"Tonight." She almost choked on the word.

Amaris had tumbled from the sheets and was already searching for her clothes before he'd finished speaking. She didn't miss the trouble that clouded Gadriel at her hunt. He helped her locate her tunic. He grabbed her hand to make her pause. "Is everything okay?"

She swallowed. "Nox might be with them."

His expression softened. "Nox, your childhood friend? The one who met you in the dungeon?"

She didn't know how she could possibly correct him. She had no idea what she could say. Yes, Nox, the one who had spent years protecting her, loving her, being her only companion in this world. Nox, whom she had abandoned as she ran off to Uaimh Reev. Nox, who had freed her and saved her in the dungeons of Aubade. Nox, who had kissed her and held her. Nox, who had told her that she loved her. And what had Amaris said in response to the declaration? She had told Nox to save her brothers. She'd failed Nox again and

459

again. She'd never done enough, never said enough, never been enough.

Amaris felt a wicked sense of betrayal as the night-haired girl colored her vision. All she knew was that for now, she needed to get out of Gadriel's bed.

He was doing his best to maintain his sense of casual control. "Amaris, you're under no obligation to stay here. I'd also like to hear how you're feeling before you go. If you're having complicated emotions, you're allowed to say so. Even if you regret—"

"No," she cut him off, suddenly feeling fully lucid. She straightened her spine, meeting his look as she weighted her look with sincerity. "I don't regret anything."

"It's okay if you do. Whatever you're feeling…"

Amaris rejoined him on the bed and met his gaze for a serious moment. He was so big, so strong, and some part of him also craved the care and reassurance that she had needed. "I don't want to take back anything that happened between us, Gad. Truth be told, I'd hoped you'd fill me senseless, and maybe if things go my way, you still might."

He offered a half smile at that.

"If Nox is on her way, I can't focus on anything else. This isn't about you. This is about her."

He wove a large hand through the strands of her hair at the back of her head and pressed a kiss onto her crown. She found herself unable to fully enjoy it as she wanted to. It was meant to be such a sweet, reassuring kiss. She finished dressing and stole her way out of his room, heading directly for the bath that adjoined her room. Amaris scrubbed herself without knowing why she felt the need to wash away his scent. She didn't regret anything that had happened between them, yet she also couldn't explain the emotions that pounded inside her at the thought that Nox might have crossed the Raascot border and be only one day away. She wasn't scrubbing away his memory but instead readying herself for something that she had spent weeks thinking about.

She couldn't name what she felt, other than to admit to herself that she was exceptionally nervous.

Amaris submerged herself under the warm water, immersing herself fully in the ripples and bubbles until the waves of the bathwater stopped moving altogether. She opened her eyes from beneath the warm water and looked up through the bleary haze. Her mind was anything but still.

When Nox had kissed her in the prison, Amaris had felt something she'd spent months—years, even—suspecting click into place. She liked men. She liked the way they looked, the way they smelled, the way their hands were so much larger and bodies were so much heavier than hers. She liked the idea of being able to hand over power in a world that so often felt out of control. This was exactly how she had felt when she was with Nox.

Amaris broke the surface of the bathwater, gasping for air as she struggled to get control of her thoughts.

Nox was a fierce, goddess-like authority that neither man nor fae could tackle. She always knew what to do, where to go, and what to say. Where Gadriel was dominant, Nox's strength was peerless. While men had used their size to intimidate, Nox had been a force of nature irrespective of her frame. She was crafted from things that the gods had set aside solely for her. Men smelled of weapons and sweat and steel. Nox had smelled of dark spices and plums. Her hair had always been ink and night and starlight. No human's or fae's eyes sparkled like the deep wells of Nox's. Amaris liked men for their broad shoulders and the firm crush of their abdominals, and in an entirely separate but equal strength, it was the softness of Nox's curves and pillows of her breasts that made her just as formidable. When Gadriel smiled, it was powerful and terrifying. When Nox smiled, Amaris knew that the same smile that sent others to their knees had been softened, kinder just for her.

Gadriel could take sexuality off the table and just play the role of general in their efforts to save the kingdoms. Nox could remove all romantic components from their relationship and be simply her oldest and dearest friend.

But was that what she wanted?

As a reever, Amaris had grown into examining her body and her womanhood.

Once she had been set free of the constraints of the mill and allowed to discover her power, she found deep, unexplored waters beneath the surface of her emotions. Amaris liked men, but she loved Nox. The idea of seeing her again tonight—the first time since the fateful parting in the dungeons—was the only thought that consumed her. She wouldn't even consider regretting Gadriel's touch, as she wanted it still. She wanted Gadriel in the bath, hands moving against her soap-slicked skin even now as she prepared herself to see Nox. She wanted Gadriel's mouth on her throat while she braided her hair. She wanted his hands fighting against her shirt while she tucked herself into clean clothes. Her wants and her needs battled each other in a confusing internal rivalry with blood on both sides.

Amaris stayed sequestered in her rooms with her thoughts for the majority of the day. These rooms weren't grand like the suite she'd been allowed in Queen Moirai's castle, nor were they purely perfunctory like the medical rooms in the healers' hall. They were decorated with simplicity—comfortable enough to allow for sleep while remaining boring enough to offer no distractions.

She attempted to make an appearance for lunch, but once she discovered nearly every resident from Odrin and Elil to Yazlyn and Gadriel in the dining room, she had made an excuse about her stomach and taken a plate to her quarters.

Amaris was too nauseous to even attempt dinner. Odrin checked on her to see if whatever had afflicted her stomach was still bothering her and left her a plate of some bland foods that would be easy on the bug that ailed her. She loved the man so deeply, not only for saving her from her fate at Farleigh but also for being a constant force for resilience, education, and hope in her life. His face had creased with kindness as he'd set the plate on her writing desk and returned to whatever the crew was discussing in the dining room, always a bit too uncomfortable to attempt discussing his feelings outright.

She waited in her room, wondering if Gadriel would stop by, and was glad when he didn't. It wasn't that she didn't want to see him. She vowed to explain everything to him eventually. She would tell him anything he needed to know. But this moment in time was not about him, and he seemed to possess the wisdom to understand that.

Amaris's mind rocked like a boat in the stormy sea. No events, no people, no futures or pasts accompanied her. Instead, she was splashed with wave after wave of raw, incomprehensible emotion. It was the longest day of her young life.

The summer sun stayed up for far too long. It seemed to peak above the horizon for hours past its welcome in the north. She remembered the long, midsummer evenings in Farleigh, but Gwydir seemed to take liberty with its stolen hours, turning it into the day that never ended. The sun had barely begun to set by the ninth bell, finally coloring the sky with red as she paced the length of her room. Night was not a time defined by the colors of the sky, but the sun did keep the house awake. Sometime past the tenth bell, a commotion sounded in the hall.

This had to be it.

Amaris emerged from her room to find herself trapped behind the bodies of others. Everyone had exited their rooms and headed down the hall toward the stairs in response to the noise. She heard familiar voices as men hugged and clasped one another in amicable greeting. She felt as though the fae in front of her were moving slowly just to irritate her. Her fingers flexed as she fought the urge to push them, knowing Gadriel would probably snatch her shoving hands out of the air.

Their stupid, giant wings were practically wallpaper between her and what she needed to see. Then she heard the first recognizable sound. Ash's voice reached her ears. Malik was speaking. Her anxiety bubbled as the intense urge to reach the landing surged through her. She wanted to give Gadriel a shove, though she knew it to be both horribly impolite and also utterly irrational. The iridescent curtain of his wings continued impeding her sight as voices filled the dining room and entry hall of the town house, as wide and comfortable as any tavern.

After a day of making herself scarce, angry pushing would win her no favors.

She put her hand on Gadriel's shoulder to gently press herself past him when she heard Yazlyn mutter, "I call dibs on that one."

She knew what one Yazlyn was referring to before their eyes met.

Amaris had heard songs about moments like this. She had been told stories and read novels about exactly what occurred in the town house as a pair of lavender eyes and two, large eyes darker than coal locked from across the room. The sound around her faded into little more than the buzz of honeybees. The colors and faces and people became a blur, much like the smear of paint on a canvas, unable to be discerned one from the other. The ringing thud of her heart in her ears was the only thing she could hear. Her face slipped from something pale and wide-eyed to a raw, honest joy.

It was her. Nox was here. She was real.

Nox's hair hung loosely at her side, her black tunic and leather pants as dark as her night-dark eyes. Somehow, despite the depth of the charcoal colors that clung to her, she was the only light in the room. Nox's lips parted in a half greeting, attempting to breathe a hello as she fixed on Amaris.

It was almost like a dream, a song, a poem. It was too good to be true. It was a fiction, her imagination, an invention, a lie. Amaris's feet remained glued to the final step for two heartbeats, then three.

Something within her snapped when she saw Nox's

chest rise and fall, knowing that she was also too overcome to move. Amaris's soul left her body as her feet carried her forward. She flung her arms around her long-lost other half, and the two of them released partial sobs, sounds unknown to man or nature. Each one breathed in the other, juniper and spice and white winter and plums. Fingers twisted against fabric and hair, bodies clutched and pressed, and hot, wet tears stained cheeks and shirts and the very air around them as they held each other. Though the noises of the home in Gwydir had faded away long before this moment, Amaris was vaguely aware that the others had become even quieter as they embraced.

This wasn't reuniting after a long journey. This wasn't friendship or brotherhood or missing someone not seen in a long while. This was the magma core at the center of the world. This was the bond that forged the universe. This was sacred. Together, they were whole.

Amaris was scarcely present for the formalities, too numbed with awe to acknowledge the others who shook hands.

They were loosely aware of the words that passed their lips as introductions were made, never allowing each other's hands to drop. The fae introduced themselves to the new parties, and Nox did her best to say hello to all the faces in the room. So many names. Grem and Odrin and Elil and Gadriel and Yazlyn. Amaris watched all the names flit in one of Nox's ears and out the other as if she hadn't been present at all to receive them. Amaris gripped Nox's arm as if afraid she would vanish into the night if she released her.

Of course she'd missed her brothers, but Amaris wouldn't even drop Nox's hand for the moments it took to wrap an arm around Malik or Ash, using a singular arm to press herself lovingly into each of them as they held her tightly in reunion. She continued to clutch Nox's hand while the stunning young woman shook Gadriel's outstretched hand in greeting and left her frost-white fingers intertwined with

Nox's sun-kissed ones as she exchanged niceties with an awe-struck, slack-jawed Yazlyn. Knowing as she did that Yazlyn preferred women, Amaris wryly imagined this must be similar to meeting a goddess.

That was what Nox was, after all. She was a goddess. They were right to see her as such.

Amaris sought Gadriel's gaze only once and was curious at what she saw behind his dark, evaluating eyes. He wasn't angry or disapproving or jealous. He wasn't disrespectful or doubtful or perplexed. She saw only recognition. He saw, and he understood. Amaris knew with that one look that Gadriel identified her bond with Nox as more than friendship. She'd tell him. She'd explain everything to him once she had something real to share. First, she needed to tell Nox. Before that, she needed to admit it to herself.

Enough time had come and gone in the common room. She loved the reevers, but she'd spent years around them. They were safe. They were fine. They didn't need her right now. She could spend her life catching up with them. Now that they'd undergone whatever social norms were required of them, she needed the two of them to be alone.

"Are you ready to get out of here?" Amaris asked.

"Goddess, please," Nox whispered back.

The party would surely continue downstairs late into the night. The reevers and the fae would undoubtedly have plenty of war stories to swap, monsters to compare, and opinions to share on kings and queens and curses. They had enough beer and food and fire to occupy them well into the earliest hours of the morning, should they choose.

Amaris led Nox up the stairs and pulled her into her room. She didn't look over her shoulder to see who was watching. Maybe no one. Maybe Gadriel. Maybe every single set of eyes, curious and nosy and wondering what gossip may or may not emerge from the night. It didn't matter. The transition from the gathering room, up the stairs, down the hall, and into her room was an absolute blur.

She shut the bedroom door behind her. Nox was normally the one who took the lead in their relationship, but this was Amaris's room. She knew the people. She knew the land. She knew the town house, and right now, she knew what she wanted. The moment the sounds from the town house drowned out behind the click of a lock, any and all emotions that had waited patiently to emerge sprang forth.

Nox's fingers grazed Amaris's jaw as they pushed below her ear, holding the back of her neck, fingers landing in her hair. "I can't believe you're real."

Amaris grabbed the hand against her neck and pressed it in more tightly. She closed her eyes, leaning into it. A spike of hot tears threatened to spill over her lids. "I dream of you all the fucking time."

Nox giggled.

"What?"

"I just...I don't know if I've ever heard you curse."

Amaris laughed. "Goddess, so much has changed."

They stared at each other for a long moment. "And some things never change at all."

The moment collapsed, each girl twining their hands, their arms, their faces into each other like a dying star, fully sucked into the other's gravitational pull. They could barely breathe, let alone cry as they clutched each other. Amaris relaxed into the freedom of finally being away from the prying eyes of the room around them. They had no obligations to anyone but each other. There would be time for tenderness and declarations of feeling. There would be time to discuss all that had passed between them. There would be time for what they had discovered and what had happened since their moments in the jail cell. Amaris would tell her of the curse she had seen in the orb, and hopefully Nox would find the time to tell her all that had passed in her journeys with the reevers. For now, they were simply holding each other as if they might float away. This was not the passionate urgency of greed, nor was it anything that resembled platonic companionship.

"Do you need anything?" Amaris asked, still not lifting her face from the cloud of hair.

"What?" Nox pulled away long enough to study her face.

Amaris searched her gaze in return. "Food? Water? A bath? Because I don't want to let you go, so if you need something, tell me now. Get it now. Do it now. After that, I don't think I can let you out of my arms."

"I don't need anything. Just to be here."

And so they were.

Amaris's eyes went to the bed, then back to Nox. Her eyebrows turned up in the center—a question, a hope.

Once more, Nox's hand brushed a path against Amaris's jaw, slower this time. It carved a slow line from her chin, brushing her neck, her earlobe, stopping just where her hair met her neck. Amaris leaned backward into the door and Nox followed the motion, lowering her forehead to meet Amaris's.

Her heart skipped at Nox's nearness, mind flitting through cloudy, unnamed want as she hoped Nox wouldn't stop. They pressed into each other, allowing the question to stretch between them. It was hesitancy and curiosity and want and uncertainty all at once. There was a pattern that they'd lived out in dreams. Amaris knew every step that led up to this moment. Time and time again, just before waking, they'd bring their lips so close that a single breath was shared. The heat, the taste, the temptation as each wondered if the other would close the gap between them.

They'd done it once before. They'd held each other through iron bars. Their mouths had met, kisses tasting of tears. Nox had shouted her truth across the sands of the coliseum before they'd been ripped apart. Amaris wondered if Nox could feel the way adrenaline made her heart pound against her ribs. She wondered if the wet, hopeful rush of her want was mutual. She waited and prayed, and just as she rolled her hips closer to beg for every part of them to unite, she realized that Nox had already said everything she needed to say. If Amaris wanted this, it would be up to her to close the gap.

The moment stretched between with the sticky slowness of burnt molasses.

Their shared, frenzied kiss in the dungeons had been love, panic, fear, and desperation, but now there was no dungeon, no queen, no dragon. The tension in the town house knew no rush, no threat, no fear, save for whether they wanted the same thing.

When they connected, it was with the electric shock of lightning. Oceans coursed between them. Fires blazed and snow fell and wind howled all within the movements of lips and tongues and hands and hair. Nox leaned into the intensity as if Amaris's unspoken declaration of action was all she'd needed to unleash herself. Amaris's back and head thudded against the door as she gave herself over wholly. Her back stayed pressed to the door as she pulled Nox against her more urgently, her need, her want, her acceptance so overpowering. Her body responded on instinct, every part of her calling out for more. She wanted soft lips on her neck. She wanted their clothes on the floor. She wanted to know how it would feel to be kissed in places that, until now, only hands had explored.

Her leg swept up to pin Nox close to her, and she felt only soaking, aching need in return.

This was love.

Nox's hands didn't knot in her hair with possession. They weren't angry, they weren't demanding or furious, nor were they too tender, too soft. There was the intensity of a thirst that had needed quenching for years behind every kiss, every movement, every press of the hips, every taste, every desperate, unrealized want that had hung between them.

Nox broke the kiss first. She pressed her forehead into Amaris's once more, practically choking against what sounded like the urge to sob. A smile spread across her face as tears lined her eyes.

"Nox…" Amaris caught her breath as she struggled to make sense of the cornucopia of emotions on Nox's face. She tried blink through the passionate fog but knew she'd be able to discern anything that mattered if she remained flattened against the door with soft, perfect breasts pressed into her, a warm stomach touching her own, and her leg hooked around Nox's thigh.

The bed was large enough for four, as it had undoubtedly been made to accommodate Raascot fae and their enormous wings. Amaris tugged Nox away from the door, pulling her onto the bed. They curled into the middle, enveloped by the pillows and down comforters and blankets at its center. Their emotions were deeper than want. It was more than sex, more than hunger, more than flesh and fingers and tongues and the exchange of bodies and pleasure that they could share. For this moment, what they needed was simply to be together. They held each other on Amaris's bed, Amaris's starlit hair on Nox's stomach. Nox stroked Amaris's hair, and Amaris looked up into Nox's dark eyes.

Amaris felt Nox's energy drift away.

"I have so much to tell you," Nox said, voice distant.

"And I you," Amaris agreed. So much had happened. She continued to look up into Nox's face from where she rested against her. "Can we just enjoy this? For right now?"

Nox's tears caught on her laugh, half cry, half chuckle, as if the weight of her message was more than she could manage. "I would love nothing more. All I want is to be here with you. Tomorrow's problems can wait for tomorrow."

This was something they'd never been allowed. Their small gap in age had been enough to separate their dorms for more than half their years at Farleigh, forcing them into a friendship that existed only in the daylight. Even if they'd been the same age, they never would have been permitted to fall asleep in each other's arms. Their moments together, even the companionable ones, had all been stolen. They'd never been permitted to explore who they were, what they were, or what they could be.

Being together now, on this bed, was spiritual. It was as if they'd stepped out of their shared dreams, holding each other in a way that only their subconsciouses had allowed. They took turns tracing disbelieving paths along the arms and waists and curves of each other's bodies, unwilling to cease touching the other, until the lines they drew lulled them into a hypnotic sense of relaxation. Between the love that cast its soothing hand over the room and the comfort of reuniting, they fell asleep, drunk on each other's presence.

Neither of them had been willing to break the spell of their night with the realities of the world around them. Their gentle, unrelenting touches had been acknowledgment enough of what they knew to be true. They were more to each other than any friend, family, or companion. They were everything.

Dreams had been challenging to distinguish from reality, as even under the blanket of sleep, they held each other tightly, their never-ending dream finding a different, sweeter ending as their mouths connected at long last.

When the morning came, Amaris's heart picked up against the realization that this had been no dream. She hadn't moved from where she'd fallen asleep on her stomach and could feel the undoubtedly pink lines of indention where clothes had creased her face. Nox was still in her arms, glossy hair puffing gently with each dozing breath that escaped her full, beautiful lips. Amaris felt like she might melt into her own smile as her heart pulled the edges of her mouth upward. She nuzzled into Nox's side until she stirred. The light had an early, dreamlike quality. The dawn was too dim to be the bright glare of sunlight. Everything was cast against the soft, shadowless light of the early hour.

"I can't believe you're real."

It was a sentiment they'd echoed again and again.

Amaris tucked her face in closer, brushing Nox's soft stomach and grazing her breast against her cheek. A small sound escaped Nox's throat, and her hands were once again in Amaris's hair, the gentle touches of disbelief tracing lines against the soft, silvery strands. They had hugged so many years ago. They had held hands, they had touched, they had spent so much time together unsure of the other's feelings, never naming what lingered between them. This was something wholly different and entirely beautiful. Their kiss in the dungeon had been born of panic. No confusion remained. They'd opened a door and crossed a threshold that could never be closed.

"I thought I'd never see you again." Amaris's words were low to keep the emotion from her voice. Neither of them dared to be loud enough to break the beautiful magic that encompassed the room.

Nox smiled as she tugged Amaris's chin to look up at her, the way she had in her sleeping mind. Amaris loved the familiar motion, if only from her dreams. Her chest tightened at the confidence of the simple, wordless command. She knew this was where she had developed her unyielding love for authority. The trust, the safety she felt whenever Nox had taken control and saved her from monster after monster— whether it be a matron, a bully, or the queen of Farehold and her dragon—had created a pocket that could be filled only in moments where she knew she could trust the hands that held her. Those moments that had been intended for fear at the hands of the bishop or the market had crafted something lovely, something stronger. Amaris had learned to lean into trust as its own beautiful form of submission. It had grown from friendship and faith into a shape that anchored her, that formed her.

"I love you too," Amaris said with a low, firm declaration. She was answering Nox's words from so long ago as Amaris had been dragged into the dirt and sand of the coliseum. She knew it with every stitch of her being. There was no question. There was no doubt. She would spend her days at Nox's side if fate allowed. They could never be parted again.

Amaris knew from her stories that some relationships

were the torrential downpour of flash floods. One might find themselves drowning, caught and swept up in the waters. The deluge was wild and all-encompassing. Perhaps with Gadriel, it did feel like a flood. She was washed away in his rainwater as it covered her, soaking her and consuming her. Floods came on quickly, suddenly and powerfully. They were nothing to be trifled with, as they were destructive, intense, and forceful. But Nox was a river carving its way through a canyon, forging the contours of the world. There was no beginning and no end to her path. When the waters between them flowed, the whole earth bowed to them.

Amaris had spent enough years looking into Nox's face to recognize when something was amiss. Nox's brows furrowed ever so imperceptibly in a way that may have been unbecoming on anyone else, but even in her worry, she was utterly stunning, despite having just woken up. Amaris didn't remember Nox looking so effervescent. Had she always been this beautiful?

"Amaris—" Nox began, but Amaris didn't need to hear the excuses or worries that held her back. Whatever tugged at her mind could be addressed, as she had doubtlessly experienced countless things over the past three years that they'd never had the chance to discuss. None of it mattered. Nox had revealed her cards while the iron bars had separated them.

Amaris raised her head from where she had spent the night in Nox's arms and pressed her lips into the bare skin of her shoulder. Nox's lids fluttered shut the moment Amaris's mouth made contact. Amaris lifted herself further, closing her eyes in return as she grazed the barest tips of teeth along Nox's collarbone, waiting again for the encouraging sound of consent. Another tiny gasp from Nox urged Amaris forward as she closed the final space between them. She lowered her body until they connected, her mouth against Nox's full, parted lips. The kiss began slowly, increasing with rhythmic intensity as Nox's hands clutched Amaris. It was a gentle, warm dance intermingled with the gasping sounds of breath. She wanted this. Not just sex, not just intimacy, but all of it.

Nox's breath broke as if she were about to cry. She pulled away. "There's something I have to tell you."

Amaris couldn't discern if Nox was overwhelmed by what had been years of culmination all crashing into one moment or if there was something more. It could be any number of things. Given her years at Uaimh Reev and how drastically her life had changed, she couldn't begin to imagine the things unspoken between them. Maybe Nox wanted to share the other lovers she'd taken, the lives she'd lived, the path she'd forged.

None of it mattered.

Whoever they were—whoever they'd become—was something they could face together.

Nox turned her face away and held her, pressing her in more tightly. Amaris folded herself into Nox. The smell of plum was so sweet. The softness was so all-encompassing. Whatever she had to say, it didn't matter.

"It can wait."

Nox wrapped her hands around Amaris, holding her close. One hand twisted in Amaris's hair, the other pressing into her back to bring her as close as possible. "I've missed you so much." Her words were thick with emotion. "But what I have to say—"

"We're together now," Amaris responded. She couldn't think of anything more intelligent to share, any promises, any regrets, or anything that could change their fates, so instead she repeated, "We're together now."

"This is big," Nox emphasized, voice pained. "This is really important. I did something. I saw something, and... Amaris, I have so much to tell you."

"And I you, but we have nothing but time."

If Amaris were to have the opportunity to think back on their beautiful night and their morning together, she would have recognized her mistake. She had spoken five words responsible for undoing the very fabric of time. These five words may as well have been a witch's curse, a djinn's double cross, a spell caster's jinx.

There are a few phrases in this world that are said to aggravate the gods and goddesses, old and new. Some plans make the fates laugh, and others anger destiny and draw consequence like a magnet.

These five words had been her undoing.

Forty–Three

W*E HAVE NOTHING BUT TIME.*
This sentence had triggered the All Mother's cruelest brand of correction. Amaris's assertion prompted an avalanche to break free from the snowiest of Raascot's peaks, tumbling into their moment of shelter as it cascaded into their perfect world. Her innocent sentence ended as another swelled, one fading as the other began. At first, the noise was too unfamiliar, too confusing to rally either girl to move from where they had clung to each other. Perhaps it would settle itself and prove utterly irrelevant. Maybe someone had tripped in the kitchen. Maybe there was a disagreement among the reevers.

No, Amaris realized. This was wrong.

She didn't need combat training to tell her that something was amiss. As the noises burbled and grew nearer and voices joined the commotion, they brought themselves into tense, sitting positions. Something was terribly wrong in the house. The sounds swelled until they were on the stairs.

Amaris scrambled off the bed, tugging Nox along with her so they wouldn't be caught prone. She had just begun to test the windows when the door was flung open with a bang, clattering against the wall of Amaris's chamber. Those who had invaded the house filled the hall as several armed men poured into Amaris's room.

Amaris had barely pried the window open before they were at her arm. She rendered the first man utterly unconscious, fae though he was. A swift elbow in a sharp, upward strike had sent him to his back. Amaris drove her foot into another assailant while someone else closed in from the side. They pushed past Nox to get to her. She didn't know why, but she was their target. She had taken three in combat once before. She could take four. But now five, six—so many were in the room. She dropped to the ground, swinging her leg to disarm the man from his footing. She thrust the heel of her palm into another man's nose, breaking it where he stood. It didn't matter how many she disarmed, she was outnumbered. These were no drunk mercenaries in a farm town. The men before her were armed members of Raascot's military.

"Get off me!" she shouted at the men as she continued to disarm one, then the next. She had no weapons. She had no way out. Maybe if she could get to the window...

Nox shouted several unintelligible threats, but the men paid no mind. Amaris had stayed low for another sweeping kick, but they pressed down on her, grabbing her by her arm while she knelt. She continued to kick, shouting and using every ounce of strength she possessed. Her persuasion was nothing to the winged fae who grabbed her. She'd been overpowered. Her commands were useless.

"Stop resisting or we'll have to restrain you," one said.

"Don't you fucking dare!" A man's voice—Gadriel's—was in the hall. He'd burst out of his room, half-dressed.

Amaris was vaguely aware of the chaos around her. Nox had been left in the wake of their calamity. Gadriel continued pushing the men while barely clothed. His voice attempted to command the men to release her as she was dragged down the stairs. He pulled rank. He shouted names. He ordered them to stand down. Gadriel's voice was louder than Nox's as she tumbled down the stairs after them.

Everyone was roused from their rooms. There were so many bodies, so many people, so many fae. Too many. The noise, the press of hands, the confusion, the pain of gripping, the blood still dripping from the centurion with the broken nose, the fruitless commands of the general, the ever-growing cries that belonged to Nox.

Amaris had no idea what use training would do her. There was nothing she could use. Her only comparison had been the moment she'd been overpowered by Moirai's guards. Helpless. Utterly useless.

She'd learned from the men, the guards, the humans. She knew she should turn her attention and focus on those before her...but these were fae. Her persuasion was useless. She had nothing—she was nothing.

It had been three against everyone in Aubade. Now she had a small army of reevers. She had Gadriel. She had Nox and Yazlyn and Odrin and everyone in the world who mattered to her. She was not alone.

She heard his voice then. The father she'd never had. The man who'd adopted her, who'd saved her, who'd trained her and taught her and loved her. He had no authority in Raascot that could supersede Gadriel's fruitlessly attempted commands, yet Odrin's voice bellowed through the room. It was too much of a blur. Too much confusion, hands, bruising grips, noise, so much noise, color, panic, and pain.

She focused on Odrin. He was coming for her. She could hear him chasing after the men. She heard the steel scrape of his sword as it unsheathed, barking demands in his deep, powerful voice. Odrin's tone was ripe with the same desperation Amaris felt as he watched the child whom he'd considered a daughter taken from him, dragged by armed guards from the house.

Amaris twisted enough to see him. She caught his face, her violet eyes wild. She didn't want to worry him. Some part of her forced her to stop from crying out. She didn't want him to panic. She was a reever. She could handle this. She didn't want him hurt. The hold of their eyes told her it was too late. Worry was a dot on his horizon. He'd gone mad with his attempts to free her. She'd scarcely been able to comprehend the wildness of his emotion before the other reevers had to intervene. Odrin had been seconds away from committing crimes against Raascot. Grem and Elil held him back, forcing Odrin to keep his sword down as they fought to reason with the guards, hardly able to contain the bearded reever and his violence.

Gadriel, still shirtless from his recent sleep, shot his way into the sky over the scuffling reevers as he pushed to his men.

She recognized the sorrowful face of the kind, winged man waiting by the horse.

"Zaccai?" She gasped his name, voice hoarse with confusion as she eyed the commander.

Guilt and pain dripped from his face to his voice. "Amaris, I'm so sorry. I—"

Gadriel planted himself firmly between them, holding his hand up to stop the ones who'd been holding her arms.

Amaris whipped her head to face him. His eyes met hers for the briefest of seconds before turning to his troops. He thundered to the ground and raised a hand to stop them. Amaris looked at him helplessly, uncomprehending as his wings stretched to their full expanse. She'd never seen him with this particular brand of fury.

"I don't know what the fuck you think you're doing." His voice was the gravel of white-hot embers and hate. "But as your general, I command you to release her." His authority carried across the lawn as his bare feet planted in front of them on the grass outside the town house.

The men looked at one another.

"We're sorry, Gadriel." One's voice was thick with apology, cringing a bow to their general. "Our orders come directly from the king."

"Gad—" She met his eyes, her eyebrows bunched together with their turmoil. It wasn't a plea. It wasn't fear or begging or any of the worming emotions one might have expected from their captive. She was confused in a way that infuriated her. This wasn't right. There was no rationale. There was no reason. These were Gadriel's men. They should have bent to his command.

"Amaris, I've got this." His eyebrows pinched for the briefest of moments before he returned his attention to his men, white-hot fury overcoming his expression once more.

"Don't—"

"Call you by your right name. Now's not the time, witchling!" He backpedaled to create more space as the men advanced, fluttering his wings to stop them. He still wasn't looking at her. "I know what Ceres has told you! I'm his general, I'm his cousin, and I'm his right-hand man. I'm telling you—"

Zaccai put a hand on his shoulder, forcing him to spin and look at his second-in-command. "Gad, the men were specifically told that you would defy this order. It's not their fault. They're under orders to disregard your intervention."

"No." Gadriel shook his head. His face twisted in anger at Zaccai. "How could you?"

"It wasn't me, Gad." Zaccai's expression would have broken Amaris's heart if her very life hadn't been on the line.

Gadriel turned to Amaris, begging her to listen, to stay calm. "I'm going to get you out of this." Then he turned back to Zaccai and said, "Don't let anything happen to her."

"I..." Zaccai was probably about to tell him that he had no say in the matter.

"If anyone touches her, Cai...if anyone hurts her..." Gadriel left his threat unfinished.

Zaccai's face said what his mouth couldn't. His hands were tied. He was as much of a pawn in the game as the others around him, moved by the hands of the powerful. His agency had been snipped. Instead, he just nodded, agreeing to a promise that he'd have no way of keeping.

"Zaccai!" Gadriel practically begged, voice fierce with the single word.

"I won't," Zaccai said, though they both knew his promise was useless.

The information deflated Gadriel with an instantaneous, drenching effect. His wings went limp behind him in a way that allowed the men to press through him, marching Amaris forward.

Anger overtook Amaris. Her body remained too stricken with surprise and dread at being torn from Nox's arms to remember any further training or defense. She'd broken a nose, rendered one unconscious. How many could she possibly disarm if they wouldn't even stand down to their general? Who could she fight if even the reevers at her door weren't helping?

She looked over her shoulder again with large, lilac eyes as Odrin chased after them. She did her best to shake her head, giving him a reassuring glance—one she did not believe. Gadriel watched helplessly. Nox spilled out the door to the town house with the winged sergeant holding her back from where she threatened to thrash and claw at the men who dragged Amaris away. Nox's voice was loud and high with her anger, her threats burning through the air. Yazlyn did her best to contain Nox's wrath, though even from her far-off place, Amaris could see that Nox was scratching the sergeant to bloodied ribbons.

"Where are you taking me?" Amaris aimed her question at Zaccai. She tried to count how many flanked her, but the number of escorts Ceres had sent had been pure overkill. Perhaps it really had been in response to Gadriel's presence. She was outnumbered twelve to one at the most modest of estimations. Her voice hitched into higher, more panicked tones as she looked to the guards again, shooting her question for anyone who might respond. "Where are you taking me!"

"I've got her." Zaccai extended a hand, taking her arm with a lot more gentleness than the men before him had used. "We're going to the castle. And believe me when I tell you that from the bottom of my heart, no one wants to see you get hurt. If you ride with me, can you promise you won't do anything stupid?"

She was absolutely baffled. "Don't do anything stupid? What am I supposed to do? You dragged me from the house! You aren't telling me why! No one has told me—"

"We're going to see King Ceres. He wants to speak with you."

Her heart dropped into her stomach. She had come to Raascot to see the king. This was not how she'd envisioned their meeting.

"Amaris, please trust me," Zaccai said, voice broken. "No one wants anything to happen to you. I don't want anything to happen to you. I won't leave your side."

Amaris looked over her shoulder to where she could still hear the shock and violence erupting from the town house. She heard the shouts. She heard the panic and anger and screams. Though she could not see her, the evidence of Nox tearing at the people around her as she tried to launch herself forward carried over the grass. Men's voices joined the cacophony as Gadriel spoke to Odrin, though she couldn't discern what he was saying. He kept shooting angered, desperate looks after her as he used his arms and wings to stop those who attempted to chase after her.

Zaccai didn't need a horse. He could fly. Given the nature of their mission, fae and human centurions had all joined for accountability. Perhaps a single, rogue commander could not be trusted to deliver the captive to the castle. Maybe that was why he swung his legs into the saddle, offering her a hand. Maybe that was why she took it, sitting numbly on a large, dark horse. Maybe that was why two dozen or more men remained tightly knit as they continued on their mission. Amaris's heart remained in the pit of her stomach as she watched the residents of the town house grow smaller and smaller as they headed to the castle of Gwydir.

Forty-Four

G ADRIEL SPUN BACK TO THE HOUSE, MIND CRACKLING AS IT filled with lightning. He was trained to create order from chaos. There had to be a solution, and he would find it. If he could just…

"No!" came an angered shout.

He turned his attention to the woman he'd met the night before and saw nothing but rage. Nox looked like she might tear out the eyes of the first person who spoke. She was fierce and feral, fingers flexed at her sides like claws. "Not again! How could this happen again! Where have they taken her! Where did they take her!" Nox was not asking. She made her fury known.

The reevers flanked behind her in a way he attempted to discern. He didn't know who Nox was to them, but the newcomers made their allegiances clear. His gaze flicked to the flash of wings in the corner of the room as he caught sight of his sergeant.

The energy in the town house was palpable. Anxiety, anguish, and betrayal could have been cut with a knife as it hung as a thick fog in the air. The room had divided in a way that found the winged fae dramatically outnumbered. Gadriel held out an arm in front of Yazlyn as the two of them faced off against an army of reevers. Nox positioned herself toward the middle as if she didn't care where she landed in the battle so long as she got Amaris back.

Gadriel attempted to create order from chaos as he addressed the room. "Ceres wants to see her—"

"How does your king even know she's here?" came the boom of Odrin's voice. The effect it had on the others told Gadriel that this was a man who was rarely loud. Amaris had reacted to their reunion as if she were a child meeting a parent, and it was the same fatherly command that filled the space.

Gadriel knew better than to react before he had the information he needed. He studied the war-ready postures and faces dripping with anger. He searched his memory for anything that had been said or shared by Zaccai or the men. He tensed at the horrid message overruling his authority he'd been given by his second-in-command.

They could sip the anxiety from the very air they breathed as tension pulsed with every heartbeat.

Yazlyn's voice was quiet when she finally broke the silence. "I sent word."

Everyone in the room wheeled on her in a way that let her know her next few words would determine whether she lived or died. Gadriel's lips pulled back from his teeth in a snarl.

She only looked to her general. "I had to, Gad. If the goddess's promise is the only who will stop this fucking point-less bloodshed, if she's the only thing on this goddess-damned earth…if Ceres will stop sending us to die—"

Gadriel's face went fully animalistic. He chuckled a black, humorless laugh and balled his hands into his hair. "He will never stop, Yaz! Ceres has lost his mind! There will be no sacrifice great enough to quench whatever fire has burned him from the inside out for the last twenty years while he's searched for his child. How could you think sending Amaris to him would solve anything?"

Yazlyn barked back, clearly not afraid to fight. She

doubled down, fists clenching at her sides. "How many have to die? How many of your men do you need to watch die, Gadriel? We've lost so many men for nothing! For this child who doesn't exist! We've lost too many for me to do nothing. I don't want anything to happen to her, but if the good of the many—"

Gadriel rarely lost his temper. "There is no good of the many! You are delusional if you think this will stop him!"

"But you brought her here. You brought her to Raascot." Her voice was heavy with some implication. The others looked to Gadriel, but he was struggling to compose himself.

"Goddess's promise—" Nox could barely choke out two bewildered words before the others spoke over her.

Odrin's voice broke through their argument. He spoke for everyone in the room as he demanded an explanation from Gadriel. The room had no patience, anger gripping at their throats. "What is she talking about? Why would Ceres want Amaris?"

Gadriel forced the heels of his hands into his eyes as Yazlyn spoke for him, drawing their eyes. "Nearly a year ago—"

"Yaz, don't."

"What?" she screamed, looking at the men in the room. "What, you don't want to lie to them now? I'm still supposed to keep it from them? How's that gone for you! For any of us! You had weeks—*months*—to tell Amaris. You want to keep it from all the reevers? It's done, Gadriel! It's over! What I did was far more honorable—"

"Don't talk to me of your honor, Sergeant!" He bit out her rank like it was a curse.

Ash hadn't spoken until this moment. Gadriel knew the half-fae reever had only been exposed to Raascot fae in their ag'imni form, and even if he'd technically met this very man on more than one occasion in Farehold, they'd never truly spoken. Ash looked to Odrin, then Yazlyn, then finally at Gadriel. "What is she talking about?"

"Tell them!" Yazlyn demanded.

Gadriel shook his head.

"I am not the villain here, Gadriel!"

"Yes," he said quietly, "you are."

She glowered at her general, fists flexed so tightly that her nails nearly drew blood from where they punctured her palms. She looked to Ash, then to the other reevers. "Our mission changed nearly a year ago. For twenty years, Ceres looked for his son, and then in the twenty-first... On a scouting mission, someone captured a priestess."

It was too late to keep his sergeant from sharing military secrets. Gadriel forced himself to face the reality and watch the others as she told the story. He didn't miss how Nox stiffened while Yazlyn spoke.

"The priestess told the scout everything. She told him how Ceres's beloved had died and how she had brought their son to the temple. The woman saw the little boy's dead body. It was only a year ago that Ceres learned his son was gone. Not only that but that it had been his lover's final prayer that the goddess would send someone for vengeance. Moirai may have brought a curse on the land, but Daphne was not powerless. Her counter curse was supposed to be just as potent."

And though Yazlyn had been an excellent soldier, a friend for decades, and was speaking every word of truth, Gadriel was still certain he wanted to kill her.

✦

Nox shook her head silently. She'd seen this memory. She knew of this prayer. This wasn't right. None of what Yazlyn was saying was right. No one looked her way as her lips parted in silent dismay, hair moving noiselessly against her shoulders as she shook her head.

"Listen," Yazlyn continued, using her hands to attempt to still the furious reevers who had tensed for battle. "We didn't think anything of it! Everything Ceres does is insane!" She looked to her general. "I'm not sorry. It is. Ceres is. Why were we supposed to think any differently of this goddess-damned mission? Just another reason to be in the south. Just another reason for our brothers and friends and men to die. And then you found her."

Gadriel's voice was a snarl. "And you thought you knew better than me, Yaz? You've known Amaris for three days! I've spent months with her! Did you really think you were qualified to make this call?"

Yazlyn's curled auburn hair shook with her fury. "I do know better! I know better because I'm not blinded! I'm not thinking with my dick!"

"Back the fuck down, Sergeant."

"She meets the description, Gad!"

While Nox hated Yazlyn with a fiery passion, she agreed that the time for listening to calls for silence had come and gone.

Yazlyn bit with the righteous knowledge of someone who knew her general's authority had been usurped. "That has to be why you brought her to Gwydir! I only had to spend a day with the two of you to know you were too close to it to make a judgment-free order. Anyone else would have been able to see it. You've spent too much time with her. You can't see what's right in front of you. You can't see what your people need you to do, but you still brought her to Raascot. You brought her north because you knew it was the mission. I knew I had to finish it for you because you wouldn't. I did this for you, for all of us, so it wasn't on your hands, Gadriel."

A speechlessness throttled the house. Nox shot a look to the others and felt an undeniable surge of solidarity. It was unclear whether they were going to murder Yazlyn or have Gadriel hanged and quartered.

"She's a person, Yaz." His dark eyes dripped with hate as he stared into hers.

The fae sergeant straightened. "Of course she is! She's a person, just like I'm a person, and you're a person, and so is everyone else Ceres has sent to their death! How many of your men need to die? How many northerners need to be sent to the slaughter? Isn't the death of one better than the deaths of countless others?"

The question shook the other half of the room from their shell-shocked silence. The Raascot fae had spent enough time tearing each other apart that they'd needed very little help from Nox and the reevers. If left to their own devices, it seemed as though the two would kill each other before the day was over.

Nox's voice was low but not quiet. She burned with the controlled rage of a fire within a kiln, ready for its door to be opened. "You sent Amaris to her death?"

Yazlyn raised her hand as if to steady her from the anger she sensed impending. She gave Nox her full attention as she said, "No. No one said she would be hurt. King Ceres has a vested interest in keeping her alive. Ever since he learned his child was dead—"

There was no patience in Odrin's voice when he spoke beside her. He demanded answers. "What do you know of Ceres's child?"

Gadriel cut over both of them, attempting—and failing—to regain control of the room. He exhaled with frustrated anger like a man tortured by duty-bound secrecy and the reality of their present crisis. He looked briefly at Nox, then the reevers, and settled on Odrin before he answered. "A priestess was taken prisoner in Farehold. It's not our usual technique. It wasn't me or my team. But this woman had a lot to tell Ceres. She gave over everything she knew. She told him everything had been shared with her by the priestess at the Temple of the All Mother: that Daphne had brought their son's body and both were laid to rest in the temple."

Malik shook his head. "You're holding a priestess? That's unconscionable. That's—"

"It wasn't me," Gadriel reiterated. "There are so many outposts in Farehold. The men were desperate. They've been on dispatch for decades without answers. I don't know why

they thought the answers might be with the church but..."
He shook his head a second time. "This woman is in the jail
cells now and has been for nearly a year. She's not treated
unkindly, but her secret was not closely guarded. It was almost
as if she wanted to share everything. The priestess that Ceres
has been holding told him all about the child that the goddess
sent to break the curse. Daphne's final prayer was one of
vengeance, and now that Ceres knows that he has no hope of
finding his son, he is consumed with avenging his love with
her dying wish. When I met Amaris, she met the description
the priestess had given. She was born as white as snow, with
violet eyes. When she could see us for who we rightly were,
I knew she was the curse breaker that the goddess had sent. I
didn't realize—"

Nox fought to listen as the militant fae shouted over one
another. In one heartbeat, she valued Gadriel for not giving
Amaris over to the king and despised him for sticking to
whatever code had vowed him to secrecy, even now. In the
next beat, she loathed and appreciated Yazlyn for betraying
Amaris, then telling the truth. Nox's hate was up for grabs
depending largely on what they said next.

Yazlyn cut through Nox's murderous contemplation,
interjecting, "You didn't realize she'd be beautiful, witty,
strong, and a wonderful companion? What kind of general
are you, Gadriel! Of course you didn't realize she'd be pretty!
And what if she had been sour and unintelligent? Would her
life have been any less meaningful if you weren't attracted to
her? What if she had been an ugly wretch? Would you fight for
her still? Everyone's life matters, Gad. *Everyone's.* Your men's
lives matter! Raascot matters! My life matters! You can't scrap
the mission just because she's kind or funny. You can't let
your judgment cloud just because you're attracted to her or
because of whatever relationship you two have developed—"

"You should have trusted me. I have a plan."

"What fucking plan!"

Nox struggled against the urge to hold her head at the

angry burble of voices that crashed through the room. One could hardly be distinguished from the other. The shouts were the clanging of swords as voices dueled. Ash and Malik had grown quiet beside Nox, filled with knowledge only the three of them held after Nox had left her meeting in Farleigh. They hadn't needed to look at one another to understand the weight of the information that had been pressed onto them.

The fire still crackled, happily unaware of the turmoil in the hall in front it. It snapped and popped at the logs in its mouth, greedily devouring the wood in its maw with the cheerful sound of a hearth. Something about the jolly, familiar noise of the fire helped Nox focus.

The information couldn't stay within her.

"Excuse me?" She was rarely quiet, but she was having trouble hearing anything other than the pop of the fire. She could see the lifeless body of the boy that had been passed off as the crown prince. She saw his limp form as the princess said her husband knew it wasn't his—because it wasn't hers either. It had been the orphan child who had gone to the palace in Nox's stead.

The reevers and fae around her continued fighting, Odrin's and Gadriel's and Yazlyn's red-hot voices pouring over one another as they battled for attention.

"Sorry?" Nox attempted to be a bit louder, but she wasn't really looking at any of them. Her voice was so seldom polite. She was angry. She was confused. Everything was so unfamiliar. The situation. The emotion. The sound of her words. The eruption of sounds that battled over her as she knew she had to share a key piece of information. Her eyes were somewhere in the middle distance as she saw nothing of the town house. Her vision contained only the temple and the dreams that had been given to her by the apple. The wood of the room, the walls of the home, the shouts of the men, the flared wings of the arguing fae, none of it really connected to her and the small ember of information that glowed inside her.

Malik took an angry step forward and bellowed a single word from his diaphragm. "Hey!"

Everyone paused in a frigid motion, frozen to where they had been in their argument. Their agitated eyes flitted to him as he gestured to give Nox the platform she deserved.

"Did you say that Princess Daphne's lover was King Ceres?"

They looked at her, something between agitation and whatever strangled feeling of being cut off mid thought holding them by the throat.

Nox had known for several days that Daphne had been her mother. She had also known that the changeling prince had not contained a drop of royal blood, and that revelation had led to his death. It wasn't until the angered arguments of the winged fae that she first learned who had sired her. Her father. The king.

She repeated her thought, this time finding her feet. Malik put his hand on her back briefly in a comforting, supportive motion to usher her forward. He released his hand just as quickly. She didn't need his help. She could do this. She blinked against the wildly unfamiliar uncertainty that threatened her very footing. Nox had never been one to lack assertiveness, but the information had knocked her wholly off-kilter. She looked at the fae.

Regaining her authority, she demanded, "Who was Princess Daphne's lover?"

They furrowed their brows. She recognized the searching look as the others struggled to see the relevance of her or her questions.

Malik positioned himself slightly behind Nox so that when they looked at her, they'd see the support of the reevers at her side.

It was Ash who spoke, his father in the middle of the room raising a hand to silence the noise. Ash's voice was loud and cold, leaving little room for argument. "Nox is Princess Daphne's daughter. She has proof. Answer her question."

Time froze. The fire stilled within the hearth. No one moved. Nothing stirred.

The fae wilted at once. Their wings went limp at their backs. Their faces drained of blood. They looked to her as if they had inhaled some numbing agent that had slackened every muscle within their bodies. Any argument they had felt, any anger they had contained had slipped from their tendons and disappeared into wherever their feet had anchored them.

The general was the first who seemed to truly consider her. His eyes shifted from whatever oblique regard he'd been offering to a true, drilling stare. He examined every part of the dark-haired woman in front of him. He scanned her for her bronze features, her bottomless eyes, her black hair. With every pass of his eyes, he seemed to see the familial traits of King Ceres.

Nox felt rawer and more laid bare than she had in her days in the brothel. Fully clothed, surrounded by friends, she was being examined as if her very worth depended on whatever he saw in her features. Aside from the days following the jarring revelation the tree had given her of Amaris's bizarre and terrifying heritage, Nox had never found her voice lacking. But now in the face of the morning's events, in having Amaris ripped from her bed and strangers shouting about the woman she had learned to be her mother, she hadn't found a drop of strength in her words. Nox held up a finger, urging them to wait.

"I *do* have proof." She excused herself and ran across the room and up the stairs.

No one so much as breathed in her absence. By the time she reappeared, no one had relaxed a single muscle.

She returned holding a small crown. "I'm told my mother switched me for a human babe when I bore northern resemblance in order to hide me." She handed the crown to Gadriel. "I was told only three people in the world knew Daphne's secret: the princess, her handmaiden, and the Gray Matron at Farleigh who took me in. The matron told me that Daphne chose a human boy of peasant birth who may have passed for resemblance to her human husband. It's why she left me at an orphanage so close to Raascot's borders, in hopes that whoever had fathered me might find me. At least that's what the matron said. No word was left of my father. I don't think Daphne trusted the secret with anyone. At least that's my guess. The Gray Matron did her best to shield me without ever letting anyone know of my heritage. I didn't know. No one did. The only clues she left me were my name and my crown."

"Nox." Gadriel repeated the name quietly to himself, turning the tiara over in his hands. She understood why he rolled her name over in his mind. Her very name meant "night," the representation of those who for centuries had been called the dark fae, their powers banished to the shadows of the north. Daphne had hidden her in plain sight. She watched the calculating look in his eyes as he stared at the tiara, black jewels gleaming in the firelight— the same black gems that sat embedded in Ceres's crown in the portrait hanging above the fireplace.

"If that's true, then—" Gadriel began, but Yazlyn cut him off with a tone of reverie.

"Then you're the heir to the Raascot throne."

"No," Malik corrected, his voice soft. "Nox is the only surviving heir to the continent."

Forty–Five

A MARIS HAD NOT BEEN HURT, THOUGH THE JOURNEY had battered and bruised her in other ways. The men who forced her to cross from the outskirts of Gwydir to its castle were not violent or cruel as Moirai's centurions had been, but they also had to work twice as hard to keep her still. Amaris had been knocked unconscious, bound and gagged in Aubade. She was certain their mutual fates would have ended in bloodshed if Zaccai weren't the one transporting her.

Amaris had been in three structures she had considered to be castles. Uaimh Reev was formed from light-gray granite, hewn from the mountain itself, and it had been her first exposure to what she might consider a castle. Aubade had been the cream and caramel rounded brick of the seaside and stood as the enormous seat of power of the southern kingdom. Amaris's lips parted in horror as she found herself in the dark, cold stones of the north. The high ceilings were flanked with wooden pillars that seemed more for show of strength than any structural need. So long ago, she had entered the castle of Aubade and marveled at the warmth and rainbow colors of the stained-glass lighting. She entered

Gwydir now and shrank at its shadows and the weight of its midnight-blue stone.

"What do I do?" she whispered to the commander. Zaccai wasn't her enemy, though she didn't count him as a friend now either.

"I don't know," he answered honestly, voice quiet. "All I know is that Ceres wants you. I'll be in the throne room the whole time." He'd meant it to be comforting, but it wasn't. It hurt her to know that even if she needed help, he'd be powerless.

She suspected that he continued to loosely grip her arm as a show of support rather than restraint. Perhaps the small physical comfort was all he could offer. She didn't know if it helped or made things worse. This was a game with no winners.

They did not stop until they'd marched directly into King Ceres's throne room. The large wooden pillars seemed out of place in this enormous room. The structures would have been better suited as the ornate bows of carved northern ships or the whittled heights of a mast. They had no place holding up the dark stones, so bluish black they seemed to glint with the fabled aurora borealis of labradorite within the depths of their features when caught in the light.

Gwydir wasn't far from the northeastern sea. Perhaps Amaris would have seen ships in the dark river that ran through Raascot's capital. Maybe the bay just beyond the alpine cliffs was filled with large boats, hulls for trade, and enormous canvas sails. Somehow, she doubted it. This room had the energy of one that had existed for a millennium. Perhaps they'd been an oceanic people once, exploring the cold, northern waters long before flight had become their defining feature. She didn't know. She didn't care. None of it mattered.

She'd walked into Moirai's throne room, bathed and dressed as a guest of the castle and ambassador of Uaimh Reev. She'd gone in with confidence, knowing Moirai to be human and persuasion to be radically effective, and it had ended in tragedy.

She was escorted into Ceres's as a blindsided captive.

Queen Moirai had sat on a gilded throne, while King Ceres was on an elaborate throne of solid wood, matching the wood of his seafaring pillars. The chair appeared to have no seams, as if the tree from which it had been carved were as tall and infinite as time itself. The seat was as wide as it was tall, each rootlike tendril of its wooden spokes carved with intricate runes. The king who sat on it did not have the cruel, proud face of Moirai. The man may have been beautiful. If he could smile, if he could relax his shoulders and find joy, perhaps he would have been lovely.

His features were jarringly familiar in so many ways. His dark eyes and the curve of his jaw were the same ones she'd looked into as she'd spent every night for weeks with his cousin. Gadriel had been tired from the road and had worn the weight of a general and his men, but it was nothing like the existential fatigue on the face before her now. King Ceres carried the weight of the entire kingdom not only on his back but in the sunken crescents underlining his glossy stare and in the red, bloodshot capillaries of the eyes themselves. He did not seem angry or sadistic as the men brought Amaris before him. He was distant, almost as if he were not present at all.

"So this is the one?" he asked.

Zaccai removed his hand from Amaris's arm once they reached the base of the pedestal. He nodded but said no more. Amaris held her arms at a slightly bent angle, confused at the sudden release. Part of her mind urged her to run, but another voice forced her to listen to the king. She wondered how much time had passed between when she had been dragged from the soft comfort of Nox's stomach to the cold throne room before Ceres. It was as if Raascot's king had been left in a permanent state of waiting for precisely a moment such as this.

496

"What's your name?" the king asked.

Amaris blinked. "Do you not know me?"

She didn't ask the question facetiously. She was genuinely confused as to why the king of Raascot would have her pulled from her room without notice, away from her loved ones, especially if he didn't even know who she was.

His face wasn't unkind as he examined her. It was almost as if he understood precisely what she asked. The exchange was so bizarre, so jarring, she felt as if this might just be a nightmare.

"Bring her in." The king waved a hand at one of his guards.

Nothing constrained her to where she stood rigidly in the middle of the throne room. She examined the beautiful, exhausted, half-mad fae king and his raven wings. He sank into the enormous wooden throne that looked as if it had been carved to fit him and him alone. Amaris scanned the room for an exit, for a plan, for information. She examined the face of the guards who lined the throne room, fae and human alike, all uniformly dressed in the bronze and black of their kingdom. While the king was fae, there seemed to be no strong differentiation in who he employed, nor who remained loyal to him. It was so different from the pale, homogenous human crowd in Aubade.

No one laughed or glowered as they had in Aubade. There were no frills, no obnoxious air of condescension. This throne room seemed to ring with something distinctly sad. Perhaps it was that emotion, a feeling of dampening on her spirit, that prevented any fight from bubbling up within her. It had a soaking effect, keeping her feet on the floor and her hands at her sides as she stared, waiting.

"Your Majesty, why have you brought me here?"

He exhaled slowly through his nose. King Ceres wore a shade of midnight blue that seemed to refract the same deep, iridescent shimmer of the northern lights in the stone. The color matched the energy around him, as if his veins had opened and leached their misery into the fabric. His crown wasn't overly ostentatious but a simple ringlet of white gold set with black gems. Amaris felt a hint of familiarity as she eyed the crown, but she couldn't place where she'd seen a similar piece before. The memory seemed important but too far away for her to wrap her hands around, like a dream upon waking.

"Who are we waiting for?" Amaris asked, trying once more to get Ceres to talk to her. She wasn't sure if speaking was a mistake, but the fae life span was long, and perhaps he intended for them to stand silently until the leaves changed, the river froze, and snow fell all around them.

He looked vaguely surprised that she'd spoken again but not bothered. Neither the king nor anyone in the throne room spoke while they waited. The quiet made it easy to hear movement from a distant hall. The opening and closing of doors. The sounds of feet on stone.

Finally, Ceres displayed a recognizable emotion. Sorrow. A chilly, sickly sweet flavor of regret, pain, and tragedy filled her mouth. Then she saw the reason for what saddened him. Amaris tensed, readying herself to run to the woman's side. The woman was neither young nor old. She was in what had once surely been a beautiful, silvery gown that had grown disgusting with age and dirt, as if she hadn't bathed nor changed in months. She wore a thick woolen cloak of northern colors over her shoulders for warmth. She didn't look starved or battered, but she was truly filthy. While she appeared physically uninjured, her eyes told a different story. Time, isolation, and trauma were their own forms of torture. Her foggy, glazed sight drifted from the king to Amaris in a way that suggested she no longer had a firm grip on her sanity.

Ceres spoke to the strange woman. "Is this her?"

The woman attempted to see Amaris, but her eyes were caught in the hazy distance. Focus evaded her. The words that left her mouth were a garble of nonsense.

498

"The goddess gave us a baby of snow."

The king did his best to temper his impatience. Amaris watched his face as it flicked against annoyance, eyes closed and pinching until he calmed himself. She felt confident this man was not intentionally cruel, but neither were his actions kind. He kept his eyes closed while using a hand to vaguely gesture. "Is this your baby of snow?"

The woman looked in Amaris's direction, but her eyes did not see her. "The goddess answered a prayer that we facilitated. It was not our place to intervene."

King Ceres massaged his temples as if he had a headache that never truly went away. "You described her as white of skin, hair, and eyelash. The babe's eyes were lavender in color. Can you confirm that this is the baby born to the All Mother?"

The woman muttered, "The All Mother heard the prayers of the faithful. We helped the miracle come to life. Destiny has done the rest."

Ceres made some command that sounded like sending the woman to see a healer and have a bath. Amaris felt angry. She felt empathetic for the stranger, yet she didn't feel as if the king before her were evil. Gadriel loved his cousin. He'd spoken fondly of him. He believed in the man, and maybe she could too. Perhaps they could still be allies.

She found her voice once more as she addressed him, hoping she was right. "King Ceres, may I speak?"

He opened his eyes and looked at her. He had the sort of fae face that may have been twenty-five or two thousand years old. Their agelessness was as beautiful as it was aggravating and intimidating. He had Gadriel's night-black hair. It was the same dark, glossy hair she had nuzzled into only yesterday morning, and she wondered how many people with Raascot blood littered the continent without knowing their king had lost his touch on sanity. Gadriel had said that Ceres was good. Yazlyn had the voice of a true believer. If he was a good man, perhaps he would hear her words.

"Your Majesty, I'm Amaris. I'm trained as a reever from Uaimh Reev. I was sent on dispatch to the south to discover why Queen Moirai was ordering the slaughter of northerners on her land."

"Amaris," he repeated, tasting the name. King Ceres was both listening and absent. He was awake and asleep. The throne room seemed so truly large and dark in the presence left by his voice. Amaris didn't feel ignored, but neither did she feel truly heard.

She went on, "I was in the throne room before Queen Moirai when I saw that she was using an illusion to create the image of a crown prince. It's why she gave the order to have me killed."

Amaris had expected more of a reaction from this, but Ceres merely blinked as if to acknowledge that he was listening. Little emotion showed on his features.

"I fought an ag'drurath with your cousin Gadriel."

Still, Ceres was unmoved.

She fought a gnawing discomfort within her. Surely, he should have reacted to the news of a demonic dragon or mention of his general. Amaris had, along with the rest of the continent, heard that King Ceres had gone mad. She had been expecting a raving lunatic. She'd been prepared for yelling, for accusations, for peculiar, erratic behavior. His madness wore a different mask entirely.

"King Ceres," she said, wrestling with her rising tension, "I've been on dispatch to help your cause—to help stop the slaughter of northern men. After learning about the curse, Gadriel and I went to the university and witnessed the curse that the southern queen cast on the land. I saw you in the curse's memory, Your Majesty. Moirai damned the northerners to the perception spell while you shielded someone. Perhaps we share a common goal, Your Majesty. I've come north to Raascot to ask you of your lover. Was the woman with you Princess Daphne? Is that why Moirai has cursed the north?"

Her voice had lost its strength by the end. Amaris was only loud enough to be heard by the king and the men standing nearest to him. He did not smile. He did not move. His brows collected toward the center in a single pained motion. It seemed as though the picture she had painted must have colored itself onto the inside of his eyelids, forcing him to remember his wings as they shielded Daphne from the wrath of her mother and the swell of the woman's magic. To her surprise, the king responded.

"She was never able to see me again."

Amaris's face lifted in encouragement. She felt her hands flex and relax at her sides as she did her best to maintain a sense of calm. She was desperate to have some grip on the king's absent mind. Perhaps if she could connect with him, if she could make him see reason, they'd be able to find some solution.

"I visited her so often." He didn't look at Amaris while the painful memories played in his mind.

She wanted to look at the guards, to look at Zaccai to see if this was normal behavior, but she supposed it would win her no favors. She remained focused on the king as he told his story.

"I tried time after time to see her, but she only saw a demon. She couldn't hear me or see me. She wouldn't even dream of me. Even my dreams..." He smiled with the cracked, heartbroken smile that only came before tears. It took the man a moment to steady himself before he could continue. "If we hadn't changed tactics and found the priestess... Well, until one year ago, I didn't even know if Daphne had understood it was her mother's curse that barred us from each other."

Amaris dared a prompt. "One year ago?"

King Ceres nearly laughed, though the sound was humorless. He gestured to the empty place where the strange, filthy woman had been. Her memory was a shadow on the blue-black stones now. "My men have grown as desperate as I have. I would never have ordered infiltration of a holy place, and yet…"

Amaris recalled stepping into the moonlit blue-green glen with Ash, Malik, Gadriel, and Zaccai. She could still hear the waterfall and feel its mist against her face. The priestess had stood at its steps, welcoming her into the temple as if the woman had always expected her. The two of them had walked slowly and patiently around the Tree of Life. "This woman was a priestess?"

Ceres had neither the time nor the energy for Amaris's emotions. "She was there at your birth. She had been told of Princess Daphne's dying wish, and once my men interrogated her, she was quick to relinquish her secrets. A prayer was made, then answered. The goddess sent vengeance in the form of a moon-white child."

Amaris shook her head, not understanding.

"You're a weapon," he said, emphasizing it as if it should have meant something to her.

"I'm sorry. I'm not sure I…" She looked around, eyes briefly catching Zaccai before she returned to the king. "I don't know what you're implying."

Ceres sighed. "I know enough of your birth and your upbringing to know that you were not told, nor do you understand your role in the coming battle. Hardly your fault, snow child. This worries me not. Until one year ago, I believed my son to be alive. It wasn't until the priestess told me of his lifeless body that accompanied Daphne—" His voice broke with emotion.

Amaris stared at him, uncomprehending. Ceres was not angry. He was no hateful, barbarous villain. He was heartbroken. His grief had consumed him. The king finally found his voice and continued again. His voice, though the intonation of a man in his twenties, held the weight of someone far, far older. "I know that Daphne implored the goddess to send someone, and the goddess answered. You are the All Mother's answer. You're the last thing Daphne gave me. Her final gift."

Amaris shook her head. Nothing he said was registering. There was no logic in his words.

"You...you said it once. Your name is?"

She repeated it slowly.

"Amaris, sure." Ceres nodded, chewing on the name once more, rolling it over in his mouth until something clicked. He smiled then. "What a lovely name, for both the All Mother and for the kingdom of night. Do you know what your name means?"

Amaris felt her throat constricting. "The recvers told me it meant 'child of the moon,' but you seem to know that."

He smiled. It was an honest, disarming smile, as if truly experiencing a sliver of delight. "So it does! Isn't that beautiful for a kingdom of the night? Do you know the other meaning of your name? It's quite lovely, actually. *Promised by the goddess.* Isn't that appropriate? You were made for Raascot in more ways than one, Amaris."

She couldn't swallow. She tried again and again, finding only cotton in her throat. Her eyes felt strangely dry. Yes, that was what the matrons had said. It was what she had been raised to believe. She had been named as if she were a gift from the goddess, a rare treasure that would line their pockets with crowns and fill their purses for years.

"Amaris," he repeated yet again. "You're alarmed, and that's to be expected. I'm sure you have so many questions. In a way, you're my child. The last thing Daphne gave to me was a weapon. You were sent as Daphne's dying act of revenge. The All Mother unleashed your birth on this world in an expression of her wrath to avenge my lover. You have been delivered by the goddess as my champion."

So there it was. The fabled madness. Amaris took a step backward, then another. No one in the throne room had moved until she began to back away. She bumped into the leather-clad chest of a fae who she didn't know to be friend or foe. Apology was etched on Zaccai's features as he put steadying hands gently on her arms.

"I'm sorry," he said quietly, and she believed he meant it. His low voice was melancholy as he prevented her backward retreat. No one in this throne room had experienced joy or victory in a long, long time. This was a kingdom of the broken.

She looked into his face for help, but he merely shook his head once, urging her to stop moving.

The king spoke again. "Amaris, the child of the moon, promised by the goddess, are you ready to help me find Daphne's vengeance against the south?"

Amaris flinched against his words. "I'm a reever," she responded. "We're trained for balance. We don't fight on behalf of the kingdoms."

Ceres began massaging his temples as he had before. Some pounding headache had never left the man, eating at his mind from within for years and years. He pressed his fingers harder and closed his eyes.

Her heart stuttered as fear began to bubble up within her. She'd been anxious before. Now she was terrified. What vengeance? What weapon? What lunacy had driven this madman to—

A sharp sound interrupted their conversation, slicing her thoughts as her mind scrambled for reason. She whipped her head to the noise.

The carved, wooden doors to the throne room opened with a clang, and everyone lifted their heads and watched as Gadriel entered. She looked over Zaccai's dipped shoulder as the general advanced. Gadriel made a curt attempt at bowing before his cousin, the king.

"Gad—"

He passed Amaris, shooting her a single, pleading look before addressing his cousin. "Ceres, you've made a mistake."

Ceres clapped his hands together. His face lit in a mockery of delight as he said, "Gadriel! How nice that you should join us. Thank you for bringing her to Gwydir."

Amaris's eyes tightened as her stare bore into the back of Gadriel's head. Her confusion churned into anger.

"What do you know of this?" she demanded of Gadriel. She saw the muscles in his neck and shoulders tighten at her question, but his eyes remained on his cousin.

Ceres continued, voice tinged with a bitter note. "It's been months since you sent word of finding a snow-white girl who could see through the enchantment. You really know how to leave your king in the dark! Given that your second-in-command was posted outside Aubade and saw the ag'drurath take flight, I was prone to giving you the benefit of the doubt. If your sergeant hadn't found a raven a few days ago, I might have thought you both had even been scattered to the wind or assumed the worst of you, cousin."

Gadriel sucked in a breath to steady himself. He raised a single hand, flattening it against the implication. "It's not like that."

Amaris choked on the information. She ignored the king entirely as she made a move for Gadriel, but Zaccai put a gentle hand on her arm, stopping her advance. "You meant to bring me here for this?"

Gadriel looked between her and the king. He dropped his volume as he implored her to listen. His eyes were flooded with a silent plea for her to hear him. "Amaris, please, let me speak to him."

She shook her head in horror and disbelief. She hated the way her name sounded on his lips. Her eyes were stricken with pain. "You knew that night? When you found me in the glen? You knew you meant to bring me here to the king for this?" Her voice dropped again. "The ag'imni... Even the demons knew you were betraying me. Everyone knew."

"Amaris—"

She took another step backward, prevented from her retreat only by Zaccai as she said in horror, "You didn't want me to talk to it," disgust bleeding into her voice. "You told me not to open my mouth because you didn't want me to talk to the ag'imni. It was going to give you away."

Frustration and desperation clouded Gadriel's face. He

spoke quickly, trying to appease her while the looming threat of the king sat amidst the petrified roots of his spindly throne. "I know how it looks. Please, you have to hear me. Amaris, the priestess told us of some fabled moonlit girl one year ago. No one thought it meant anything. We were going to continue to be sent to our deaths, at first in search of an heir and then in search of some fictional weapon, some tool for revenge. I didn't believe any of it. And then I met you." He put his back to her as he faced his cousin. "Ceres, I have information—"

"Gadriel, stop," Ceres cut him off.

Gadriel disobeyed, straightening his spine and staring into the king's eyes. "I have learned of your heir."

"Yes, yes." The king continued to rub at his temples. "I have made my peace with the child's death."

"You're wrong. Your child lives." Gadriel's voice was powerful, but Amaris heard it for the bluff it was. He was a liar. He'd deceived her for months. He had never said anything to her of an heir. Even Zaccai looked up at him, forehead creased with quizzical brows.

She was so overcome with disgusted incredulity that Gadriel had knowingly brought her to meet this fate. Her chin quivered as her lips raised as if she had consumed something rotten. She'd swallowed his lies, his charm, his very fucking essence in the bedroom. This was so much worse than the centurions pulling her into the coliseum. This was worse than Moirai or the bishop or the threat of the brothel. He had known since his first night with her that he would have her dragged to this very throne room to serve Raascot's dark agenda.

"Is this why you call me a witch?" she said breathlessly from behind him. "Because you thought I wasn't fae? Because you think I'm some...what? To think I trusted you...to think I—"

"Amaris—"

"Don't you dare say my name."

A muscle in his jaw ticked. Through gritted teeth, he turned his back on her with singular focus. Tendons flexed in his forearms and hands as he faced his cousin. "Ceres, I've found your child. I—"

Ceres laughed to interrupt Gadriel, but the sound was hollow. His eyes were mirthless, flat-black coals. "Of course you have new information! Your sergeant mentioned your affections for this white-haired weapon. She informed me that it's why you didn't bring the girl to me yourself. She meant it as an excuse, as an attempt to forgive you, but I have to say, it's quite the disappointment. Now the same moment your new pet is brought before me, you have the first news in twenty years of my dead son. What a charming coincidence, cousin! I never took you for a sop."

Gadriel shook his head, taking a half step forward, "You didn't have a son—"

Amaris felt like she might vomit. It wasn't just their moments in the glen or him fighting the beseul. It wasn't him seeking her in the castle or helping her in the coliseum. It was every moment since then, from how she had held him in the forest to how he'd brought her to Raascot, holding her naked and vulnerable, asking her to trust him. The ag'imni had told her in the forest that Gadriel knew what she was. The demon had told her that he knew how she would die.

She knew Ceres and Gadriel were still speaking, but she couldn't keep the words from coming up like bile in her throat. She thought of the ag'imni's words as she saw how King Ceres planned to march her south as his champion. "You're killing me."

"Amaris, no—"

"You brought me here to die!" She thrashed toward Gadriel, ready to claw out his eyes.

Zaccai could no longer afford the luxury of gentleness. He grabbed for her again, doing his best not to hurt her as he constrained her. She didn't care about Zaccai. She drove an elbow into the commander's center to release his hold, sending the air from his lungs as she lunged again for the general. Gadriel's face was crushed with hopelessness.

507

Hostility burned from the pit of her stomach like acid and bile and pain all hurled in one hate-filled look of betrayal. The grief washed over her to form an impenetrable wall between them. He looked back at her with his heart utterly shattered.

Gadriel hadn't moved to defend himself, but Zaccai had been quicker to recover than she'd given him credit for. He swept two large arms around her, pinning her against his chest so she couldn't harm anyone in the throne room. She kicked, thrashing against Zaccai's hold as she allowed the weight of her loathing to sink into Gadriel.

"Guards!" Ceres waved his hands in a loose command, but they weren't coming for Amaris. "Cousin, I hold no ill will toward you. You're a good man, and once you've had a night to sleep off this infatuation you've formed, maybe—"

Gadriel tore his pleading eyes from Amaris as the guards approached him, imploring the king to hear him. "Daphne bore you a daughter!"

Ceres remained completely disengaged as Gadriel was taken away, the sounds of his feet and the scuffle of his struggle muted against the sheer number of armed men who overpowered him. It took nearly six to contain him.

Gadriel beat his wings against the force of the guards as he shouted, "Your child lives! She's here, Ceres! She's here!"

Ceres's stare cut through the arctic energy of the throne room, as he had eyes only for Amaris. He was evidently tired of this exchange as he asked, "Are you ready to fight as my champion against the south?"

Amaris was mortified. She wanted to spit. Between Gadriel's betrayal and the king's sick usage, she'd had enough. "I've told you, I'm a reever. We don't fight on behalf of kings or their agendas."

Ceres threw his hands up. "You're a reever because you didn't know your destiny! And how beautiful that the goddess would lead you down a path to train you as an assassin. The All Mother wouldn't let a weapon so valuable live a life as a gardener or a baker or a scribe. She sent you to Uaimh

Reev to prepare for your purpose. Everything points to her will! You were born for this vengeance. The goddess created you for exactly this moment!" This was the first time Ceres looked truly and utterly insane. Lunacy sparkled in his eyes as he stared down at her, disconnected from whatever small hope of finding his child had tethered him to this earth.

She shook her head defiantly, looking after the empty space where Gadriel had been taken away. Rage burned within her, mingled with some desperate, painful wound. She didn't know why she bothered to ask. "What are you going to do with him?"

Ceres frowned deeply. "How about you answer my question, and then I'll answer yours? You have been born for this purpose, child of the moon, promised by the goddess. Daphne's dying words brought you your very life. I heard it from the priestess's mouth herself. This is why you exist, Amaris. This is why you're on this continent. Vengeance is why you live!"

He had lost his mind. There was no doubt.

Stepping backward was not an option while Zaccai remained a wall of restraint and support. She snarled, "I have no idea what you're talking about."

Ceres shot to his feet as impatience flared to anger. "I don't have the time for you to see the thread of destiny! You were created for this purpose. You were born for this moment, and our time has come!" The dark stones echoed his voice. His guards were immobile as he shouted.

Amaris could see the carved lines of madness etched into his face. His eyes were red with countless sleepless nights. The mauve half-moons under his eyes were not merely evidence of sleeplessness but of how deranged he had become.

He shouted his final sentence to the room as a whole. "Tomorrow, we will depart for the south."

Zaccai had slackened his hold but left a hand on each of her arms. Her back remained against his chest as he continued to block retreat. She wanted to punch the fae she had thought

509

so good, so kind. Instead, she shouted at the psychotic man on his throne. "I've been to the south, King Ceres! I've spoken with Queen Moirai! There's nothing I can do. I tried! I was sent by the reevers for exactly that purpose!"

He refused to hear her. "I will ask you one more time. I will ask once more, and then I will tell. You will have no more chances after this. Will you be the champion for the north that the goddess has birthed you to be?"

Amaris was repulsed by his insistence on their intertwined destiny. Her outrage echoed on the blue stones of the great cold room. "No! Absolutely not! I will not feed into your delusion!"

He scoffed.

Through bared teeth, she said, "I am not who you think I am. I will not march with you to the south on whatever misguided mission of vengeance you have for me."

"I'm king, Amaris." He said it as fact. "You don't get to decide what you will and won't do when speaking to a king."

"I have taken an oath to serve no king. If you know anything of the reevers, then you know I'm forbidden by rite and blood from serving your agenda."

Ceres sank back into his wooden throne, the wooden spirals of its once-great roots like a halo of madness encircling him. Whatever anger had filled him ebbed into the exhaustion of years. He sounded so tired as he spoke again. His voice might truly be one of pain and regret.

"I'm not a cruel man. I did say I would ask only once, but here I find myself." His voice had dropped to a crushed, pained register. "I can only ask you once more, Amaris. You will agree to do precisely what the All Mother has sent you to do, or you will see the consequences that befall the disobedience of fate."

Amaris didn't know what possessed her to be filled with such venom, but his threat overwhelmed her with a flame unlike any she'd known before. She hurled her angry defiance at the king like a blazing stone.

"I don't know who the fuck you think you are, demanding a reever as your kingdom's champion, but I am not doing anything for you."

Ceres had reached the end of whatever rope he had possessed. He flicked the fingers of his left hand forward, though his right hand held his forehead, his gaze buried in the carved arm of his throne. He was too lost to his thoughts to witness a nightmare more heartbreaking than her sleeping mind could have fathomed as the doors banged open and a reever was dragged before the king.

Forty-Six

D EEP, IRATE YELLING ENTERED THE THRONE ROOM.
No.

Her soul left her body as her heart dropped to depths
below the earth's core. She twisted to look over the block of
Zaccai's wings to see the man being marched down the labradorite stones of the floor, protesting every step of the way.
His angry outcry reverberated off the walls. His shouts were
far older and deeper than the king's or those of his men. He
was not yelling in fear but in outrage. These were demands
for explanation. Reevers could not be treated this way by any
crown.

Odrin called to her, but not for help. He called out against
injustice. She had never heard him yell, had never heard him
speak out in anger. Hoarfrost filled her veins, freezing her
solid as fear coursed through her. Her eyes whipped between
Odrin and the king, erratic heart unable to find a place within
her chest.

Amaris's voice pitched into hysterics as she began to beg.
"Ceres, no! Ceres, listen to me! Ceres—" Her desperate pleas
were ignored. He didn't even look at her.

Odrin was pulled up in front of her.

She fell to her needs as she pleaded, "Ceres! Ceres, please!"

Odrin was forced between her and King Ceres. Though still angry over the blatant disrespect, he made no effort to fight the men around him. She wanted to shout to him to start, to run, to punch, to flee.

Zaccai's hands tightened around Amaris's arms while several others flanked the reever before her. Zaccai muttered words over and over that sounded like a muffled, agonized apology. His words were unintelligible as his fingers dug into her. Amaris's eyes widened. Her mouth opened in the loudest scream she possessed. It tore from somewhere deeper than her belly, somewhere sharper than her lungs. Her sound filled the hall.

His booming protestations ceased the moment they forced Odrin to his knees.

A high-pitched ringing filled her ears as she knew exactly what the king intended. She felt the air as if it had been sucked from the room.

"Ceres!" she cried, tears streaming down her face as she threw elbows, thrashed, and cried. She could barely spit out the words as she wailed, "No! Ceres, no! Listen to me! I'll fight! No!"

Amaris shrieked that she would do whatever he wanted. She cried that she would seek his vengeance, that she would kill Moirai, that she would do anything, be anything. Her desperate begging resounded off the rocks. Her words were nonsensical babbles, tearful promises and oaths, and the loud, pleading sounds of the hopeless. She was little more than a woman screaming at the grim reaper.

Amaris understood what was happening before Odrin did. She fell into her training and used the methods that had been drilled into her, dropping to her knees, twisting, fighting free from Zaccai's grasp. She'd kill the commander if she had to. She didn't care. She had to get to Odrin.

Amaris managed to get one arm free, grasping for the sword hilt Zaccai had sheathed with her small liberation. She used her legs to spring upward, fighting against the fae who did his best to restrain her, though Zaccai fought his own silent tears, begging for forgiveness through gritted teeth. It was something more than desperation that fueled her. It was a deep well of love for the man she knew to be her only father. The notes rang both high and low, animal and human as they throbbed through every crevice of the room, soaking the soul of every bone, fae and human alike, as the order was given. Her throat was raw with her screams.

If Odrin hadn't known what was happening when he was dragged into the room, the slump of his shoulders revealed that the wild desperation in Amaris's voice told him. His back remained to her as he bowed his head in resolution.

Odrin wasn't able to look into her eyes as he spoke his final, gruff message to his daughter. Through her tears, she heard two words.

"Be strong."

She hadn't even seen the blade.

The sword was raised and descended in a swift, sharp motion.

There was no crunch. There was no wet noise, no sound of flesh or bone or blood. There was merely the thud as her final, primal wail echoed off the walls of the throne room and gave way to the pressure of her silence.

The rolling noise of skin against stone was too much. She clenched her eyes tightly against the horror. Zaccai collapsed with her, holding her in his bastardized attempt at empty comfort as she sank to her knees and allowing her whatever heaving and retching racked her body.

The sound of a horrid, feral animal filled the vaulted ceilings and echoed from wall to wall. The raw tear of her throat made her aware the sound was coming from her. With teeth bared in a snarl, she threw out a hand and unleashed an earth-shattering shock that rocked the world around her. Though her eyes had been tightly shut, she felt the release as Zaccai was thrown from his holding place behind her and sent careening into a pillar. A crash sounded as the royal seat overturned, Ceres barely able to catch himself with the use of his wings in his fall from the great roots of the throne. The wooden pillars rippled against the power she'd unleashed as if they were little more than trees in the forest. The walls themselves buckled against her powerful earthquake. Dust snowed down on them from where the stones had clanged against one another. No one was left standing by the time the shock wave ebbed, leaving only their yelps of surprise and the clattering sounds of wings, weapons, and bodies collapsing to the ground around them.

Just as quickly as it began, it was over.

She ran from the epicenter of the shock wave to Odrin's body.

The guards rushed to contain her, but she was on her knees over the man's crumpled torso. She had no control over her power. If she could have called to it before the blade had descended, Odrin might still be alive. If she could have summoned the ability that stayed so uselessly dormant now, she could have saved him. Ceres raised a hand to stop the men's advances as Amaris's sobs were the only sound in the room. The metallic scent of blood filled her nose as the hot, wet liquid began to seep into the fabric of her pants where she knelt, the lake of his life surrounding them both.

After getting to his feet, Zaccai made a reassuring gesture to the bewildered guards around him, urging them to stand down. Even his eyes were wild from the demonstration of power. Not knowing what to do or how to help, he knelt beside her where she remained draped over Odrin's torso.

King Ceres didn't look at any of them. She glared up at him with hateful eyes for the barest of moments, but his eyes were focused somewhere off to the side, as if he'd been present for none of it.

"You truly are the child of the goddess. Your display of power proves you're the weapon promised by the All Mother," said the king.

His words exacerbated her sorrow.

Zaccai didn't dare touch her as she cried. She was allowed the mourning wails of the grieving. The remaining guards did not relish in her pain, though they seemed torn between heartache and fear at the wild display of ability that had knocked them from their feet. Their lips remained pursed in their sympathy, their eyes closed against her cries.

The king didn't face her as she broke. Maybe if Gadriel was to believed, King Ceres knew grief and loss better than anyone in the kingdom. Maybe that was why he knew precisely how effective a broken heart could be. Perhaps if he must suffer, so should they all. Even as he spoke, he did not look at her.

"There are many more, child of the moon." He stood to the side of his toppled throne, gazing vacantly into the distance once more. "I don't relish in blood, but it won't stop me from doing what needs to be done. Four more reevers are held in my dungeon as we speak, along with your child-hood friend. I don't want to have to slay my general—he's a brother to me, Amaris—but the goddess does not care about our familial ties if her will is done. It brings me no joy to bring death and sorrow to this place."

Her mourning broke into the dry, heaving sobs of primal pain. Her lungs refused to fill with air. The water of salty tears would not come. She could not vomit. She was caught in some horrible, suffocating in-between.

Four more reevers, he had said. Four more of her men. Ash and Malik were in his dungeon, along with Grem and Elil. Nox was held by this mad king. He had Nox. He'd hurt her. He'd kill her. He'd kill his own cousin.

Amaris didn't know how to speak. She had lost the capacity for words.

"Amaris," Zaccai said quietly, trying to help her to her feet.

"Get off me!" she choked as she jerked fruitlessly from his hold. The guards exchanged pathetic looks and refused to grab on to her. She flung herself wholly onto what remained of Odrin's body. She didn't care how she sounded. She didn't care how she looked.

King Ceres's face was pained, which only angered Amaris further. His brows remained pinched in the center; his lips stayed in a tight line. He buried his face farther into his hand as if it caused him agony as well.

She hated her power. She hated that she'd seen the demons in the glen. She hated that her shock wave hadn't brought the stones down around them, burying them alive in the justice they deserved.

Amaris clung to Odrin's back, burying her face against what remained of his lifeless shoulders. Her sobs had lost their volume, silent as she shook.

Ceres moved his hand from his brow to his mouth as if preventing himself from voicing whatever emotion he held back.

"I understand pain, but this was what had to be done for the All Mother to usher justice unto the land. This is the price of Moirai's actions. She is to blame."

Through gritted teeth, she said, "I only see one murderer here, and it isn't Moirai."

"Amaris." He said her name through closed eyes and the muffle of his hand where he slumped in his wooden throne. The fae king disgusted her. There was nothing beautiful or whole left in the man.

She could not let go. Her fingers gripped uselessly at Odrin's back. The guards edged around her, none daring to move.

"Amaris," Ceres said again. "Don't let this happen to anyone else."

She stilled her crying long enough to look up at him. She summoned all the blackness into her body she could muster. She knew in the deepest parts of her soul that her eyes, normally the soft color of lilac in the spring, burned with the dark amethyst of nightfall. Her face was swollen with her anguish. Her hair had plastered to her face with her own tears. She had never known such loathing. Every fiber of her being was overrun with how much she despised the mad king on the throne of Gwydir.

"Amaris." He said her name once more, and she felt bile rise in the back of her throat. Her name sounded like poison on his lips. She never wanted her name in his mouth again. "Don't let this be your reevers. Don't let this be your dark-haired friend."

She pulled breath in like guttural shards of glass rather than air. A headache consumed her, thundering through her skull. She felt dizzy at the thought of Nox, Ash, and Malik scattered amongst the corpses. Rage overcame her grief.

"Don't touch them," she sobbed in one dry, angered command.

"Tell me you'll fulfill your destiny, and no one else needs to be harmed."

"Don't touch any of them. The reevers, Nox, Gadriel, they all need to be set free." She stared into the king's eyes, watching what little lucidity he had left as he returned her stare.

"I swear it."

Amaris could barely find the strength to pull herself from Odrin's back. Zaccai helped her to her feet. He made some half-hearted attempt to comfort her, one hand uselessly trying to hold her head to his chest as he would for a friend, as if it might offer her any solace. She hated him. She hated all of them. They were not her friends. They had done this.

She closed her eyes, pushing herself away from Zaccai to stand fully in front of the king. Her pants were wet, already itchy with the blood that stuck to her legs. Her hands balled into fists at her sides. Amaris bent her head before Ceres, but not in reverence. "Let them go, and I will fight for you."

"I promise you: they will go free, and no harm will befall them."

"Now. They will go free now."

"The moment we depart for Farehold, I'll have my guards release them. Once we're beyond Gwydir's city limits, they'll walk out of here unscathed."

It was over.

Ceres motioned for her to be taken away. Zaccai remained at her side, guiding her out of the throne room, then several floors away, deeper into the castle. She moved as if through time and space, unaware of the sounds or rooms or halls that moved underfoot. She blinked without realizing she'd moved rooms and levels and corridors, relocated entirely.

"This is where you'll stay tonight," Zaccai said.

She didn't look at him.

"I'm so sorry—"

"Spare me your apologies."

He nodded. She was right, and they both knew it. Her anger, her betrayal, her hate was right. Everyone in Raascot deserved every drop of vitriol she contained. Before leaving, he told her that he'd return to fetch her by morning. The commander's voice had been ripe with whatever withheld hurt he'd trained himself to conceal, however poorly.

Amaris found the smallest, most shadowed corner of the room and pulled her bloodied knees to her chest. She clutched herself into the smallest ball, wishing she could disappear into whatever scraps of darkness found her. She clutched herself tighter and tighter, but no escape found her. No sleep would come to her. There would be no relief. She wasn't sure if she'd ever rest again. She wasn't sure if she'd ever know joy, comfort, or peace for whatever remained of her days. All she knew was that for the next few moments, her friends were alive. No one else would be beheaded on the mad king's floor because of her.

No, she amended to herself. There would be one more beheading.

If it was the last thing she did, she would see the king of Raascot's head roll in precisely the same fate he had forced on Odrin. This was her prayer as she clutched her knees. If it were her last action on this earth, whatever power she possessed or whatever bargains she must make with the goddess, the regents of the continent would pay for their crimes against their kingdoms with their final, undeserving breaths.

Epilogue

Y OU SAID YOU WOULD FIX THIS! YOU SAID YOU WOULD GET her back!" Nox didn't care that she was wounding herself more than Gadriel. She continued to thrash with every drop of fury she possessed. "Now they're saying they've left the city? I can't do this again," she cried, face soaked with tears. "Not again!"

It was the second time in twenty-four hours she'd assaulted Gadriel. He'd deserved it in the town house, and he deserved it now.

Gadriel shot her a single, pained look before his gaze darkened as he descended on Yazlyn. The sergeant had been waiting for the imprisoned on the castle grounds, knowing they were set to be released. Her eyes were already red with whatever guilt she battled. She ran her hands through her hair in a desperate raking motion.

"Why are you here!" he growled.

"Gadriel, I need you to listen to me," she begged.

Nox wasn't sure if she trusted Gadriel, but she liked him a hell of a lot more than Yazlyn. The sergeant's tear-rimmed eyes did nothing for her as Nox watched her plead with her general. To Gadriel's credit, he seemed every bit as angry as she was.

"You should be marching south with Ceres, Sergeant. You are neither needed nor welcome."

"I was sparing the kingdom, Gad. I was sparing our men!"

Each word came out in a sharp snarl. "You're a fool, Yaz. I did not train you to be such a gullible fool."

Nox took a backward step until she felt Malik at her side. She was grateful for his support as she glared at the sergeant.

"Tell me you wouldn't have done the same thing in my place!" Yazlyn was near hysterics. "If you had been me, if you had first laid eyes on the girl and thought she could spare our men the slaughter after everything the priestess had said! Once he knew his child was dead—"

"His child is not dead!" Gadriel raised his hand in angry emphasis.

Nox knew enough of men to understand the significance of Yazlyn's unwavering stare. From her defiant glare to her posture, it was clear she knew he would not hit her. He was angry. He was terrifying. But even in his worst moment, he would not lose control on his soldier. Yazlyn told the world with her unflinching stance that she knew it.

Gadriel's hand lowered into a fist that clenched and then opened. His voice was thick with disgust as he gestured to Nox. "Look at his dead child, Yaz."

Nox didn't have the energy to watch their spat any longer as her face fell into her hands. The curtain of her black hair fell around her where she rocked with noiseless sobs.

"It's why I'm here," Yazlyn said finally.

Nox forced herself to look up at the words in time to see Gadriel shake his head.

Yazlyn continued, "If she's our princess, then she's owed. I know I can't make it right, but..."

Nox's eyes widened, hate clawing through her. "You're here to help *me*? You, the one who sent Amaris to her death? You think I want your help?"

Yazlyn's face scrunched. "You don't have to want it. You have it anyway. You're Ceres's child. That makes you my—"

"I am not your *anything*." Nox shredded Yazlyn's peace offering to ribbons.

Ash and Malik had remained near Nox, but their expressions and stances betrayed their struggle as they had no idea how to comfort her. They appeared just as shocked and furious as anyone else, but helplessness wouldn't serve anyone.

Elil found his place near Grem, both remaining despondently in the distance. Nox had learned enough from Ash and Malik in their time together to know reevers had been revered by both kingdoms for a millennium. Uaimh Reev had been sponsored by the church, honored by civilians, and protected by all. Now the south had proclaimed Uaimh Reev to be enemies of Farehold, and the north had murdered one in cold blood while abducting another. Their entire lives had changed in mere moments.

"You said you can help?" Malik's voice was quiet behind them. He shifted beside Nox once more, hands twitching as if to reach out and hold her, but the tendons in his arms flexed as if he absorbed his pain like a sponge. Her grief and anger were echoed through him as he asked, "What do we do?"

Grem spoke first. "We do what reevers do. We balance. We figure out where the imbalance is and what unnatural powers are being wielded, and we intervene. Right now, the south is using a curse to force magic in its favor, and the north is using some product of the goddess in its favor. There is no balance on the continent."

Nox pursed her lips, watching carefully as the sides converged.

Gadriel nodded. "Neither the king of Raascot nor the queen of Farehold honor any harmony. They're both wielding powers that don't belong on the continent. The monarchs have lost their minds. It's time we face those consequences. I'm going to do more than help."

Yazlyn was aghast. "Gadriel, if you're saying what I think you're saying, you're suggesting treason."

He shook his head, eyes hard. His voice was resolute. "I'm not. There is an heir to both thrones. The king has dedicated the last twenty years of his life to recognizing his child's claim to his throne. What he's done to his kingdom, his people... He's not our monarch anymore. I don't recognize him. We have an obligation to Raascot. We have an answer to the balance the reevers have been charged to seek."

Nox held her breath as she looked between them, but Yazlyn may as well have forgotten Nox was there. Her wings slumped behind her as she paled.

Yazlyn's tone verged on hysteria. "We are not reevers! Our allegiance is to the king—"

Gadriel turned to face his sergeant, standing scarcely more than a few inches away. As he towered over her, there was no doubt as to who was in charge. "You're right. We've served our king. He's sent us to be butchered for twenty years, and then you did the very last thing you thought you could to prevent that bloodshed and handed Amaris over as a lamb to slaughter. Has it ended his bloodshed, Sergeant? Tell me."

Gadriel remained a threatening force of power until Nox spoke.

"How long?" Any uncertainty had long since gone as Nox demanded an answer.

Gadriel broke his glare from Yazlyn's defiant, unmoving face long enough to shake his head.

"How long, Gadriel!" Nox burned as she yelled at him. "How long until you undo what you've done! How long until we get her back! How long!"

"Three days," he said, voice cold with certainty. "They left this morning, so they're less than a day ahead. We wait until they get to the choke point at the gully. We get to her before they get to the border."

"And then what? Ceres will remain a threat! We wait until your king takes her away again? Then she's ripped out of my arms by every fucking monarch on the continent?"

"You're the monarch now, Nox." He said it with such

conviction that it sent a chill through her spine. "I won't let this happen. Never again."

Yazlyn shook her head, voice growing louder over their exchange, eyes going from Nox to her general. "Gadriel, listen to yourself! Listen to what you're saying. You'll be tried. You'll be—"

"Goddess dammit." He rounded on his sergeant once more as only a commanding authority could. "Yazlyn, the next words out of your mouth had better be asking how to help unfuck the situation that *you* put us in. You think you're here to help the princess? You want to look out for Ceres's heir? Then get on board, because your new princess's first order of business is to get Amaris back. I'm rescuing her, and you're either with me or you're against me. Decide right now, or I don't want to see you again."

Yazlyn didn't back down, though her chin trembled. Her hands balled tightly into fists as she refused to blink under the weight of Gadriel's stare.

Nox's fingers bit into her palms as she waited impatiently for the most important answer of her life.

Gadriel didn't wait for Yazlyn's response. "You want to go your route, Yaz? More will die than ever before if Ceres marches into open war. When his troops cross the border, it won't be only Farehold's trained soldiers who pick up their swords but every citizen and civilian who sees an army of the damned cross the border. You handed over the last key he needed to unlock the door to our genocide."

Yazlyn did not move. She could not breathe.

Nox looked at all of them. She wiped at her tear-stained face and scanned between the reevers and the fae. Her question was thick with her suffering. "What do we do?"

Gadriel relaxed from his posture over Yazlyn as he looked at Nox and the reevers. "We do three things. First, we do everything we can to intercept Ceres and Amaris before she and the king reach the border. Three days. Second, we keep you alive, Nox, because without an heir to the thrones, the continent will descend into anarchy."

Yazlyn's chin quivered defiantly as she dared to prompt, "And third?"

Gadriel nodded. "And third, we get the princess on her throne."

This was not the sport of toying with men in the Selkie or the match of soldiers plied for information. Nox understood strategy. She knew high stakes. Life was a board, each black or white square a strategic move toward winning or losing. The players were different, but the pieces were the same. This would require every skill in cunning, every lesson she'd learned, and everything it had taken her to reach checkmate time and time again. The chess match unfolded before her as she steeled her heart against what must be done. Her face went cold as she saw the pawns, the knights, the king, and the queen. With a single dark exhale, she said, "Fine. Let the game begin."

Acknowledgments

Thank you to the women who support women's wrongs: Kelley, Grace, Allison, Claire, Bela, Lucy, Meg, Tracy, Christa, Jada, and everyone else who's walked with me down this winding path to make these books the best they could be.

And thank you to my chaos goblins, the children of Mrs. Piper Jareth the Goblin Queen (an author, girl, and sleepy TikTokker who likes *Labyrinth* an amount that is normal, not an amount that is weird) for going on this journey from folklore to fantasy, and for trusting that even if I do something terribly cruel and sad and mean in book two that objectively had to happen, I will return in book three with love and magic and adventure and make it all better.

Thank you to the LGBTQIA+ community and for everyone who's reached out in support and felt represented by *The Night and Its Moon* and who walked through *The Sun and Its Shade* knowing that our identity is ours and ours alone, not something defined by the gender identity of our partner. Bi erasure has no place in Gyrradin. I see you, I am you, and everyone in Gyrradin champions that we are who *we* are no matter who we love.

About the Author

Piper CJ, author of the bisexual fantasy series *The Night and Its Moon*, is a photographer, hobby linguist, and french fry enthusiast. She has an MA in folklore and a BA in broadcasting, which she used in her former life as a morning-show weather girl and hockey podcaster and in audio documentary work. Now when she isn't playing with her dogs, Arrow and Applesauce, she's making TikToks, studying fairy tales, or writing fantasy very, very quickly.